ever since new york

THE LOVE ON THE SETLIST SERIES
BOOK 1

COLLEEN MCNAMARA

Cover Art Illustrated by Sophie Riley

Edited by Sabrina Grimaldi

Author Photo by Kymberlea Dehoney

To anyone who has ever felt like they have been "too much" or "too broken" to be loved – may you find the kind of love that shows you that you deserve to live as your most authentic self.

And to my younger self – thank you for helping me reclaim my love for writing, giving me the gift of creating this story.

content warnings and a note from the author

A few warnings for content present in this story:

- Explicit language/cursing
- Open door, explicit, descriptive sexual content
- Descriptions of OCD
- Descriptions of eating disorders, including restricting + purging
- Mention of sexual assault (no graphic details)
- Mentions of suicidal ideation (no planning/attempts)
- Mentions of pregnancy (not a main plot point)
- Brief scene of physical violence (one bar fight)
- Mentions of PTSD flashbacks + nightmares

For anyone who wants to skip sexual content (or find it more quickly), the following chapters contain open door/explicit sexual content – please note that these correspond with the paperback pages and may vary in the ebook format depending on your device settings:

- Chapter 10, pages 80-86
- Chapter 13, page 107-second to last paragraph of page 110
- Chapter 16, pages 136-137
- Chapter 24, bottom of page 206-209
- Chapter 27, bottom of page 242-244
- Chapter 29, page 269-middle of page 271
- Chapter 32, bottom half of page 294

On the next few pages, I have included a carefully curated playlist, with one song corresponding to each chapter. Music is an important part of my creative process, and listening to this playlist while reading may enhance your experience.

playlist

APPLE MUSIC PLAYLIST QR CODE

SPOTIFY PLAYLIST QR CODE

1. greedy - Tate McRae
2. Shelter - Dermot Kennedy
3. pretty isn't pretty - Olivia Rodrigo
4. Woman - Harry Styles
5. Deep End - Holly Humberstone
6. Can I Be Him - James Arthur
7. Run the World (Girls) - Beyoncé
8. rejecter (one take) - nothing,nowhere.
9. Endless Summer Nights - James Bay
10. Dress - Taylor Swift
11. Everywhere, Everything - Noah Kahan
12. Grow As We Go – Ben Platt
13. PILLOWTALK (the living room session) - ZAYN
14. ILYSB - LANY
15. Body Back - Brye
16. Small Talk (Live) – Niall Horan
17. Control - Halsey
18. Carry You (feat. Fleurie) - Ruelle
19. Dancing With The Devil - Demi Lovato
20. Hold On - Chord Overstreet
21. Black Friday - Tom Odell
22. Your Needs, My Needs - Noah Kahan
23. Science - Niall Horan
24. Little Things - One Direction
25. Home (slowed) - Edith Whiskers
26. Someone To Stay (Acoustic) - Vancouver Sleep Clinic
27. Simply the Best – Noah Reid
28. Rome – Dermot Kennedy
29. All Your'n - Tyler Childers
30. Shine – Years & Years
31. Golden - Harry Styles
32. Coming Home - Leon Bridges

emaline

THE AIR IS FILLED with the stench of weed and bad decisions, and all I can think about is this girl's lips on my neck. Music is blaring, and I'm at yet another party in Los Angeles at some artist's house that I don't care to remember at this point because of how much tequila is coursing through my veins.

Sometimes I drink to celebrate. Sometimes I drink to distract. Tonight is the distracting kind of night. I've been working on a new album for months, and I've been having major writer's block with the last two songs. I keep getting caught up in my brain and second-guessing myself even though my last album broke the top five on the charts, and I leave for my biggest tour to date in a few weeks. I guess when one of your exes, who used to be one of your producers, fucks with your head and tries to convince you you're talentless, it doesn't matter how many objective markers of success there are. So, here I am, drinking to try to get the imposter syndrome and self-pity out of my head.

Warmth spreads through my lower abdomen as she pushes me against the door of some random room, her kisses gradually inching closer to my mouth. One of her hands grips my shoulder and the other dances down my curves, touching the skin exposed between my cropped pink lace corset and low-rise jeans.

"I can't wait to tell my friends that I hooked up with *the* Emaline Levine."

The urge to vomit radiates through my bones, and it's not because of the alcohol. I push her hands off of me, get out from under her, and say, "Absolutely fucking not. I'm not some damn object or trophy to kiss and tell. And if you're at this party to try to collect hookups with celebrities, see yourself out."

"This isn't even your house..."

"And do you think I give a fuck? Now, excuse me while I try to erase your pathetic statement from my brain."

Unfortunately, I'm no stranger to people trying to hook up with me as a status symbol or a way to social climb. All of these industry parties are filled with people who are either cocky as hell or want to hook up with successful people for clout. And while I can't say I've *never* hooked up with someone to try to get something I wanted, it has certainly never been to be able to brag that I fucked XYZ celebrity—and hearing my name and body used as something to be thrown in a group chat just feels disgusting.

After walking away from that girl and trying to rid myself of the gross feeling, I scan the living room to try to find my best friend Kieran. We've been best friends practically since we were born. My parents moved into his parents' neighborhood shortly after my mom got pregnant, and after working at the same company for a few weeks, our moms quickly learned they were both expecting and due around the same time. My birthday is August 7th, and Kieran's is July 20th. I've never known a life without him, and we spent nearly every waking moment together as kids, completely inseparable. He's also my main co-writer, in addition to playing guitar for my touring band. I count on him for everything... including getting the hell out of this party so that I can put sweatpants on and stuff my face with some In-N-Out.

I walk through the living room, trying to avoid any potential conversations, feeling the room spinning ever so slightly. Kieran is sitting alone in the corner of a couch, nursing a beer as he scrolls on his phone. His short, dark brunette waves are falling into his eyes, and he's clearly enjoying this party about as much as I am.

"What's up, Em? You all good?"

"Can we get out of here? I was about to hook up with a girl until she said, and I quote, 'I can't wait to tell my friends that I hooked up with *the* Emaline Levine.'"

He shakes his head and says, "Ew. People at these parties can be so disgusting. Wanna get some burgers and then we can drive home?"

"You read my mind."

We wade through the intoxicated people littered through the house, to the front door, and fresh air has never felt so good. I sigh and my shoulders drop, releasing an amount of tension I didn't realize I was holding.

I love making a living from my music, but I hate the gross undertones that are part of it. In the grand scheme of things, a girl trying to get with me at a party because of who I am isn't *that* bad. But, when I've had countless times of just being a body to people, it still makes me feel dirty. It's unfortunately part of being in this industry, but that doesn't mean I have to like it.

Kieran opens the passenger door of his black Jeep for me, always a gentleman.

Why can't more people be like him?

It seems like the bare minimum, but when you've been in shitty relationship after shitty relationship and just want the kind of love where someone treats you like you're deserving of respect and acts like they actually love you, bare minimum feels pretty good. Even when it's from just a friend.

"Your head's running in circles, Emmie. Did something else happen in there that you didn't tell me about?"

After knowing me for all twenty-five years of our lives, Kieran can always tell what's going on. There's no hiding from him, even when all I want to do is go back to forgetting about the swarm of thoughts ricocheting through my brain. And it's not just the last two tracks of the album... it's *everything*.

"Can we talk about it tomorrow? Nothing else happened, just my brain not wanting to shut up. In-N-Out and Gossip Girl are what I need right now."

"Fine, but this escapism shit only works for so long. You know that."

"I know, I know. I promise we can talk tomorrow. But, can you start driving? I'm starving."

"Your wish is my command. I need to see what nonsense Chuck Bass is up to anyway."

Thanks to it being midnight, there's magically next to no traffic as we breeze down the Pacific Coast Highway. *Alive* by Pearl Jam is playing, and everything is starting to feel more at ease. Driving away from the chaos of downtown LA back to Santa Monica, where Kieran and I both live, is always a weight off my chest. It's close enough to the city where I can easily get to the studio and quickly get to LAX, but it's far enough away that I can breathe. Santa Monica isn't the middle of nowhere by any stretch of the imagination, but it's more chill. As the city lights get further and further away, my brain finally starts to quiet.

We pull up to the drive-through and Kieran says, "Your usual?" I nod in agreement.

"Can we please get two double-doubles, both animal style, two orders of light well fries, and two chocolate shakes?"

After grabbing our food from the window, Kieran finishes the remaining five minutes of the drive back to my apartment. I say my apartment, but we live in the same building, a few doors apart. Everyone always asks why we don't just live together, but I feel like it would get too complicated, and the last thing I'd want is to ruin our friendship if living together didn't work out.

We take the elevator up to our floor, and he says, "So, how many people do you think have fucked in this elevator?"

"Are you seriously asking this right now, Kier?"

"Is that you saying you've fucked someone in this elevator?"

"Ew, no. It's disgusting in here. Get your head out of the gutter before I dump this shake on you."

The elevator stops at our floor and he shakes his head playfully. "You're no fun."

I scoff. "Oh, I'm plenty of fun. For the record, I've fucked in more than one elevator. I don't like to think about doing it in one with an inspection that expired nearly a year ago and a carpet that probably hasn't been cleaned in months."

He unlocks the door to my apartment as he says, "Fair enough, getting stuck on the elevator would probably kill the vibe."

"Exactly."

For some reason, it's funny to me to think about a golden-retriever-like guy like Kieran fucking someone in an elevator... but I have heard enough stories of his sexual exploits that I suppose this shouldn't surprise me. The man is multifaceted.

We walk into my living room, welcomed as usual by the

lived-in but still organized vibe. I could easily afford a bigger apartment, but it's spacious enough for what I need and definitely cozy. I hate the look of bare walls, so I have a variety of art pieces and prints strewn about, mostly created by friends and local artists. My favorite one is a framed print with cherries tied together with a pink bow and the words "ma chérie" over the curve of the loops of the ribbon.

Kieran grabs plates and takes our food out of the greasy bags as the aroma of the burgers permeates the room. He then gets us metal straws from my drawer, knowing how much I despise the paper ones that are an LA default. I'm all for saving the environment, but the sensation of a soggy paper straw will quickly kill the enjoyment of a milkshake.

As he brings the plates to the dark wood coffee table in the living room, I say, "I'm gonna go change real quick."

Desperate to inhale my burger, I rip off my corset and jeans and pull on the oversized black sweatpants and baggy tie-dye t-shirt that I threw on my floor this morning. Any other guy, I'd want to look cute for, but Kieran has seen me in pretty much every possible state of disrepair. And it's not like I'm trying to impress him—we're just best friends, and that's all we'll ever be.

I walk back to the living room, and Kieran has Gossip Girl queued up. We watched the entirety of it together back in middle school, so it's a comfort rewatch. I plop onto the emerald green couch, pulling one of my many cushy throw blankets over my lap before digging into my food.

"You look much comfier now," Kieran says.

"Yeah, that fit was cute, but underwires and denim don't exactly make for very good 'lay on the couch and stuff my face with fries' attire."

After demolishing my burger, fries, and shake, I lean into Kieran's side. To anyone else, cuddling like this may look like something a couple would do, but it's just our thing. Sure, he's an amazing friend and treats me wonderfully, but I don't think I've ever seen him as any more than a friend, and I know that he sure as hell doesn't see me as more than a friend. He just knows me better than anyone and likes to do things that make me happy, because isn't that what best friends do?

I lay my head in his lap, all the stress of the day melting away. Suddenly, the combo of my exhaustion from the alcohol and my stomach's satisfaction from the food is making the edges of everything fuzzy, and I involuntarily drift off to sleep.

kieran

EMALINE'S long blonde hair is splayed across my lap, in effortless-looking curls that I know took at least half an hour for her to do before we left for the party. She still has little pink rhinestones in the corners of her eyes that match the corset she wore tonight. The rise and fall of her breath as she sleeps peacefully calms me, and I can't help but notice the depth of her beauty as she lies here, not trying to impress anyone or be the manufactured version this industry pressures her to be. She's just Emmie.

From us singing in her childhood bedroom on her karaoke machine to now preparing for her sold-out tour, I'm so lucky to exist in her magical presence. As much as I don't want to admit it, I'm pretty sure I've been in love with her for years. But, I'd never act on it. Relationships I've had that started off as friendships have only ever met painful demises. And with her being my best friend, I can't risk losing the person who's most important to me, even if we could be good together. Plus, I don't think she'll ever see me as anything other than her best friend, which is okay. I'm just grateful to be in her world.

It's a gift to be able to see this version of her, one that so few people get to see. Even though it's nearly 2 am and I'm trapped with her on my lap, I can't bear to move her yet. She looks so at ease and worry-free, something that doesn't happen often. So, instead, I lightly rub her back, wishing there was a way to bottle up this feeling. This feeling of being here while she doesn't have a care in the world. Being the purest version of herself.

After another half hour of scrolling through my phone while she's out cold, my eyes start to get heavy. The urge to just lay back, pull her close to me, and go to sleep here is so strong, but that would be way too much. So, instead, I file that dream away in my brain and gently tap her saying, "Hey, Em, it's getting pretty late. Want me to help you get to your room?"

"Shit, I fell asleep? What time is it?" she says groggily.

"It's 2:15. You fell asleep almost an hour ago, but you were so peaceful, and I didn't want to wake you."

Looking up at me with her sparkling blue-green eyes, little flecks of mascara under them, she says, "Kieran Hayes, were you watching me sleep?"

"No, I was half watching Gossip Girl while I scrolled through social media. You seemed really comfy, so I figured I wouldn't disturb you."

I was totally watching.

"Hmm, whatever you say...but yeah, I should probably go wash my face and head to bed," she says as she rolls off my lap and stands up, stumbling ever-so-slightly from the combination of just waking up and still having some tequila in her system.

I get up off the couch, start folding the throw blanket, and reply, "Good idea, I'm pretty tired, too."

She pulls me in for a hug. "Sweet dreams, Kiki."

"Sweet dreams, Emmie," I say, squeezing her back, noticing the lingering rose and cherry scent of her perfume.

I grab my wallet and keys and head out the door, taking the ten foot walk to my apartment. After kicking off my black and white Converse and throwing my wallet and keys on the marble kitchen counter, I walk to my bedroom to get ready to sleep. I've never been a skincare guy, but Emmie's obsession with trying to have perfect skin and her insistence on me having a skincare routine has me in the habit of washing and moisturizing my face every night, even when I'm as dead tired as I am right now.

As I lay in bed, wrapped in my light gray comforter, my brain is hyper-fixated on every detail of the night. Especially how perfect Emmie looked at the party and how I felt a slight twinge of jealousy when seeing her with that girl... *but I can't be jealous, right?* We're best friends, and there's no way she'd want more than that. Unless her little remark after I said I wasn't watching her sleep was her flirting? That had to have been her joking around because she's never expressed even a little bit of romantic interest, at least not directly. Even if she was a little attracted to me, Emmie could get pretty much any guy (or girl) she could ever want, and while I know I'm not unattractive, I'm just... me. She's the star, I'm just here in the background.

I turn off the faucet of my kitchen sink for the third time, completing one of my brain's stupid rituals that has become more frequent thanks to the stress of the upcoming tour, only interrupted by my phone vibrating.

NOAH

Hey man! I know it's been a bit since we've caught up. I know you're busy with the album and tour but would love to FaceTime sometime soon, miss you. How are you doing?

Noah and I met as first-year roommates at NYU, and we very quickly became like brothers. Em and I majored in songwriting, and he majored in music business. He moved to London pretty quickly after graduating because of a job offer at a label, and the drastic difference in time zones coupled with chaotic schedules has made it tricky to stay in touch as much as I'd like.

It takes me a second to figure out how to reply to his text because I'm not sure the last time I paused to think about how I've been feeling.

KIERAN

Hey!! Miss you too bro

I'm doing alright, things have been all over the place with leaving for NY so soon. Trying to wrap up this album has been a struggle. How about you? And if you're free later tonight I can give you a call?

NOAH

Damn yeah I'm sure that's hard. Wish I could make it to one of the shows but work's been killin me. Tonight's perfect, I'll be home all night

KIERAN

Great, I'll hit you up when I get home

Maybe talking to Noah later will help get my mind off my feelings about Emaline.

Just as I slide my phone back into my pocket, the alarm reminding me that it's time to leave starts to ring. Em and I have a Sunday morning tradition, getting bagels and chilling in the nearby park. It's reminiscent of childhood when our dads would go grab bagels for our families, and we'd all hang out in one of our backyards, enjoying shared company. I grab my keys and head out the door. I wait by the elevator, and about a minute later, she walks over.

"So, how's the hangover?" I say.

Emmie grumbles at me and rolls her eyes. "Pretty sure you already know the answer to that one."

"Hey, you're the one who decided all those shots were a good idea. I was the smart one who had two beers and called it a night. Alcohol doesn't hit the same at twenty-five as it did when we were eighteen."

"Thanks, *Mr. I Told You So*. What novel information."

We get in my car and head over to our favorite breakfast spot. I know a lot has been running through Emmie's head over the past few days, with finishing the album and our tour coming up, so I'm hoping that having a chill morning and talking it out can help calm her nerves a bit. After parking my car, we go inside.

I order us both our go-to, an asiago bagel with cream cheese for Em, an everything bagel with butter for me, and two iced oat milk brown sugar lattes.

As I slide my wallet out of my pocket, Emmie tries to beat me to the chase, pulling her card out. I shake my head. "Nope, you know the drill. Sunday breakfast is on me."

She sighs. "Fine, but I'm going to beat you to it one of these days."

The cashier smiles at us. "You two are a very cute couple. I'll have your order out in a few minutes."

In sync, we both reply, "Oh, we're not a couple." Even though I wish that answer was different.

"Oh, my mistake. Have a wonderful day!"

Em never seems bothered by people thinking we're a couple, despite it happening frequently. I wonder if she's ever thought about me like that.

We grab our bagels and lattes and drive over to the park. As I pull a checkered picnic blanket out of the trunk of my car, I say, "So, what's been running through your mind? Last night when you were asleep was the calmest I've seen you in weeks."

We walk to our usual spot under a large bay fig tree, and she replies, "Honestly, a bit of everything. These last two tracks can't seem to get out of my brain and into existence. The comment that stupid bitch said last night had me thinking about Chris. My sleep has been shit. I can't stop thinking about how my body is going to look at the album shoot tomorrow, especially after some of those comments about my cellulite in the bikini pic I posted the other day. I'm all over the place with these interviews we have coming up for the tour. It's so much."

Chris is Em's abusive ex who I wish I could kill after what he did to her last year.

"Okay, let's pause for a moment and take a breath. We can worry about the work shit later. Do you want to talk about what the comment brought up about Chris? We don't have to, but I'm all ears if you do," I say, taking a bite of my bagel.

She shakes her head and looks at the ground, smoothing her matching charcoal-gray crop top and joggers. "I don't think I can right now. It brings up so much shame. I know you've never judged me for it, I hate how much brain space it takes up even though it's stupid, and I should be over it."

"Hey, it's not stupid. And it's okay that you don't want to talk about it right now. How about the interviews? What's worrying you with those?"

The abuse she faced from Chris went on for months, and one night last year, he did unspeakable things to her. And if it was up to me, I would've murdered him. Or at least hurt him enough that he would've wished to be dead. But, she asked me not to intervene, so I didn't. The last thing I wanted to do at that moment was take more autonomy from her.

I hate that Emmie feels like she has to discount her trauma and feels so much shame about not being "over it." She doesn't deserve what she experienced, and I have plenty of things that are nowhere close to as bad that I haven't gotten over. Even though she's opened up to me a bit, her walls are a thousand feet tall, despite me being her best friend. I know that she says she can't talk about it right now, but I wish she would so that I could try to make things even just a little better.

She fidgets her hands. "Just imposter syndrome, ya know? Yeah, this is a big tour and my old tracks have stayed on the charts, but I don't get why these major outlets want to cover me. Like why is someone from Yahoo writing an article about me? I know I'm talented, but I'm not really special."

"Hold the fuck up, Em. Don't ever say you're not special. You're about to play some of the same venues that Harry fucking Styles has played. You're about to release your third album, you've gone viral on TikTok practically a million times at this point, you've been on so many Spotify playlists, everyone on Instagram is beyond obsessed with you...what more do I need to add to the list? You're not an imposter, you're fucking iconic."

She takes her hair down from its messy bun, laying back on the blanket. "I...I just sometimes don't understand how this all happened. It's really hard to wrap my head around, and sometimes I wonder if I deserve it all. And when I see people who make comments online saying I don't, my brain immediately hyper-focuses on those. It's so much easier to believe the nega-tive than the positive."

I flop onto my stomach next to her, trying not to let my eyes linger over her for too long, even though that feels impos-sible. "I know it's hard. Sometimes I can't believe that we're in this place either. But you've worked incredibly hard and deserve all of these major opportunities you have. I'm so proud of you and how far you've come, Emmie. I wish you could believe in yourself as much as the rest of the world does."

emaline

THE STUDIO IS dead quiet as I get ready to lay down my first take of vocals for the final track on my upcoming album, *Getting Back To Me*. This final track is titled *Wild Mind*, and it's about the battle I'm continuously fighting with my brain, between my history of an eating disorder, my trauma, and all the other shit that makes it run a mile a minute, all exacerbated by being in this industry. After two weeks of struggling to finish the final lyrics, Kieran and I pulled an all-nighter (after smoking a considerable amount of weed) and finally completed it.

"And I love this wild mind, but sometimes I just wish it would go silent," I sing then sigh, happy to be done with the first take.

"That was great. Let's take a break for a sec so you can get some water, but then let's do another take of the bridge, maybe a little softer?" Quinn, my recording engineer, says.

I nod as I walk out of the booth. "Yeah, I agree. I'm shocked that I didn't hate that take. You know how I usually tear it apart." I plop down on the black leather couch next to Kieran, chugging some water to hydrate my vocal cords.

He ruffles my hair before saying, "Look at you being nice to yourself. Progress. It sounded incredible, you'll probably only need a few more takes."

I lightly lay my head on his shoulder and reply, "It only took recording the entire fucking album for me to be semi-pleased with a first run. I guess it's fitting with the track title."

I'm a compulsive perfectionist in every aspect of my life, music being one of the most prominent areas. The title track took me nearly forty takes to be happy with, much to the chagrin of everyone involved. When your words and voice are heard by millions of people, it's hard not to be so obsessive. I want everyone who hears my music to hear it in the exact way I intended it, the exact way it runs through my brain, and the way I know I have the potential to deliver. I'm my own worst critic, which I suppose is commonplace in this industry. I've been this way since I was a little girl, and with my ex Chris producing my last album, it was amplified even more. It got to a point where it was hard for anyone other than me, him, and Quinn to be at our recording sessions because of how much everyone hated what he was doing to me.

"Okay, time for round two. I'm starving, but I'm determined to at least get half done with the final vocals before we break for lunch," I say, getting off the couch and walking back to the recording booth.

Kieran turns to stretch out his lanky legs on the couch and then says, "You've got this. Now go dazzle us with that beautiful voice." His eyes seem to linger a little longer than usual, and I'm starting to wonder if he could somehow want to be more than just friends, but I doubt that's true... but the little compliments he throws in that give more than just best friend energy get the wheels in my brain turning. The times he says things like "you look absolutely stunning" instead of "your outfit looks great," the way he was definitely watching me sleep the other night... it all makes a girl wonder.

I smooth my denim shorts and white t-shirt and put my pink headphones back on, turning towards the mic. As I open my mouth to start the second take of the bridge, everything seems to magically flow. My voice is light and airy, a contrast to the stronger, more belted quality of the chorus. There's a momentary quiet feeling in my brain as I sing, being in the moment, completely in flow.

While I'm often caught up in my mind when recording, there are moments like this where I feel so completely connected to my body and soul, that remind me of why I do this, *why I love this.* Making music can be stressful, but ultimately I do it because it's an outlet for me. It's a space where I can make sense of and express things in a way that just speaking can't adequately capture. Sure, when I sing, I'm saying words, but it's different than speaking in a conversation. I speak my mind about a lot of things, especially with the people closest to me, but my music still captures it in a deeper, more authentic way. The backing instrumentation, vocal dynamics, and lyricism add a level of complexity that more adequately captures my internal experiences.

After I finish the last line of the bridge, everyone starts to clap. My manager Ruby walked in part way through, and she has a huge smile on her face. What's even more obvious than Ruby's smile is the way Kieran is looking at me. It doesn't look like just a proud best friend. It looks like adoration. But that has to be me making things up in my head or reading into something.

"You killed it. I'll let you listen to it back, but if you're happy, I don't think we need another take," Quinn says, tucking her ashy blonde hair behind her ears.

She hits play, and I'm immediately satisfied with what I

hear, even though it's just the raw vocals without editing. I'm perfectly on key, my breath support is solid, and the dynamics are exactly how I want them to be. Some days I'm reminded of my ability, and today is one of those days.

"Okay, I can't believe I'm saying this, but I think we can go with that take. What does everyone else think?" I say, walking out of the booth. As I push Kieran's legs out of the way to sit next to him on the couch, Ruby comes over and high fives me. She's wearing a simple black tank top and mom jeans, with her light brunette hair in a half-up ponytail and her signature "ruby" red lipstick.

"It's perfect. Love to see an efficient recording session. If the rest of the track sounds like this, I think you're on your way to a number one," Ruby says.

Kieran grins and says, "She's right. I'm so proud of you and this album. It's really coming together, just in time for that stealth release date before tour."

For my previous albums, I've always done the traditional kind of rollout with a few singles and a ton of promo before-hand, but when I discussed the plan with Ruby and my label, we decided to do a surprise release with this one. The night before my tour starts. As a result, the first time I perform these songs live will be during the opening night of tour. While I'm a little nervous about not having the usual amount of marketing for the album, I know that there's a ton of marketing for the tour. Plus, surprise album drops tend to lead to even more press and social media buzz with the shock and excitement that accompanies it for the fans. But, I still worry that somehow the album might not do well, so I've been extra hard on myself not just during our recording sessions, but during rehearsals, too.

I've had a lot of growth in the number of streams over the past year, but I know there's still always the chance of things flopping… which would be extra embarrassing. You never know what people are going to think of an album, even if you've put your heart and soul into it. Music is so subjective, and with how quickly this industry changes, it's hard to predict how things may go. Hence all of the sleepless nights and recording sessions where we'd record one line so many times that Ruby and Quinn would force me to take a break.

But, somehow, today my brain is a little nicer to me than usual. I guess you've gotta take the wins where you can get them and not question it too much. Even though I'm still anxious.

"I'm feeling really good about this one, guys. I know it's been a winding road to getting this album done, but we're finally almost there. Now, how about some lunch? I'm shocked that the sound of my stomach growling didn't bleed into the vocals."

Countless racks of clothing are spread through my stylist Brie's studio, and I'm completely overwhelmed, my thoughts flying through my brain like a swarm of bees. After finishing recording the rest of the final track, Ruby came with me to try to figure out my wardrobe for each show. We leave for tour in under three weeks, and I have twenty five dates to figure out looks for. I don't even know where to start. I know my music is what people really come to my shows for, but it is a performance, and the right or wrong outfit can make a big difference. Especially in the age of social media where every performance is blasted online before the show is even done. My heart is running a marathon, and the room is making me feel like a lizard in a terrarium, even though the air conditioning is blasting.

Likely sensing my typical anxiety, Brie says, "I know, it's a lot. The most shows you've ever needed to be styled for. How about you take a few minutes to peek through everything and see what's speaking to you most?"

"Yeah, I can do that. Sorry that I always make this so difficult," I say, walking over to the racks.

She shakes her head. "Em, you really need to stop apologizing. It's literally my job. It's what I'm here for."

Ruby adds, "You have so much going on, but don't forget, this part is supposed to be fun."

They're both right. I get to play dress up for an entire evening, something my younger self would've been all over. If you had told me when I was four years old that I'd be spending my night getting to try on fun outfits as part of my job, I would've been losing my mind from the excitement. I wish that in moments like this, I could see myself as more than just my body. *Come on, little Emaline, I know you're in there somewhere.*

I take a deep breath, trying to absorb the fun energy of the colorful walls of the studio. As I piece my way through the first rack, a super fun hot pink feather top that is very different from what I've worn in previous performances jumps out at me. I grab it and then notice a pair of hot pink wide-leg trousers that would be a perfect match. Holding onto both hangers, I continue sorting through them. I find several other pieces that feel like potential winners, including a little cherry-covered bralette, a cute nod to Harry Styles that only fellow fans will pick up on. It's a little weird being a touring musician who is also a huge fangirl, but it's not my fault that One Direction was in their prime when I was a teenager. I've yet to meet Harry despite running in some of the same circles, and if I do end up meeting him someday, trying to come across as a colleague versus a super fan will certainly be a feat.

Now it's time for the part my childhood self would've found the most fun but my adult self finds the most challenging—trying everything on.

I walk into the little partitioned changing area in the corner of the studio, pull off the jeans and t-shirt I'm wearing, and start to pull on the hot pink outfit. After zipping up the pants, I walk out and look in the mirror. Because they're somewhere between low and mid-rise, my gaze is immediately laser-focused on my stomach, one of the parts I'm most insecure about...even though last week I felt hot as hell in low-rise jeans and a cropped corset. I have a societally accepted body type, but even with that, I've gotten plenty of shitty comments about it over the years, on social media and in tabloids. I still struggle to see my body for what it actually is, not the distorted version my brain tries to convince me of. Even though I've spent countless hours in therapy, at this moment, I want to crawl out of my skin. The not-so-linear journey of body image healing is truly a mindfuck.

Brie looks at me and says, "I'm obsessed. The feathers are so bold. A pair of white sneakers, some sparkly earrings, and you'll be set. What do you think?"

I bite my lip anxiously. "Not sure how I feel about my stomach in this...but the top is so cute and playful. Maybe I need to say screw you to my brain and wear it anyway. I want to get Kieran's thoughts before I give it a definite yes, though."

Clearly suppressing a true laugh, Ruby snickers. "It's kind of cute how much you always need that boy's feedback."

"I mean, sometimes he knows me better than I know myself," I say, and then snap a mirror selfie.

EMALINE

thoughts?

KIERAN

Looks amazing. Feathers suit you

Reassurance from Kieran always takes a weight off my shoulders. He has never steered me wrong, aside from some questionable drunk decisions we've made, so when he says something looks good, I know he means it.

"Okay, let's go with this one for sure. Maybe for opening night?" I say.

Brie says, "I was just going to suggest that. Starting with a bold statement piece is a smart move."

"Yep, I agree," Ruby adds. "It's going to photograph so well, too. And you can do some pink rhinestones in your makeup or a pink lip...or even both. A sassy Barbie moment."

Feeling a little better after everyone's positive feedback on the look, I try on several more options, finding outfits for half of the shows before calling it a night. A girl can only look at her body in the mirror so much in one day without completely losing her mind.

FOUR

kieran

AFTER TWENTY FIVE years of being Emaline's best friend, I should know that when she says, "I'll be ready in five minutes," she means "I'll be ready in twenty minutes." Instead, I'm sitting on her couch, still waiting for her to be ready to go to the club, even though she told me to come over a half hour ago. She's changed her outfit seven times because none of them have been "the vibe," which is only mildly infuriating.

I usually don't take too much time to get ready, tonight wearing a simple, tight black tee that lets my tattoos peek out, paired with dark charcoal jeans and some slightly scuffed white Vans. As usual, I let my hair dry naturally, adding a tiny bit of pomade to enhance my natural waves.

"How's this look?"

Emmie finally walks out to the living room, and she is beyond radiant. She's wearing a v-cut black bralette, high-rise black jeans, a cropped leather jacket, and white sneakers, her blonde hair straightened and in a half-up ponytail. Her bold red lipstick perfectly accentuates her already immaculate lips, and it's probably very obvious that I'm checking her out. It's hard not to when she looks like a walking wet dream.

"Hey, earth to Kieran. I asked how the fit looks?" Emmie says, tapping my shoulder.

Yep, pretty damn obvious.

"Sorry, zoned out there for a sec. You look great. Ready to head out? Everyone's probably waiting for us," I say, trying to quickly change the subject in hopes that my staring seems less apparent.

We're meeting Ruby, Brie, Quinn, the rest of the band, some of the crew, and my older sister Madison at a club to celebrate the completion of the album. It's been a winding road to get here, but it feels so freeing to be done and another step closer to sharing this project with the world. This will be our last big celebration before heading into our final round of rehearsals and then leaving for tour, so it's probably going to be a bit of a wild night. I tend to keep my intoxication to a minimum when I'm out with Em since I get paranoid that some guy will try to take advantage of her when she's drunk. I know she's a strong woman who can take care of herself, but I still worry and want to make sure that I'm of sound enough mind to intervene if I need to. Guys can be pretty brazen around her, and I'm always on guard because of my general mistrust and disdain for most men... despite being a man.

Seemingly glossing over my staring, Emmie says, "Yeah, I'll order an Uber."

After a few minutes, she gets a notification that the Uber is approaching, so we head outside. I check the license plate and then open the door for Em. The driver confirms her name, types in the code from the app, and I climb in. As we get on the interstate and get closer to downtown, my mind continues to race. I'm not sure why these thoughts and feelings about Em have gotten stronger over the past few weeks. But they're becoming impossible to ignore. With how close we are, I think we could make a good couple. But, even if she does somehow feel the same way as I do, I can't risk losing the one person who knows me better than anyone else. And with my OCD and the baggage of my past relationships, I don't know if I could be a good enough boyfriend for her. So, I'm going to push these feelings down. Since Em is looking out the window and not towards me, I shake my head to try to get the thoughts to leave, even though I know it's illogical.

We walk into the bar, and I need alcohol to shove down these feelings ASAP. I don't like pushing down my emotions. I pride myself on being the kind of guy who doesn't buy into the toxic masculinity, "feelings are bad" bullshit. But there's too much at risk with Emaline. So, emotion suppression it is.

Almost everyone is at a booth in the corner, and while I have an urge to grab Emmie's hand as we keep walking, I don't.

Isabelle, our keys player, says, "Hey guys! How's it going?"

"Good, feels nice to have had a day free from the walls of the studio," I reply.

Em nods. "You can say that again. Loved making this album, but the exhaustion is real."

"And now it's almost time for a different type of exhaustion with tour rehearsals," Kenzie, our front-of-house engineer/production manager says.

Front-of-house is what the audience hears, and a production manager makes sure that everything with the actual run of the show goes smoothly. With the size of this upcoming tour, we might just hire a separate production manager so that Kenzie can really focus just on front-of-house, but she's just so good at her job. So for now, she'll keep doing both which isn't uncommon in the music industry.

Delia, our bass player, looks towards Kenzie and says, "Yeah, and you had the luxury of not having the stress of studio sessions, unlike most of us."

Some crew members are part of the recording process, but not all. Everyone has different roles, both on and off the road, that all make it possible to do what we do.

"Hey, it's not like I'm just sitting on the couch all day even though I'm not in the studio. Your monitor tracks don't appear out of thin air," Jake says. He's our monitor engineer, who handles what we hear in our in-ear monitors during every show.

Kenzie nods. "Exactly. And the production doesn't manage itself."

I laugh and say, "You know we're joking. We couldn't do it without all of you."

Madison, my older sister, runs over. Her dark brunette hair is twisted up in a claw clip, and she's wearing a teal slip dress with a pair of Dr. Martens.

"Mads! Hi!" Em says.

I pull Madison in for a hug. "How's your day been, baby brother?"

She's only five years older than me, but she always makes sure to remind me that I'm the younger one. As a little kid, it used to make me angry. But now I'm just grateful to have such a supportive big sister who will drop everything at a moment's notice if I need help. She's been married to her husband Matt for three years now, and he's the only guy she's been with that I've ever approved of. And with Emaline being an only child, they're like sisters which I love.

"It's been good. Super chill day. Looking forward to celebrating now though. How about you?"

"Pretty chill, too. Worked from home, decided to take the day off tomorrow since I have extra PTO, and I figured I could start the weekend early. And because working with a potential hangover tomorrow didn't sound like the vibe."

Before I can respond to her, Nick, our drummer, and Ryan, our tour manager, come over balancing a massive tray of shots. Austin, our lighting director, trails behind them.

"Cheers to finally wrapping this project and getting ready to share it with the world. Every moment was worth it," Em says, raising her glass and tapping it to each of ours.

After I throw mine back, I pull her in for a side hug and say, "So fucking proud of you, Emmie girl. Proud of all of us, but especially you. I know this was a hard one with how personal and deep it is, but you did the thing. Even if I may have wanted to kill you with how many takes we did."

And in a few weeks, the world will get to be as proud of her as we all are.

I'm pretty proud of myself, too. I was a co-writer on all of the songs, and getting to have those credits is big for my career as well. Even though I don't think I'd ever want to become a solo artist. But, never say never, I guess. There's a lot on the line with this album and tour for all of us, not just Emaline.

I let my fingers linger on her waist for a moment longer than I probably should, and a big smile spreads across her face. "I know, I know, I wanted to knock myself out, too. You guys all know how hard it is for me to be proud of myself, but I'm honestly so proud of this album. I haven't put out anything this vulnerable before, and I think the fans are really going to connect with it."

"I know they're going to," Ruby says, hugging Emmie's other side. "It's the perfect blend of raw pieces and more cute, bubble-gummy ones. I can already visualize the late-night show appearances."

Still beaming with pride, Emmie replies, "Now we just have to shoot the cover, and we'll be officially done. Enough work talk, time to get fucked up."

Even though we're surrounded by tons of very attractive people, the only person my eyes are on is Em. She downs another shot, and her natural ease in social situations radiates, flitting around and talking to all of our team members, while I'm here, a bit caught up in my brain and my now unignorable desire for her. My heart is beating out of my chest, a sensation heavier than the bass of the music. Which is saying a lot, with how much the speakers are shaking. My eyes are completely glued to her, stuck on the sliver of exposed skin between the edge of her bralette and the waist of her jeans, until she turns my way.

She walks back to me and places her hand on my shoulder, saying, "I'm gonna go grab another drink and dance a bit. Want to come with?"

I want to say yes, but I feel like if I start dancing with her, I won't be able to hide how I'm feeling. I mean, I'm not even sure if I'm hiding it now. And if she knows how I'm feeling, it's going to make everything weird and ruin the night. I can't ruin this celebration that she's earned. So, time for an at least slightly plausible excuse.

"I want to catch up with Mads for a few, but then maybe I'll come find you?"

"Sounds good, take your time!" she says, strutting over to the bar.

As much as I want to stay truly present, my eyes stay on Emmie, watching as she grabs her drink and then heads to the dance floor. She dances on her own briefly, her perfect body highlighted by the bright lights. But she shines brighter than any light in the room.

Madison puts her hand on my back and says, "You good,

Kier? Your eyes haven't left Emaline the entire time we've been here. Is there something going on that I don't know about?"

Madison always has a crystal clear vision of what's going on for me. She's almost as close to me as Emmie is, and she never lets me get away with not talking to her about what's going on in my head. Most of the time, other people kinda let me get away with not sharing my feelings if I'm not forthright with them. But Mads always calls me on my bullshit. Which sometimes is good. Other times, I hate it. She does it because she loves me and wants the best for me, but it never feels good when you want to ignore what you're feeling and someone knows you too well to let you.

"Oh, nothing, just making sure she's okay. She had a shitty experience at a party we were at a few weeks ago and I want to make sure nothing bad happens."

Shaking her head at me, Madison says, "You know, you're a real shit liar. The look you're giving her isn't just protection, it's adoration. And I'm pretty sure all of us saw your hand on her waist. Be honest with me, do you have feelings for her?"

I want to lie, breeze past this conversation, and not have to speak these feelings out loud because I don't want to seem like too much, like I've been told by so many people, But Madison will see right through my bullshit. And I know she won't think I'm too much, even if my mind likes to tell me otherwise sometimes.

My voice cracking slightly, I look at the ground and quietly say, "Yeah."

She shoves my side and replies, "Shut up!!! Since when? And when were you going to tell me this?!"

"Honestly, I think it's been for years. But, over the past few weeks, it's gotten to the point where I can't seem to ignore it or push it down. I never thought I'd see her as more than my best friend, but everything about her is taking over all of my thoughts. I'm not sure if it's all the extra time we've spent together with the new album or tour or what. We've always spent all our time together. Maybe it's because she's single now and not with Chris? Who knows."

"Are you going to tell her?" she says, smirking.

Continuing to look at the ground, I reply, "No, there's no way she has the same feelings, and I think it would make everything weird. I'd hate to ruin everything we have. You know how many times she's been hurt. And I can't lose my best friend."

"I mean, I've seen the way she looks at you sometimes, and while I don't know for sure, I think there's a chance she likes you like that, too. And even if you don't tell her, she's going to notice the way you fucking stare at her like she's the sun at some point."

I just need to push it down, that's all I need to do. If I push it down, the feelings will eventually go away. And I won't lose one of the only people I've never been too much for.

Lifting my head and glancing to the dance floor, I see Emmie dancing with a guy. My already racing heart picks up speed, and I don't think I've ever felt this feeling towards her. My face is hot, my hands are tingling, and my whole body is starting to tense up. It's like I'm a washcloth being wrung out.

Madison shakes my shoulders and says, "If you're so committed to not telling her about your feelings, you at least need to come drink with the rest of us or find some other girl or guy to dance with. You're not hiding anything, and it won't be good if you let this keep festering."

"Okay, okay. It's not like I have any right to be jealous anyway. She deserves to enjoy her night and celebrate, and I need to get my mind on something else."

It's going to take a *lot* of alcohol for me to focus on

anything else. Especially when another man's hands are currently on Em's waist.

"Four shots of tequila, please," I say to the bartender. He pours them, and Madison snickers.

"Ahh, trying to drink her out of your mind, I see. Something tells me that this is going to make things worse, but hey, whatever you think will work."

Without a word, I down the shots, even though getting out of my head is probably a hopeless cause at this point. My phone vibrates.

EMALINE

hitting it off with this guy and gonna take him home lolol, see you tomorrow?

KIERAN

K, see you in the morning?

My blood is boiling, and I hate it. I hate that the thought of her with another guy is making me want to vomit. I hate that I want to tell her not to go home with him. I hate that I'm this jealous—if I can't even tell her what I'm feeling, how am I allowed to be jealous? It's not like me to feel this way, but I'm pissed. At myself for being too weak to share my feelings and at that guy who's about to be living my dream, even though he could never even hold a candle to how good I could make her feel. I try to wipe the anger off my face and show the texts to Madison.

"That could've been you if you'd man up and tell her how you feel. But, since we both know you're not going to do that, more drinks?"

Tomorrow's hangover is going to fucking suck.

emaline

I STUMBLE through my front door and kick off my shoes. The hands of the man I brought home from the club are dancing all along my curves, sending goosebumps throughout my body. His name is Stefan, and in a refreshing change of pace, he didn't know who I was when I started dancing with him. I know pretty much nothing about him aside from the fact that he's visiting from New York and works in finance.

He lightly presses me against the wall and sprinkles kisses along my body, starting at my cheekbones and making his way down my chest. He pauses for a moment to run his hands along my cleavage, and I run my fingers through his hair to gently pull it. I moan out, "Fuuuckkk, that feels so good."

He smirks and says, "It should," followed by kissing down my exposed stomach. Warmth and tension grow in my lower abdomen, aching for more of his touch. His hands continue to slide lower, approaching the place where I need them most.

Too impatient to wait any longer, we rush to my bedroom. He opens the door, revealing my all-pink paradise. His eyes are immediately drawn to my king-sized bed, which is covered in a subtly floral comforter. I don't frequently bring people home, so letting someone into my space is pretty vulnerable. While I'm an extrovert and not ashamed of frequently having hookups, having my room as somewhere that's my own space, safe from all of the stressors and judgment and bullshit of the outside world is really important to me. But between the level of alcohol in my body and how turned on I am, I don't care.

We finish about as quickly as we started—which isn't necessarily bad, just kinda... meh.

"Want me to help you clean up?"

While the offer is sweet, I feel like taking care of myself and getting under my covers, alone. I either do purely hookups or relationships, not anywhere in between, except for the one friends-with-benefits situation I had while in college at NYU, which ended rather poorly.

"Oh, I can take care of myself. Thank you though, this was great. Want me to walk you to the door?" I reply, standing up.

Seemingly a bit frustrated by my abrupt ending and lack of inviting him to stay the night, he narrows his eyes at me and says, "That's fine, I'll show myself out. Thanks, this was a lot of fun." He pulls his pants back on quickly and then walks out of my room. After the front door slams, I walk to my ensuite bathroom to pee and get ready for bed.

As soon as I climb into my bed, my brain goes into overdrive. There was nothing wrong with this hookup. It physically felt good, but there was something missing. It's been nearly a year since I was last in a real relationship, and while I've overall loved being in my chaotic hookup era, it's not truly satisfying for me anymore. The tricky part is that the idea of trying to date and get into a relationship is terrifying. After so many shitty relationships, including one very abusive one, my hopes aren't very high for finding someone who will treat me the way I deserve.

Plus with my growing career, it's hard to know if someone

is actually into me because of who I am at my core or if it's because of my fame. The almost-hookup with the girl at that party I was at a few weeks ago wasn't the first time of someone only being into me because of my success. When dating is already so vulnerable, having the added layer of trying to decipher people's intentions almost makes me want to avoid it completely. That and the struggle of tour life—dating while on the road is a whole other can of worms that most people just don't understand.

Why can't I find someone like Kieran? He's a true gentleman, he's funny as hell, he's treated every partner he's ever had wonderfully, and if the stories he's told me are true and not exaggerations, he's pretty good in bed.

I want a deeper connection and relationship with someone, where it's not just phenomenal sex, but also emotional safety that isn't the gaslighting and manipulative BS I've dealt with in the past. I want someone who can be like a best friend, that also happens to be my partner. And I know Kieran could technically be that person. But it feels too risky.

I need to get these thoughts out of my head, but obviously, Kieran isn't the one to share them with. She's probably busy or asleep, but I text my college bestie, Alaina. Even if she doesn't reply, it's good to just get things out to someone.

EMALINE

super drunk and just had another subpar hookup

why do I never learn??

also why aren't more men like kieran? ugh

I wait a few minutes to see if she'll reply, but the heaviness of my eyes and the pre-emptive embarrassment I know I'll be feeling in the morning tell me to lock my phone and go to bed.

kieran

I THROW BACK another shot of whiskey, now at a total of seven shots in the span of two hours. After that text from Emmie, something shifted in me. Hell knows that after the stress she's been dealing with, she deserves to have a release. But, I wish I was the guy going home with her, even though I know that it would completely destroy our friendship if things went south. That I could lose the girl who has been at my side through every painful moment. She's been there through every happy moment, too. And living a life where I can't share both my horrible moments and my incredible moments with Emaline would destroy me. Those inklings of being into her have been subtly present for years, even when I hadn't quite acknowledged them, but now they are loud and clear, to the point where I can't ignore them. I wish that I could follow through on the feelings and see if she feels the same way, instead of just stewing in them like I am now, but there's too much at stake.

Madison comes up behind me and places her hand on my shoulder. "Hey, are you good?"

I could lie, but she always has too good of a read on me.

"Not really. I feel like an absolute ass for being this jealous and angry. Especially when I haven't vocalized my feelings to her. I'm pathetic," I reply, my words slurring.

Her face gives a combination of sympathy and pity. "Kier, let's pause. You can't control what your brain decides to present you with, but it doesn't take a genius to gather that you've felt like this for a while. And it's natural to be jealous, but you're an idiot for not telling her how you feel."

"I don't know. She's blowing up to be this major pop star who can get pretty much any person she wants, and I'm just me. She has no reason to feel the same about me, and I'll fuck it all up if I ever tell her. You know how it's gone with every relationship I've ever had. I pour my heart into people and then they hurt me. And I can't be the one to hurt her." I say, looking at the ground.

"I know that she has this insane trajectory, but you know as well as I do that you've been best friends your entire lives, far before she was famous. So stop using that as a bullshit excuse. I get not wanting to risk it, but letting this fester isn't good either. It's going to make its way out sometime," she replies.

Ruby strolls over with her usually confident stature, but with a hint of concern in her eyes.

"Everything okay?" she says.

Madison looks at her and then at me, saying, "So, are you going to tell her, or do I have to?"

Way to go, Kieran. Couldn't push down the feelings and ignore them. Now you're ruining everyone's night.

Unable to look anyone in the eye, I sigh and mumble, "I... I love Emaline."

"Okay, I love her too—what's the problem?" Ruby says.

"No. Like, I'm *in* love with her, and she went home with some guy, and I feel like I'm crawling out of my skin. I've been downing shots to try to get her out of my head," I reply, wringing my hands together.

Her eyes widen. "Oh. Well, I can see the problem now. How long has this been going on? Does she know?"

I'm far too drunk to make sense of all that's flowing through my brain. I can't even explain these feelings to myself, never mind anyone else.

I press my lips together. "I mean...I honestly have no idea. Since forever, maybe? Who the fuck knows. Of course, I haven't told her. Last thing I need to do is screw everything up right before tour starts. She's already been anxious about it. I don't need to add to that. I don't need to tell her. What I need to do is figure out how to delete these feelings."

Ruby gives me a weak smile. "You've been drinking alcohol like it's water. I figured that was you celebrating. She hasn't said anything, but I've seen the way she looks at you sometimes. Not saying you *have* to tell her, but I don't know if your fears are totally accurate."

Madison shoves my shoulder and says, "Wait, you're in love with her? I thought you just started having a crush on her. This is huge! Mom is going to lose her shit."

"Mom will not know a single word about this. You know she can't keep her mouth shut, which means Em's mom will know because she can never keep a secret from her. This needs to stay on the DL, especially because I don't even know if I'm going to do anything about it."

Madison shakes her head. "Fine, fine. But you know that I'm going to be your biggest fan if this does happen. Let's go hang out with everyone else, and maybe cool it on the drinks a bit? I don't want you to do anything you'll regret."

The last thing I need is for anyone else to find out about my feelings for Emmie, and clearly, I'm already not doing a stellar job hiding them. I should call it a night, even if being alone with my thoughts may not be the healthiest thing.

I open the Uber app on my phone. "Actually, I think I might head home. Don't want to ruin the vibe, and I think I need to go to bed."

"Promise me that you'll text me as soon as you get home and that you won't do anything stupid? I worry about you sometimes, Kiki," Madison says.

"Thanks, Mads. Matt is going to pick you up to drive you home later, right?"

She nods. "Yep, and I'll text you when he gets here and when we get home. Be safe."

After I get the notification that my Uber has arrived, I head outside and get in. Thankfully my driver doesn't try to spark a conversation.

One door down, Emmie is hooking up with someone who isn't me. The tension throughout my body and the pounding in my chest that started earlier is amplified, and it's unbearable. All I want to do is to completely disconnect from reality and not have to feel anything.

I unlock the door to my apartment and throw my wallet and keys down on the counter. After changing into sweats and a hoodie, I open the liquor cabinet to pour myself a whiskey on the rocks. Mads was right when she said to cool it on the drinks, but my drunk brain doesn't have enough judgment to care. I sip it as my thoughts flood incessantly.

Did she see me staring?

Can she tell I'm acting weird?

If she saw me staring, does she think I don't want her to be happy?

Did everyone else see me staring?

Did she think my reply to her text was weird or rude?

Should I say something to her?

Should I text her?

Should I go over to her apartment?

Should I pull away and spend less time with her so that my feelings don't come out?

With all sense of judgment out the window, I chug the rest of my drink. My OCD is telling me that to get the thoughts out of my brain, I need to pace. I start to pace back and forth, taking five steps in one direction, and then taking five steps in the other direction, stumbling a bit because of the alcohol.

I hope my downstairs neighbor doesn't hear me.

This goes on for nearly a half hour until my phone vibrates.

MADISON

Did you get home okay?

KIERAN

Oh yeah, sorry meant to text you. Getting ready for bed now. Glad you got home alright

I feel bad that I forgot to text Madison, but I'm grateful her text got me out of my pacing loop. He's likely asleep, but I decide to call Noah, hoping that maybe he'll have some advice or can help me chill out.

"Hey, man, everything okay?" he says, groggily.

I slur, "Fuck, did I wake you up? I'm sorry. I'm actually having a really bad night."

"Nah, I woke up like five minutes ago. What's wrong?"

I fight the overwhelming urge to drink more and instead walk over to my couch.

"Long story. But the other day I realized I'm in love with Em and we were out at a bar celebrating being done with the album and she left with another guy and she's probably down the hall fucking him and I started spiraling and now I'm like eight drinks deep and I don't know what to do. Sorry for bothering you."

"Hey, don't apologize. If I were you I'd be spiraling, too. I hate to say I saw this coming, but I've kinda thought you had feelings for her for years. I just didn't want to assume or make anything weird. And yeah, she went home with some guy, but you know as well as I do that she's always been more of the relationship type anyway. It's probably not the best timing with the tour coming up, but I feel like you should say something to her. You two would be really good together. Not just really good. Perfect."

Exactly what I was hoping he *wouldn't* say. Noah is third in line of the people who know me best, so if both he and Mads are saying this, my feelings for Emaline must be getting really obvious.

"I dunno, man. She's everything to me. And with my luck, it'll just crash and burn. You know how it turned out with Jamie. I can't lose Em. It would destroy both of us. And she's worked so hard for this career and she's been so stressed and still struggling with all the Chris shit. Yeah, we could be good together. But what if that's not enough?"

He sighs. "I get why you're afraid, but you can't let fear get in the way of what could be something incredible for both of you. I know it's really late for you and with how drunk you are, you may just want to sleep on it. But I'm here for you, whatever you decide."

"Yeah, I should probably go to bed. Thanks for hearing me out. Love ya."

"Love you too, bro. Talk to you soon."

My mind is still in overdrive, and forcing myself to go to bed is probably the smartest option before I do something I regret. I walk into my bathroom to do my nighttime routine.

Sometimes, when my OCD isn't flaring up, I don't have to

do things in a particular pattern. But on nights like tonight, I need to do the routine in threes. Having no desire to fight the compulsion even though I know it will make things worse, I wash my face three times, brush my teeth three times, and wash my hands three times before getting in bed.

As I place my phone on the nightstand, I get the urge to text Emmie. I start typing a text saying, "Hope you had a great night. Excited for the shoot tomorrow. See you in the morning," but immediately delete it. Sending it will make it seem like I can't give her space.

We're at a photo studio in LA, getting ready to shoot the album cover. Usually, band members wouldn't be present for this, but Emmie asked if I could come along to give my input. I was tempted to call her and say I wasn't feeling well and couldn't make it, but despite my excruciating hangover and inability to find my sanity, I'm here.

She's currently finishing up in hair and makeup, and she is stunning, as always. Her hair is in beachy waves, and her makeup is subtle, just enough to further enhance her natural beauty. A simple pink tank top and a basic light-wash pair of jeans wait for her on a rack on the other side of the room. As I sit on the couch scrolling on my phone, Ruby struts over.

"How's your head, lover boy?" she laughs, handing me a coffee.

Making a "shh" sign, I say, "I need to sleep for a week. Is it that obvious?"

"Oh, not at all. Figured based on how you left last night that you'd be feeling rough today. Glad you made it though, I know Em was insistent on you being here," she says.

"Kier! Can you come here for a sec?" Emmie shouts from the other side of the room.

Just. Act. Normal.

I walk over, making sure I don't get in the way of all of the people setting up equipment. I try to paint a natural-ish looking smile on my face instead of the anxiety that's swirling through my head.

"What's up, Em?"

She passes me her phone. "What do you think of this inspo?"

There are several photos of her, a few side profiles, one sitting on a chair, and one laying on the ground with her legs in the air. Unsurprisingly, she looks amazing in all of them, but there's one side profile shot where she's glancing down at the ground that I think is best.

"I think this one fits the vibe best, but all of them look great. It's simple but gorgeous, and you look deep in thought," I say, passing her phone back.

She flashes me a smile. "I hoped you would say that. Wasn't sure if it was too plain, but I think it'll be perfect. How was the rest of your night after I left?"

Breathe, Kieran, breathe.

"It was nice. Got to catch up with Madison, then called it an early night. Wanted to do some reading and get to bed early. How about you?"

I'm secretly hoping her night was terrible.

"Ehh, wasn't bad. Sex was alright, but honestly, I'm getting tired of the whole hookup game. And he got all pissy when I asked him to leave, but you know how I feel about having people in my space."

Emmie is very particular about who she lets in her room. I'm one of the few people who she lets chill in there. We've spent countless evenings hanging out on her floor, smoking, and talking about everything from industry gossip, to reminiscing on childhood memories, to talking about our dreams for the future. Her space is sacred to her, and it makes me angry. What sort of losers is she picking up that act like babies when she asks them to leave?

I wouldn't do that.

Maybe Noah is right and she's ready to settle down in a relationship. But that still doesn't mean she wants me.

"That's shitty. He should feel lucky that he had the night with you. It's not like you were on a date or something. I feel you on the hookup thing, it isn't doing it for me anymore. I guess when you're twenty-five, doing the same shit you've done since you were eighteen gets old."

She nods. "Yeah, while I'm kinda scared for something more after everything that happened with Chris, I'm also tired of doing the same old, unsatisfying, shit over and over."

"Don't let that criminal keep you from finding happiness, he doesn't deserve to continue taking up residence in your brain. But enough about shitty guys, you ready to shoot this cover?"

It seems like she wasn't bothered by the text I sent last night saying "K" when she was leaving the bar, and I'm not sure how to feel about that. Not that I wanted her to be mad at me, but part of me was hoping it would elicit some sort of response. Some sign of her somehow having feelings for me.

She stands up from her chair and pulls me in for a hug. "Yep, let's do this so we can go get ourselves some very delayed Sunday bagels."

Moments like this make me wonder if there could be some sliver of a chance of her sharing my feelings. This hug feels different. It feels like she's holding me a little longer than usual. And sure, it could just be her commiserating about hookups getting old, but the glimmer in her eye when she pulls away from the hug hints at something different.

"Alright, let's get this show on the road," says Lydia, the creative director. "Em, let's get you dressed while Callie gets the camera and lights situated."

I stretch my legs and finish up my coffee, taking in the set. Umbrella lights and shiny reflective photography screens burn my eyes, and I squint through the last few sips of my coffee. The brightness is not helping my hangover in the least. This is far from the first time I've been at this kind of photoshoot, but it's still never lost on me how far we both have come. We're not the little kids playing karaoke anymore.

Emmie walks out from the changing area. The pink top brings out her blue-green eyes, paired with jeans slung so low on her hips that I can't help but fantasize about what's underneath them. She heads over to Callie's setup, transitioning into "work mode," focused and serious.

"Okay, have you decided which pose you want to go with?" Callie says.

"Yeah, Kier and I were talking, and I think the one of me turned to the side, glancing at the floor, is the best option. What do you think?"

"Let's do it. Should only take us a few shots, and then we can see what you think."

They both get into position and while Em looks beautiful, all I can think about is her taking that douche home last night. About his hands running down her curves. About how he could never please her in the way I know I could. About how I wish I was him.

Callie snaps a few shots, and as they pop up on the display monitor, I'm even more certain of how successful this new album is going to be. Emaline puts her heart and soul into everything she does, and it's why I love her the way I do. It's scary to think about how much I love her. Because we've always been a package deal. Taking that to the next level could possibly be great. But it could also ruin everything we have. I know that losing Em wouldn't just ruin music for me. It would ruin everything. It's terrifying to think that risking the thing that could possibly bring me the most joy I'll ever have also has the potential to rip the best person in my life away from me.

But, maybe, scary doesn't have to be a bad thing.

emaline

IT'S FRIDAY, and today is a day full of press and tour promo before heading to San Diego for a girls' weekend. Alaina, my college bestie who I don't see super often, will be coming and I can't wait to spend time with her. She moved to LA around the same time as I did for her dance career. With our mutually chaotic schedules, we don't get to see each other super frequently, but we text all the time. I'm really excited that she'll be coming this weekend and to a few of my tour dates.

I stare at my closet, trying to figure out what I want to wear for my Yahoo interview and SiriusXM performance, knowing that whatever I wear needs to look good on camera. I decide on a simple olive green crocheted crop top, medium wash jeans, and my well-loved white sneakers. It'll bring out my eyes and be cute but casual. I put the outfit on, shocked that I like how I look today, despite the eating disorder that has ruled my brain since I was a preteen.

While I've been in recovery for years and I've done a ton of therapy, my body image still fluctuates from day to day, and honestly, moment to moment. One day I can be wearing the skimpiest outfit and feel hot as hell, and another day I can pick apart every single aspect of my appearance that I hate—even when my body doesn't look any different.

Being in this appearance-focused industry doesn't help things either. While there has been some progress, the music industry is an amplified version of the toxic body ideals that exist in our world as a whole. There's constant talk of who's on what diet, who had liposuction, or who "let themselves go." My fans are usually pretty supportive, but from time to time, I've seen shitty things said about me online. Instead of being able to focus on talent and art, there's this constant looming worry of someone judging or commenting on my body. And, sometimes, so that I don't have to wait for the other shoe to drop, I criticize myself before anyone else does.

While my struggles with my body are sort of about my physical appearance, they are also about something deeper beneath the surface. I've experienced a lot of trauma, so my eating disorder has been a safety blanket. I've been clean from eating disorder behaviors for a few years now, but in the past, when I needed to feel in control, I would restrict my food. When I felt like I needed to get what I was feeling out of my body but couldn't find the words for it, I would throw up or overexercise.

The thing is, eating disorders lie to you. Sure, they sometimes "help" in the moment, but when I thought I was finding control, I was finding the opposite—and when I was trying to get those feelings out of my body, I was continuing to dig myself into a deeper and deeper addictive spiral. My brain thought it was protecting me, but it was killing me.

I'm just grateful that at this moment, my brain is being kind to me. Especially because it's about to be a chaotic day, and I need all the brain space I can get.

I'm usually a last-minute packer, but knowing how

stressful today was going to be, I packed my bags last night so that all I have to do is throw them in Ruby's car. We'll be driving straight to San Diego from the SiriusXM performance, so I figured it would be best to be prepared instead of scrambling this morning when I'm already pressed for time.

KIERAN

Good luck with the interview! You'll be amazing. See you over at Sirius

EMALINE

thanks, i'm hoping it goes well! see you later on <3

Kieran often tags along for my interviews, but he's getting breakfast with his mom before the performance this afternoon. He's a true mama's boy, and it's always hard for him when we're on tour and he can't see her for a few weeks. Whether it's FaceTiming in the greenroom or paying for flights so that they can come out to shows, he makes every effort to stay connected to his family, despite our crazy schedules. His mom raised him right, and unfortunately, his kind, loving, selfless nature has often been unappreciated or abused by past romantic partners, which I hate. He deserves to have someone love him in the way that he loves. I guess we both do.

After getting dressed, I throw on some light makeup and pull my hair into a high ponytail because I don't have the energy to wash it. With how stressed I've been the past few weeks, sometimes I need to do the bare minimum. Luckily, I've developed the art of it not being obvious to anyone else.

Forever an over-packer, even for a two-day trip, I grab all of my things and take the elevator down to meet Ruby.

"Feeling ready?" she asks as I get into the passenger seat of her SUV, after shoving my bags in her trunk. "I know it's been a bit since your last interview."

I nod. "I think so. A little worried that I'll accidentally blurt something about the album, but trying to keep my mind on the tour so that nothing slips."

"You're going to be great. And if they ask if you're working on new music, say something to the effect of 'I'm always writing, but right now all of my energy is going into this tour'."

"That's what I figured. I'm determined to keep this a total secret. It's always wild when fans already know the songs just a day after they're released. It blows my mind how dedicated they are to my music. I'm so lucky."

She starts driving and replies, "I mean, yeah, you're lucky, but you've also worked your ass off since you were a little kid. Sure, some luck is involved, but you didn't fall into success. You put so much effort, not just into your music, but into connecting with your fans, which is why they're so committed to you. It's no surprise that you are where you are, and that's not me saying that because I'm supposed to be your number one fan."

Logically, she's right, but with going from writing songs on a shitty guitar in my childhood bedroom, to living in a tiny dorm at NYU, to performing at iconic venues, it can be hard to reconcile in my head.

"So many people in this industry are just as talented but don't have the same level of success, so sometimes it feels like I fell into this instead of earning it."

She taps the music icon on her car display. "Okay, let's get you out of your head before this interview. Who do you want to listen to?"

Knowing she won't judge, I say, "One Direction. Hard to be anxious when belting *Best Song Ever*."

After a photographer shot a few photos of me, I'm sitting on a purple velvet couch at the Yahoo offices, being interviewed by a reporter.

"So, how does it feel getting ready for this tour? Your opening show is at Radio City Music Hall, one of the most iconic venues in the world, and it's completely sold out. That must be surreal, especially with going to college in New York," the reporter says.

With my typical "I'm bubbly and not at all socially awkward," face on, I reply, "I'm a little nervous, but mostly so excited. It's a dream come true to have the opportunity to perform at so many famous venues on this tour. After seeing so many concerts at Radio City during my time at NYU and seeing the Christmas Spectacular there as a little girl, it's mind blowing to me that in less than two weeks, me and the band will be on that stage."

"Any other cities you're most excited about?"

"So hard to choose... but I think Nashville will be pretty fun, and I'm really excited to get to close out the tour here in LA at The Troubadour. My family will be there, and while I grew up in the suburbs and not LA proper, it's kind of a homecoming. And I love that it's a smaller, more intimate venue."

She nods and says, "Last question. Do you have any new music on the way?"

Control your face, Emaline. Don't be suspicious.

"I mean, I'm always writing, but right now I'm super focused on this tour. A lot of preparation has gone into it, so I haven't really had time to put energy into anything else. My second album was very special to me, and I'm excited to get to play those songs again and hear everyone scream the words back at me."

She stands up to shake my hand and says, "Thank you so much for your time. It was lovely meeting you, and looking forward to seeing you perform on closing night."

"It was lovely meeting you as well, thank you so much for the opportunity, and excited for you to see the show!"

Now that the interview is done, it's time to shift into performance mode. We'll only be doing two songs, but the pressure is high, especially with the number of listeners this particular show gets. It's a stripped-down, acoustic set, which means that fewer things can go wrong technically, but there's also a lot less to hide behind vocally—so I have to sound perfect.

"You were great. We need to speed over to Sirius now so we don't have time to stop for food. But drink this for your vocal cords, and Kieran grabbed you something to eat between soundcheck and the performance," Ruby says, passing me a cup of hot tea. I haven't had an entire day of having to be "on" and be *Emaline Levine* instead of just Emmie in months, but it's good prep for the two months we're about to have on the road. All I have to do is make it through the next four hours, and then I'll have a full weekend to just be me, no cameras or expectations.

After not eating since breakfast, scarfing down this chicken caesar salad wrap in the green room while stretching my legs out across Kieran's lap feels glorious. Soundcheck went off without a hitch, and now we're chilling until go time.

"Alright, we're live in fifteen minutes. Em, you can finish

eating, but then everyone needs to get into their places," our tour manager, Ryan, says.

Kieran is looking down and playing with my shoelaces, his gorgeous, slightly wavy, dark-brown hair falling slightly into his ocean-blue eyes. I'm not sure if I've ever noticed how pretty he is. As I look at him, slight butterflies start in my stomach, but I quickly try to suppress them when I realize I haven't acknowledged what Ryan said.

"Copy, I'll be finished with this in a sec," I reply.

I've had butterflies for plenty of other guys and girls throughout my life, but having them for Kieran? That's completely foreign... and for some reason, I almost don't want to ignore it. But, now is not the time. I need to be on my game, and my brain can't be wandering. Shaking my head to try to refocus, I finish the last bite of my wrap and abruptly stand up.

After he stands up, Kieran pulls me into a hug and says, "Ready to knock 'em dead, Emmie?"

This hug feels different than any hug we've had before, but I don't think he's hugging me any differently than usual. It's kind of unsettling, but surprisingly nice? But, I don't have time to sort through this right now. I need to go be my performance persona, not the girl trying to figure out if she somehow has feelings for her best friend.

I hug him back and say, "Yep, let's do this thing, Kiki."

I quickly check my teeth to make sure no lettuce got stuck and chug the rest of my tea. We walk over to the set and I grab my in-ear monitors from my monitor engineer, Jake. I clip the pack to the waistband of my jeans and loosely put them in my ears, not yet fully having them in so that I can still hear everyone else. I sit down, and Kieran grabs his guitar before sitting down on the stool next to me. The rest of the band has already taken their places.

The host of the show points at us, saying, "And we're live in three, two, one. Welcome back to SiriusXM Hits 1, I'm your host Nola Hart, and today we have a special guest, Emaline Levine, here to perform two of her hit songs and share more about her upcoming sold-out tour. Emaline, it's wonderful to have you here. I know you haven't been on the show before, but we've met a few times, and I've been a fan of your music for years. You're such a genuinely cool person, and I'm so excited you're here."

Putting my smiley performance face on, I say, "Thank you so much for having us on the show, Nola. It's a dream to be here."

"I know everyone listening is dying to hear you perform and learn more about the tour, so let's get into it. Starting on June 1st, you have a twenty-five date sold-out run opening at Radio City Music Hall and closing here in LA at The Trou-badour, which is a pretty impressive feat. How does it feel to be heading out on a tour of this magnitude?"

"It's incredible. I'm so grateful for how my journey as an artist has continued to evolve, and it's such a privilege to get to share my music with so many people. I'm truly at home on stage, and it's magical getting to see the audience every night. After nearly a year off of tour, I'm excited to get back on the road."

"Your fans are so dedicated, and it's amazing to see. We can talk more about the tour in a minute, but I know you're really here to perform for us. So, *Shut Down*. Super powerful lyrics, really heart-wrenching. This one must have been hard to write. What inspired it?"

While I haven't publicly disclosed the specific person this is about, I wrote it about my destructive, toxic relationship with Chris, and how he constantly tore me apart. Maybe one day I'll share the full story with the world, but for now, vagueness is where it's at.

Trying not to appear too emotional, I say, "A few years ago, I was in a really bad situation, that I'm luckily not in anymore. It's all about that and what my internal experience was like when going through it."

"I'm sure that, unfortunately, many people, myself included, can relate. Without further ado, this is *Shut Down* by Emaline Levine."

As usual, I get lost in the music, having an experience where I'm pouring my heart out like there's no one else in the room. Closing out the song, I sing, "...you rip apart my body and tell me how much you hate me, and all I can do is take it and shut down." Everyone in the studio claps, and I'm brought back to the present moment.

Wine-filled glasses clink together, toasting to a successful performance and a much-needed work free weekend. We got to the rental house in San Diego about an hour ago, and I'm so glad to be in sweatpants and a bralette, laying on what's probably the comfiest couch in existence. These women are the people I'm most comfortable with, aside from Kieran. While I met all of them except Alaina through my music, they've gone past coworkers to now being some of my best friends. I can be my truest, most unfiltered self with them, with zero fear of judgment.

My phone vibrates. I plan on trying to stay off it most of the trip, but I check it to make sure it's not anything important.

KIERAN

Have fun with the girls! Sad we won't get our Sunday bagels though 😔

> And say hi to Mads for me

EMALINE

> i will!! have fun at the dodgers' game with your dad! 🦴

> and you better not get sunday bagels without me 🥯

KIERAN

> I wouldn't dare

I laugh to myself about the exchange. Or, at least I thought it was just to myself.

Alaina sits down next to me and says, "Whose texts have you giggling?"

"Oh, it was just Kieran. He said to say hi to everyone," I reply.

"I saw how you were looking at him earlier...what's up with that?" Delia says, flopping down on the floor, wearing a pink pajama set.

Cover blown, apparently.

Blushing, I chug some of my pinot grigio and reply, "What do you mean? How was I looking at him?"

Ruby snickers. "I saw that, too. Is there something going on that we don't know about?"

"N-No. I mean, yes. But also, no. I think I may have a crush on him or something? I'm not sure what's happening, but when we were chilling on the couch I started getting butterflies out of nowhere, and then when he hugged me it felt... different."

A huge smile spreads across her face, and Alaina adds, "Oh. My. God. This is everything. I've been waiting for this chapter for years."

"Uhhhh... what chapter are you referring to?" I say.

Kenzie places her wine glass down on the light wood coffee table and says, "The one where you and Kieran both pull your heads out of your asses and realize you're in love with each other and become the cutest couple known to man."

Both of us? They asked if there was something they didn't know, but is there something I don't know?

Furrowing my brow, I say, "Both of us? I'm confused."

"Uhh... I'm definitely not supposed to tell you this... but Kieran is head over heels for you. Has been for years. Well, he hasn't known about it until recently, but it's definitely been for years," Madison says.

Have I been living under a rock? Am I oblivious? This can't be true. If it was true, I'd have to have picked up on signals at some point.

"There's no way. I mean, if it was true, I would've noticed at some point. He's my best friend, we tell each other everything."

Laughing, Ruby says, "Except this apparently. I promise we're not lying. He'd kill me if he knew I'm telling you this, but last weekend at the club, he was losing it when you took that guy home. Nearly cleared the bartender out of whiskey trying to lie to himself, until Madison noticed something was up."

Madison nods. "Yep, she's telling the truth. He definitely didn't realize it until recently, but he's down bad. I'm surprised it hasn't slipped yet, he's not exactly good at hiding his emotions. I don't think I've ever seen him as angry as he was the other night."

Isabelle glances up from her phone and says, "You have to be oblivious if you haven't seen the way that boy looks at you."

I didn't think anything of him just saying "K" in reply to my text to him last weekend when I was leaving the bar, but was that him trying to get some response out of me?

"Wait. When I was leaving the bar last weekend and told

him I was going home with that guy, he just said 'K see you tomorrow' but I figured he was trying to be quick and get back to hanging with you guys. Was that him wanting me to stay? Or, him wanting to be the one I was going home with? Holy shit. I need more wine," I say, throwing my face into my hands.

Mads shakes her head. "Nope, I already dealt with drunk Kieran sorting through these feelings the other night, and alcohol made things significantly worse. No more wine for you tonight."

"She's right. You need a clear head for making sense of this. I know your mind is already all over the place, but trying to numb the feelings away isn't going to help," Ruby adds.

Alaina gently places her hand on my back and says, "You don't have to sort it all out tonight, Em. But even though it's coming as a surprise to you, I promise none of us are lying. I just never said anything back when we were in school because I figured you may have had a thing as kids that didn't work out and I didn't want to make it weird."

My brain is in overdrive, and I'm not quite sure what to do with this information. I only just realized that I have feelings for him, and now I find out, not from him, that he has feelings for me too? It's all so risky. Tour starts in a week and a half, the album is about to drop... even if I wanted to do something about it, is it worth it? There's no taking this back. It would change everything. Sure, it could be for the better, but what if it's for the worse?

kieran

IT TURNS out that trying to ignore the fact that you're in love with your best friend is fucking hard when you're rehearsing to go on tour with her.

Who would've thought?

It's our last day of rehearsals before we leave for New York tomorrow night. All week, I've been trying to push my feelings down. With no success. I mean, even before I knew I felt this way about Emaline, I thought about her all the time since we're always together. But now? It's to a level that is impossible to keep out of my head. I've been able to keep myself together enough to play my guitar well. But aside from that, my brain is consumed with trying to not love her. Well, not not love her in general... to not love her in *that* way. My efforts are proving futile, especially since my goal is to not think about my feelings. And now I'm thinking about them more than I was before. Which I didn't think was possible.

Part of me wants to not ignore the feelings. But part of me wants to tell her. To take her on dates. To hold her hand as we walk through the airport. To take silly pictures in a photo booth where I kiss her and she has that intoxicating smile painted across her face—and not the one that she sometimes puts on for performances. The one where she's truly happy from the inside out. Where she has that cute little giggle that I know she's self-conscious about but that I'm addicted to hearing.

I keep getting this image in my head of us finishing a show and her sprinting to me, going up on her tiptoes to kiss me, and me picking her up and swinging her around, knowing that while the rest of the world just got to see her perform for ninety minutes, I get to see her and know her in a way that no one else does. I want to love her in the way she deserves to be loved. Not in the way that all of her asshole exes, especially Chris, have.

"Okay, let's take *Growth* from the top one more time. Overall, great, but Kieran, maybe you can throw in a harmony on the chorus?" Emaline says.

I nod. "Yeah, I can do that. Should I add some on the bridge, too? Could sound good."

"Sure, let's give that a try, good thinking," she replies.

We run through the song again, and, as usual, I'm completely in awe of her. Her pitch is impeccable, and she manages to sound better than the studio recording, which isn't super typical of live performances. She constantly doubts herself and references "luck," but this isn't luck. This is natural talent combined with working her ass off. I'd say that it blows my mind how quickly her fame is rising, but it's no surprise with the quality of her work. Being able to be just a small part of her success is such a privilege.

Emaline walks over and high fives me as she says, "That was perfect. Let's break for lunch, and then we can do one more full run through before we call it a night."

We place our in-ear monitor packs down and head over to the table where catering is. There's a big assortment of tacos in addition to a salad, some tortilla chips, guac, and queso, which is exactly what I need after only having coffee this morning. I don't often run late, but this morning I slept through my alarm. And no matter how late I'm running, I always make sure I get to Emaline on time. Even if it means being starving all morning.

We make ourselves plates, and I grab our utensils. We walk over to a couch in the corner. She immediately inhales her tacos, which makes me smile internally. Seeing her struggle with food and her body for so many years was extremely painful. Recovery isn't a linear journey and she still has hard days, but I love it when I see her enjoying food and nourishing her body. She used to constantly only eat salads with dressing on the side when we got food anywhere, and now, most of the time, she eats pretty much all types of food without shame. For so long, I was afraid she'd die or permanently destroy her health, and seeing how much she has grown and healed is such a relief.

"Ready to head to New York tomorrow?" I say.

Finishing a bite of her salad, she replies, "I think so. Still have to pack my day off clothes and makeup and everything. Brie has all of my show outfits packed. I'm also honestly so excited to get some real bagels and pizza. The shit here isn't the same as New York."

"I'm not packed at all, going to have a hot date with my closet and suitcase tonight. And, same. I love that we're back living in LA now, but sometimes I miss our NYU days, especially the food. Well, not the dining hall. All of the other food, though," I say with a laugh at the end.

"The dining hall food left a lot to be desired, to say the least. I'm glad we have two days off after the show, I'm excited to see all of our old fave spots. Professor Smith is going to come to the show, too, and it's going to be great to see her."

Professor Smith was our main songwriting professor, and she's arguably Emaline's biggest fan. After me, of course. Emaline was a legend at NYU. People constantly asked why she was still in school and not working in the industry full-time, but it was important to her to continue working on the technical aspects of her craft. Even if she could've easily dropped out and still been as successful as she is now.

"Wouldn't mind doing a little picnic in Washington Square Park like we used to. Maybe that guy who was always covered in pigeons will still be there," I say.

She giggles and says, "I'm not sure if he ever leaves. Feeding those birds is seemingly his full-time job."

She places her plate on the ground and then lays down on the couch, her legs across my lap, which seems to be her go-to spot when we're chilling together on breaks—and I'm not complaining. I'm trying to control my eyes, but I can't help but scan over her body, noticing her in a way that I haven't quite seen before. My attraction to her is rooted in her personality and the incredible woman she is. But I'd be lying if I didn't say that she's easily the most stunning person I've ever laid my eyes on. She's wearing a thin-strapped, maroon crop top with a pair of gray low rise sweatpants. She has a tasteful level of cleavage peeking out, and the curves of her waist and hips are accentuated by her pants. I'm trying so hard not to stare, but it's impossible when she looks like a piece of artwork, with zero makeup and her hair in a messy bun. She's effortlessly beautiful, and it's not just her body—it's her heart and soul, too. I thank whatever higher power exists that she's scrolling on her phone, unable to see how embarrassingly I am engrossed with her.

After finishing our final run through, I drove home, grabbing In-N-Out on the way. Em had a meeting with Ruby after, so we drove separately. I grab two suitcases out of my closet and place them on my bed. I walk back over to the closet, looking at everything to decide what I want to pack for our two-month trip. Sometimes I'll buy new stuff when we're on the road, but I still want to make sure I've got my bases covered. As I peek through, my heart rate suddenly skyrockets, and it feels like it's going to burst out of my chest. And not in a good way. I have the urge to start pacing, and I'm not sure if I can fight it. My brain is playing all of my interactions with Emaline from the past two weeks on repeat, analyzing if I somehow made my feelings obvious to her. I try to resist the urge to pace because I need to pack and don't have the extra time, but the compulsion is too strong to stop.

My thoughts start with the SiriusXM performance, remembering playing with her shoelaces and the hug we had afterward.

Did I hug her too tightly? Could she feel how my heart was beating a mile a minute? Did I hug her for too long?

Then my thoughts leap to when we were on the couch earlier, and I worry about if even though she was scrolling on her phone, she could sense my eye. She's extremely perceptive of everything, and what if she knew? What would she have been thinking? Would she like it? Would she think I was creepy?

The pacing won't make my brain shut up, so I walk into my bathroom. I turn on the faucet of the sink as hot as it can go and start washing my hands, trying to wash the thoughts out of my head. When I'm in these spirals, I'll do anything I can to try to eliminate the obsessive thoughts, even if it's not logical. Despite the pain, I continue scrubbing my hands, my skin turning beet red from the scorching hot water. The thoughts still won't stop even though the water is searing my hands, but I know that if I don't stop this snowball soon, A) I won't be able to play guitar for opening night, and B) I won't be able to start packing.

To make matters worse, I'm reminded of the night when my ex Jamie dumped me. My ears are flooded with her telling me I was too broken and that I was a hopeless cause. That no one would ever be able to love me or deal with me. It's so pathetic that I can't just stop this. It's embarrassing that instead of being able to pack like a normal person, I'm wasting time being held hostage by my brain.

I scrub for a few more seconds, but then with every ounce of effort I have left, I turn off the faucet and walk back over to my bed. I sit down cross legged, chest heaving, and grab my phone to call Madison. Of all of the people in my support system, aside from Emaline, Madison knows me and my OCD best. Even in the deepest of spirals, she can usually still help me pull myself out. I go to her contact and hit call, hoping she answers because I'm not sure what I'll do if she doesn't.

"Hey, what's up?"

My voice shakes. "I can't stop thinking about Emmie. I started trying to pack, and as soon as I was looking in my closet, every interaction we've had in the past two weeks started replaying in my head. Paced for twenty minutes. Washed my hands with scalding water for fifteen minutes. Then all of the shit Jamie said started coming back to me. I don't know what to do."

"Kier, pause for a minute. Breathe in... and out. What are you thinking about?"

Trying to get my heart rate back under control, I let out a huge sigh.

"When we did that Sirius performance last week, we were on a break eating, and we were on a couch and she had her feet in my lap and I was playing with her shoelaces and then afterward I hugged her and I think I may have hugged her too tight or too long for what a friend would do. Today, we were on a break again, and she was laying in the same way, and she was scrolling on her phone, and I couldn't stop staring. I mean she was on her phone, but she notices the smallest things. That probably seemed creepy as hell and I can't stop thinking about how much I love her and want to be with her and I don't know what to do."

"Breathe. Breathe. She's given you long hugs plenty of times. And sure, maybe she could've somehow sensed your eyes today, but honestly, I'm sure her thoughts are consumed with this tour and that she was too much in her own thoughts to notice. And if she did notice, I think she may have some similar feelings. I've seen how she looks at you, and I could be wrong, but something tells me that she may be as anxious as you are. Do you want me to come over to help you pack?"

Still firmly gripping my phone, I walk to the kitchen and open the freezer, grabbing an ice pack to put on my face. It's a coping skill I learned in therapy years ago that's supposed to really quickly calm your nervous system. As I grab the ice pack, I say, "I mean...I don't want to be a bother...but if you can, that might be a good idea."

I hate asking for help, but if I don't have some extra support right now, I'm never going to actually pack or get sleep, which will only make things worse. I'd usually ask Emaline for support in a situation like this... but since it's about her, that's not exactly an option right now.

"It's not a bother at all, I promise. It'll be nice to see you before you leave, anyway. Matt is out with friends watching a football game, so I've just been watching Real Housewives anyway. I'll be there in fifteen."

I sit down on the gray suede sofa in my living room and turn on an old episode of Saturday Night Live, hoping that laughing can keep my brain distracted until Madison gets here.

> **EMALINE**
>
> how's packing going??

> **KIERAN**
>
> Indecisive as always…but going okay!

> **EMALINE**
>
> oh good!! i'm about to have some ice cream and call it an early night but see ya in the AM?

> **KIERAN**
>
> Sleep well, see you then!!

I hate lying to Em. But she has enough to worry about right now. I can't have her worrying about me.

There's a knock at my door, followed by the sound of it unlocking. Madison steps inside, wearing a pair of Matt's baggy shorts and a big t-shirt, along with fluffy slippers. I'm guilty about messing up her chill time. But I wasn't sure what else to do.

She steps over to hug me. "Ready to conquer your suitcase, Kiki?"

I nod sheepishly. "Yeah. Well, not really. But I think I can do it now that you're here. Thanks for coming to help, I know you were having a much-needed chill night. Sorry for interrupting that."

She shakes her head. "Don't apologize. I needed something to stop me from letting the reality TV rot my brain anyway."

I stand up and pull her into my chest, grateful for the sense of grounding and calm. I'm far from calm internally. But some of her peace is transferring to me, in a way. We break the hug and walk to my room.

She spreads out my navy blue packing cubes on my bed between the suitcases.

"Okay, let's get your bases covered. Basics first. Do you think five simple tees are enough? I figure you'll have plenty of not-basics too."

I nod and say, "Yeah, that'll be perfect."

I open one of the drawers of my dark wood dresser, pulling out a few white and black t-shirts. Already meticulously folded, I place them into one of the larger packing cubes.

She grabs a hoodie from my closet. As she turns around, I notice that it's my favorite one, one that my mom bought me when we all saw *Pearl Jam*, my favorite band, together a few years ago.

"Figured you'd want to pack your fave hoodie. I know it's summer, but hotel AC can be so cold," she says.

I tend to remember everyone else's favorites, so having someone remember one of mine, especially on a night when I'm so caught up in my head and feeling like too much, feels really nice.

"Didn't think you'd remember it was my favorite. And for sure, always gotta have a few hoodies in my bag on the road."

After about an hour, we finished packing all of my clothing, only having my toiletries and a few other random things left to add.

Plopping down on the edge of the bed, I say, "I know it's summer, but would you wanna have some hot cocoa before you head home? Like old times."

A smile spreads across Madison's face. "Of course, I would."

emaline

MY NEW ALBUM *Getting Back To Me* dropped at
midnight, and the internet is going wild. It was incredibly
difficult for everyone involved to keep it a secret, but it was
beyond worth it. Some of the comments on social media have
included:

- OH MY GOD. I GET TO HEAR THIS LIVE TONIGHT
  I'VE WON AT LIFE!!!
- okay but literally every song is so fucking relatable.
  zero skips
- cursing myself for not getting tickets to night one
- BUT CAN WE TALK ABOUT THE ALBUM COVER???
- how did she manage to keep this a secret?? zero
  leaks is unheard of these days

The stealth release worked exactly as planned, and I'm
giddy thinking about tonight's show. Aside from the SiriusXM
show last week, it's been nearly a year since I've performed,
and Radio City Music Hall is one of the most famous venues
I've ever headlined. It's always so special getting to play

through songs live for the first time, and while there isn't a true pit since all seats are assigned, something tells me that everyone in the first few rows will already have some of the lyrics memorized... which will be an unreal experience. It's really cool to see everyone's reactions, but I'm going to try to stay off social media most of the day so that I'm not distracted before the show. And so that I don't risk seeing inevitable negative comments. Not every album is for everyone, but that doesn't mean it's not hard to see people say they thought it sucked.

Our flight got in pretty late last night so we stayed at a hotel near the airport, but for the next two days, we'll be staying at a hotel right near the venue. Kieran and I almost always share a room on tour, which feels reminiscent of the countless sleepovers we had as kids. As we sit in the sprinter van and drive over the Queensboro Bridge, Ruby passes us all the bagels we ordered—a true New York staple.

"Which outfit are you wearing tonight?" Kieran says, pushing his hair out of his face.

I unwrap my everything bagel with cream cheese. "The hot pink feather one. I figured it would be a great statement piece to start out with."

"Iconic outfit for an iconic woman at an iconic venue. You're going to look stunning," he replies with a big smile.

Ever since the girls' weekend, I've been reading into every interaction I have with Kieran, trying to decipher if what everyone said about his feelings for me is true. They wouldn't lie to me, but with how risky it is, I need to be absolutely certain before I even think about saying something, if I decide to do that. He's complimented me before, but something about this does seem a little *different.* He's seemed more anxious around me than usual, which could have to do with the tour, but he usually doesn't get too anxious about performing.

We've been doing this for years, and it's second nature to both of us at this point. So maybe there's more behind his words?

I eat a few bites of my bagel and then say, "I was a little in my head about how my body would look in it, but I think it's worth the risk."

"Everyone's there to hear you sing, not to see your body. But if it helps, you looked amazing in the selfie you sent me from Brie's studio."

Trying not to get too much in my own head about the interaction, I say, "Thanks, Kiki," and look out the window while eating my bagel for the rest of the drive.

I sit down on the massive stage and flop onto my back, pleased with our now completed soundcheck. The lights are a bit blinding, but I want to soak up this feeling.

"That was amazing, everyone. Now, if you can perform just like that tonight, it may be our best show ever," Ruby says.

Kieran plops down next to me and gives me a high-five. "We fucking killed it. Well, I sounded decent, but you're the one who really killed it, Em."

Deciding to slightly test the waters without it *really* being obvious, I lay my head on his shoulder. "Don't be modest. You were amazing, too. Those harmonies we added sealed the deal."

He leans his head back into mine. "Fiiiine, didn't want to seem cocky, but yeah, I killed it, too."

Ruby yells over, "Hey, Em, I have a quick question for you, can you come here for a sec?"

Something tells me her question has nothing to do with the show and everything about her watching my interactions with Kieran like a goddamn hawk. I get up and walk over to her, saying, "What's up?"

She puts her hand on my shoulder. "You need to say something to him. The two of you are so clearly into each other, and if you both keep this in, it's going to end up interfering with your being able to focus on the show. You're good at trying to hide these things and trying to distract yourself, but you're not *that* good."

"It could also distract us even more. What, am I supposed to be like 'Hey, I'm obsessed with you, let's go do a show'?"

Shaking her head at me, she says, "I mean, maybe not like that. But, just saying, if you don't say something soon, it's going to become a problem. I'd hate for either of you to get so stuck in your head that it keeps you from performing at your best."

I look at the ground, sigh, and quietly say, "I'll think about it."

Focus, Em, focus.

The lights of the vanity in my dressing room illuminate my face as I finish my makeup while on FaceTime with my mom. She couldn't come to the first show because of a work commitment, but I wanted to have her as part of my getting ready ritual. I've been hesitant to say anything to her about the whole Kieran thing because she's not exactly good at keeping secrets, but, at this point, I'm desperate.

As I place little pink rhinestones in the corners of my eyes with eyelash glue, making sure I don't get them too close to my eye but also not too far away, I say, "So, I need advice on something. But, you can't tell a single soul."

"Please don't tell me you're pregnant, Emaline."

I snort. "Oh, absolutely fucking not. It's about Kieran. I think I have feelings for him. Well, not think. I know I do. And, according to literally everyone, he does too. But I don't know what to do about it."

She presses her lips together giddily. "Oh, I've known that boy was in love with you since you were in middle school. He's never said anything, but it's clear as day. I'm shocked it took someone else telling you, you're usually pretty perceptive of these kinds of things."

I roll my eyes. "So I've been told. But that doesn't answer the question... what am I supposed to do?"

"Well, ultimately, that's a question for you to answer for yourself. But, you know that he's an incredible man, and I have no doubt that he would treat you wonderfully. You already know each other inside and out, and I can tell you, without a doubt, that he has stronger feelings for you than you have for him. I can understand being worried about what could happen, but I think it would be a shame to miss out on what could be a beautiful relationship because you're anxious about 'what ifs'. You're perfect for each other."

So, I've been completely oblivious to his feelings forever. Cool.

I sigh. "You're right, you're right. I just would hate for it to make things weird or something. Like, what if everyone else is just reading into it and he doesn't actually feel that way?"

She shakes her head. "Emaline Rose Levine, You're a smart girl, and you're not being very smart right now. All of the important people in your life wouldn't be telling you the same thing, especially about something like this, if it wasn't true. We love you, we're not trying to sabotage you. It's up to you, but I think it would be awfully stupid to not say something."

"I'll think about it. I'm not sure how I would say it. But, I have to go so that I can finish getting ready. Show starts in thirty. I'll text you later," I say.

"Have a great show, baby. Love you so much."

"Love you too, mom."

I finish getting ready and head backstage, grabbing my in-ears from Jake. As I put them in, Kieran walks up beside me, putting his hand on my shoulder.

"Ready for go time, Emmie?"

"So ready. It's mind-blowing how many people are out there. Let's do this thing!"

We do our pre-show handshake, one that we started doing as kids and has now become a tradition. The band takes their places on stage with the lights still down, and I jump up and down a few times, getting myself pumped up. The grounding sensation of my feet hitting the ground reminds me of the magnitude of this moment. They start playing the intro of *Getting Back to Me*, and I run out, the crowd going wild. I'm not thinking about my feelings for Kieran, I'm just fully immersed in the song as it flows through my body. I sing the last note, and the volume of applause and screaming is almost over-whelming. My huge smile won't leave my face, so proud of myself and in awe of what I've accomplished. I've dreamed of moments like this since I was that little girl playing karaoke in my bedroom with Kieran, and, now, I'm living it.

"Hi! I'm Emaline Levine, this is my incredible band, and I'm so overjoyed to be playing for you all tonight, on the release day of my new album. It's a dream come true getting to be here, and it wouldn't be possible without each and every one of you. We have a jam-packed set with a few surprises thrown in, and I hope you all have the time of your life tonight, just like we are. Now, here's *Wild Mind*."

Ninety minutes later, the last note of the encore plays. I throw my body forward in my final bow and walk off stage. Kieran runs over to me and we high-five each other with both hands, high off of the adrenaline.

Ruby struts over to me in her typical all-black show attire and pulls me in for a huge hug. "So fucking proud of you. That was amazing. Not a single flaw, and the energy of the crowd was infectious."

I squeeze her back. "It felt incredible. I know I can be hard on myself after shows, but tonight, I'm proud of myself. Like, I just did that!"

The rest of the band walks over and Delia says, "Yeah, you fucking did!" We have a huge group hug, and then go backstage to pack our things up from the dressing rooms while the crew loads out. I take off my makeup, peeling off the rhinestones and trying to get the residue of the glue off. I change into hot pink sweatpants, glad to be rid of the itchy feathers, despite them looking good. After packing everything up, I swing my bag over my shoulder, and walk to the stage door, heading outside. Kieran is already out there waiting for me.

"Ready to go get some sleep? I'm fucking exhausted," he says.

I nod. "I think I'm going to knock out immediately. The chaos has definitely caught up with me." The hotel is only a block away, but our driver brings us there in an effort to avoid fans. We pull up and walk inside, and Ruby is standing near the front desk with our bags.

She passes us our room keys. "Get some rest, and enjoy your day off. Text me if ya need anything!"

"Thanks, Rube! Sleep well," I reply, grabbing the key from her.

Always a gentleman, Kieran grabs a gold and black luggage cart and places our multitude of bags on it before we take the elevator up to our room. I open the door with the keycard and while the emerald green and gold accents are beautiful, there is only a singular king bed—not the two queen beds that were requested.

"Uhhhhh…" I mumble.

Bringing everything into the room, Kieran says, "Fuck. That's a problem. I'll call down to the front desk and see if they can change our room."

As kids, we shared a bed plenty of times on family trips, but we've never shared one as adults. And with how I feel about him, I'm not sure if it would be a good idea. Scratch that. It would be a terrible idea.

"Yeah, that would be great."

He dials the front desk on speaker. "Hello, this is Kieran Hayes from room 355. We were supposed to have two queen beds, but this is a king bedroom. Is it possible to change rooms?"

"Hello Mr. Hayes, I'm so sorry for the inconvenience, but there are no other rooms available."

I press my lips together and look at the ground. Kieran replies, "Is there any way you can bring us a rollaway bed or something?"

"Unfortunately, we don't offer those. Again, so sorry for the inconvenience. Is there anything else I can help you with, Mr. Hayes?"

"No, that will be all. Have a good evening."

Welp. This is going to be a problem. There's a large chair in the corner, but certainly not one that would be manageable for other of us to semi-comfortably sleep on. I have a feeling that the universe putting us at a sold-out hotel that also doesn't have rollaway beds isn't a coincidence.

"I can try to sleep on that chair, I don't want you to be uncomfortable," Kieran says.

I'm worried about the prospect of us sharing our bed, but we've both had a long day and desperately need a comfortable spot to sleep.

I shake my head. "No, there's no way that'll be comfy, especially with how long your legs are. We can make it work. I'll put pillows between us or something if that'll make you feel better."

"You sure?"

I nod. "At this point, all I care about is getting in bed after how exhausting today has been."

I slide my shoes off and pull off my hoodie before climbing into bed.

Kieran cautiously climbs in next to me and says, "I'm okay without pillows between us if you are."

It makes me anxious, but since I don't want to make things weird, I reply, "That's fine."

We spend a few minutes debriefing about the show, and I can't stop looking at him. I love how his eyes light up when he talks about things he's passionate about. And one of those things happens to be performing with me. My eyes drift to his lips, and I'm overcome with the curiosity of what it would be like to kiss him. His lips look so soft, and I'm desperate to know how they'd feel on mine. I try everything I can to push it out of my brain, but it's not working.

Fuck it.

"I'm a little cold, do you mind if I scoot closer to you?" I say.

He lifts his arm and puts it over the pillows. "Well, I'd hate for you to be cold, c'mere."

I scoot into his side, and my heart is running a marathon. It feels so right to be here next to him... while also feeling so wrong. My head lays on his chest, and his heart is beating nearly as fast as mine. Maybe what everyone has been saying *is* true.

He looks down at me and smiles. "Comfy?"

Smiling while trying to hide my anxiety, I reply, "Very."

The butterflies in my stomach are going a mile a minute, but, somehow, as he places his arm around me, I'm more at ease. I don't feel as anxious, and something feels natural about this, even though it shouldn't. Even though the racing of his heart is still apparent, it seems to be slowing a bit, his side melting into me.

"What happened to you saying you were going to go to sleep right away?" he says, with a slight smirk that is completely out of left field.

Glancing at him and unintentionally dancing my fingers along his arm, I reply, "Not sure, on a bit of a high from the show and kinda liking cuddling with my best friend. The comments on your Instagram lead me to believe that there are plenty of women who would kill for this, so might as well take advantage of it."

His hand rests on my waist, sending goosebumps throughout my body.

"Well, those DMs you've shown me make it obvious that thousands of guys dream of having a second like this with you, so I guess I'd be an idiot to go to sleep and waste the moment."

"Oh, really? A moment like *what*?" I say, scrunching my nose.

Lightly running a finger over my curves, he replies, "A moment laying in bed with the prettiest, most talented girl in the world."

Completely unsure of what words I should say in response

since flirting with Kieran is foreign to me, I look up at him, my eyes darting to his lips. Part of me feels like this is a terrible idea...and part of me feels like it's a really good one. Channeling what everyone has been saying over the past two weeks, along with the energy he's giving in this moment, I decide to listen to my gut and take the risk. This could go very wrong.

But, couldn't it go right?

I scoot up closer to his face and lean my face close to his. His eyes widen, but he leans in closer. As I continue inching in, he blushes and says, "Are you trying to do what I think you are?"

"Y-yes."

"You know there's no going back from this, right, Em?" he replies, placing his hand on my cheek.

Looking away for a second and my heart rate increasing again, I say, "I know," and then press my lips to his, not waiting for a reply.

TEN

kieran

IN COMPLETE SHOCK, I kiss Emmie back, one hand on her cheek and the other on her shoulder. This kiss is electrifying, and nothing has ever felt so right.

I know she was obviously flirting with me, but kissing me? I never saw this coming.

One of her hands rests on my chest as she continues the kiss, running her tongue along my bottom lip. Wanting to get more comfortable and see her better, I take a chance and start gently pulling her on top of me. She lays on me, and I follow her lead, slowly sliding my tongue into her mouth. She dances our tongues together in sync and sighs, her body melting into mine. I bite her bottom lip lightly before breaking the kiss to catch my breath.

"Fuck, Em, you have no idea how long I've been wanting to do that," I say, placing my hand on her back.

She sighs and smiles. "Honestly... same. Not sure what came over me but couldn't wait any longer. Everyone's been saying that you've been having *more than friends* feelings for me, and I was scared to do something, even though I've felt the same way."

I shake my head and blush. "Of course, they fucking told you. No one can keep a damn secret. In fairness, Madison kinda told me about your feelings, too. I was lowkey freaking out about it. Can we please do that again?"

"Fuck, yes, please."

I smirk, tempted to take things further than just a kiss, but wanting to take it slow while I try to sense what her body is communicating.

"Want to sit up, pretty girl? Wanna hold you while I kiss you."

As she sits up, her crotch grazes mine, and I will my dick to not get hard, not wanting to freak her out. She sits on my lap, and I pull her into me, running my hands through her soft blonde hair. I press my lips to hers, kissing a little harder than before. She presses me against the headboard, sighing into my mouth, and my arousal builds quickly. Even if it doesn't go further than this, I think I can die a happy man.

I slide my hands down her curves, lightly grazing the sides of her boobs through her top, then resting them on her waist. She bites my lip roughly and grabs my hands. I worry that she's going to think it was too much and move them off of her completely, but instead, she moves them back up to her boobs.

"Fucking love when a woman knows what she wants," I say lowly through the kiss.

She lightly grinds her hips into me and says, "Is this okay?"

Is that a necessary question?

Trying to stifle a moan, I reply, "More than okay." I lightly squeeze her boobs and her nipples start to harden through the material, thanks to her being braless. I get bolder and trail my kisses down to her jaw and neck. She moans quietly, and I'm intoxicated by the sound, wanting to play it on repeat. This is moving fast, and I don't want to mess anything up, but I'm also done with fear running the show.

"Can I take this off?" I say, playing with the straps of her top.

Rolling her hips into me, she sighs, "Please, Kier."

Something about hearing her say one of my nicknames flips a switch in me, and all I can think about is how badly I want her hands or mouth or pussy or any part of her on my cock. I hook my fingers under the band of her top and pull it off, completely entranced by the gorgeous sight in front of me. Her boobs are a perfect handful, and I'm addicted to their softness. I plant kisses from her collarbones down to her boobs and run my tongue over one of her nipples. She moans softly, and I can tell she's trying to hold back.

"You don't have to be quiet, Emmie girl. This is all about making you feel good, and I want to hear how good I'm making you feel."

My tongue moves to her other nipple and she moans louder, leading me to say, "Good girl," in response. Just like hearing her say my nickname flipped a switch in me, hearing me say 'good girl' has clearly flipped one in her. She grinds quicker, pressing her hips more deeply into me. She runs her hands down my body, pulling my shirt off. She's seen me shirtless countless times, but I've never seen her look at me like this. Her eyes dart all across my body, staring at my tattoos, particularly the roses I have on either side of my hip bones.

She grazes my abs with her hands, saying, "Why haven't we done this sooner?"

I laugh slightly. "Guess we were both so caught up in our anxious brains that we couldn't see it."

She runs her hands lower, lightly touching the thin trail of hair sticking out of my pants.

I breathe in sharply, saying, "You can go lower if you want to," desperately hoping that she does.

She smirks. "Never thought I'd say this, but I'm dying to know what your cock would feel like in my mouth."

Jesus fucking Christ. I know that Emmie is a confident, and fairly sexual, woman, but hearing her say that is something that's never crossed my mind.

"Fuck, I mean, I'm not gonna say no to that. But I don't want you to feel like you have to, I know sometimes guys do that."

She drags her tongue from my sternum down to one of my rose tattoos and looks up at me with fire in her eyes. "Kieran, I love that you're so sweet and considerate, but I don't need you sweet right now. I need your dick down my throat."

Add this to more things I never thought I'd hear come out of her mouth. It feels wrong to be anything but sweet with Emmie. But what Emmie wants, Emmie gets.

"Oh yeah? You want me to take these off so that I can push your head down until you're choking on my cock? Think you can take that?" I say, gesturing at my sweatpants and the waistband of my boxer briefs that's peeking out of them.

"I know I can," she says, rolling off of me to pull off her sweatpants. I'm shocked when she is completely bare. I've seen her in bikinis that don't leave much to the imagination before, but seeing her naked like this for the first time is a gorgeous sight that I wish I could take a photo of in my mind. She has this timeless beauty with a little bit of edge, and the feistiness of her personality that is peeking out has me more attracted to her than I already was.

"Goddamn. You mean to tell me that you were on the streets of Manhattan, commando under your sweatpants?"

"You'd be surprised to know how often I've been commando in your presence, I guess just neither of us was able to take advantage of it," she smirks.

I never expected this kind of dynamic to be happening between us, but it's going to be so fucking fun.

I stand up and pull off my sweatpants and boxer briefs in one motion, throwing them in the corner. As I lay back down, she walks over and sits down next to me, her eyes trailing down to my dick. Desperate to feel her touch again, I say, "Em, please don't make me wait any longer."

"Well, since you asked so nicely," she says, sinking between my legs. She swirls her tongue around the head and my back arches. The combination of the pleasure from her mouth combined with the shock of the sight in front of me has me completely entranced, no other thoughts running through my head. I run my hand through her hair and moan as my cock starts to graze her throat.

"Fuck, you're so good at that," I say, gently pushing her head down. She moans, and the vibration along with the tightness of her throat leads me to grunt loudly. All I want to do now is give her more pleasure than she's given me.

I lightly rub her shoulders and say, "Can I taste you, baby?"

Baby... I didn't really intend to say that. I hope it's not too much for her.

"You sure you don't want more?"

"You feel fucking amazing, but I want to make you feel good, too. And, something tells me that blowing me has you drenched."

She blushes and says, "Maaaaybe."

I smirk. "Don't get all shy on me now, Em. How about you lay back so that I can give your pretty pussy the attention it deserves? Dying to taste you."

She crawls up next to me, and before she lays back, I pull her face into mine to kiss her.

"Need your mouth on me now," she whines.

"You've already got my mouth on you, where do you want it, pretty girl?"

Rolling her eyes, she says, "You know what I mean, Kieran."

I trail my hand down her body. "Yeah, but I want to hear you say it. If you want it, gotta tell me, babe."

"I want your mouth on my pussy," she says, moving my hand to her crotch.

Crawling between her legs, I say, "There you go...now you better not hold out on me, Emmie. Want to hear those pretty moans." I lower my mouth to drag my tongue through her slit, not wanting her to have to wait any longer. Especially after how good she made me feel. As much as teasing her is fun, I don't want to do it to a torturous level...or at least *not right now*. Her wetness coats my tongue, and I relish in the slightly musky, yet slightly sweet taste. She arches her back and whimpers as I look up at her, obsessed with seeing her in this way.

"You taste so good, could stay between your legs all night. Can I slide some fingers in?"

She tangles her fingers in my waves and moans, "Yes, please. Need more."

Knowing how wet she is, I decide to skip going with only one finger and immediately slide in both my pointer and middle fingers, her tight entrance stretching around them. All I can think about is how badly I want to be inside her, but I'm determined to hold off and make her come at least once before suggesting that. I suck her clit into my mouth while gently curving my fingers up, wanting to find her g-spot. She starts to squeeze her thighs around my head, letting me know that I've definitely found it. I go back to flicking my tongue over her clit and continue curving my fingers up, and she cries out, "I'm gonna come."

Music to my ears. I pull my mouth off but don't stop my

fingers, saying, "There you go, pretty girl. Come all over me. Drown me in it."

After she comes down from her high, I pull my fingers out. "If you've had enough, I will gladly stop here, but if not, I'd really love to get inside you, Em."

Sighing while smiling, she replies, "I wasn't sure if that would be too far, but I want that, too. So fucking bad. But, I don't think I have any condoms with me."

I scoot up next to her while she continues to catch her breath. "I have a few in my backpack. And you're sure you want this, right?"

"I wouldn't have said it if I didn't. Do you not want to?"

Shaking my head, I say, "Of course, I want to. Just want to make sure I'm not doing anything wrong or taking anything too far. Never want you to feel like you have to do something just because I want to."

"I thought we talked about dropping the sweet and considerate? I *need* you to fuck me. I'm all yours. However you want me."

I walk over to my backpack, grabbing a condom out of one of the pockets. I take it out of the foil wrapper and roll it on, walking back over to the bed.

"Well, if you don't want me to be sweet, how about you get on your hands and knees like a good little slut?"

She hesitates for a moment, but there's desperation in her eyes. "Or I can put you on your hands and knees, your choice, Emaline."

She crawls down the bed closer to me and gets on all fours. I line myself up with her entrance and push in gently, though I plan on not being gentle in a moment. Her walls squeeze me, and I groan, knowing that at this moment, she's ruined me, and I'm never going to want anyone other than her. She pushes her hips back to meet mine, and I sink all the way in. She told me not to be sweet, so I pick up my pace and drill into her roughly, making sure I'm angling myself in a way that also grinds into her clit.

"Fuck, Kieran, you feel so good," she whines.

"So..do..you," I say, my breath quickening. I grab a handful of her hair and pull it back, hoping she likes it. Her walls tighten more around me, and her moans start to get uncontrollable. Despite it not taking very much time, my orgasm is approaching. I usually last pretty long, but with it being our first time together and the unreal blow job she gave me earlier, I'm going to be over the edge soon. I reach my hand between us and start to play with her clit, thrusting as deeply as I can.

She starts to shake a bit, and I say, "Em, I can't hold off much longer."

Continuing to throw her hips back, she moans out, "Come for me, Kieran." Hearing her say my name again puts me past my peak, and I spill into the condom, completely satiated and exhausted. I pull out of her and say, "I'll be back in a sec, want to clean this up real quick." I walk into the bathroom to get rid of the condom and come back to her all cuddled up in the sheets with a huge smile across her face.

"That good, huh?" I say.

She playfully hits my shoulder and says, "I'd say don't get too cocky, but that was fucking amazing. Never in a million years saw that happening, but I'm so glad it did."

I lay down next to her, snuggling her into my side, and say, "Me too. Can't find words for everything I'm feeling right now."

She lays her head on me. "I'd love to just fall asleep like this, but maybe we should both go clean up a bit? I saw that it's a pretty big shower, we could shower together?"

Fucking is one thing...showering together after fucking,

that's another level of intimacy—and one that I'm certainly not going to turn down.

"Only if you wash my hair for me, Emmie girl."

"Only if you wash mine, too, Kiki."

We're both back under the blankets, and Emmie is currently completely knocked out with her head on my chest and one of her arms and legs thrown across me. She's wearing my t-shirt, which is adorable. Her heartbeat radiates, which is simultaneously soothing and anxiety-provoking.

She said, and clearly showed, that she enjoyed it all, but was I too much? What does this mean for us? Is it just a "Oh, we got it out of our systems and now we'll get back to normal?" Are we going to be in a relationship? Would she want to be in a relationship? Will I freak her out if I ask? Will I freak her out if I don't ask?

I try to quiet my mind a bit and focus on the rise and fall of her chest, knowing that I don't need to worry about this right now. Right now, I need to enjoy having this beautiful woman that I love sleeping in my arms and get some much-needed rest.

emaline

MY EYES FLUTTER OPEN, and Kieran's arm is draped across my chest as he continues to sleep. Last night was a fever dream—one I want to repeat over and over again. Somehow everything between us just *worked*, even with it being our first time together. I suppose it makes sense that we would be able to read each other well since we've known each other for our entire lives, but it's still a little shocking.

Part of me wants to keep this as our little secret for now, but another part of me is absolutely dying to tell the girls.

ERL TEAM GIRLIES GROUP CHAT

EMALINE

guys...you're about to have the biggest i told you so moment

DELIA

oh my god, pls tell me that you're in bed with kieran

RUBY

YOU GUYS FUCKED DIDN'T YOU!!!!!

ISABELLE

girl you can't leave us hanging!!!!

EMALINE

there was only a king bed in our room. there were no other rooms left in the hotel and no rollaway beds.

we decided to try to make sleeping in the same bed work and we like were first laying far apart but then cuddled

and then i kissed him and he kissed me and we fucked and then we showered and he washed my hair and we fell asleep together and now he's still sleeping next to me

and HOLY FUCK i think i'm in love with him??? who am i

KENZIE

LETS FUCKING GOOOOOOOOO

BRIE

I FUCKING CALLED IT

RUBY

This is the best news I've heard all week, and considering the playlists the new album is already on, that's saying a lot

DELIA

PICS OR IT DIDN'T HAPPEN!!!

Whether our feelings for each other end up going somewhere or not, I want to have this memory of pure bliss to hold onto. Being careful not to move too much and wake him up, I snap a selfie of both of us, smiling big as I feel the rise and fall of his chest.

ISABELLE

STOPPPPP you're the fucking cutest i want to frame this

DELIA

power couple of the year!!!

EMALINE

pls don't get ahead of yourselves guys. it's def obvious he's into me at least as much as i'm into him, but idk if he wants to go anywhere with it or not

RUBY

Oh he absolutely does, trust me

Kieran starts to stir, and I lock my phone and put it down on the nightstand. He wipes his eyes and I ruffle his hair, saying, "Morning, cutie."

Cutie. Never thought I'd be saying that to Kieran.

"Good morning to you, too. So, did last night actually happen, or was that just a really good dream?"

Laughing, I reply, "Oh, it definitely happened. Wouldn't mind that happening again sometime."

He stretches out for a second and says, "I definitely wouldn't mind that either. Also, we don't have to have this conversation right now if you don't want to. It may be too soon or may be dumb or may be too much or may be unnecessary or may not be the time for it but I was kinda wondering what this all means for us."

Kieran's mind is always running a mile a minute, which is both endearing and exhausting. Mostly endearing.

"Pause your rambling for a moment and breathe, Kier. It's not dumb or too soon. I've been thinking about it too, and I mean, I think it can mean whatever we want it to? This is obviously different than people who just met each other, so the conversation is worth having. But maybe we can take some time to just soak this all in before jumping to putting a label on it?"

Before last night, even though I knew I had feelings for Kieran, I wasn't sure if I could see myself as being his girlfriend or something like that. But, somehow, now I can.

"Sounds perfect to me, Emmie girl."

The first people I text? Alaina and Ruby, of course.

Kieran's holding my hand, swinging our arms as we walk through Washington Square Park, and I couldn't be happier. Successful album launch, perfect first show of tour, and now I might end up dating my best friend? I've been in a lot of shitty relationships, so I've struggled to believe that it's worth putting myself out there and being vulnerable, versus getting caught up in the endless cycle of hookups. Don't get me wrong, I don't think there's anything wrong with enjoying hookups. I think that my hookup phase was really important for me in terms of exploring sex and my sexuality. But it wasn't fun anymore. Instead, it was me being afraid to look for more after how badly I had been hurt, and not feeling like I deserved more. I don't think this struggle with feeling like I'm worthy of being treated well in relationships is one that I've suddenly "conquered," especially since who knows if we'll actually end up boyfriend and girlfriend. But, I trust Kieran more than I trust anyone else, and I'm trying to trust that I deserve this. I'm trying to trust that I deserve far more than what Chris put me through.

We spent most of the day laying around in bed and watching Gossip Girl while eating room service, but then he suggested we leave our hotel room to have a picnic like he mentioned the other day. We haven't put a label on anything, but Kieran said we should at least go on a date while we think about it. Instead of getting anything too fancy, we grabbed a bunch of things from Westside Market, figuring we can bring leftovers back to the hotel. Despite trying to convince him otherwise, he also insisted that he get me flowers to put in the middle of our picnic blanket... even though I have no idea what we're going to do with them afterward. He claims that it's not a proper date without flowers, which I suppose is a sweet sentiment that isn't worth fighting.

A few fans noticed us when we were in the checkout line at the market, but since we're best friends and hang out all the time, no one seemed to think anything of it. It was two teenage girls with their mom, and they said they were at the show last night. The shock and joy on their faces when they recognized us was priceless and reminded me that I'm pretty famous, even though I forget about it sometimes. We took a few photos with them and then bought our food and got on our way.

We find a spot that isn't completely secluded but is far enough away from larger groups of people that we'll be able to hopefully have some level of privacy. It was fun getting to meet those fans earlier, but I want us to be able to have this moment of being... whatever we are. Kieran places the grocery bag down while I spread out the picnic blanket that was in his backpack. I sit down, smoothing out my sundress over my lap, the pink and white floral print perfectly matching the vibe of our date. He starts to spread out our multitude of food options, and I'm reminded of how grateful I am for the work I've put into my eating disorder recovery. A few years ago, this would've been terrifying, but now, I'm enjoying it instead of being caught up in my brain trying to figure out how many miles I'd need to run to compensate.

Kieran arranges the flowers in the middle of the blanket. "Pretty view completed by the prettiest girl."

I lay my head on his shoulder. "You're so cute that it's almost sickening. *Almost.*"

"Hard not to be with you. Making up for so much lost time," he says, booping my nose.

We both make ourselves plates with some roasted veggies, pita chips, and hummus and start eating. I soak up the sunshine and the little bit of calm that this spot is amidst the chaos that is New York City – just like how Kieran is the bit of calm amidst the chaos of the rest of my life. No matter how chaotic things are, he has always been a constant, and I feel lucky to now have that on a deeper level. It may seem a little counterintuitive that a guy who is fairly anxious would feel like calm, but even when he doesn't know how to make *himself* calm, he knows how to make *me* calm. And, somehow, I'm able to do the same for him. We've always complemented each other like that. It helps that we mostly struggle with different things, so there's not often something that we both are really distressed about in the same way at the same time. But, with this new added layer of closeness and trust, something tells me that if we get into some really dark moments, we'll be able to carry each other through.

Kieran places his plate down on the blanket and anxiously fidgets his hands together.

"Whatcha thinking about, Kiki?"

He sighs. "I'm sure it's too early to ask this. And I'm panicking just thinking about saying this because I don't want to fuck everything up. But today has been perfect, and I want more days just like this. I really want you to be my girlfriend, if you want that, too."

I place my hand on his thigh. "Breathe, Kier. Of course, I

want to be your girlfriend. If it was anyone else, I'd say it's way too fast. But, I think we're made for each other."

"Oh, thank god. And I know we are, pretty girl."

Already putting a label on things may be moving a little fast, but for once, I'm going to trust my gut and go with it. A giant smile is plastered across my face, like when little girls are told to smile on stage at their first dance recital. I grab a sea salt chocolate chip cookie from the bag, break off a piece of it, and feed it to Kieran.

Sickening, I know.

"So, I'm not supposed to tell anyone yet since not everything is completely finalized but since I already tell you everything and now I have the added excuse of you being my boyfriend, Ruby's cousin is friends with the owner of a venue in Paris, and they've arranged for me to do a special show in August on my birthday."

Kieran looks at me with a shocked-but-happy expression on his face. "Paris?! You've been wanting to go there since we were kids. And now you're going to perform there? I'm so fucking proud of you, Emmie."

"Well, *we're* going to perform there, not just *me*. But, I know, I can't fucking believe it. When Ruby asked me about it a few days ago, I was fully convinced she was joking. But, when I realized she was serious, I lost it and was jumping up and down. We're waiting on one more contract and then everything will be official. It's a little last minute, but with how fast this tour sold out, I'm not too worried."

He takes another bite of the cookie and then opens his arms for a hug. "Well, now I'm going to have to plan the most perfect Parisian birthday date. Can't believe that we're going to get to experience Paris together for the first time, not just as best friends, but as boyfriend and girlfriend. We're going to do every little sappy, romantic, cliché thing possible while we're there."

"I'd expect no less. It's going to be pretty fun getting to be the girl who enjoys all of your romantic plans instead of just being the one who helps you plan them," I say, hugging him back.

"And it's going to be pretty fun knowing that I'm with someone who *actually* appreciates the effort instead of them thinking it's silly or later using me. We get to be hopeful romantics this time instead of hopeless ones."

Hopeful romantics. I love the sound of that. We're both the type of people who stay sunshiney despite the ways we've been burned. While books may say that sometimes you need a grumpy to balance out the sunshine, I think it's pretty cool that we get to amplify each other's brightness.

"Hopeful Romantics sounds like a song title," I say.

Running his fingers through my hair, he replies, "Hmm, guess we'll have to keep that one in mind."

After eating and talking for another hour, we decide to pack up so that we can drop the rest of the food off at the hotel before going to a few of our other favorite NYC spots. We got everything back in our bags, but I'm still not sure what to do with the flowers. I don't want to throw them away, but bringing them back to the hotel sounds annoying. We start to walk, and across the way, there's a little girl who must be two or three years old, running around with who seems to be her dad while she wears a Cinderella dress and tiara.

Kieran pauses and says, "I have an idea," walking us in the direction of the girl and her dad.

"Hi, Cinderella! If it's okay with your dad, I was wondering if you might want these flowers? We're leaving and can't take them with us, so we figured who better to give them to than a princess," he says, walking up to the girl but keeping a distance.

Her face lights up and she looks over to her dad. "Daddy, peez?"

"Yes, of course, sweetie," he replies.

Kieran crouches down to her height and passes her the flowers. She carefully grabs them before jumping up and down, saying, "Tank you!"

He stands back up and says, "You're welcome, Cinderella!"

Her dad looks at us and smiles. "Thank you both, that was so kind. Have a wonderful rest of your day."

While I've never been quite sure if I want kids or not, seeing that interaction makes it where I can't help but envision Kieran being the most amazing dad one day. I've always loved him as a friend, but I think I might be starting to *love* him.

kieran

"HOW COULD you have not told me sooner? You tell me everything!"

Even though my mom is thousands of miles away and I'm only seeing her on my phone screen on FaceTime, her excitement about me and Emaline is palpable. We flew to New York for the first show of the tour, but we'll be on the bus for most of the run. My long legs make my small bunk less than comfortable, but it's manageable.

"You're not always the best at keeping secrets, and since you tell Kim everything, I didn't want to risk Em finding out before I had sorted through it all."

Like how Emmie and I are best friends, our moms are, too.

She shakes her head and smiles. "You're not wrong, it would have been pretty hard to not say anything to her. I'm thrilled for you both. I've known since you were a little boy that you loved her, and ever since then, I've hoped that you would end up together. Has she told Kim yet?"

It's continually becoming more painfully obvious that everyone except us already knew that we needed to be together. It's a little annoying that people sometimes seem to know me better than I know myself, but I also think the best kind of love is the kind that's so palpable that other people can't help but see it. The kind of love where there is no doubt that it's real. The kind of love that isn't as perfect as what you see in movies or read in romance novels but is as undeniably apparent.

I nod. "Yep, she told her last night. She had the sweetest reaction. And, of course also said that she's known for years. Wish someone would've let us know, but I guess it's better that it unfolded like this naturally instead of being forced."

"I agree. You were able to figure this out for yourselves without having all of the pressure and expectations of others."

"Well... we did have a little pressure. Mads found out and kinda wouldn't let me not tell Em because of how it was eating me alive. And apparently Ruby and the rest of the girls knew about Em's feelings and also wouldn't let her not tell me. But, still different than having people push it for years, only for a few weeks," I say, running my fingers through my hair.

It was really hard keeping this from my mom, but I'm glad that I was able to have the space to process my feelings without worrying about potentially disappointing her. I wanted to do this for me and Emmie, not for anyone else. Sure, there was a little pressure from Madison, but that was just her encouraging what she knew I wanted to do. With moms, it's a different kind of pressure. The kind that's like, "Oh my god, my little boy is going to marry his best friend." And while I hope that will be true someday, having that pressure when all you want to do is know if someone feels the same way about you is a lot.

"Very true, I'm glad that Maddie was able to talk some sense into you. Have you taken Em on a proper date yet?"

"We had a picnic in Washington Square Park, complete

with a bouquet of flowers that we then gave to a sweet little girl when we were leaving."

Her face lights up. "I know this is too soon, but you both are going to make beautiful babies someday."

Shaking my head and blushing, I say, "Mom, please stop, she's going to hear you. Last thing I need is to freak her out and scare her away only a few days into dating."

"Alright, alright, I know, I'm getting ahead of myself. Now, how about I let you go so that you can spend time with your sweet Emaline? I need to get ready for work, anyway."

I nod and say, "Sounds good, love you mom."

"Love you too, Kier."

We're almost in Philadelphia, and Emmie and I are cuddled up in the back lounge. Since everyone else was so obsessed with us getting together, they luckily haven't been bothered by our PDA, but give it a few days and we'll see if they're telling us to "get a bunk." Unsurprisingly, Em told me that she had told the girls about us in their group chat yesterday, and the way they were freaking out in the lobby at bus call filled the guys in, too.

Tonight will be our first show together as a couple, and although we've played countless shows together since we were teenagers, something about this newness feels like it's that first show all over again. It was our fifth-grade talent show, and we did a cover of *Today Was A Fairytale* by Taylor Swift. Em, of course, sang, and I played guitar with a hint of background vocals. Without any formal vocal training, she still had such control over her voice, and everyone knew she was going to be famous someday. It's funny to look back at the song choice and think about how we performed a love song as a duet, even though we were oblivious to our feelings. Now I know that the level of admiration I had (and still have) for her went beyond being a supportive best friend. But at eleven-years-old, I had no idea.

I stretch my legs out and my feet touch an ottoman as Emaline's hair is splayed across my lap. She's been complaining all morning about it "being greasy," but it looks perfect to me. I run my fingers through it, the softness still there from when she blew it out on Saturday. The rise and fall of her breath is so soothing, and I wish I could bottle up this feeling—where everything is at ease and slow, nowhere to be, no one to impress, completely ourselves. With every other partner I've ever had, I've been terrified of judgment, but with Em, I know that she only ever wants me to be my truest self, bad jokes and overprotective nature included.

"I love that we get to have little moments like this," I say.

Looking up at me, she replies, "Me too. I don't know if I've ever felt this relaxed before a show. Pretty wild that tonight is going to be our first show together as a couple, but no one will know except us and the band and crew. Well, unless anyone other than those girls saw us back in New York and got any ideas. I don't want us to be a secret forever, but I do like that we get to have this short time of it just being us without the whole world knowing."

Even though I'm eager for the whole world to know about us, it's nice to have this little window where only the people we care about most know. Not subject to the opinions of fans or the internet. We'll still be us when the public knows, but with how much Em's been blowing up, people are bound to have thoughts and opinions. Which I hope will be positive.

"Definitely. I'm excited for whenever we reveal it, but I like being able to be in our own little world, too. What outfit are you wearing tonight?"

She stretches out her back. "I think I'm gonna keep it a surprise so that I can see your reaction when I'm fully ready. Maybe a new tradition?"

Ruffling her hair, I say, "I'm impatient, but I like the idea of making new traditions with you, so I can deal."

As usual, soundcheck went off without a hitch, and now we just finished a late lunch. It's 2 pm and the show doesn't start until 9 pm, so we have several hours to kill before we need to start getting ready. We're all chilling in one of the green rooms, and Emaline doesn't know this, but I asked Ruby to add the game Twister to our tour rider for this show. A rider is a list of things that you ask a venue to provide as part of your contract. We played it together all the time as kids, so I thought it would be a sweet, nostalgic moment. Plus, what's wrong with a little healthy competition for team bonding?

"So, you're probably going to think it's silly, but I maaay have secretly put Twister on the rider," I say to everyone.

Em's face lights up. "Oh my god, that's not silly at all! We haven't played that since we were like ten years old, it'll be so fun. Plus, with how it makes you contort your body, we can consider it part of our warm-up for the show."

"I haven't thought of that game in years, this is going to be a blast. Everyone else in?" Kenzie says.

Everyone nods, and I say, "Let's do it!"

We decide to make groups to rotate since you can only have three people play at one time. Then, the winners of each group will play against each other for one more round. Em, Ruby, and I are in one group. Nick, Isabelle, and Delia are in another. The last group is Jake, Kenzie, and Austin, and then Ryan is playing referee.

"Okay, Em, Kieran, and Ruby, you're up first," Ryan says.

Emaline and I face each other on opposite ends of the mat, near the word Twister. We each place one foot on the yellow circle and the other foot on the blue circle closest to each of our ends of the mat. Ruby faces the center from the red-circle side of the mat, placing one foot on each of the two middle red circles.

Ryan spins the wheel. "Right hand red."

The first move is always the easiest, but I know this is going to get more complicated as we go.

"Next, left foot green."

Laughing as she moves her foot cautiously, Emaline says, "I really hope I don't get eliminated first."

"Left hand, blue."

Still not too bad. Maybe I can win.

"Right foot, red."

Well, shit. This one is going to be hard, given my right hand is on red, my left hand is on blue, my right foot is on yellow, and my left foot is on green.

I immediately lose my balance and fall flat on my ass. Ryan chuckles, saying, "Well, Kier, you're the first to lose. Gotta knock that competitive ego down a few pegs anyway."

I don't have an ego about many things, but when it comes to games, I do.

Em ends up winning our round, and then in the last round, she goes against Isabelle and Kenzie, ultimately winning it all.

"I'd say it was rigged because you're the star, Emmie, but you can't really rig Twister. So, I'll stop being a sore loser," Ruby says with a joking grumble.

While we're all in 100 percent focus and professional mode

while on stage, I love that we all get to have these silly, unfiltered moments together—especially with Em.

Emaline walks over and pulls me into her chest. "Thanks for doing this. Exactly what I needed before this show. It's pretty special getting to do all of this with you, and I'm excited to keep building these fun memories together, like when we were kids."

My mind runs through so many of the moments we had playing together when we were young, and, suddenly, I realize that I've truly loved her all along, even when I didn't know it.

emaline

THERE'S a light knock on the door of my green room. "Ready for me to see you yet, baby?"

"Come in, Kiki," I reply, dying to see his reaction to my outfit for the night.

I'm wearing a tiny black lace bralette that *just* about covers my boobs, along with faux leather pants that hug my waist and hips and flow out into a wider leg. My hair is in two high messy buns, and I have a red lip with little cherry earrings. While I have plenty of days where I hate my body, tonight I know without a doubt that I look hot as hell.

Kieran walks in and practically fucks me with his eyes, glancing over my entire body. Placing his hands against my shoulders, he says, "Fucking hell. I have half a mind to pull this off of you and bend you over this couch right now."

"Down, boy. I'd love that, too, but we have a show in thirty minutes, and redoing my hair and makeup wouldn't be the vibe."

"I can be careful..." he says.

I smirk. "I promise, as soon as we get back to the hotel, you can do whatever you want to me. But, it's game time."

"Let's knock 'em dead, Emmie girl."

We finish the last note of the encore, the audience goes wild, and while I'm completely sober, I feel high. The energy of the crowd is coursing through my body, and it's like I'm floating. I'm always exhilarated after a show, but tonight was something special. The show wasn't any different than usual, but the sheer bliss that's enveloping me now that I'm Kieran's girlfriend is next level.

As I walk off the stage after everyone else, Kieran is standing backstage, arms wide open with a huge smile. I jump onto him, wrapping my legs around his waist and my arms around his neck. He scoops his hands under my ass to hold me and presses his lips to mine. I kiss him back, feeling like we're the only two people in the room. The electric feeling is interrupted when there's a camera flash and I peek over to see Ruby holding her phone up, with an "awwww" look on her face.

"Way to interrupt the moment, Rube," Kieran says.

She shakes her head. "Trust me, you wanted that moment captured. You guys are fucking adorable."

I plop myself down out of his arms and walk towards her, saying, "AirDrop it to me. My mom is going to lose her shit."

She sends the photo, and pure joy washes over me. You can't see our faces, but the love is palpable.

Love... am I in love?

I thought the prospect of being in love with Kieran would be terrifying, but it feels *right*. It feels like it's always been this way. Some people may say that this is going too fast, but we've known each other for our entire lives—we just both finally realized what was here all along.

"What do you think about me putting this on my Instagram story, Kier?"

He smiles and says, "I'd love that, but are you sure you're ready for it? Do you think the label will say anything about it?"

"I think I'm ready. They can't see your face, and I won't tag you, but people will still probably pick up on it, which I'm fine with. It's hard having the opinions of the world, but I don't want to tiptoe around. I'm so fucking happy, and I want everyone to know it. And screw what the label may think. This whole damn album and tour is about finding myself, and if they have a problem with it, we can deal with it later."

Ruby nods. "If any pricks at the label try to pull something, they can take it up with me. Do what feels right for you, Em."

"Then let's do it, pretty girl," Kieran says, his arm draped around my shoulder.

I throw a film-like filter on the photo and open up Instagram, posting it on my story. I know this is a "soft launch," but I'm so excited for the world to know how I'm on cloud nine.

"Damn, making moves. I'm gonna head back to the hotel, see you guys at call time in the morning?" Ruby says.

I nod. "Yeah, I'm gonna go get changed and pack my things up, and then I think we're going to head back to the hotel, too. Dying to become one with bed, I'm exhausted."

Exhausted is now code for, "I need to get back to the hotel ASAP so that my boyfriend can fuck my brains out."

I scan my keycard on the door of our hotel room, and we burst inside, desperate to rip each other's clothes off. In the sprinter van on the way back to the hotel, we could barely keep our hands to ourselves but did our best to keep it *classy*. But now? We can be exactly how we want to be.

"Em, as much as I still want to have slow, romantic sex sometime soon, I want to be anything but slow and romantic with you right now."

Thank fucking God.

Running my hand down his body and squeezing his cock through his pants, I say, "I was hoping you'd say that."

All I want is for him to throw me around and use me in whatever way he wants. It's a side I never thought I'd see from Kieran, and it's one that I now crave constantly. He's sweet and gentle most of the time, and then rough and dominant when our clothes come off. It's the perfect combination, and I love that I'm the only one who gets to see this side of him. It may be counterintuitive to some people to think that someone who has survived a sexual assault would be into rough sex, but it's different when you're the one actively choosing it. And Kieran and I have had a lot of conversations around boundaries, which is key.

"How rough can I get with you?"

Hoping to get a rise out of him, I reply, "Show me your worst."

"You sure you can take that?"

"You sure you can give that?" I smirk.

While I don't exactly know Kieran is going to react, I'm pretty sure I'm in deep shit. And I can't fucking wait.

Something switches in his eyes, and his voice gets low, almost growling, as he says, "If you're going to be a brat, I'm going to show you exactly how I treat brats."

Feigning innocence, I flutter my eyes up at him. "And how do you treat brats, Kieran?"

"That's for you to find out," he says, roughly grabbing my neck.

I've never had someone be this dominant with me, and it's something I've been craving intensely. Now, it's time to see if I can really take it.

I nod, and he says, "I need more than a nod. I need words. This doesn't happen without verbal consent, Emaline."

There's something about him using my full first name and not a nickname that makes this infinitely hotter.

"Yes, you're being clear."

"Good girl. Clothes off, and then I want you to grab a pillow from the bed and get on your knees for me."

Not wanting to test my luck any further, I undress. I walk over to the bed and grab a pillow, gently placing it on the ground as I sink down to my knees. Kieran walks towards me with a devious grin, and I look up at him, already getting wet. He pulls his pants off, followed by his boxers, and places his hands on my shoulders.

"Now, are you going to let me fuck that pretty mouth?"

Boldly, I say, "Please fuck my mouth, Kieran."

His face softens for a moment, and he runs a finger over my cheek before whispering, "Let me know if I get too rough, baby. This only goes as far as you want it to."

Some women may think it's demeaning, but I personally think few things are more powerful than knowing exactly how badly someone wants you and having the power to control their pleasure, even if at face value it seems like they're controlling you. Sure, Kieran is being dominant, but the power is all in my hands... or my mouth, I guess.

I open my mouth, and, without a word, Kieran shoves his full length in, thrusting hard and fast. He laces his hands behind my head, pulling it forward and back. The sound of his moans is intoxicating, and knowing that I'm the one who is making him feel this way has me drenched. As he hits my throat, I gag a little and close my eyes, not because I don't want to see him, but because it's hard to keep them open like this.

The soft look he had on his face a moment ago is replaced with intensity, but I know the softness is still there.

"Eyes open, or I'll be the only one coming tonight."

I blink my eyes open, doing everything I can to keep them that way.

"That's my good girl," he says. After I choke again, he pulls out. "Get on the bed and get on all fours."

I obey, wiping some spit from the corners of my mouth. I get up off the floor and climb up on the bed, quickly getting on my hands and knees. I don't want to make him wait, and I'm dying to have his hands back on me. He firmly places a hand on my back, slightly pushing me into the bed.

He grabs my ass and says, "Do you think you deserve a bit of a punishment after doubting me earlier?"

Don't talk back. Don't talk back. Don't talk back.

"Yes, I do."

"That's what I thought," he says, pushing me fully down onto the bed so that I'm no longer on all fours. He takes his hand off my ass, and I prepare for what I can only assume is him spanking me. His hand crashes down and I flinch, despite expecting it.

"Think you can take more, baby?"

I love that he's weaving in "baby," even when being this rough.

"I think I can," I say breathily.

He spanks me again, and the sting is intensifying in the best way. Seeing this rough side of him come out has me beyond feral, and I'm dying to have him inside me.

"I know you can, pretty girl. Taking your punishment so well. Keep being good and you'll get a reward soon."

After the final spank, he gently rubs over the red welts. I've always had a pain kink, and while I thought I was wet earlier, I'm definitely dripping now. He lightly rubs his fingers through my slit, sending shivers down my spine. He roughly shoves two fingers in, not giving me a second to prepare. The pleasure is consuming me and my moans get louder, leading him to quicken the speed.

"Fuck, Em. I need to get in there."

"Please," I moan.

He lines himself up with my entrance and aggressively slides all the way in. He grabs my hair, pulling my head back. Despite trying to remain rough, his body starts to melt into mine. I smirk, knowing the power I have over him, even when he's having power over me. His speed quickens and his grunts and moans are getting louder, seemingly uncontrollable at this point.

Pressure builds in my belly, and I cry out, "Kieran, I'm gonna come," hoping that he rewards me like he said he would.

He flips me onto my back and then drops his dominance, stroking my cheek as he says, "I need to see your pretty face, Emmie girl."

My back arches and I almost see stars, pleasure radiating throughout my whole body. He slams into me one more time, grunts, and fills me with his cum—a feeling I've been dying to experience. Thank god for having an IUD.

He gently collapses onto me. "Fuck, I love you, Em."

Without a second thought, I wrap my arms around him and reply, "I love you, too, Kieran."

If it were anyone else, I'd say that saying "I love you" so soon was a terrible idea or untrue, but with Kieran, it just feels like it's always been this way.

kieran

EMALINE LOVES ME. She LOVES me. And I can't stop smiling.

I've heard the words "I love you" come out of her mouth before, but only as a friend. Not like this. I've known for a bit now that I love her, but I didn't expect those words to blurt out like they did. Seems like it's working out perfectly fine though.

"You don't know how long I've been dying to hear those words, Emmie girl," I say, trying to get up.

She keeps her legs wrapped around my waist, trapping me.

"I could say the same thing. Please don't get up yet," she pouts.

Stroking her cheek, I say, "Let's clean up real quick, baby, and then we can cuddle before we knock out."

"Fiiiiine," she grumbles playfully, unwrapping her legs.

I grab a few tissues from the bedside table and lightly wipe us off before scooping her into my arms and walking to the bathroom. I place her down on the marble counter, soaking up how lucky I am to have her and be loved by her. Love is hard for Em, but when she loves? She loves hard. I grab a washcloth and run it under warm water, gently wiping her clean. After placing a kiss on her nose, I take her down off the counter so that she can use the bathroom while I clean myself.

Smirking at me, she says, "Never thought I'd see that side of you, Kier. And I'm definitely not complaining. Most guys seem to think getting rough is spanking me once and maybe throwing in a 'what a dirty girl,' but that was so fucking good. Wouldn't mind more of that in the future."

"This is the byproduct of shamelessly reading romance novels, and spending way too much time on parts of the internet I had no business looking at when we were in high school. And something tells me you want it rougher than that."

"Kieran Hayes reads romance novels? I thought I knew everything about you. And you're not wrong," she says, blushing a little.

There is a lot that men can learn from reading romance novels. Many guys say that "they're too girly" or that reading them "isn't what real men do," but women don't say that they want "a man written by a woman" for no reason. Men need to drop the toxic masculinity and step up their game.

"Obviously every woman likes different things, but those books don't become bestsellers for no reason...and BookTok definitely has infiltrated my feed. Seems like it's already paid off."

She laughs, "Hey, I wasn't complaining, just making an observation."

We climb back in bed. My phone vibrates.

MADISON

THE PICTURE ON EM'S STORY!!!!!!!! OH MY FUCKING GOD

KIERAN

What can I say? We're in love and want everyone to know it...even if it's only a soft launch for now

MADISON

oh there is no way that everyone hasn't
figured it out

KIERAN

Kinda what I was secretly hoping...about to
go to sleep so I'll talk to you tomorrow,
love you

MADISON

love you too!!

I pull Em into my chest and squeeze her tightly, her heartbeat
radiating. I love that we don't have to have the usual initial
awkwardness and 'getting to know you' phase that happens in
new relationships. It's a little weird and kinda scary to admit,
but it feels like we've somehow skipped the first few months of
a relationship, even though we've only been a couple for a few
days. I guess when you've been best friends for your whole life,
it works like that. Her breathing slows and she melts further
into me mumbling, "I love you, Kiki," as she starts to fall
asleep.

"I love you too, Emmie. Sweet dreams."

My eyes blink open as sunlight pours into our hotel room,
Emmie still snuggled into my side. I carefully reach over to the
bedside table to grab my Zoloft, not wanting to wake her. But if
I don't take it now, I'll forget.

OCD has plagued my brain since I was a kid. The first time
someone noticed was when my third-grade teacher saw that I
had ripped a hole in a piece of paper with my eraser. I was

erasing and rewriting over and over again because my brain was telling me that if I handed in an assignment with a mistake, something bad would happen to my family. My teacher told my parents, and after I told them more, they brought me to a therapist. At first, we would just play games. Over time, once I got to know her more, we started doing some exposure therapy. Erasing holes into my paper wasn't the only way my OCD showed up back then. I also had to line all of my books up in alphabetical order on my bookshelf, put my clothing on in the same order every day, would repeatedly ask my mom to check if the door was really locked when we left the house, always washed my hands three times, turning the faucet on and off in between each rinse, and had to have everything on my desk at school lined up in a very exact order.

I was bullied a lot because of it. People didn't understand me and thought I was "weird." Boys in the bathroom would turn the faucet off and stand in front of me so that I couldn't complete my ritual, leaving me crying. They'd also intentionally move things around on my desk and knock them onto the floor. The only person who really saw and understood me was Emmie, and, for most of my life, she was my only friend. I have a few friends now, but the trauma of my bullying makes it hard to trust people. I always fear that people will judge me for my OCD. I've been in and out of therapy since that first therapist I saw, and I've taken Zoloft daily since I was 10, but I still struggle. My struggles aren't as apparent now, but they can still be visible at times.

OCD also makes relationships and sex challenging. I obsessively think through my relationships and constantly worry that someone is going to leave me or isn't interested in me anymore. Most people worry about those things sometimes, but I've had times of spending hours reviewing every interaction in my head until my brain was so exhausted that I could no longer stay awake. It doesn't help that I've been dumped because my OCD made me "too much."

My most recent ex, Jamie, broke up with me while I was in a compulsion spiral. I'd been having a particularly difficult few weeks and wasn't sleeping well, and then the band had a shitty writing session. Stressful times like that fuel my OCD because meds and therapy can only do so much. She came home from work, and I was in the kitchen, unable to stop washing my hands, even though I had already been going for a half hour. She was yelling at me to stop, saying it was stupid and that I needed more willpower. I started sobbing because between my brain telling me I needed to wash off my mistakes and her telling me how weak I was, it was too much to take. She stormed out of the apartment saying, "I can't keep dating someone who's this fucked up in the head, I'm done." In some ways, I don't blame her. It's so painful seeing someone you love suffer. But doing it in that way was pretty cruel.

Luckily, Emaline barged into my apartment fifteen minutes later, worried because I hadn't been answering her texts and calls all night, and she knows how I get after rough sessions. She talked me out of the spiral, got me to let her turn off the faucet, and rubbed lotion on my raw hands as we watched Gossip Girl until she fell asleep on the couch. I'm not sure how neither of us saw it in that moment, but we've always been it for each other.

And while I've managed to not majorly fuck up anything with Em's struggles, I worry, especially with her sexual trauma. Everything's been fine on that front so far, but I want to make sure I do everything right and learn everything I can.

I swallow the pill and wash it down with water, feeling Em starting to stir next to me.

"Morning, my love. How'd you sleep?" I say, brushing her hair out of her face.

She nuzzles into me. "Like a rock. Wish I started sleeping in your arms years ago."

"Makes two of us. Your presence is so soothing."

She grabs her phone and opens Instagram. As usual, she has hundreds of DMs. This time, they're a bit different. She occasionally replies to fans, but most of the time, she tries not to stay too absorbed with social media. Her fanbase is pretty non-judgmental and genuinely supportive of her, but there are always assholes.

- *"OH MY GODDDDD IS THAT KIERAN?!?"*
- *"MOM AND DAD!!!!!"*
- *"Oh that is SO Kieran I'm SO HAPPY FOR YOU"*
- *"okay but this is actually the sweetest pic ever"*

Countless messages, all thankfully supportive. She rarely gets hate from fans, but with a new relationship, you never know. I just hope the label doesn't give her any shit about being "less marketable" with being in a relationship. It sounds horrible, but it's how this industry is. And I'd hate to somehow destroy everything she's put her blood, sweat, and tears into.

She peeks at her mentions, and a fan update account posted a screenshot of the story with the caption, *"FROM EMALINE'S STORY LAST NIGHT!"* There are thousands of comments, all similar to the DMs. I can't help but smile, ecstatic that her fans are as excited about our relationship as we both are, even if we haven't officially announced it yet.

She locks her phone and says, "Wow, that was a lot. All so supportive, but still really overwhelming. I love how they immediately knew without seeing your face."

"May have forgotten about the whole seeing my outfit during the show piece. Not that that bothers me, it's honestly really sweet seeing how much they already love us together."

Flopping onto my chest, she replies, "Guess we might as well make an actual post soon, no use waiting at this point."

"I'm here for whatever pace you want to go at, pretty girl."

Today's a day off in Philly, and Em and I decided to each have a guys' day and girls' day with the rest of the band and crew. Sure, before being in a relationship we spent almost all of our time together, but we both want to keep up with friendships and spending time with other people. She's having a spa day with Ruby, Brie, Isabelle, Delia, and Kenzie, and I'm having a chill video game day with Jake, Ryan, Austin, and Nick. We'll probably grab lunch somewhere, but for now, we're going to shoot the shit and see how many rounds of Mario Kart we can play before wanting to kill each other.

"So, you and Em? About fucking time," Ryan says.

As Jake places his water bottle down on the table, he adds, "You can say that again."

Nick plops down on the couch next to me. "Saw this coming miles away. You've always looked at her like she hung the moon. It's good to see you this happy."

"I think it's always been meant to be, but we couldn't see it. It's going to make making music together that much more special," I reply.

Ryan nods. "100%. It's like a weight has been lifted off of both of you. There had been so much tension there, but you both seem so at ease. After that abusive piece of shit Chris, I didn't know if she was going to find someone who could treat her well, but clearly, you fit the bill more than any other person could."

"And you best believe, if you somehow hurt her, we will all

take you down. She's like our little sister, and we'll always be on her side," Austin says.

"I could never do that to her. She is absolutely everything to me. It may be soon to say, but I really think we're endgame."

Ryan grabs one of the game controllers. "Oh, I know you are. Zero doubts in my mind. There aren't two people more made for each other."

Nick adds, "And I don't think it's too soon. You've known each other for your entire lives. You've practically been in a relationship for that long, you just never called it that. I'm usually not one for romance, but you guys are a match made in fucking heaven."

"Exactly. We're all rooting for you, and that's not me trying to be cheesy," Austin says.

I've never been "one of the guys," and having this kind of connection and support from someone other than my family, Noah, and Emaline feels amazing. I'm an open book with the people I trust, but getting my trust can be hard. It's not that I don't want to trust people, I just have been hurt so many times that the reward doesn't seem to be worth the risk.

"Thanks, guys. It means a lot. I was worried that us becoming a thing would make work weird, but it seems like it's actually made everything better. But, enough sappy relationship talk for now. Who's ready for me to beat their ass in Mario Kart?"

FIFTEEN

emaline

TONIGHT WE'RE IN BOSTON, and we just finished our third show of tour. While I sometimes shower at the venue, tonight I'm opting to shower back at the hotel so that I can take my time. It was our first show with the relationship being fully public, and it felt so good to kiss Kieran before we ran off stage. Everyone's been so supportive, and our relationship feels easy. It's not that I'm not putting effort into it, but it helps that I'm already so comfortable completely being myself with him, zero filters. He's seen me at my absolute best and absolute worst, and I trust him more than anyone. I don't need to do anything excessive to impress him or "keep him interested," which is refreshing. I'm almost worried about how things seem so easy, but I'm trying to just embrace it and not question it.

After the drive back to the hotel, we put our things down. Desperate to wash the sweat and glitter off my body, I look at Kieran and say, "Babe, I'm gonna shower first if that's okay with you?"

"Go for it, baby."

I grab my pink toiletry bag and walk into the bathroom,

placing everything down. I pull off my sweatpants and crop top and undo my high ponytail, sighing at the release of tension. I walk over to the shower and turn on the faucet, letting steam fill the room. I step in, and as soon as the water starts running down my body, my heart races. It's like the walls are closing in on me, and my throat tightens. A crushing sensation overcomes me, and breathing feels impossible.

Fuck fuck fuck. Why is this happening again?

Once again, the shower that I took in my apartment the night I broke up with Chris last year is replaying in my head. I found out he was cheating on me, so I went to his apartment to confront him. He had been emotionally abusing me for months, and I'd never been able to find the strength to end things. But, the cheating was the final straw. Instead of owning up to his shit, he decided to accuse me of being the one who was cheating. But I never did. He called me a useless whore, saying the only thing I was good for was sex, while also saying I had a horrible body. He then sexually assaulted me, and my body went into freeze mode, not allowing me to fight back. That night, I was telling myself, "You didn't say no strongly enough. You didn't try to fight. You let this happen." Eventually, he stopped, and I managed to escape. I drove back to my apartment, sobbing the entire way, too ashamed to tell a single soul.

Throughout the drive, I felt like I was going to die, vomit, or both. I'd been living in my apartment for over a year, but it was like I was in an alternate dimension. I tore off my clothing and got in the shower, trying everything I could to wash the unbearable feeling off of me. And it didn't work. I scrubbed at my skin for over an hour, finding no relief. And, now, here I am, trying to do that again.

I aggressively scrub my arms, trying to rid myself of the

dirty, shameful feeling, and like that night, it's not working. The temperature of the shower is turned as high as possible, but I can't feel it, even though my skin is turning bright red. "It's your fault, you deserved it," is running in my mind on repeat, and no matter how much I scratch at my arms, nothing is making the feeling of crawling out of my skin go away. My head spins, and tears pour down my face. Feeling like I'm going to pass out, I grab the marble wall and slide down to the ground, putting my head between my knees. My sobs are uncontrollable, and I can't stop shaking. Water pools around me, and my soaked hair covers my eyes. In this moment, I'm not in a hotel room in Boston. I'm back in my apartment that night, reliving every excruciating detail. Remembering how aggressive he was and all of the demeaning things he said. Remembering how I didn't even feel like a human, just an object.

This can't be happening. I can't let Kieran see this. I've been doing so well, and I can't have him worrying about me. I can't fuck this all up.

As I continue bawling, the bathroom door creaks open. My head is still between my knees, desperately clinging to consciousness.

"Emmie? What's going on? Are you okay?"

I continue sobbing, unable to speak. He slides open the shower door as I shake on the floor. All that is running on repeat in my mind is Chris assaulting me and how badly I want to rid my body of the sensation. How I feel like I'm not in my body and like I'm just watching it as if I'm in a movie.

"This is my fault. This is my fault. I should have done something. This is my fault," I choke out as I sob.

"Baby, let's get you up. What's your fault? What's happening?"

He pulls me up from the ground, and my body is dead

weight. All I want to do is hide from shame and the feeling of being a burden, but I also need comfort and safety.

As I look at the ground and more tears stream from my eyes than I ever thought possible, Kieran grabs a towel and wraps it around my body. The sensation helps me find a slight sense of grounding, and I don't feel like I'm dying anymore. As much as I'm ashamed of being a burden and having this reaction, I throw myself into his arms and sob into his chest. He pulls me as close into him as he can, whispering in my ear, "You're okay. You're okay. You're safe here. You're safe here."

His heartbeat starts to feel a bit calmer. He's not freaking out. He's not saying I'm a burden. He's trying to comfort me.

"Can I help you get some clothes on and get your hair in a towel, baby?"

Glancing at him with mascara running down my face, I nod yes.

He kisses the top of my head, pulls the crop top I was wearing earlier over my head, and then picks up each of my feet to slide my sweatpants up my body. Grabbing another towel, he gently tips my head forward and wraps my hair up in it. He hugs me again and then places me up on the cold counter, grabbing a makeup wipe. He gently wipes my makeup off, quietly singing to me. It's such a simple action that means so much and is helping me come back to earth.

"Can I dry your hair for you? I know you hate going to bed with it wet, but I don't want to overwhelm you."

I nod and quietly say, "Yes, please."

He kisses my forehead and unwraps the towel from my head, gently brushing out my hair before drying it.

After my hair is all dry, he takes me off the counter, hugs me, and says, "We don't have to talk about it if you don't want to, but can we at least get into bed?"

I mumble "yes," and walk with him towards the bedroom.

He pulls back the blankets, and I climb in, tempted to hide under the covers. But Kieran already knows the story of that night, and he has never once judged me or said I'm too much. When I told him about it the day after it happened, he wanted to call the police, but I didn't let him for fear of it making things worse. If I told him the night it happened and not the next day, I think he would've gone and tried to kill him.

I can't keep running from talking about these feelings. I mean, I can, but it's just going to keep me in this endless spiral.

After he climbs in next to me, I lay my head on his chest. "I was having a flashback to the night I broke up with Chris. I'm sorry for worrying you, it's not a big deal."

Gently rubbing my back, he says, "Please don't apologize, Em. You have nothing to be sorry for. It is a big deal. I hate that that criminal still steals so much from you. You never need to apologize for having feelings. I promise you will never be too much for me."

As always, Kieran has the perfect response.

"I hate that I'm not over it. I mean, it was last year. I could have done more. It could have been worse."

"You know as well as I do that discounting your feelings doesn't help anything. You did everything you could in that moment. None of it was your fault, it was all his. You didn't deserve any of it, and I wish you could give yourself a sliver of the compassion and care you give everyone else."

"It's hard to believe that sometimes, you know? Before that night, he got so deep and twisted in my head that it's hard to unlearn. I probably need to go back to therapy."

Intertwining my hand with his, he replies, "You know how much I can relate to shitty partners infiltrating your mind. Going back to therapy would be a really good idea. I'm always here to support you, but therapy is important."

I processed some of the trauma of my relationship with

Chris with my most recent therapist, but after a bit, it felt too scary and like I wasn't ready. I'm still not sure if I'm ready, but clearly, if I'm having these kinds of reactions still, I need to do something before things get worse than they already are.

"It feels scary to start processing this again, but it's scarier thinking of things getting worse. After we get done with tour I'll text my old therapist and see if I can make an appointment."

He delicately runs his fingers through my hair. "I'm always here for you, every step of the way, no matter what. How about I make you some tea and we can watch some Gossip Girl until we fall asleep?"

"That'd be perfect."

Last night was fucking rough. Despite drinking a ton of water to hydrate after how much I cried, I still have a pounding headache that's like a hangover, and my body feels like it was hit by a bus. I'm grateful we have a day off because if I had to directly go into another show day, I don't think I could've handled it.

Kieran and I are taking it easy today instead of trying to explore the whole city of Boston. We've decided to find a bookstore, browse around, and take some time to read. I love having moments where we're in the same space but also able to be in our own little worlds. When we were preschoolers, my grandma used to bring us to our local bookstore every Wednesday morning for their weekly storytime, and afterward, she'd let us each pick a book to buy. It fostered my love for reading, and every time I step foot in a bookstore, it's like she's there with me. One of the sweetest parts of being in a relationship with Kieran now is getting to do things together as adults that we once did as kids. It's very nostalgic and reminds me that no matter how hard things are, he's here for the long haul. I don't really believe in a god, but I'd like to think my grandma is smiling down on us as we walk into this bookstore.

The smell of book pages permeates my nostrils, immediately grounding me. A little corgi runs over to us, and my face lights up. I love dogs so much, and I'm desperate to get a corgi of my own someday. I look at its pink collar and see the name "Toast," aptly fitting with how corgis look like little loaves of bread. We crouch down, and Toast starts covering me in kisses.

"According to that sign, it seems that Toast is the most valuable employee," Kieran says, pointing to a sign that has a photo of the dog.

Booping her nose, I say, "The universe may be on my side today. This seems like the sweetest shop and corgi kisses are exactly what I need."

We pet Toast for a few more moments and then stand back up, starting to wander through the books. My phone vibrates, and there's a text from Madison.

> **MADISON**
>
> hey are you okay? kieran said you had a rough night. he didn't tell me any details

> **EMALINE**
>
> thanks for asking <3 i am now. or at least i will be. some PTSD stuff, but kier was really helpful. today's a day off so we're just taking it easy

> **MADISON**
>
> glad you're okay – text or call if you need anything 🤍

I slide my phone back into my pocket and continue walking through the aisles, looking for a fluffy romance novel that can be a good distraction. I read the backs of a few and then pick one before finding Kieran. We head over to the checkout, and he has a book about managing OCD. I know it could just be proactive, but I'm worried that things have been getting harder for him and he's just not saying anything.

Putting his arm around my waist, he says, "Find anything good, baby?"

I nod. "Just a cute rom-com, thought it might help me get out of my head a bit. How about you?"

"I've been worried about my OCD kinda creeping in again, so I thought it might be good to get something about that. I'm sure I've heard most of it before, but you never know. Now, let me buy that for you, this is a date after all," he says, grabbing my book from my hands.

"Well, I won't say no to a free book. And I'm proud of you, I know it's hard to confront your demons."

We check out and head over to the lounge area that has several very comfy-looking couches and chairs, along with a little cafe. I plop down on one of the big couches, placing my new book on my lap.

"I'm gonna grab us some coffees, want your usual?" Kieran says.

"Yes, please. And maybe a muffin or something? I'm kinda hungry."

"That sounds perfect," he replies, walking over to order.

I start reading, immediately transported to another place. Books have always been a safe haven for me, and being in a bookstore is an added layer of comfort. I don't need to think about any worries or responsibilities. I can let my mind soak up the story.

After a few minutes, Kieran walks back over with two brown sugar oat milk lattes, a chocolate chip muffin, and a blueberry muffin. He sits down next to me and says, "I think your grandma would've loved this place."

"I was thinking the same thing. Especially Toast. You know how much she bothered my grandpa about getting a dog."

He smiles, sliding the chocolate chip muffin my way—my favorite.

"Something tells me she also would've loved knowing that we're on a date together at a bookstore," he replies.

"She would've been gossiping about it to all of her friends. I miss her, but her energy is here," I say.

"I miss her, too. I know that somewhere, she's so proud of you."

SIXTEEN

kieran

WE'RE ABOUT to play the Ryman Auditorium in Nashville, and the anticipation of waiting to see what Emaline is wearing tonight is killing me.

It was a rough few days after her flashback in the shower, but after a few good shows, she seems to be doing much better. I'm still worried about her, but her decision to go back to therapy seems like a genuine one, not just one to placate me. And I'll be keeping an extra close watch until then. She tends to close off because of not wanting people to worry, pretending like everything's okay.

She's terrified of being a burden, but she could never be a burden to me. No amount of tears, anxiety, flashbacks, meltdowns, disordered eating, sleepless nights, depression, or anything else could be too much for me. We've seen each other through our highest highs and lowest lows without an ounce of judgment, and I intend to do the same for the rest of our lives. Seeing a smile on her face and seeing her continuing to live her dreams, despite the vile things that piece of shit said and did to her, is reassuring. He took so much from her, and he doesn't deserve to be able to take anything else, especially her ability to live life to the fullest.

My intrusive thoughts from my OCD have been spiking up a bit again, and I should probably do something about it and read more of that book I bought, but I'm more worried about making sure Em is okay.

I stand outside the door of her dressing room, not so patiently waiting for her to be done getting ready.

"Okay, you can come in, Kiki."

I open the door and step inside. She's wearing a low-rise denim mini skirt and a baby pink rhinestoned, strapless crop top that has a heart cutout highlighting her cleavage. Her long, blonde hair is in loose waves, and there are little pink rhinestones in the corners of her eyes—one of her signature makeup looks. She's always gorgeous, but tonight is a new level of beauty.

"Goddamn, Emmie. You look perfect. It's beautiful on you, but I can't wait to take it off of you later." What can I say? It's impossible to keep my mind out of the gutter with her.

She smirks and then flashes me a playful smile. "Glad you like it, baby. Wish we had time to do something now, but we've gotta get backstage or Ruby will kill us."

I playfully roll my eyes at her. "Guess I have to practice that whole patience is a virtue thing."

We head backstage and do our pre-show ritual, ready for game time.

"Hellooooo Nashville! I'm Emaline Levine, and I am so excited and grateful to be able to perform for you all tonight. Before we play any more music for you all, I'd love to introduce you to my incredible band. We have Nick Miller on the drums, Isabelle Jones on the keys, Delia Murphy on bass, and, of course, my amazing boyfriend, Kieran Hayes, on guitar."

As the crowd goes wild, Em walks over to give me a quick kiss. When we break the kiss, I have a huge, stupid smile that is seemingly impossible to wipe off my face.

I've known that we've been in this music thing together since we started, but, for some reason, now it *really* feels like we're in it together. We're both living our dreams, and we're not holding each other back. In fact, being together is helping us live these dreams in a more fulfilling way.

We've been worried about whether the label will say anything about our relationship being public, but so far they haven't. Or if they have, Ruby hasn't told us. I suppose no news is good news.

The number of phones in the crowd pointing toward us is overwhelming, but it's cool that we get to have these kinds of moments preserved forever. We get out of lovebird mode and back into performance mode, somehow seamlessly transitioning. For some people, performing with their significant other may be a distraction, but, for us, it's only made us better. Now that the sexual tension and hidden love are out of the way, we're both able to be present instead of being distracted and stuck in our heads.

When I'm on stage, even though there are thousands of people in the crowd, everything but the music fades away. For me, it's the ultimate form of mindfulness. Occasionally, my OCD will pop up during shows, but usually, the sensation of strumming my guitar, as well as hearing my voice as I sing the background vocals grounds me. The level of focus it takes to perform at this level gets me out of my head and into my body.

As we pause between songs, I take in the intricate stained glass windows of the Ryman Auditorium. Awe and gratitude wash over me, feeling so proud that we get to perform at such iconic venues like this one. The rainbow of colors radiates and I'm filled with pride. I can be really hard on myself, but I've worked so hard to get here, and it's all paying off.

We finish the rest of the set, and Em performs perfectly as always – including a surprise cover of *Landslide* by Fleetwood Mac, which compliments her voice beautifully. As she takes her final bow, my heart flutters, feeling so lucky that this wildly talented, stunning, intelligent, loving woman is all mine.

Forgetting that we all planned to go to a bar post-show, Em said I'd have to deal with waiting to fuck her for a little while longer. I've got a plan that I think both of us will enjoy, but it depends on how risky she's willing to be.

I finish packing up my things for the crew to bring back to the hotel and then walk across the hall to her dressing room. As I open the door, she's wearing a tiny black mini skirt that barely covers her ass and a strappy lace bralette that doesn't leave much to the imagination. Her hair is pulled into a half up half down ponytail, and all I can think about is how much I can't wait to pull it later.

Doing a little twirl, she says, "What do you think?"

"You look absolutely stunning. Not that you don't always," I reply, pulling her body into mine.

She lightly grinds against me, sadly just a tease.

"Let's go get drunk, pretty boy."

After a five-minute drive that felt like an eternity, we hop out, show our IDs to the bouncer, and go inside. This bar isn't only for celebrities, but the majority of the people here have some degree of connection to fame. In some ways, it's nice to not have to stand out. But in other ways, I get caught up in my head when Emaline is surrounded by a bunch of famous guys drooling over her, the majority of which are more talented than I am... or, at the very least, more attractive than I am.

After walking inside, we make a beeline for the bar.

"Hey, can we please get a double vodka cran and a double Jack and Coke?" I say.

The night isn't getting any younger, and with a day off tomorrow, Em wants to get completely fucked up. And so do I.

"Sure thing," the bartender replies.

He passes us our drinks and swipes my credit card to open a tab. I down half my drink and we find the elevator to make our way to the rooftop, where the rest of the band is. With my free hand, I run my hand over Emmie's barely covered ass, slip it under her skirt, and give a squeeze. She presses back into me, and I smirk, excited for what'll hopefully happen soon.

She turns to face me, bites her lip, and says, "I can't wait to have you inside me."

Before I can mention the idea of a quickie, the elevator doors open. As we step out, I whisper in her ear, "I bet you're already soaked for me."

She smirks. "Have been since you killed that solo during Wild Mind."

I have half a mind to push her into a bathroom and fuck her against the wall, but if I do, we're going to be desperate to go back to the hotel—and Em wants to have at least a *little* time on the rooftop soaking up the Nashville skyline. Instead, I decide to tease her, my fingers grazing her thong. Pulling her body into mine, I whisper, "Dirty girl, already so ready for me."

She sighs. "Such a damn tease. Let's go show our faces, get another drink or two, and get the hell out of here."

We walk out onto the rooftop, and Isabelle waves at us,

standing near Delia and Kenzie. I'd usually be glad to party with the team, but tonight I have one goal: to get absolutely hammered before using my body to show Em how much I love her. I suppose that's two goals, but same difference.

"Who's ready for some shots? First round on me," Ryan says, walking over to us, still in his typical show attire of black joggers and a black t-shirt.

"Only if they're tequila," Em replies.

Delia laughs. "Kieran, you're going to be a lucky man tonight."

Em blushes and shoves her arm.

"Please, we all know you're far from some angel. Might I remind you that the bus isn't soundproof?" Isabelle chuckles.

Note to self – do a better job at covering Em's mouth if we're going to fuck on the bus.

We both shake our heads and I say, "Guilty as charged."

Kenzie puts her arm around Em. "Hey, I know we give you guys shit about it, but I'm so happy for you. You're sickeningly cute together, and everyone deserves that kind of love."

"Aww, thanks Kenz," I say.

Ruby struts over, and she's traded her black show attire for a dress and cowgirl boots–when in Nashville, I guess.

"Hey guys, sorry I'm a little late," she says.

Emaline gives her a hug and says, "You're just in time. Ryan is grabbing shots."

With an exaggerated sigh, she replies, "Oh thank god. By the way, now's probably not the time you want to hear this, but one of the old dudes over at the label emailed me with some stupid shit about you announcing the relationship without consulting them. I told him it's a bunch of bullshit, especially considering the numbers the album is doing, so hopefully he doesn't reach out to you. Just figured I'd give you both a warning."

This is exactly what I was afraid of. Sure, it could end up just being water under the bridge, but what if it ruins everything she's worked so tirelessly for? I love her too much to even entertain ending things, but knowing that I'm part of making the label angry at her has my stomach in knots.

Isabelle grumbles, "Fuck the patriarchy. You know how I feel about relationships, but you guys should be allowed to do whatever you want. You're not some puppet. And Ruby is right, the numbers don't lie. Not like that should matter anyway."

Leaning against a high-top table, Austin adds, "It's so stupid. You've worked so hard, and I've seen all the comments of how obsessed all the fans are about you and Kieran being together. If they spent even a moment in the crowd at one of these shows I'm sure they'd change their tune."

Em leans into me. "Exactly. I don't regret a thing. A few months ago, I would've probably said something different. But I'm done letting assholes tell me how to live my life. Especially assholes that I'm making rich."

Ryan comes over with a tray of shots, looking like he owns the bar.

"Jesus, that's a lot of shots," I say.

He laughs, "We've got a day off tomorrow, and we deserve to celebrate."

We each grab a glass and Delia says, "Cheers to saying fuck old men in the music industry and doing whatever the hell we want. Well, not actually fuck them. Because that would be gross. But, you know what I mean."

We all chuckle and say "cheers" in unison.

As I place my shot glass down on a table, there's a random girl walking towards us with a shocked look on her face.

"Oh my god, you're Emaline Levine, right? I'm such a big fan, your music has changed my life," she says.

Emaline beams, saying, "Aww, thank you so much, that

means the world. What's your name? Do you want to get a selfie together? Or Kieran, maybe you can just take a pic of us?"

"Please! I'm Gabby, I can't believe I'm meeting you. I was just at your show. And you two are so cute together."

Gabby passes me her phone and she and Emaline pose for the photo.

"I hope you enjoyed the show! And thank you so much for supporting us. We couldn't do it without the fans," I say, passing her phone back.

"It was incredible. One of the best concerts I've ever been to, and living in Nashville I go to a lot of shows. I'll let you guys enjoy your night, but thanks so much for talking to me and taking a photo."

After three rounds of shots, Em is draped all over me. Her kisses have progressively gone from subtle to practically shoving her tongue down my throat. I've tried to patiently wait and spend time with our friends, but I can't wait any longer.

Feigning tiredness, I force a yawn. "Hey guys, this has been great, but I'm exhausted. See you all tomorrow?"

"That's the fakest yawn I've ever seen, but I'll let it slide because of how good Em looks. Go defile your hotel room, lovebirds," Kenzie says.

No longer embarrassed because of the alcohol, Emaline rolls her eyes. "I've got a hot boyfriend, what can I say? See you guys at dinner tomorrow."

We walk back towards the elevators, and there's an all-gender, single-stall bathroom with a "vacant" sign over the handle. Em gives me a look that shows she clearly has the same idea I do. She peeks to see if the coast is clear, as if she cares about that, and opens the door. Not giving a fuck about if the floor is going to get my pants dirty, I sink down to my knees, push her skirt up over her hips, and rip her thong off.

"Hey, that's one of my favorites!" she whisper shouts.

"I'll buy you a new one," I say, moving my head between her legs.

My nose nudges against her clit, and I go down on her, eliciting the most obscene moans. Her eyes start to roll, and her body shakes as she melts into the wall. In what feels like record-setting time, she finishes, whimpering my name repeatedly.

"Jesus fucking christ, Em. I need to fuck you now," I say as I rise up to standing. I quickly unbutton my pants and pull down my boxers, desperate for a release. She unzips her skirt and throws it to the floor, running her hands down my body.

Positioning myself directly at her entrance, I hook one of her legs around my waist and say, "Jump, baby."

Not wasting a second, she hops up and wraps her other leg around my waist, her arms draped around my neck. I push into her roughly, and she latches her mouth to my neck, lightly biting me.

"You can do better than that," I moan.

She roughly sinks her teeth into me, sending shockwaves through my body.

"Fuck, Em. Such a good girl."

The praise makes her clench around me, and after how pent up I've been all day, I know I'm not going to last very long. I slide my hand between us, finding her clit with my thumb. I lightly but quickly dance it over, and she moans out, "Please don't stop."

"Wouldn't dream of it, Emmie girl."

I thrust as hard as I can, my orgasm dangerously close.

"Come for me. Now," I say lowly.

Her legs tense up and she lets out a chorus of expletives and my name, leading my own orgasm to wash over me. I unhook her legs from my waist and kiss her lightly before grabbing some paper towels.

"Hope you know I'm not done with you yet, pretty girl."

"I was hoping you'd say that."

emaline

MY HEART IS BURSTING out of my chest, my eyes open abruptly, and tears stream down my face. I'm shocked that somehow I'm silent. Kieran is sleeping next to me, completely knocked out. I'm grateful that I somehow haven't woken him up because the last thing I want to do is ruin the perfect day we had yesterday, worry him, and have to explain that my nightmares have become progressively worse since that night in the shower.

More nights than not, my dreams have been violently plagued by Chris, each one more vivid and real than the last. Even though the night I broke up with him was the most traumatic experience I had with him, there were plenty of other terrible moments we had together, giving plenty of nightmare fuel. The one I had this time was a replay of a day on my last tour. I hadn't quite sold out the venue, even though it wasn't a massive one. We were in a hotel room, and he kept screaming at me, telling me how pathetic it was that there were still tickets left and that clearly my album wasn't good enough to make people in that city want to come to the show. He said I was giving his production skills a bad name by not being able to sell out a tour for a project that he put his name on. At the time, part of me knew it was bullshit, especially because there were maybe five tickets left, but when you already judge yourself so harshly, having someone who has even a small amount of influence in the industry berating you will make you fall apart.

Meanwhile, now I've sold out this tour, and the album he said I was giving a bad name hit number three on the charts. Even though I objectively know that he's wrong, the things he said still run in my mind on repeat, even when I'm asleep.

It's not good to keep Kieran in the dark, but he's seemed so happy, and I'd hate to be the one to bring that down. Or to make his OCD spiral, especially since he bought that book the other day.

Despite having some great days, the nightmares have been overshadowing it all. Yesterday was almost as perfect as a day off can be. We got room service pancakes for breakfast, walked through the iconic Centennial Park, got barbecue from a little hole in the wall for lunch, walked through the sweetest local bookstore, and had classic Nashville hot chicken for dinner—followed by a glass of wine on the rooftop of our hotel. Well, two glasses actually. We giggled and roasted each other, and for a few hours, everything felt normal. Blissful even. But, now, here I am, once again plagued by my fucking brain.

Sometimes, it's easier to not tell anyone and suffer in silence. Feeling alone in the struggle is hard, but feeling like everyone is pitying me or watching like a hawk to see if I'm not doing okay is exhausting, too.

As my PTSD has crept in more obtrusively, my eating disorder is also trying to creep back in. The urge to pick off and throw away parts of meals, order the dressing on the side so that I can add the smallest possible amount, only get water to drink, and blot the oil off of my food is getting stronger. All of my body imperfections have seemed more visible, feeling like all my eyes can do is hyperfocus on every stretch mark and bit of cellulite. I've been wishing that there would be scales in our hotel bathrooms, and when there is one, it takes everything in me to not step on it. I should probably be concerned, but the volume of the intrusive memories is clouding my ability to try to push down the eating disorder. And despite the body checking, I haven't engaged in any sort of unhealthy behaviors, so does it matter? It's not like when I was 13 and barely eating at all and purging everything I did eat, so it's not *that* bad. Everyone in this industry, and honestly, our world in general, does weird shit with their food and bodies, so why does it matter if I do too?

I look over at the clock, see it's 3 am, and do some breathing exercises my therapist taught me, hoping that I can at least get a tiny bit more sleep.

"Emmie baby, time to wake up. We've gotta get down to bus call in less than an hour," Kieran says, gently shaking me awake.

Despite being afraid to go back to sleep, I managed to knock out. I roll towards him and open my eyes, seeing that the clock says 7 am and all of our bags are already repacked.

Smiling at him, I say, "You didn't have to do that, I could've helped."

"You were so peaceful, I could tell you needed the rest. And it wasn't that hard, you didn't take too much out. I already showered, but do you wanna hop in? I ordered us some break-fast that should get here in fifteen minutes or so."

The eating disorder voice in my brain is hoping he ordered

something light, but, knowing Kieran, he probably ordered my favorite—chocolate chip waffles. I don't want to show my anxiety, so I nod and get out of bed.

"You really thought of everything, didn't you?"

He flashes me a grin. "Anything to make your life easier, pretty girl."

"I love you so much," I reply, ruffling his still slightly damp hair.

His lips melt into mine as he says, "I love you more."

I walk into the bathroom, and my reflection stares back at me. I force my gaze away, determined not to pick apart my body. It'll just make everything worse. I put on the flimsy, scratchy, throwaway shower cap and get in the shower, trying not to get my hair wet since I don't have the energy to wash it today. I try to mindfully focus on the water hitting my skin to distract me from the negative thought. The lavender scent of the shower gel soothes my anxiety, and, for a moment, I feel calm. After hearing the room service arrive, I quickly finish showering and getting myself together so that we can eat while still checking out on time.

The sweet smell of waffles permeates the room, creating a mix of fear and excitement. People often think that people with eating disorders hate food. But so many of us love food; our brains just make it really hard to enjoy it. I'm trying to remind myself of weekend mornings after sleepovers when Kieran's mom would make us waffles, bacon, and hot cocoa loaded up with marshmallows. There wasn't a single thought about it being "bad" or "wrong" or "unhealthy." It was delicious food, not the enemy.

"Ordered your favorite," Kieran says as I walk out of the bathroom.

They're just waffles. They're just waffles.

I pull him in for a hug from behind. "Thanks, baby. Perfect start to the day."

We sit down at the little table, and I take what's hopefully an inconspicuous deep breath as I add butter and syrup to my waffle. I take a bite and it's the perfect blend of crisp on the outside and fluffy on the inside, with just enough chocolate chips. I take every ounce of effort in my brain to focus on the texture and taste instead of the anxious thoughts that are weaseling their way in.

"These are so fucking good," I say.

Kieran nods and smiles. "Exactly what I need before a long bus ride."

If only he knew everything that was floating through my brain right now. I am enjoying the waffle... just with a side of anxiety and guilt.

We finish eating and I pack up my toiletries before we head down to the lobby for bus call.

The ride to Austin is almost over, and Kieran asked me to paint his nails, which is a questionable choice on a moving bus, especially with my lackluster manicure skills. He picked yellow—the perfect complement to his sunshiney demeanor. Even in the darkest moments, Kieran radiates pure sunshine. I wish I was the same way, but he brings enough of it to balance us out. For a guy, he has surprisingly well-kept nails–not bitten and neatly trimmed.

"So, what possessed you to think that having me paint your nails on the bus is a good idea?"

He laughs. "I like doing things that challenge you to not always try to be so perfect. I'll always think you're perfect, but it's fun to do things out of your comfort zone. Plus, this twelve-hour bus ride is making me lose my mind just a little."

Kieran forever has an endearing answer for everything. And, the man has a point. I far prefer long bus rides that happen overnight versus during the day, even if it means having to sleep on a bus instead of in a hotel room. Bunks aren't the comfiest, but boredom is worse. I apply a base coat and let it dry, somehow followed by an even first coat.

"Told ya you'd do a good job, Emmie girl."

I snicker. "We've still got another coat and a top coat to go, plenty of space to fuck it up."

"Shhhhh, stop being mean to my girlfriend."

"It's not mean if it's true," I say, rolling my eyes.

"Evidence so far shows that it's not true, so, until proven otherwise, I'm right. If you want to see a bad job, you can let me paint yours."

"I'd love to take you up on that offer, but these cherry nails are too cute to change right now. Sit still so I can finish these up and they have time to dry before we get to the hotel."

I methodically apply the final coat on his left hand, and Kieran uses his right hand to take a picture of me. My focus breaks for a second and I smile, grateful that he's capturing this sweet little moment, even though I'm a mess in my bralette and sweatpants. It's this weird juxtaposition of having made so much progress on accepting and loving myself, while simultaneously being acutely aware of the backslide that's currently morphing into a high-speed train. Right now, I'm choosing to soak up the joy, regardless of the other shit.

After the second coat dries, I finish the top coat and admire the shockingly clean and precise job I did.

"Well, guess you can say I told you so. I'm surprised, but I guess I should start trusting how much you believe in me after all."

"You know I'd never steer you wrong, pretty girl. I know I need to let these dry so they don't get smushed, but get over here and cuddle me."

I twist the nail polish bottle closed and climb onto the couch, scooting into his side while making sure I don't graze his hands accidentally.

After about thirty more minutes the bus comes to a halt, arriving at the hotel. Eager to get out, stretch my legs, and get whatever room service is hopefully still available, I pop up and grab Kieran's hand. There's a hint of nervous excitement on his face and I wonder what he's hiding.

"I know that look, and it usually means you're up to something."

He looks at the ground. "Oh, nothing. Just excited to stuff my face with food and take a nice, long shower."

"Whatever you say," I reply, shaking my head.

We get off the bus, grab our suitcases, and walk into the lobby of the hotel. My jaw drops because my mom is sitting on a couch near the check-in desk. I drop my pink backpack on the ground and sprint over to her.

She stands up, and I throw my arms around her. "MOM!!!! What are you doing here?"

"Kieran and I have been planning this for weeks. I know your LA show is less than two weeks away, but I had to see my girl. FaceTime and videos on Instagram weren't enough," she says, hugging me back as a huge smile spreads across her face.

My mom is my second biggest fan, only beat by Kieran, and having her here is the exact mood boost and distraction I need after this morning.

Kieran walks up next to us, and I look at him. "I'm shocked you managed to not let on at all until a few minutes ago. You're not usually one for keeping surprises."

"Hey, you're better at doing nails than you thought, I'm

better at keeping surprises than I thought. We're both full of wins today."

"Put those bags down and get over here and hug me, Kieran. It's about time you both pulled your heads out of your asses. Your mother and I have been waiting to see you guys get together since you were toddlers."

He places the bags back on the ground and gives her a huge hug. Moments like this remind me that we're not going too fast and that it's so beautiful and easy that Kieran is basically already part of the family. There's no awkward "meeting the parents" phase and no anxiety-provoking, "Are they going to like him?" moments. She's seen him as her son practically forever, and now it's in the way that it's always been meant to be.

They break the hug and my mom says, "Now, I know it's nearly 10 pm, but how about we go grab a glass of wine? You have so much to catch me up on, and I won't keep you up too late."

Even though I want to get into bed, I'm dying to have some girl time with my mom. When I'm on the road, we so rarely get this, and I've missed it dearly.

"That sounds perfect. Can I go change real quick?"

"Oh, nonsense. No one cares what you look like right now, and I don't want to lose any more precious time with my baby."

I shake my head. "Fine. Kier, are you going to come with us, too?"

"I figured I'd give you some time just the two of you. I've been meaning to FaceTime my mom, so it's good timing. I'll get our room key from Ruby and come down to give you a key in an hour or so if that sounds good?"

"Perfect."

"So, how has it been being on the road together while actually being in a relationship? I know you've toured together for years, but of course, I'm sure some things are different now."

After finishing a sip of my wine, I reply, "It's been so nice. Things were a little awkward when we were both realizing it all, but since admitting it, it's felt pretty perfect. He's always been so supportive, but it's on a different level. I guess I have to thank that hotel back in New York for only having a king-size room left. Without that, I'm not sure we ever would have gone for it."

"Oh my goodness, you didn't tell me about that. The universe has always had this in the cards for you both, and I knew it was just a matter of time. It's so wonderful seeing how he treats you after everything you've been through with Chris."

My throat catches a little with the mention of Chris, but I play it off as a tickle in my throat from the dryness of the wine.

"With him being here through it all, I know that I can trust he's not going to let me down. We just fit together like a puzzle piece."

She smiles after taking another sip of her sauvignon blanc. "Sounds like you're both pretty serious about each other. I hear wedding bells in the future."

I blush. "As much as I'd love to say that you're saying that too soon, I can see it too. We're not gonna rush into anything, but I know he's as in it for the long haul as I am. Not sure how I got so lucky."

"I don't think this was luck, Em. You've both been there for each other your entire lives, and you consciously built a friendship rooted in love, respect, and support. This was something you worked for and helped blossom, luck has nothing to do with it. You deserve every moment. Your father and I couldn't have hoped to see you with anyone better. I'm so glad we moved into our house when we did."

It's the butterfly effect. If my parents never bought that house, my mom would've never had the job she had when she met Kieran's mom, and we would've never met each other or become best friends. If the hotel had a room with two queen beds, we wouldn't be where we are now. The universe is a weird and magical thing, and it's wild how every moment and choice creates a domino effect that makes the rest of our lives.

"I'm so glad, too. I've never been more sure about anything as I have been with this. It may have taken us forever and a million shitty relationships to get here, but now we're here, and it's more than I could've ever dreamed of."

With a little happy tear in her eye, she replies, "My baby is all grown up."

kieran

SINCE THINGS HAVE BEEN rough for Em, Madison decided to fly to Austin to surprise her for the show. Her flight got in early this morning, right after we finished soundcheck. The show doesn't start until 9 pm, so we have plenty of time to chill instead of having to stay at the venue. Em is having a cute mother-daughter self-care and shopping day, so Mads and I are having lunch at a cute little park tucked away in a corner of downtown Austin. When she'd visit me while I was going to NYU, we'd do little picnics in Washington Square Park, so it's very nostalgic.

We brought books to read after we finished eating—reminiscent of our teenage years when we'd read out in the treehouse our dad built us when we were kids. She glances over at the book I have sitting on the picnic blanket. I picked it up at a bookstore near our hotel, and it's about loving someone with sexual trauma. Even though I don't think I've messed anything up yet, I want to do everything in my power to be the best boyfriend I can.

"It's really sweet that you're reading that book. How's Em been doing?"

How much do I share where I can be honest but also not air out Emmie's business?

Reminding myself that sharing this with Madison is different than sharing it with some random person, I say, "Honestly? It's been pretty hard. She had a really bad panic attack the other night—the worst I've ever seen. She's been kinda off since then. Trying not to worry too much, but you know how dark things have gotten for her before. I just hope things aren't heading back in that direction, you know?"

She puts her hand on my shoulder, and a sense of calm immediately rushes over me.

"It makes a lot of sense that you're worried. Seeing someone you love so much struggle like that is so scary, especially when you don't know exactly what's going on inside their head. All you can do is be there for her and hope that she's being honest with you about where she's at and what she needs."

After finishing a bite of my sandwich, I say, "That's the thing... I know she's usually really honest with me, but back in high school, she wasn't honest with anyone until it couldn't be ignored. I don't want to assume anything or be overbearing, but I worry about her more than she knows."

"You're a great boyfriend, you know that, right? You're doing the best you can. And don't forget to take care of yourself, too. I know you were struggling a few weeks ago, and I don't want you to feel like you can't voice your own shit because Em is struggling," she replies, then taking a sip of her iced vanilla latte.

It's really hard to think about myself when my Emmie girl is struggling because she's my everything. I haven't been doing the best, but it's nothing compared to what she's been going through. She doesn't need to worry about me. She has enough to worry about.

"I know, I know. And it hasn't been all bad. We had a really nice day off in Nashville. Went to Centennial Park and got to read on Taylor Swift's bench because there wasn't a line of people wanting to take pictures on it. The dark moments have been really dark, but the bright moments are like when the sun finally peeks through the clouds after a storm."

"The way you two love each other is almost sickening. If it was anyone else, I'd say you were crazy for going this fast, but you've been it for each other since you were teenagers. I'm so glad you both have each other."

"I'm really glad, too. Not sure how I got so lucky."

"And how have you been doing, especially with your OCD? I probably should have asked about that before asking about Emaline," she says before grabbing her latte.

Wanting support but also not wanting to have to talk about how you've been struggling is a hard combo.

"Ehh, things have been a little rough. I've been getting stuck in doing my night routine in threes again. I've also been doing this thing of tapping my fingers together before we get in bed because my brain tells me if I don't, Emaline is gonna die. Even though I know that's not true. It's just hard to want to focus on myself when things have been so heavy for her, you know?"

She nods. "I get it. When Matt is having a rough time with his anxiety, it makes me struggle to share anything I'm struggling with. But it's not fair for you to expect Em to be open about what's going on for her if you're not being fully honest about what's going on for you."

I take a sip of my vanilla sweet cream cold brew and then say, "I know, you're right. I just don't want her to spiral more if she thinks too much about me struggling. Enough about us though, anything new with you and Matt?"

A little smile comes across her face as she says, "So, you

have to promise not to tell mom, but we're going to start trying to get pregnant. Now that we've been married for a year and he got that promotion a few months ago, the timing seems right. But seriously, you can't tell mom. You know she'll tell Kim and then the whole neighborhood will know. And the last thing I need is the neighborhood thinking about my sex life."

Our mom is nothing if not a yapper. There's a reason Madison knew about me and Emaline far before her.

"I promise I won't. Honestly, I don't want to think about your sex life either, but I'm so fucking happy for you guys. I know it can take some time, but I can't wait to have a little niece or nephew running around."

It's almost show time, and after drying my hair post-shower, I'm about to walk over to Em's dressing room. I wish I could just share a dressing room with her. But for now, I'll continue entertaining her desire to surprise me with her outfit every night.

I knock on the door. "Ready for me, pretty girl?"

She opens the door, and I scan my eyes over her whole body, taking in her beauty. She's wearing mid-rise, wide-leg white jeans that hit just below her belly button, paired with a crop top covered in cherries and accented with a red lip. I love that she changes it up between more casual looks and more extra ones. And I swear that she gets more and more stunning with each passing day.

"Goddamn, Em. The red lipstick and your ass in those jeans is doing something to me."

She laughs playfully and shakes her head. "I know I can always count on your dirty thoughts to hype me up."

"Glad to be of service, baby."

She walks back over to the mirror. I assume she's going to do something with her hair or makeup, but, instead, she turns sideways and grabs at the skin on her stomach. Her expression sinks as she turns back to face herself, and she wraps her fingers around her wrist.

I've seen her get stuck looking at herself in the mirror a few times recently, but I haven't seen her do the wrist thing in years. She said it's called body checking, and from what I've heard, it's easy for it to become something that consumes your whole brain, like my OCD. I can tell she's stuck in a loop, like when my obsessions and compulsions take over my mind.

Hoping to gently get her out of the loop, I walk over and hug her from behind. "You okay, my love?"

"Oh, yeah, I'm fine," she says unconvincingly.

"Then what was going on in the mirror and with your hand on your wrist?"

She looks at the ground. "I've been body checking a bit again recently, but I promise it's no big deal, you have nothing to worry about."

The way she averted her eyes tells me that there is *everything* to worry about.

With her flashback the other night, I've seen less light in her eyes. And it terrifies me. I want to trust what she says, but her eating disorder has made her lie in the past. Maybe it isn't a big deal, but something tells me to trust my gut instinct over her word right now.

Wanting to communicate my support and concern while also not starting some sort of fight before we get on stage, I dance my fingers along her shoulders and say, "We don't have to talk about it right now, but I want you to know that if you are ever struggling more, I'll never be angry at you. I'm here for all of you, even during those low moments. Now, how about we go play Austin a kickass concert?"

She smooths out her jeans, turns to me, and says, "Let's do it."

After she sings the last note of the encore and I put my guitar down, Emaline yells, "Thank you, Austin!" and jumps onto my back for a piggyback ride.

Please tell me that a fan got a video of that.

Having a relationship in the public eye has its challenges, but it's also pretty cool that we get to have special moments like this captured. We also get the whole invasion of privacy thing, but having so many people cheer us on and having these moments documented to have for the rest of our lives makes it worth it. That and the rest of our relationship, of course.

At the same time, I know that being in the public eye definitely contributes to Emaline's struggles. It's hard because she absolutely loves performing with every inch of her being. Right now, the pros of her being a touring recording artist outweigh the cons, and I hope with all of my heart it stays that way forever—that she never has to choose between her well-being and one of the things she loves most.

emaline

AFTER TWO MORE WEEKS OF shows, we just finished soundchecking in Las Vegas. We only have two more shows after tonight, San Diego and LA. While I love being on tour, I desperately need a break from bus/hotel life and having to be "on" almost every night.

As much as I want to ignore it, the voice in my head that has been telling me I need to be smaller and need to control my food (and honestly, everything in general) has been getting progressively louder. Every night, I've had multiple nightmares, and I usually lie awake for several hours, terrified to go back to sleep because I know that as soon as I close my eyes, horrific scenes will play on repeat. It's getting harder and harder to hide how bad I'm doing. I hate that I haven't been fully honest with Kieran, but I don't want him to worry when I feel like, once I get more than one day off in a row, I'll be back to my normal mental state. Sure, things haven't been this rough in a while, but I haven't been this busy in a while. It's not that big of a deal.

It doesn't help that I got some shitty comments on a social media post I made recently where I was wearing a bikini by the pool. It had a few photos, including one looking over my shoulder and one sitting down, where you could see cellulite and a stomach roll—which are pretty standard things to see in a picture of an adult woman in a swimsuit. Most of the comments were nice, but there were a few saying things like, "Yikes, cellulite at 25," "She's def gained weight this year," and "These are so unflattering". Even though hundreds of the comments were really nice, the handful of critical ones have made me go further into a tailspin.

It's lunchtime, and I'm glad that on show days I don't have as many urges to restrict because I'm moving around so much. It means less anxiety and less having to pretend like I'm okay, even if it's only temporary.

"This all looks fucking amazing," Kieran says, gesturing to the catering table that's covered with an assortment of roasted vegetables, grilled chicken that looks like it's in some sort of balsamic glaze, salmon, a giant caesar salad, roasted potatoes, and garlic bread. Despite the anxiety, my mouth is watering.

"Seriously, I need this to be our catering for every show," I reply, walking towards the wide array of food.

Instead of listening to the voice in my brain telling me I should only take the minimum amount that wouldn't raise concern with anyone, I listen to what I want and scoop a little bit of everything onto my plate. It reminds me of neighborhood barbecues when we were younger, where everyone would bring a variety of dishes to Kieran's house to share, and then we'd each try a bit of it all. When my eating disorder first got bad back in middle school, I lost the joy of that, but I'm determined not to lose it again.

Kieran pulls my chair out for me, and I sit down at the table, immediately devouring my food.

"I swear it tastes better than it looks," he says after taking a bite of his chicken.

"We need to try to get Ryan to get this marinade recipe from the caterer, it's so fucking good."

For some reason, I'm genuinely enjoying this food right now and not feeling anxious or guilty... so here's to trying not to question it and to hoping it stays this way.

"I know I say this after every show, but you were absolutely incredible, Emmie girl," Kieran says, swinging me around in a circle and enveloping me in a giant bear hug.

The post-show high is coursing through me, and I'm so glad we're heading to a club to celebrate because there's no way I'm letting this feeling go to waste by going back to the hotel and going to bed. I don't want to stay out too late, but, for now, it's time to party. Gotta live up to the "Everything that happens in Vegas, stays in Vegas" cliche.

"I could say the same about you, Kiki. Those riffs you improvised were everything."

"It's all the extra playing I've been doing while singing to you in the bunk. Seems like lulling my girlfriend to sleep doubles as practice time," he says.

"We've always been great performing together, but dating has made us even better. Another thing to add to the list of reasons why we should've realized our love sooner."

He kisses me and then says, "That and so that I could've been kissing you and messing up your lipstick sooner."

"If you really want to mess up my lipstick, we need to get changed and go soak up Vegas before we head back to the hotel for the night."

He places me back on the ground. "Sounds like a perfect plan with my perfect girl."

We walk back to our dressing rooms, and as we reach his, I say, "Meet you out here when I'm ready?"

He nods and pulls the door shut behind him. As I step into my dressing room, I toss my phone down onto the couch, knowing that if I don't, I'll get stuck in a loop of watching TikToks and we'll never end up leaving.

Sometimes my show outfits outshine my going-out outfits, and sometimes it's the other way around—tonight is one of the nights where it's the other way around. I wore jeans on stage, and now I'm changing into a hot pink mini slip dress that accentuates my curves. I'm not totally sure how I feel about the way it hugs them and shows the imperfections, but I don't want to go out in what I wore for the show and I don't have anything else here other than the shorts and t-shirt I was wearing this morning, so I guess I'm going to have to go with it.

I add some dry shampoo to my slightly sweaty hair and pull it into a top knot, keeping a few waves out in the front. I refresh my makeup with a tiny bit of setting powder so that I look dewy but not sweaty, and add a pink lip to accent the dress. After slipping on my trusty white sneakers, I grab my phone from the couch and head back out to the hallway to meet Kieran.

He looks hot as always, wearing a pair of beige slacks with a loose black button-up shirt that has several buttons undone.

After pulling me in for a kiss, he says, "So fucking beautiful, Em. So fucking beautiful."

I blush, ignoring the voice in my head telling me that the dress shows my curves too much.

"You need to wear shirts like this more often. Seeing your tattoos peek out does things to me."

"That can be arranged," he smirks.

We walk out the back entrance of the venue and take an Uber to the club.

As soon as we get into the club and have our IDs checked, Kieran makes a beeline for the bar.

"Hello, can we please have 4 shots of tequila?" he says.

Apparently, we're starting the night out strong. RIP to me and my hangover tomorrow... good thing we have a day off in Vegas and won't be on a bus.

"Absolutely, do you want to keep the tab open or close it?"

"You can keep it open, thank you."

After the bartender gives us the shots, Kieran immediately downs both of his like they're nothing, completely ignoring the lime.

"I'd say I'm shocked with how you took those down like they're water, but with how many college parties I went to with you, that would be a bold-faced lie."

Kieran laughs. "May not have been a frat boy, but can def keep up."

I choke back my shots, nowhere near as gracefully as him, and aggressively bite into the lime to help neutralize the flavor. The alcohol starts to hit, and I say, "Want to go dance?"

"Isn't that the whole point of us coming here? Of course, baby."

We start dancing, Kieran's hands on my waist, moving in rhythm to the loud music. Suddenly, I'm laser focused on the sea of bodies around us. Every woman here looks so perfect. So much thinner than me, so toned, so *everything I'm not.*

My thoughts are consumed by every bump and curve this dress shows, the massive plate of food I had at lunch, the sugary latte I had before the show, the social media comments, and the In-N-Out Kieran wants to grab on the way back to the hotel.

All I can see are all of the perfectly flat stomachs and tiny waists, and my brain can't stop repeating every negative thing Chris ever said about my body, how he would monitor what I would eat in the same way I used to when I was a teenager. How in so many ways he was an external representation of all of the demons inside my brain.

I don't want Kieran to worry, but I can tell I'm about to have a panic attack. The way my heart is racing has me thinking that I can't stop it in its tracks.

"Babe, I need to run to the bathroom. I'll meet you over by that booth when I'm done?" I say.

"Sounds good, take your time, baby."

I quickly make my way through the crowd, willing my brain to let me be and begging any god that exists to not let anyone notice me. Grateful that there's a single stall restroom and that it's open, I burst inside, look at myself in the mirror, and start to sob. My hands brace the sides of the sink, and my breath quickens as my heart pounds harder than the bass of the music outside.

I haven't had the urge to purge in nearly a year, and it's been two years since I've done it, but an all-consuming urge is washing over me.

"Don't do this. Don't do this. You're stronger than this. Don't do this," I whisper to myself, tears streaming down my face, willing myself not to vomit. I know I should call Kieran or Ruby or Madison or my mom, but I'm too ashamed to ask for help. I know they wouldn't judge me, but I can't help but judge myself.

Hundreds of thousands of dollars spent by my parents on my treatment, hundreds of hours in therapy, and here I fucking am, a pathetic sobbing mess trying to convince herself not to puke in the bathroom of a bar in Vegas after playing one of the best shows I've ever had.

My brain won't quiet down, and "You need to throw up. You ate too much today. You don't deserve the success you're having. All of those shitty comments are right. Chris was right. You don't deserve the love Kieran gives you. The label is going to drop you because of you being less marketable. You need to throw up," is running on repeat. I'm trying to calm myself with the breathing exercises I've learned in therapy, but nothing is working.

I start crying harder and sink down to my knees, flipping the toilet seat up. Here I am, in this same familiar position I've been in more times than I can count. I'm living a fucking dream life, having opportunities that most people could only dream of. Dating my childhood best friend who loves me more than humanly possible. Selling out countless shows. Having my new album on the biggest playlists and climbing the charts. But yet, this is where I'm at, letting my goddamn eating disorder win. About to purge because I'm too fucking weak not to.

Any semblance of control has left me, and I'm completely ruled by the thoughts plaguing my brain. I stick my fingers down my throat and vomit. A combination of relief and immense shame washes over me. My eating disorder is telling me I did something good. The healthy part of my brain is telling me that I fucked up massively.

And now I'm sitting here on the bathroom floor, mascara smeared all over my face, continuing to sob. The coldness of the ground sends chills down my spine, a stark contrast to the burning sensation in my throat. I don't want to tell Kieran, but he's going to find out sooner or later when I go back out there looking like this. I dial his number.

"Hey babe, you good?"

Trying to stop crying, my voice cracks. "Kieran...I...I did something really stupid."

"What's wrong? What do you mean?"

"I...I started having a panic attack, and I just purged for the first time in two years, and I can't stop crying, and I'm sitting on the bathroom floor, and I'm so sorry," I sob.

"Baby, you have nothing to be sorry for. I'm on my way."

My head pounds from the dehydration, and my body feels weak.

What the fuck have I done? How am I back in this place again?

IT FEELS like my heart was ripped out of my chest. My head is spinning, and I know that we need to get out of here. Quickly.

How didn't I see that Emaline wasn't doing okay ten minutes ago? How didn't I see that the woman I love with my entire being was so distressed that she relapsed after two years of being clean from purging? I should've known. I should've been able to see some sort of sign. She's clearly been struggling more recently, but I didn't realize it was this bad.

What kind of boyfriend and best friend isn't able to see that?

I need to find a way for us to get the fuck out of here without anyone seeing that she isn't okay and hope that there aren't somehow paparazzi outside if people noticed us earlier and posted any photos. These days, we get recognized all the time. And the last thing we need right now is for this to somehow get blasted across the internet, especially with the tour still going on. I pull out my phone to text Ruby.

KIERAN

SOS. I need you to come get us from the bar.
Bad situation, don't want to risk anyone out
front seeing us. Will explain more later

RUBY

On my way

I shove through the sea of people, not caring who I bump into or if anyone thinks I'm an asshole. I need to be with Emaline. Now.

After pushing my way through, I get to the bathrooms. One is open and the other has a closed door. Knocking on the door, hearing excruciating sobs on the other side, I say, "Emmie, are you in here?"

"Y...yes."

Thank god she forgot to lock the door. But I would've broken it down if I had to. I'd do anything to make sure she's okay. I open the door, and she's sitting on the floor next to the toilet with her head between her knees. Her sobs are breaking me, and I sit down next to her, not giving a fuck if I get anything on my clothing.

"I'm so sorry, Kieran. I'm so stupid. I shouldn't have done this. And now I ruined our night," she says, tears still pouring down her face.

I fucking hate that she feels like she has to apologize for everything. That she's apologizing for her eating disorder consuming her brain. Having OCD has taught me that it's not as easy as saying no to those thoughts and urges. When your brain is screaming at you at 200% volume to do something, it's like you're a puppet being controlled by a puppeteer.

I cautiously place my hand on her back. "Em, you don't need to apologize. Of course, it's not good for you, and you've worked so hard for your recovery, but it's not your fault. If anything, I'm the one who should be sorry for not seeing that you weren't okay."

She leans her warm body into mine, wiping away her mascara-filled tears.

"I didn't want you to worry, so I haven't been completely honest. Things have been a lot harder recently, but I thought I had it all under control."

"I never want you to feel like you have to hide things from me, baby. No matter what time of day or night. No matter what has happened. No matter how bad it is. I always want you to be able to be completely honest with me, regardless of if I'm struggling. You have my entire heart, and you're the most important part of my life. Always have been," I say, rubbing her back. "Can I help you up and help you wash your face? I texted Ruby to come get us from the back entrance so that we don't risk there being any paps out front. I didn't give her details. Just told her something bad happened and that we needed her."

She nods, and I give her my hands, pulling her up to stand. Her face is puffy and red, covered in mascara, eyes bloodshot. And I still love her the same.

We inch towards the sink and I turn it on, making sure the temperature isn't too cold or too hot. I grab a paper towel, soaking it enough to be able to wipe her face, but not so much that it falls apart. She faces me, all hope and light devoid from her eyes. All I want is to see her inner light shine like it did earlier today... but I know more than anyone that recovery isn't a straight line, and, unfortunately, relapses do happen. I gently wipe her face, the black flecks of her mascara and eyeliner covering the paper towel. My phone rings, and Ruby's name flashes across the screen.

"Hey, are you outside?"

"Yep, out back whenever you're ready."

"Cool, thanks, Rube. We'll be out in a few."

I toss the wet paper towel in the trash and say, "You ready, Emmie girl?"

She sheepishly looks down. "Yeah, let's go."

Grateful that no one is outside the bathroom door, we make our way through the throngs of intoxicated people, desperately hoping no one notices anything is wrong or realizes who we are. We make it towards the back door, but there's a guard standing in front of it.

"Excuse me, sir, you can't go out that way. Employees only."

I try to keep my cool and not cause a scene. "I understand, but we have an emergency. She's Emaline Levine, and it's very likely that there are paparazzi outside because of the concert we had tonight. Can you please make an exception? Her manager is out back to pick us up."

This is going to be a very bad situation if we're not able to go out this way.

He grumbles, "Okay, but head out quickly before anyone gets any ideas."

I quickly open the door, thank him, and we walk out, heads down in case anyone is outside. Ruby's rental car is right in front of the door, and I open the door for Em. We slam the doors quickly, not wanting to potentially be noticed by anyone who may be passing by.

Trying to hold back tears, Emaline says, "Thanks so much for coming to get us, Rube. I know I interrupted your *The Office* binge after already being with us all day."

Ruby glances back. "It's no problem at all, it's part of my job, and even if it wasn't, I'd do anything for you, and I know you'd do the same for me. If you want to talk about whatever happened, I'm all ears. But I know you have Kier here to take care of you, so don't feel like you have to tell me anything."

I pull Em into my side, kissing her head gently. Ruby has been there for us through so many difficult moments, and she knows Em's history very well. She's always been nothing but supportive, and I'm so glad that she loves my Emaline exactly as she is. Everyone should.

She starts to cry again. "I relapsed. I was having a panic attack and purged in the bathroom."

"I'm so sorry, Em. There must be a million things running through your mind. Are you okay?"

"I'm not right now. But I will be."

"Can you please eat something for me? I really don't want you going to bed on an empty stomach, Em."

We got back to the hotel a few minutes ago, and I'm trying so hard to keep it together for her. But it's taking everything in me.

"I can't put anything in my stomach. My brain is too loud right now. And if I eat something, I'm just going to go purge."

I don't want to push her too hard, but I'm worried for her physical health, not only her mental health. We had breakfast and lunch, but we never ended up getting our In-N-Out, and her stomach is probably completely empty right now.

"Please, baby. Even if it's just a bite."

"No, I can't. It's too fucking hard. My brain is too loud."

In the past, I've been able to stay pretty chill in conversations about her eating disorder, but that was when we were teenagers. This is different.

"But you *can* do it, baby. I'm not going to be able to sleep if you don't eat something. Please eat this for me," I say, giving her a granola bar from my backpack.

Tears well up in her eyes, and she grabs the bar from my hand. She throws it across the room and starts sobbing.

Shit.

"I said I can't fucking do this. Why aren't you listening to me? It's one night. It doesn't matter," she says, with a level of anger I've never seen her have towards me.

"It does matter. It matters because you're hurting yourself, and it's breaking me," I say, my throat catching.

Don't cry, Kieran. Don't cry.

"Breaking you? How do you think I'm feeling right now? Just stop. I'll eat tomorrow. It's not a big deal."

In what's probably a stupid, risky move, I grab the granola bar. I try to pass it to her again and say, "Please, Emmie. Just take one bite for me and then we can go to bed."

She opens the wrapper, breaks the bar into pieces, and throws them in the garbage.

I fucked up. Big time.

She starts sobbing. "I said to stop. I can't do this," she says, storming off to the bathroom and slamming the door.

I did the one thing I promised Emaline and myself I'd never do. Hurt her.

But was I supposed to just let her go to bed on an empty stomach without a fight?

Everything in me wants to go into the bathroom and try to apologize and make everything better, but I already pushed too hard. I really hope that her saying, "I can't do this," was referring to eating and the conversation—not our relationship. But who knows.

I feel like a hypocrite for wanting to give in to my OCD and go pace since we just had a fight about her purging, but I can't sit here. I don't want her to think I'm abandoning her, so I knock on the door lightly, hearing her crying, at least wanting to let her know that I'm going for a walk.

"Em, can I come in?"

She mumbles, "No, I want to be alone right now."

I don't blame her.

"Okay, I'll let you be. I'm gonna go for a walk, I'll be back in a bit. Call me if you need me, I love you."

"I love you, too," she says softly.

I change out of my outfit from the bar and throw on joggers and a t-shirt. I grab my wallet and put my earbuds in before heading out the door. The good thing about being in a city where people are awake at all hours of the night is that I can walk through the hotel or outside this late without it seeming weird. Desperate for fresh air, I take the elevator down to the lobby and step outside. Even though it's after midnight, it's a million degrees out here. But it feels better than suffocating in my self pity in the hotel room.

I'm just not sure how we got here. Even though things were starting to get dark, I didn't realize how far under she'd gotten. She's never been that angry at me. And it honestly fucking hurts to get that type of response when all I was trying to do was help. It's rare that I get frustrated with Em, but her pattern of throwing her walls up when all I want to do is support her is getting increasingly more difficult to navigate. My OCD has been getting louder and louder over the past week, but I haven't been able to really take care of myself. I'd never leave her, but I'm just not sure what else I can do when I'm already losing sleep over it and putting every ounce of energy I have into trying to save her.

All I want to do right now is scream, but considering the number of people around, I can't do that. So, I start walking, pull my phone out of my pocket, and tap on Madison's contact. Even though LA is an hour behind Vegas, it's still pretty late for her, especially on a weeknight. But she's the only person I feel safe trying to process this with. I don't want to rope Ruby into it, Noah is probably asleep or at work, and I'm not about to tell my mom. So here's to hoping that Mads is awake.

"Hey Kier, is everything okay?"

Shaking my head even though she can't see me, I say, "I fucked up. Majorly."

"What happened? Are you okay? Is Em okay?"

I sigh and tell her about what happened at the club and the fight we just had, shame washing over me. She's not going to judge me, but it's excruciating having to say all of that out loud. By the time I finish the story, tears are streaming down my face.

"Breathe, Kiki, breathe. You messed up, but I promise it's nothing that can't be fixed. And Em didn't respond the best either. It's not like her to throw shit or talk to you like that, so she must be in a really dark spot. It's not your fault though, you can't know how she's feeling if she doesn't tell you. And if it were me, I would've been begging her to eat something too. You pushed a little too far, but it's because you love her so much. I'm sure once things cool down and you guys are able to talk, it'll be okay. She probably just needs a little space," she says.

It's hard to believe right now, but she's right. I hate that I hurt Emaline, but it's not like I did something unforgivable. I realize I've walked nearly a mile, so I wipe my tears off with my shirt and turn back towards the hotel.

"Yeah, you're right. Thank god we have most of the day off tomorrow before we fly to San Diego. I doubt I'm going to sleep tonight, and she's gonna be feeling rough, too. Thanks for listening to me rant, I know it's late. I just didn't know who else to call. Please don't tell anyone, I didn't even want to tell you. We don't need this getting out to anyone."

"I'm always here for you, you know that. I don't care how late it is. And I promise I won't tell anyone, not even Matt. He's on a work trip and won't be back until tomorrow anyway. You should probably get back to the hotel and see if Em is ready to talk, but if you need anything else, call me back. Even if it's 3 am, okay? I love you."

"Thanks, Mads, don't know what I'd do without you. Love you too, sleep well."

I step into the hotel lobby, begging the universe to let Em let me in.

emaline

I DIDN'T REALIZE it was possible to cry as much as I have in the past few hours. But here I am, sitting on another bathroom floor, bawling—this time alone because I pushed away the man who loves me more than life itself. Dangerous thoughts are ricocheting in my mind like one of those complicated pinball machines that has multiple balls flinging at once. The urge to purge is louder than it was at the club, which is unfathomable considering how deafening it was there. There are scarier thoughts floating around, too. Ones that I can't even bring myself to name. My back is firm against the door, on the opposite side of the room from the toilet, taking every ounce of willpower I can muster to not have a repeat of what happened in the stall an hour ago.

Unable to sit up any longer, I lay on the hard, cold tile floor, painfully aware that this is rock bottom. My stomach aches from the emptiness and the violence of the purging, a reminder of how far I've fallen. I've never felt this alone, and it's all my fault. My mind is consumed with shame—both for the relapse and for how much I've been shutting everyone out. All Kieran wants to do is support me, but the shackles of my mind have made it impossible for me to let him in.

And now I'm terrified that I may have somehow pushed him away for good. He's always said he'll never leave me, but I've never acted like this. When I said I can't do this, I meant the *interaction*, not *our relationship*. I'm praying to whatever higher power that exists that he knows that. That he knows the magnitude of my love for him, despite the dark, quicksand-filled hole I'm currently trying to claw my way out of. My eyes burn, and my head pounds from a level of dehydration that I haven't experienced in years. If I were stronger, I'd go find another granola bar that surely is in Kieran's backpack and chug some water, but even just the thought of that has me shaking uncontrollably. Rock bottom doesn't get lower than this. And being alone in this moment is of my own idiotic doing.

I don't know why I had the reaction I did to Kieran trying to get me to eat the granola bar. It's like I wasn't in my own body, and I was transported back to the kitchen table in my parents' house when I was thirteen, where they'd make me stay sitting until I finished my full meal, according to the meal plan that my doctor and dietitian gave them. They wanted to do everything they could to avoid me having to go to residential treatment, and every meal was a battle. Sometimes I'd eat without fighting, but it wasn't infrequent for me to throw food or scream at them. They were trying to keep me alive when I was desperate to die. It's devastating to admit, but back then, I didn't care if my eating disorder killed me. I didn't see a way out. A vision of a life where I wasn't at war with my body wasn't even a fleeting hope. So there I was, being thrown a lifesaver, and instead of grabbing onto it, deflating it more and more with every disordered behavior.

When Kieran said I was breaking him, it reminded me of

what my parents would whisper behind closed doors when they thought I couldn't hear them. My mom would sob to my dad about how she was terrified that her baby girl would die and that she wasn't sure if there was anything more she could do about it. Even though they weren't trying to be manipulative or center themselves in my struggles, my sick brain took it as that. It took it as them trying to make me something I wasn't, even though they were trying to help me get back to who I really was. Because when my eating disorder is running the show, I'm not really Emaline. I'm a shell of myself that puts up a façade to seem like I have it all together when deep inside, I've spiraled so far that I've lost all sense of identity.

That's the thing about eating disorders. They lie and tell you that you have it all under control. That it's okay to skip one more meal or vomit one more time. But one time turns into two times. Two times turns into four times. Four times turns into eight times. Until you're so far underwater that you can no longer differentiate between your disorder and yourself. In this moment, it feels one and the same.

Wiping enough tears from my eyes so that I can see, I grab my phone and hit call on Alaina's contact. I know it's the middle of the night, but I'm not sure where else to turn. Lainie had an eating disorder when she was younger, too, so she gets it in a way that no one else does.

"Hey, is everything okay? You don't usually call this late," she says.

Voice cracking, barely able to speak, I say, "I fucked up so bad. So bad."

The concern in her voice feels like it's gripping me through the phone.

"What happened? Are you safe? Where's Kieran?"

Through my tears, I talk her through the relapse and the

fight with Kieran, each sentence stabbing me in the heart. I've never been more ashamed.

After pausing to make sure I was done talking, she replies, "Em, I'm so sorry. I had no idea things were this bad again. I hate that you didn't tell me, but I get why. Obviously, your reaction to Kieran wasn't okay, but it seems like you felt like you were backed up against a wall, and fight or flight kicked in. And regardless of what fucked up things your brain is telling you right now, you know as well as I do that he loves you far too much to run after this. I'm sure once the two of you have cooled down, you'll sort it out. The kind of love you have for each other is far stronger than your demons. But you have to let him in. You can't fight this alone."

Despite my brain trying to twist things and convince me otherwise, I know she's right. And unlike when I was thirteen, I don't want to die. And if I want to not just stay alive but also keep living my dreams, that has to start with getting up off this floor. Because while I can't fight this thing alone, the fight has to start with me.

kieran

AS I OPEN THE DOOR, Emaline is cuddled up in the bed wearing one of my hoodies, watching old One Direction videos. Specifically, one where Harry and Niall are laughing like idiots in an interview. Real Directioners know the one I'm talking about.

"Hi," I say, kicking my shoes off.

"Hi," she replies sheepishly.

Walking toward her, I say, "Can I get in next to you?"

"Please."

There's half a granola bar on the bedside table, along with an empty electrolyte packet next to her water bottle.

I gently slide under the covers, my body inching close to hers. "I'm sorry, baby. I shouldn't have pushed you so far earlier, especially after you told me to stop. I was doing it because I'm worried about you, but it still wasn't okay. I hope you can forgive me."

She puts her head on my shoulder. "Of course I forgive you, Kiki. I'm sorry too. I haven't thrown shit like that since I was a teenager with my parents, and I don't know what happened. It wasn't fair for me to react like that, even if you were pushing me. Hurting isn't an excuse for me to lash out at you."

"It's okay, Emmie girl. We both fucked up," I say, rubbing her back.

"And you probably saw, but I ate half a granola bar and didn't purge it. It was hard, but you're right, I was able to do it. I cried for a while in the bathroom, but then I called Alaina and she helped bring me down," she adds.

"I'm so proud of you, baby. I knew you could do it. We don't have to talk about it tonight, but tomorrow, can we talk more about what's been going on? I don't want to just brush over it. You can't keep running from this."

"We can. I don't want to, but we can. Can we go to sleep, though? My head hurts and I just need to turn off from the world for a bit."

I get out of bed for a second, pulling off my joggers and t-shirt so that I'm just in my boxers.

"Of course, baby."

Last night was one of the most terrifying moments I've ever had with Em. Hearing her strained, tear-filled voice on the phone nearly shattered me. She is pure sunshine, and I fucking hate that her brain torments her like this. I hate that she has been through so much, more than any human should ever have to. I hate that in that moment, everything was so over-whelming to her that she felt like she couldn't do anything but self-destruct. And I hate that she felt like she had to hide it from me. That she was masking her pain to not worry me. And I hate the fight we had.

I barely slept, replaying every moment and overanalyzing

how I missed this. Trying to figure out how we're going to move forward and get her back on the path of recovery after this relapse, while also still on tour, or if we're going to have to cancel the remaining dates.

Seeing her sleep so peacefully next to me, her gorgeous blonde hair splayed over the pillow as she lies on her stomach, is such a stark contrast to last night. In this moment, she is pure calm and serenity. And I know that's likely going to change as soon as she wakes up. My phone vibrates.

MADISON

how are you holding up? i know last night was fucking rough

KIERAN

I pretty much didn't sleep. At the very least she's still asleep so seeing her calm is grounding me a bit. Dreading having a convo about it with her today but I know it's what's needed

MADISON

i can't imagine how you're feeling right now. and i know you're worried about her, but make sure you're taking care of yourself too. lmk if you guys need anything

I place my phone down on the nightstand and feel Emaline start to move, scooting her body closer to mine.

"Morning, pretty girl. How ya feeling?"

She flops her body onto me, the warmth radiating onto my skin. With a strained voice, she says, "My throat is killing me. My head hurts. Really fucking pissed at myself."

I brush her hair out of her face and gaze into her brilliant blue-green eyes. The light has been sucked out of them, but I always see Emaline's light—even when it's hard to find.

"I can make you some tea to soothe your throat and get you

some Advil for your headache if that would be helpful? And maybe once you've had a little time to wake up, we can talk a bit about last night?"

She nods. "Yeah, that would be great. Can you order us some avocado toast, too? I really don't want to eat, but I know I need to."

Lightly pressing my lips to her forehead, I say, "Absolutely, my love. I'm so proud of you."

"Proud? After last night?"

"Yes, proud, Emmie girl. We can't change what happened last night. But right now you're choosing to help yourself, and that's what matters."

I roll out of bed, pulling on the sweatpants that I left on the floor last night. I can understand why she is so frustrated with herself, but I also wish that she could give herself some amount of grace and compassion. Shaming and hating yourself into change doesn't work. Even if I'm not good at believing that sometimes.

As I boil water in the electric kettle for our tea, I place an order on the room service app for two orders of avocado toast. I leave a note in the special requests to see if they can cut the toast into hearts, hoping that that little touch makes eating a little easier for her. Even if the chef hates me for it. We sip our tea while an episode of Gossip Girl plays in the background, and about thirty minutes later, our food arrives.

"Can we eat outside? I think the fresh air may help," she says.

"Of course we can, pretty girl."

We both eat our toast silently, and I can tell that she is caught up in a spiral in her head.

"Want to talk about whatever's running through that smart brain of yours, baby?"

She places her plate down on the patio table in front of us

and brings her hands up to her face, leaning her elbows on her thighs.

"I... I can't stop thinking about how you can do so much better than me and how I don't deserve all of the success I've been having. Seeing all of the perfect bodies in that club last night. How beautiful all of your exes are. Scrolling on my phone earlier and seeing every other person on the charts is so much more talented than me. Those shitty comments the other day. And then last night, every horrible thing Chris ever said to me was on repeat, and honestly, I believe a lot of it. My body isn't good enough. I'm not a good enough vocalist. I'm so broken. And I know that one day you're going to wake up and realize you're settling with me. That you'll get tired of picking up all of my pieces like you've done for the past twenty-five years."

I wish that for just a moment, she could see herself from my point of view and that I could bash Chris's face in for even one of the disgusting thoughts he etched into her brain. She's immeasurably beautiful, inside and out, and more talented than anyone I've ever seen. Her inner light and beauty shine through every inch of her being and through every single movement she makes.

There's far more than Emaline's body that draws me to her.

Her overflowing wisdom.

Her level of musical skill and performance quality that's far above countless other artists.

Her unconditional compassion for every person who crosses her path.

How deeply she cares for everyone she encounters, especially her fans.

The smile that comes across her face when she watches my guitar solos every night.

The way she scrunches up her nose when she's anxious.

The way she sticks her tongue in her cheek when she's trying to concentrate.

The way she loves me with every inch of her being.

"I don't know many ways I can tell you that I love every single inch of your body and soul. My exes are my exes for a reason. And I've never seen someone as absolutely gorgeous and infinitely talented as you are. I have never loved anyone in the way I love you. Beauty standards are absolute bullshit, and last night, the only person my eyes were on were you and your stunning radiance. The same body that you despise is the body I crave constantly. You're my girlfriend because of the incredible person you are and because of how well you love me. Not because of your looks or your body. And you're not broken. I know every single terrible thing you've been through. So, of course, over time, we're going to have other difficult, painful moments. But I'm here for all of it, all of you. The light and the dark. Always have been, always will be."

She angrily sighs. "You're just saying that because you don't want to hurt me. I know you've always been my best friend, but I know that you're going to get tired of dealing with me. I don't know you haven't already after an entire life of having to support me and my bullshit."

Breathe, Kieran. Breathe. We don't need a repeat of last night.

"You're not in the way. You're part of why I have every incredible thing I do and bring me joy I didn't know existed. I don't feel bad for you. I have so much overwhelming love for you that all I want is for you to be able to see yourself how I do. I could never get sick of you. Why do you keep pushing me away? Why can't you just let me be here for you?"

"Because if I push you away, then you don't have to get sick of me, and I won't get hurt when you eventually realize you're tired of dealing with me and that I'll never be enough. You're too good for me."

Oof. Suddenly, it all makes sense. Just like how Jamie broke up with me because of my mental health, Em is convinced I'm going to do that to her. I both want to scream and want to throw my arms around her. I lean in and turn her face to me, not letting her look at the ground.

"Stop pushing me away. You're it for me. I love you more than words can ever fully express. I love every single piece of you, including the pieces you think I hate. I don't want anyone else. I don't give a fuck about what any tabloid or asshole commenter or incompetent radio interviewer could ever say about you. I don't give a shit about if you're a size zero or a size four or a size eight or a size twenty-two. I don't care how many times I have to pull you out of the shower or off of bathroom floors. This is what love is. I love you because you're you. I love you because you've been more than I could ever ask for in my entire life. You've completely stolen my heart, and I never want it back. It doesn't get better than you."

"IT DOESN'T GET BETTER than you."

I don't know why my brain is trying to convince me that I don't deserve Kieran's love, when he's been by my side for my entire life and has seen me through my darkest moments without an ounce of judgment. And I don't know how he has the patience to deal with it all, especially after how I reacted last night.

But, in this moment, I'm going to try to let him be here for me.

Holding back tears, I say, "I'm sorry that I keep pushing you away. I'm so fucking pissed at myself and can't understand how you and everyone else who supports me continues to deal with this. I know how many relapses I had when I was younger and how painful that was to see, and I never saw myself being here again. When I was on that bathroom floor, all I could think about was disappointing you, disappointing everyone. And when I freaked out last night when you tried to get me to eat, I thought I destroyed everything. I thought I lost the best thing I've ever had. Sometimes I don't know how you love me through it all. I can't promise I'm never going to push you away again, but right now, I know you're here for me. And I'm going to try to focus on that instead of the lies my brain is telling me."

He pulls me into his chest, lightly running his hand along my spine, immediately grounding me.

"I'm right here for you. Always will be. I promise, Emmie girl." There's a pause for a second, but I can tell he has more to say, so I don't reply yet. "I'm sure you don't want to keep talking about this, but I think it's really important for us to talk about what triggered it. I know you mentioned the comparison and all of the shit Chris has said about your body, but there has to be more than just thoughts going on here."

The last thing I want to talk about is last night. But ignoring my struggles isn't going to make them go away. Sure, in the moment it may feel better... but in the long term, it makes it all stick around longer. It doesn't magically disappear. It festers until it eventually rears its ugly head again.

I've been in this place enough times to know that brushing over this and pretending that everything is fine is going to keep me here, stuck in the grips of my eating disorder. Stuck in the place of having momentary relief from the scary place that is my brain, but slowly killing myself in the process.

Momentary relief that is followed by more mental anguish than there was before engaging in the behavior.

Because the thing is, when at your core you really want healing, and when you know the real impact that your self-destructive behaviors make on your brain and body, you don't get the same relief that you did when you first started using those behaviors.

The relief is quickly replaced by berating myself for once again falling into the cycle.

The reality is that eating disorders lie to you. They promise relief, calm, and control, while simultaneously ripping it from your hands and walking you a step closer to death every time you engage in a behavior.

Every sixty seconds, someone dies as a direct result of an eating disorder...and as much as there have been many moments in my life where I've wanted to die, even fleeting thoughts last night, I refuse to become a statistic. I refuse to continue to let this disease consume me like it has since I was ten years old. I deserve better.

Yes, I've been in this place before. And I've also been in the place of thriving in recovery. I know I can get back to that place again—and being honest is the only path there. And that starts with telling Kieran everything.

"Yeah, about that... I started having nightmares again, like three months ago. At first, they were just like once a week. But ever since that night when I had the panic attack in the shower, they've been practically every night, and they've gotten more and more vivid. About the night Chris assaulted me. And about him in general. And then worrying about how the label has been saying I may be less marketable since we're together, so I feel like everything else about me has to be perfect, so that I can make up for it. I'm sorry I didn't say anything. It's just that everything has been going so well with us and the album and the tour, and I didn't want to worry you or bring down the happiness. I've felt like a failure."

"You don't have to apologize, Em. Of course, I wish you would've been honest with me sooner because I could tell something was up, but you've had so many times in the past where people either blew up on you or left you or both, so you're just trying to protect yourself. You're not a failure, you're a human who's been through a lot of shit. I never want you to worry about 'bringing down the happiness.' We can be having really happy moments and really painful moments, all at the same time. You've been here for me through all of my dark moments, especially everything that happened with Jamie, and I'll never leave you for not being okay. Pretending the painful parts aren't there doesn't mean they disappear."

As much as I've been incredibly pissed at myself for this relapse, this is a step back, not a complete restart. It's not like when I first started recovery or earlier relapses—I have all of the knowledge and skills I've gained over all of my years in recovery that ultimately will help me get back on track.

I haven't failed. I'm not a failure. I'm capable of getting back to where I was – it just may take some time to get there. And part of getting back on track is continuing to be honest with my people... as vulnerable and challenging as it is.

"I promise I'm going to stop hiding things. It's scary to be honest, but I know the only way to get better is to stop keeping secrets. I'm not sure who else I want to tell other than Ruby and Mads and Lainie, but I promise I won't keep you in the dark anymore."

He ruffles my hair, and while I would usually be annoyed that it could make it knot up, I let the cute gesture slide.

"Thank you, baby. I can only help you if I know what's going on, so I really appreciate that. I called Madison on my walk last night, so she may text you later. I know we have to be at the airport in a few hours, so we should probably start getting ready."

"Can we shower together? I'm worried that after last night, I may have another panic attack if I shower alone."

"Of course we can, my love."

Here's to continuing to show up for myself and continuing to ask for help when I need it.

We technically could've easily taken the bus to San Diego from Vegas, but I'm so glad that before everything that happened last night, the plan already was to fly and have the bus meet us there.

We're staying at an extremely fancy hotel on the ocean, and our room has a deck that leads out to a private beach. With living in California my whole life, the beach has always been my happy place and a place where I find solace. Even on the hardest days, coming to the beach, getting my feet in the sand, and hearing the sound of the waves brings me a sense of sheer calm and peace. Kieran and I once stayed at this hotel with our families on vacation when we were around six or seven years old, and as we sit here on the beach, my mind is filled with memories of us making sand castles... memories that I could see us recreating with our own children someday.

Kieran softly strums his guitar as I lay my head in his lap, grateful that we don't have anywhere to be tonight and that we don't have to be at the venue until 1 pm tomorrow. I'm feeling a lot better than last night, but I'm still in a weird head-space. Things aren't going to magically suddenly all be back to normal (whatever the hell *normal* is), but I'm hoping that by show time tomorrow night, everything feels at least a bit more settled. I never want to put a fake persona on onstage, but sometimes, as a public figure, you have to fake things a little so that people don't start talking about it—which would ulti-mately make things worse, both for me as a person and for my career.

"I was wondering if you might want to go walk around downtown La Jolla a bit and get some dinner? I figured it could be good for clearing our heads and feeling a little normal," Kieran says.

Food is hard today, but every bite is a step closer to being back where I was in recovery—and I know I've got Kieran in my corner.

Glancing up at him, I say, "Sure, that sounds good. I'm getting pretty hungry."

I usually would feel pressure to look "cute" while out in case anyone notices me, today I'm living the crop tank, comfy shorts, and Birkenstocks life. After all, I am just a normal girl – and despite what Shakespeare says, my whole life doesn't have to be a stage. If someone notices me, they're just getting the real me.

We walk back inside, and Kieran puts his guitar down as I order us an Uber.

"Can I please get a chicken caesar salad with a baguette on the side and a medium Coke, light ice?"

We found a cute little local salad and grain bowl shop, and despite what my eating disorder often tries to convince me of, I love carbs. When I saw the fresh baked bread, I knew I had to challenge myself to eat some of it, even if it's only a bite or two. My body needs fuel, and my taste buds need enjoyment. The temptation to only get a water was strong, but a crispy Coke sounded good enough to ignore the disordered thought.

"And I'll get the teriyaki steak bowl with double protein, chips on the side, and a large Dr. Pepper, please."

After they call our names, we bring our food and drinks out to the patio. Golden hour is starting to creep in, and the subtle warmth of the sun feels so good on my skin. Being outside doesn't suddenly cure or eliminate the deafening thoughts floating around in my brain, but it does make things a little easier. During times like this, I try my best to anchor myself to the moment and take in everything around me instead of getting too wrapped up in my thoughts.

Tonight is showing me that despite relapsing, I'm not starting over. Years ago, I would've still been restricting heavily and purging constantly after a relapse. And here I am, adequately nourishing my body and getting the food I want and need, not what my eating disorder wants. Even when you have a major backslide, you never fully go back to the start. There is always the wisdom of all of the years of recovery there. There's always the reminder that while this current reality sucks, I've had plenty of spans of time of truly being in recovery and not having my eating disorder run my life.

I can't change that the relapse happened, but I can change how I want to move forward and what I want to take from the situation. Having a raging eating disorder and continuing the trajectory I've been having with my career can't coexist—and I know which of those things I actually want.

I bite into the baguette, and instead of the anxiety I expected, I'm met with a sense of joy and satisfaction.

"It may sound silly, but seeing you smile while eating is the highlight of my day."

"It's not silly. I know how painful it is to watch someone you love struggling so much, and I know how many times you've seen me in this place before. I can't promise this is going to be a totally uphill journey, but I promise that I'll keep trying my best."

"And that's all I can ask for, baby. Healing isn't perfect. I can see how hard you're trying, and no matter how many bumps in the road there are, I'm always so proud of you. One bite at a time."

One bite at a time is a mantra I learned when I first went to residential treatment as a teenager, and all of these years later, Kieran always reminds me of it.

With eating disorders, it's not like some other struggles where you can completely avoid the substance or pattern you struggle with. You have to eat every day, multiple times a day. You have to engage with the very thing that triggers you, whether it's to binge, purge, restrict, time and time again—while trying to ignore the thoughts in your head that are screaming at you to do those things.

I finish my salad, enjoying how perfectly seasoned it is.

"One bite at a time. How's your OCD today? I know I haven't been asking as often as I should."

He finishes his soda and says, "You've had a lot going on in your own mind, baby, it's okay. My OCD has been a little louder recently, but I'm managing. I'm not really worried about tomorrow's show, but I've been having a lot more obsessive thoughts about the LA show. It's been so wild and cool seeing everything with the new album blowing up but that means that there'll be even more important people there, and I'd hate to fuck anything up. I've had to keep resisting the urge to play my solos over and over. Any time I mess it up any amount, I have to start over. I know there's no such thing as perfect, but I never want to get in the way of your success by messing something up or not being good enough."

Some of the things that have helped make me and Kieran as successful as we are are also some of our biggest downfalls. To make it in the music industry, you have to be hungry, driven, and look at your own work critically. But, there's a difference between having a healthy level of those qualities and having a level of them where you run yourself into the ground.

"I've been pretty anxious about the LA show, too. And I get

it's not as easy as telling your brain to stop, but I promise it's going to be okay. There's no such thing as a perfect show, but we've played these songs so many times now that you could play them in your sleep. And if a show didn't go well, I'd never hold it against you. Hell, I had that show back before the first album, when I lost my voice at the end, and now we're here on this sold-out tour. I think we both need to be a lot kinder to ourselves."

"I'm trying to remind myself of that. Honestly, I should put my guitar in its case in another room tonight so that I'm not tempted to over rehearse."

I put all of my utensils on my platter and get ready to bring them over to the used dishes bin.

"That sounds like a great idea. We both could use some time with our phones on Do Not Disturb, watching Gossip Girl. But maybe we can walk around a little more first? I forgot how cute La Jolla is, haven't been around here in a bit."

Before I can grab the platter, he takes it, stacks his things on top, and brings it near the trash cans.

"That sounds like a pretty perfect night to me."

We start walking down the street, taking in the cute little shops and soaking up the salty breeze. Some anxious thoughts start to creep in like, "Oh, you shouldn't have finished that whole salad," and "Did you really need that soda?" but I try to let them float by instead of engaging with them. Thoughts are just thoughts.

As we cross the street, there are some kids sitting on a bench outside of an ice cream shop, ice cream cones dripping all down their arms. It reminds me of all of the pictures my mom has of Kieran and I with ice cream all over our faces, not having a single care in the world.

"Hey, can we get some ice cream?" I ask.

"Of course we can! As soon as I saw the sign, I was hoping you'd ask, but I didn't want to push you or make you anxious."

As he opens the door for us, I say, "I hope they have butter pecan. I've been thinking about my grandma a lot, and that was always her favorite. Eating her favorite will make it a little easier."

In my lowest moments, when my parents and I were constantly fighting about my eating disorder, my grandma was always my biggest cheerleader. She never got mad at me, even the time I turned down the brownies she made me for my thirteenth birthday. I'm sure she was sad about it, but I can remember her saying, "It's okay, Emmie, I know your brain isn't being very kind to you right now. If you want any later, I'll leave the container for you on the counter, but it's okay if you don't. I know Grandpa Jack won't let them go to waste, so don't you worry." She always loved me wholeheartedly, without an ounce of judgment.

We look at the flavor board and Kieran says, "Well, the universe must have been listening because butter pecan is the first on the menu."

"Grandma's supporting me in spirit."

"Hi, what can I get for you?" the worker says.

Kieran replies, "Can we please get two small waffle bowls with butter pecan and rainbow sprinkles?"

We go to the checkout, and she brings our ice cream down the line. The waffle bowl is an added challenge, but it's one I'm willing to take because it's pretty hard to turn down a fresh, homemade waffle bowl.

Kieran opens the door and we go sit on the same bench those kids had been on, and I'm transported back to being five years old, eating ice cream on vacation with my grandma before any inkling of my eating disorder had set in. I hold that visual in my brain as I eat my ice cream, determined not to let my thoughts stop me from enjoying this moment.

I deserve to be free from these struggles that plague my mind.

I deserve to enjoy food.

I deserve to enjoy this beautiful life I've worked so hard for.

And, in each moment, I'm working to let myself do just that.

Because I'm worth fighting for.

kieran

SUN PEEKS through the blinds of our hotel room, the warmth and brightness gently waking me. The clock says it's 7 am, and while I have enough time to sleep for another hour, I might as well stay awake at this point so that I don't get more groggy.

We're not out of the woods, but yesterday gave me hope that things are on an upswing. Few things are more agonizing than seeing the person you love with all of your heart and soul in such a dark place. With how long Em has been in my life, and now being her boyfriend, she's part of me. I don't mean that I'm not myself without her or that she is my identity. But our bond is different than most relationships. When she struggles, it brings me a kind of pain similar to when I'm experiencing my own darkness. And when she finds relief, I find relief, too.

Her head is on my chest, arms splayed across, trapping me. Almost like a human weighted blanket. Her heartbeat grounds me, sensing how peacefully she's resting. It's tempting to wake her, but with tonight's show, she needs all of the sleep she can get.

I grab my phone carefully, trying not to disrupt her, and open the room service app. I scroll through the options and order us both chocolate chip waffles and bacon—Em's favorite breakfast. Food has undeniably been incredibly difficult for her over the past few days, but there are few better things to wake up to than the smell of waffles and bacon.

It's wild that we only have two shows left of this tour. Time has flown, and I'm going to miss the exhilaration that comes with being on stage almost every night. But we all need a break. Of course, we'll have the show in Paris on Emaline's birthday, but getting time away from this chaos and constant work will be really important for her recovery. She thrives on the high of performing, but it's exhausting work. It's so cool that we get to live this life where we see so many places and meet so many unique people, but it takes a toll. Even when you have the amazing crew we do, having to be "on" all the time for fans can be exhausting. I think people often forget that while artists aren't 100% different offstage, they are performers putting on a show. So, of course, they won't always have that same kind of energy or presence.

I scroll on my phone a bit and then hear a knock on the door for room service. I move carefully, trying not to wake Emaline up so that she can be surprised by the aroma of our breakfast. I take the trays from the worker and thank him before placing them on the table. Em starts to stir and blinks her eyes open.

"Morning, pretty girl."

"Morning, Kiki. That smells fucking amazing. What did you get?"

"Your favorite. Chocolate chip waffles and bacon. And iced cinnamon brown sugar oat milk lattes."

Before she has the chance to get out of bed, I bring a tray over to her side of the bed along with her latte. She sits up, and

I lean over and kiss her gently, a smile coming across her face. Every kiss with her feels like our first one, always lighting me up and giving me butterflies. I grab my tray and plop down cross-legged next to her. She seems less anxious about eating than she has been in the past few days, and while I'd love to know what's going through her brain right now, I don't ask so that I don't risk giving her more anxiety. I take a few bites of my waffle and then get up to open the curtains so that we can soak up the beautiful ocean view. The sight of waves crashing has always been grounding to me, and it's the perfect backdrop for starting the day.

"Ready for tonight?" Emaline says.

I nod. "I'm looking forward to having some of the onstage rush. I think it'll be a good energy reset."

Whenever I'm on stage, everything else falls away. All that matters is me, my guitar, and Emaline... and I guess the rest of the band. It's a kind of adrenaline rush that's impossible to describe to someone who hasn't experienced it. Few things beat seeing a crowd screaming the words to all of the songs and having the time of their lives. Knowing that you're part of that moment. That you're part of helping people also have their worries fall away. That you're part of people finding connection and belonging through everyone else in the crowd. That you're part of creating an environment where people are able to be themselves and forget about the rest of the bullshit that life brings, even if just for ninety minutes.

"I think so, too. Last night I was a little worried, but right now I think it's going to be exactly what I need. Obviously, I don't want to rely on being on stage to make me feel better, but I don't think it's going to be a distraction. Just a way of getting reconnected with myself."

It can be easy for artists to use their career as something to numb and avoid their problems, but for me and Emaline, it's a way to more fully express who we are, despite the thoughts that often plague our brains. When you're immersed on stage, it's pretty hard not to be present. I think it's one of the greatest forms of mindfulness. Feeling my hands on my guitar, hearing Em's voice, seeing the lights, feeling the reverb of the drums. My therapist talks all the time about how anxiety and trauma live in our bodies, and when I'm playing, I'm able to physically channel it into something tangible instead of it floating around in my brain.

I eat one of my pieces of bacon, the savoriness taking over my taste buds.

"100%. I know you get it in the same way I do. Being on stage with you is where I feel most at home."

Soundcheck is a necessary part of live performances, but it's a fifty-fifty toss up on whether it's helpful or just makes Emaline more anxious. And today, it's making her more anxious.

"What the fuck is wrong with me today?" she says with crossed arms and a facial expression that's the epitome of "if looks could kill"... except it's clearly only towards herself.

In "Wild Mind", there's a run of notes at the end of the bridge that is very technically challenging. But with her incredible voice, Em usually hits it with no problems. As we were playing through it, her voice cracked slightly on the middle note. Most people wouldn't have noticed, but she is hyperaware of every single thing she does. It can be a gift at times to have that level of attention to detail, but it's usually to a degree that is self-deprecating. I can be really hard on myself, too. But with her, it's on another level.

Treading lightly so that I don't make things worse, I say, "Can we take five? I need to pee."

Sometimes when she needs help getting out of her head, I do it indirectly so it doesn't draw too much attention or seem like I'm saying, "Hey, calm down," even if that's sort of what I mean.

Ruby says, "Yeah, I could use some fresh air anyway."

I pull Emaline aside.

"Don't you have to go to the bathroom?" she says, still pissed.

I put my hand on her shoulder. "I mean, sort of, but you seem like you're really in your head and could use a sec. I get that you're frustrated for messing up the run, but you know as well as I do that staying pissed at yourself is just gonna make it harder to have a good show."

She sighs, "I know, I know, you're right. It's just that it's the second to last show, and Ruby said there are some big media people coming tonight, and I want it all to be perfect. I don't want to give any sort of impression that I'm not doing okay. I can't have people speculating."

When you're in this industry and growing in the way Emaline is, there are so many eyes on you, and the smallest things can make it or break it. And it's not new news that the media will try to capitalize on anything that could possibly make for a clickbait headline, like when someone is struggling with their mental or physical health. People can be torn to shreds for the smallest things. But, if we're looking at the facts, her missing a run once that she has hit perfectly a thousand times isn't a major reason for concern. And hyperfocusing on it will only lead to it potentially happening during the actual show. Ruby also mentioned that the label wants to have a meeting with her and Emaline after we're back in LA, so I'm sure that's also weighing on her mind.

Ruffling her hair, I say, "I know the past few days have been really rough, and I get not wanting to do anything that could possibly tip off that you're struggling. But you messed it up once. And it wasn't obvious. You deserve to be gentler with yourself."

She leans her head on me and sighs.

"I hate that I can't be perfect. Especially when everyone thinks I have to be."

In my eyes, Emaline is perfect. And not in the no flaws, Barbie doll way. In the way that everything about her perfectly complements me and lights up everyone around her. She is the perfect *her*. In this chew-you-up and spit-you-out world with impossible standards, especially for women, self-criticism is unavoidable. But I hate that it gets in the way of her truly living the life she deserves. A life full of being her fullest self, without caring about the opinions of anyone else, even me. A life where she can be comfortable in her own skin, not constantly monitoring herself for flaws or shortcomings. And sure, some people may think she needs to be perfect, but the people who actually matter really don't.

"Babe, none of us think you have to be perfect. You just need to be you. This is live music. Nothing is perfect. And that's the magic of it. It's different every time, even when it's the same exact set. It's not perfectly edited, airbrushed, and auto-tuned. Your fans love you because you're you. The people whose opinions really matter are here for all of you. Not some manufactured version," I say before kissing the top of her head.

She wraps her arms around me, and the fast beating of her anxious heart resonates onto me.

"It's so hard to let all of it go when I know there are judgmental people out there who want to see my downfall. Even if they don't matter and if there are far more supporters than there are haters. My brain always wants to focus on the possible threat instead of the reality."

As I rub her back over her shirt, I reply, "I know, pretty girl. I know it's not as easy as just ignoring what those thoughts are telling you. But I promise that there are so many more people who want to see you win and succeed than those who want to see you fail. And everyone in this room? We all only ever want the best for you. And we'll fight to the death against anyone who tries to bring you down. Now, dance break before we get back on that stage?"

Ever since we were little kids, dance breaks have been our go-to way of coping when we're overwhelmed, anxious, or upset. And the go-to music since middle school has been One Direction. So, what do I pull up on my phone? "Best Song Ever", obviously.

The rest of soundcheck went off without a hitch thanks to our dance break, and we're about to have dinner. Meals on tour are weird because dinner usually happens around 4:30 pm, so we can all digest, though we usually don't get onstage until 9 pm. And there is always after show food, that without fail, everyone demolishes, even when the catering for dinner is a super heavy meal.

When we get into the communal space of the green room where the dinner buffet is set up, there's a huge spread of Mexican food. Three different kinds of tacos, rice, beans, salad, chips, guac, and churros for dessert. With San Diego being so close to Mexico, the food here is always top tier. When we were younger, Mexican was one of Emmie's biggest fear foods. She'd always skirt around things and make her plate seem more full by putting a ton of salad on it and only a tiny bit of everything else. Even when no one else noticed, I always would. Usually not knowing whether or not to comment since I was happy that she was eating at all. With how challenging food has been for her over the past few days, I'm not sure what to expect. But either way, today isn't the day to push her.

Emaline speeds over to the folding table where the food is. "Oh, this looks fucking amazing."

I breathe a quiet sigh of relief.

She fills up her plate, grabbing one of each kind of taco: fried fish, chicken, and carne asada, along with each of the sides. Before I finish plating my own dinner, she inhales one of the churros with a huge smile. I'm always elated when I see Em enjoying food. There are plenty of chairs, but she plops down cross-legged on the floor, and I join her. The rest of the team grabs their food and follows her lead, sitting in a circle on the ground.

"I can't believe that there are only two shows left of this tour. What am I going to do without seeing y'all every day?" Isabelle says with a slight frown.

Kenzie is sitting next to her, a bit closer than usual. My eyebrow raises, and I will it to go down, not wanting to draw any attention to what's going through my brain. It may be a coincidence, but there's some "more than friends" energy slightly radiating...or at least it seems like it to me. In fairness, I have no business speculating about them, considering how long I was in denial about my feelings for Em. However, if something is going on with them, I do think they'd be good together with their whole black cat and golden retriever dynamic, even if getting with your coworkers has the potential to be messy as hell.

I force my eyes towards Isabelle instead of remaining on both of them and say, "You say that as if you aren't at Em's apartment several times a week. We just won't be as sleep deprived, and your best friend won't be sad about living the no-roommate life anymore."

We are truly a family, and I don't mean that in the forced, cliché, "Oh yeah, our team is a family, but actually we secretly hate each other and don't hang out outside of work," way. When we're not on tour or recording, almost all of us see each other frequently, just not as often as being with each other practically 24/7 on the road.

Emaline finishes a bite of one of her tacos and says, "And don't forget, Paris is so soon. You know I never let you guys stay away for too long. You're all my best friends, no matter where this music stuff takes us."

"Plus, I'm sure everyone wouldn't mind a break from my 7 am wakeup calls and after-party cut-offs," Ruby chimes in.

Jokingly, Kenzie says, "I mean, you can be a bit of a buzzkill sometimes."

"What can I say? Being a paid buzzkiller is part of my job description."

I eat my churro and then place my plate on the coffee table in the middle of the circle. Desperately needing to stretch out my back before the intense workout that a show can be, I lay flat on the ground, stretching my arms over my head.

Em looks at me with a hint of judgment and says, "You know, that's bad for digestion."

"You know that's bad for digestion," I say in a playful, slightly mocking, but not disrespectful tone.

She shakes her head and snickers.

"Well, don't complain to me if you have heartburn later."

I stick my pinky out to her. "Pinky promise."

After a much-needed nap, I just finished changing into my show outfit. Em is still holding up the new "outfit reveal" tradition, so I walk over to her dressing room, even though I wish she'd share one with me. But if she wants to have this tradition, I'll let her.

I lightly knock on the door and say, "Can I see my beautiful girlfriend?"

"Only if I can see my handsome boyfriend."

I laugh. "Pretty sure that's the only way it works, silly."

She opens the door and I look her up and down. She's wearing light pink short overalls with hot pink rhinestone hearts and matching rhinestone boots, along with a lacy bralette underneath. Her hair is curled and in a half-up high ponytail, and her lipstick is the same color as the rhinestones. All I can think about is how I can't wait to mess up that lipstick later. But, for now, I need to get my mind out of the gutter and get into show mode.

"You look incredible as always, pretty girl."

"You don't look too bad yourself, Kiki," she says, glancing up and down at my outfit. I'm wearing a white button down shirt, with most of the buttons undone, along with floral pants that coincidentally have some of the same pink as her outfit. Our stylist Brie doesn't dictate which outfits we wear when, but she did strongly suggest this one today... so I guess it's not a coincidence.

Despite my better judgment, I play with fire and whisper in her ear, "I can't wait to have that lipstick all over my dick later."

Goosebumps rush over her skin, and I smirk, knowing I've accomplished my goal.

"Jesus Christ, you're evil talking like that when you know full well we have to head to stage in less than five minutes unless we want Ruby to be pissed at us."

I pull her body into mine and say, "You say I'm evil, but you fucking love it. Now let's get that hot ass backstage so we can crush this show."

Before pulling away from me, she grabs my crotch and says, "Two can play at this game, pretty boy."

I try to think of anything to keep my dick down.

Dog poop. Grandma. Paying taxes. Math tests.

Come on, body, work with me.

"You are so going to pay for that later."

Smirking, she says, "Is that a threat or a promise?"

"Both."

Kenzie presses play on our intro music, and the rest of us backstage do our pre-show ritual handshake. I quickly pick up Emaline and swing her around in a bear hug before hearing the few notes that are my cue to head out on stage. I walk onto the stage confidently and grab my guitar, taking in the magnitude of the audience. It's never lost on me how awesome it is that this is my job. That I get to play my guitar with my favorite person in the world, and that we get to create this atmosphere of joy and freedom for the fans.

Nick hits a few beats on his drums, Emmie's cue to run on stage. She runs on, and all of the rhinestones catch the light, but not shining as bright as her soul does. She can light up the darkest of rooms. Always has, always will.

The crowd roars, creating the electrifying energy that I'm pretty sure the entire band is addicted to. We play "Getting Back to Me", and the only things I focus on are Emaline's voice and my guitar. I strike my last note and then run my fingers through my hair. Knowing there will be a pause before I have to focus again, I scan my eyes over the pit, taking in the insane number of signs and all of the fans gripping the barricade. The sense of joy and excitement is infectious, and it always makes me so happy to see so many people here to support my Emaline.

"Hello, everyone! I'm Emaline Rose Levine, and this is my amazing band. Thank you for coming out to party with us tonight. I hope you all have as much fun as we are, and I hope you let loose and be your realest self, even if it's only for these ninety minutes. This is a no-judgment space. Only love and support are allowed here. Take care of one another, and have the time of your life. And now, this is 'Wild Mind'."

Just like I knew she would, she nailed the run of notes she was worried about. We play a few more songs, and after the last note of "Growing Pains", it's time for the mid-show pause for sign reading. With so many signs, it can be hard for Em to pick. Her eyes laser onto a sign that says, "It's my best friend's 21st birthday!"

"I see we have a special birthday over to the right! What's your name?" she says.

Yelling at the top of her lungs so Em can hear her, the fan says, "I'm Chloe!"

"And how about your best friend?"

"Abby!"

"Well, happy birthday, Abby! I hope you have fun tonight, but not too much. I promise you'll regret the extreme hangover. I love that you're here with your best friend, I'm here with mine too. Anyone else here with their best friend?" she says, walking over to hug me.

I place my guitar on the stand and pull her into my chest to kiss her head, creating a bunch of cheers, along with a ton of hands raised.

Emaline beams as she says, "I love this. Best friends are so important, and I love seeing all of the love in this room. And if you're here alone, say hi to everyone around you—you may meet your best friend, too. Now, let's sing happy birthday to Abby. After all, you only turn 21 once!"

We all sing to her, no need for microphones—thanks to the crowd. The rest of the set goes smoothly, and while it's always hard to finish the set and let go of the energy, I can't wait to get back to the hotel room and have Em all over me.

Everyone walks off stage, and she immediately jumps into my arms, wrapping her legs around my waist. I grab her ass and kiss her deeply, desperate for more. But we have to wait until we get back to the hotel. Sure, we could fuck in the dressing room, but I want to be able to take our time.

We break the kiss, and I lay my head against hers while she drapes her arms around my neck. In the corner of my eye, Kenzie runs over from front of house to hug Isabelle. Her face lights up similarly to how Emaline's does when she's with me. I don't want to make assumptions because they could *just* be friends, but I've known them both for a long time, and something does seem different than usual. Regardless of whether there is something going on between them or not, I'm always happy to see my friends happy.

Em lightly kisses my neck, sending shivers down my spine.

I hear the sound of a throat clearing, and Nick says, "Hey, get a room, you two."

"Oh, we will," says Emaline.

Damn right, we will.

He laughs and says, "Damn, alright then. See you guys in the morning."

I place Em on the ground and fist bump Nick as I say, "Night, man. You killed it as usual."

Just as I'm about to tell Em to get her things from the dressing room, Ruby walks out and says, "Hey, I packed your things up for you. Figured you might want to get back to the hotel ASAP since we have an early bus call."

I don't give a fuck that I'm going to be tired in the morning. We're taking our time when we get back to the hotel. We can always sleep more on the bus ride back to LA.

Ruby passes me the bags, and I grab them both.

"Thanks, Rube, I am pretty exhausted," Emaline says.

While Ruby is probably convinced Em is tired, I know that's not the truth.

I force a yawn. "Yeah, I'm gonna knock the fuck out as soon as we get back. See you bright and early."

"Sleep well, Ruby!" Emaline says.

"You too, guys. Remember, 6 am, don't be late. We've gotta beat the rush hour traffic."

"Roger that," I say.

We head out the service entrance of the venue, and our driver is waiting for us to head back to the hotel. This is going to be the longest five minutes of my life.

"On your knees. Now," I say as I close the hotel room door behind us.

Emaline immediately obeys and sinks down to her knees without taking her shoes off. She looks up angelically, but I know she's about to be anything but an angel. I unbutton and unzip my pants and then pull them down, along with my boxer briefs. She keeps her eyes on me and rises up on her knees.

"Such a good girl," I say, lightly grabbing her ponytail.

She leans forward and runs her tongue over my cock, causing me to breathe in sharply. I tighten the grip on her ponytail, and without breaking eye contact, Emaline takes the tip into her mouth. Seeing the submissiveness and desperation in her eyes is intoxicating. I love that I'm the only one who gets to see this side of her. This side where the weight of being a powerful woman melts away, and she becomes putty in my hands. This side where she lets herself free from all judgment and succumbs to her darkest desires.

"Use your hands for me, too, baby girl," I say, trying not to whine.

She reaches up, and her hand wraps around the base of my dick, squeezing it perfectly. I gently push her head down, and she moans, clearly getting pleasure, even though I haven't touched her like that yet, and she's not touching herself either. Her pink lipstick is smeared over her face and covers my cock. One of the hottest sights possible.

"You look so pretty with my cock in your mouth."

She starts bobbing her head up and down, and I moan. As perfect as this sight is and as incredible as this feels, I don't want to keep her waiting. I got her started before the show, and she's been more than patient, obeying all of my commands.

I push her head down harder, knowing how wet she always gets from it. Her body shudders, and she sucks harder.

"Okay, angel. You've been so good for me. Now, I want you to stand up for me so that I can touch you and hopefully get inside that pretty pussy soon. How does that sound?

She pulls her mouth off my cock gently and says, "Please touch me. I'll do anything."

As she stands up, I scoop her up in my arms bridal style, carefully walking through to the bedroom. I gently lay her down on the bed and say, "You don't have to do a single thing, my love. I'm gonna take good care of you, since you took such good care of me. Can you unbuckle the straps of your overalls for me?"

She nods, quickly undoing them. I gently pull down the overalls, leaving her in her bralette. After I pull them all the way off, I notice that she's not wearing underwear.

"Damn baby, didn't realize you were being such a bad girl going commando tonight."

"Every time the seam of the overalls rubbed my clit it was making me think about how bad I wanted you," she replies.

I run my hand over her pussy and it's glistening from being covered with her wetness.

"Oh, angel, you must be suffering. You're drenched for me."

She arches her back and whines, "Please get in me, Kieran."

Hearing her say my name will always flip a switch for me.

Standing up to take my shirt off, I say, "Lie back and relax for me, pretty girl. Let me relieve that ache for you."

I climb on top of her and pull off her bralette, throwing it across the room and revealing her perfect breasts. I graze her nipples with my fingers and then climb on top of her.

She whimpers, "Please, Kier. I can't take it."

I smirk. "Your wish is my command, Emmie."

She melts into the bed and moans, "Fuck me hard, please, baby."

I lean down to kiss her forehead, and slam into her harder, feeling her squeezing around me. I reach my hand down between us and quickly rub her clit. Her moans quicken, and her eyes close.

"Keep those eyes on me, pretty girl."

She opens her eyes and whimpers, getting close to coming. I speed up, desperate to see her lose control. Her hips meet mine, and she arches her back, moaning my name loudly. The volume of my moans matches hers, and her eyes start to roll back.

"There you go, baby. Come for me."

The sound of her orgasming pushes me over the edge, and I spill into her.

Sex is great. Sex when you love someone and are loved by someone this much? Beyond words.

She relaxes beneath me with a blissful smile painted across her face.

"How about you let me help you shower and then we can cuddle before we go to sleep, Emmie girl?" I say before I press a kiss to her forehead.

She runs her hand over my cheek and sleepily says, "Sounds perfect to me."

emaline

WE'RE BACK HOME in Santa Monica, and it's never felt better to use my own shower. The final show of the tour is officially here. It's at the iconic Troubadour, which is luckily only twenty minutes from my apartment. Soundcheck isn't until 2 pm, and it's only 10 am, so I have plenty of time to chill out and settle back in before we have to head to the venue.

It's weird to be back in my apartment without Kieran after so many nights on end of sharing the same bed. We haven't been back to LA since we became a couple, so it all feels new again. I mean, we spent tons of time at each other's apartments before now, so that's not new, but it's new in the sense of us being a *thing* here. I'm starting to feel like there isn't a point in us having two apartments. I don't want to assume his feelings, but considering we practically lived together before, except for sleeping, and then had all of those nights sharing a bed on tour, it's weird to think about not sleeping next to him every night. Both of our leases are up in a few months, so we should probably have a conversation about that sometime soon.

The idea of living together seems so right. I never expected that we would become more than friends, so I always worried that being roommates would ruin our friendship. But things are different now. I think it might be nice to get somewhere new for us to call our own. A place that starts out as ours, versus me moving into his place or him moving into mine. With how frequently we've been getting noticed, I've been feeling like living in an apartment complex with others around isn't the best or safest idea anymore. We haven't had any issues with fans finding us here so far, but things are growing in a way I never expected.

That's the thing about growth. It rarely looks how you'd expect it. It takes twists and turns—some of them beautiful, some of them terrifying, some of them a combination of the two. Kieran and I have always grown together, both literally and figuratively, from when we were infants. I just never thought that growth would include us becoming boyfriend and girlfriend. I never could've predicted this, but I couldn't be happier with the outcome. He is the kind of boyfriend I've always dreamed of... which I guess makes sense when we've been by each other's sides for our entire lives and when his parents raised him in the way they did.

Kieran Hayes is the kind of man people write books about. At the surface, people may only see his handsomeness, which, don't get me wrong, is swoon worthy in its own right, but there's so much more to him.

If you even have just two minutes talking with him, you'll immediately be pulled in by how he gives every person who speaks to him (unless they're being an asshole), his undivided attention and listens to you like you're telling the most enthralling story... even if you're sharing a seemingly meaningless moment of your day.

He always remembers and thinks of the little things, down to me hating paper straws and always knowing to order me "light-well" fries from In-N-Out because they are far superior to their regular ones.

He never forgets a single birthday, and he picks the most thoughtful cards and gifts, a skill he inherited from his dad.

He has a stronger work ethic than anyone else I know, putting his absolute all into everything, regardless of if it's something he hates, like bullshit papers when we were in college or meetings with label executives who only care about money, not our art.

He always makes time for his family, including when we've had sixteen-hour days and all we want to do is sleep and be dead to the world. He always makes sure that everyone in his life feels seen, known, and loved.

Every moment, I fall more and more in love with him, not for the grand gestures, but for all of the little things that really aren't so little. Now that we're back in LA and we'll finally have some time off soon, I want to make sure that we make time to just be us. We've been with each other practically 24/7 for tour, but it's still not the same as spending time together when we're not on the road. It'll be interesting to figure out what our new normal will look like.

I step out of the shower and dry my feet off, hearing the front door close. I can notice the sound and feeling of Kieran's presence from anywhere, so I immediately know it's him. I walk over to my sink to apply my moisturizer before hearing him say, "I know we already had coffee when we first got on the bus, but I figured you could use another."

He walks into the bathroom, wearing a simple black tee and black joggers, his hair slightly disheveled. While I love seeing him in more put-together outfits when we're on stage or going out, I also love seeing him like this. Comfy, relaxed, and *regular*.

I finish applying my moisturizer. "I'm still pretty exhausted from last night, so this is perfect."

He smirks. "Oh, what was so exhausting last night?"

"Oh, just being up until 1 am fucking my hot boyfriend, despite a 6 am bus call."

He gets close to me and kisses my forehead, a contrast to the energy the rest of his body is communicating.

"Hmm, if you're already exhausted, what's a little more exhaustion?" he says, running one of his hands across my shoulders.

"Down, boy. A) I just showered, and B) We have the biggest show of our careers tonight. I promise, we can celebrate later."

He pouts playfully. "Fiiiiine, I guess I can deal with that. I'll let you finish getting ready before your coffee gets too watered down."

"All I've gotta do to finish getting ready is dry my hair, since I'll be doing my makeup and everything after sound-check, and I want to let it sit in a towel for a bit anyway. So, cuddle and coffee time in my bed?"

"Sounds perfect, Emmie girl."

Sixty minutes until showtime, and my usual mix of nerves and excitement is amplified times ten with it being the last show of tour, and arguably the most important one I've ever had. Count-less reporters are here, the line for pit has been forming since long before we arrived at the venue, my family and Kieran's family are all chilling in the green room, and Alaina will be getting here shortly after her dance rehearsal. Hometown shows are always a reunion of sorts, and while some people might find it overwhelming to have so many people backstage, for me, it reminds me of all of the support I have in my corner. It also brings up all of the nostalgia around why I started making music in the first place, when I was a little five-year-old girl dancing around my bedroom playing karaoke with Kieran. Whenever I start to get too much stage anxiety, I remind myself of that little girl and little boy— since we're both still those same people, despite being adults now.

Some artists of my level like to have hair and makeup artists, but for me, doing my hair and makeup before a show is a grounding practice. I get to just be with myself, without anyone else to answer to or to have to perform for. After I finish curling the last section of my hair, I spray it all and let it cool down and set. Tonight's outfit is charcoal low-rise distressed jeans, a cropped lacy black corset-style top covered in little cherries, and a pair of red Adidas Gazelles. I unclip the jeans from the hanger and pull them on.

I was a little worried about how I'd feel about low-rise jeans after my relapse, but for some reason, I'm not caring about how my body looks today. Actually, after putting on the top, I think I look hot. I grab the red lipstick off the vanity and apply it, seeing how it pulls together the look. Before running my fingers through my curls, I add a few rhinestones in the corners of my eyes.

"Ready for me yet, baby?" Kieran says through the door.

Maybe one day I'll drop the surprising him with my outfit tradition, but today is not the day. I know it annoys him a little since he'd rather have more time together, but for me, it's fun to have something that's just *our* thing. With having a really public relationship, I always want to have things that can be just for us. It's probably a little silly, but it's special for me.

I open the door and let him in, taking in his outfit. He's wearing a black suit with a white tank top under it, the neck-line showing off his tattoos. Part of me is tempted to tell him to take the shirt off and wear the jacket on its own, but I'll save that view for myself—not the rest of the world. I'm not the type to be jealous, but I know how all of the fans thirst over Kieran, and tonight, I won't feed into that more.

He looks me up and down and whispers in my ear, "There are few times that you look hotter than when you have red lipstick on."

Shivers rush down my spine as I say, "You look pretty hot yourself, Kier."

I kiss his cheek, leaving a lipstick mark.

Without wiping it off, he wraps his arms around me. "Ready for some family time before we do this thing?"

Kieran has always been family, but hearing those words makes me think of how badly I want to marry him someday.

I look up at him and reply, "That sounds like exactly what I need."

He breaks the hug and turns to open the door. I walk out to see everyone sitting in a circle, like how we sit with the rest of the band and crew every night—except our families are there, too. The band and crew have become like family to me. When you spend so much of your time together, going to places all over the country and world, it's impossible to not get that close. Or at least it has been for me.

I haven't seen Kieran's parents, Jack and Maeve, in person since we started dating, and as soon as his mom sees me, she jumps up and runs over. She throws her arms around me, squeezes me, and says, "I'm so glad the two of you finally came to your senses. Look how perfect you are together."

I squeeze her back. "I guess everyone except for us always knew. I'm sure this is no surprise to you, but you've truly raised the perfect gentleman. He's always been an incredible friend, but he's an even more incredible boyfriend."

"And you best believe if he ever hurts you, we will be taking your side. You've always been my daughter, and you always will be."

Kieran clears his throat awkwardly, and I laugh slightly and say, "I don't think we'll have to worry about that, but thank you."

I walk over to Jack, and he pulls both me and Kieran in for a hug.

"Good to see you, kiddo. We're all so proud of you both. It's hard not to see you as often, but we wouldn't want it any other way. And clearly, you're both in good hands with each other."

I don't want to break the hug, but out of the corner of my eye, I see my dad patiently waiting for me.

"Love you, Jack. I'm so glad you're here."

I run over to my dad, and he throws his arms around me in a huge bear hug.

"My little girl really isn't so little anymore. There aren't words for how incredibly proud of you I am. Getting to see you live your dreams has been the greatest joy of my life. Even when it's on one of those crappy live streams that your fans do."

I wish my parents could be at every single show – but they, of course, have to work and have their own lives, too. It is pretty special when they get to see shows in person, though. And thinking of my dad and mom sitting in the living room watching a livestream on one of their phones almost makes me tear up.

When I was a teenager and really struggling with my eating disorder, my relationship with them wasn't the best, especially with them having to force me to go back to treatment several times. I couldn't see it then, and sure, there were plenty of things said by them that weren't okay, but at the end of the day, they were doing it because of how much they love me and how terrified they were that I would die if I didn't follow the plan my doctor and dietitian and therapist gave them. I can't imagine having to see your child suffer in that way, and while their attempts at support were misguided at times, I wouldn't be here if it weren't for them.

I hate that I haven't told either of them about my relapse, but it wouldn't help anyone and would worry them unnecessarily. I've told enough people that I know I'll be able to stay accountable with my recovery, and on Monday, I'm going to text my old therapist to make an appointment. At some point, I might tell them, and if it gets worse again, I definitely will, but for now, this is the right decision.

I squeeze my dad and say, "I'm so lucky to have the most supportive parents in the world. I always tell Kieran I feel most at home on stage, but with everyone here tonight, this feels like home."

My mom walks over, gently shoves my dad, and says, "Drew, you need to let me hug our daughter."

"Kim, you saw her a week ago. I haven't seen her in over a month."

"It's been a week and a half!"

I laugh and turn to my mom. "You know, you can both hug me at the same time."

She pulls me in, and my dad says, "Kieran, you better get in here, too, son. I've missed you. Not as much as I've missed our Emaline, but I've missed you too."

My dad calling Kieran "son" is something I could get used to.

Alaina walks through the door and runs over to me.

We embrace each other, and I say, "I'm so glad you could make it. I know your rehearsal schedule has been all over the place."

After nearly squeezing all the air out of me, she replies, "Wouldn't miss it for the world. So glad I'm not the only one in sneakers because my feet are dying after being in pointe shoes all day, and I didn't have time to throw them in an ice bath."

"Oh god, I'm sure. Do you want me to see if someone could get one for you? I'm sure Ruby or Ryan wouldn't mind."

She shakes her head. "No, don't worry about it, Em. It's your night, I don't want to draw a bunch of attention to myself. Plus, the faces I make from the temperature are pretty embarrassing."

"Well, if you change your mind, let me know."

I run out on stage, and I'm speechless. While every show on this tour has been sold out, this is different. This venue holds fewer people than every other venue we've played this tour, and yet, it feels the fullest. Countless friends and acquaintances are here and there are tons of media people. Knowing how many iconic performers have graced this stage before me is electrifying. I'm anxious about the meeting I have lined up with my label, so I'm hoping this performance will be enough to get them off my back about their patriarchal "marketing" bullshit.

As I scan the crowd, Faye, our photographer, is in the spot between the pit and the stage. She's been our tour photographer for the past two years, but she's been going through some family stuff the past few months and wasn't able to join us for this tour. She's back tonight, and I couldn't be more excited to see the shots she gets of all of us.

I grab the mic and we play "Wild Mind". It goes off without a hitch – even the run of notes that was pissing me off yesterday.

We usually play "Growth" next, but we're surprising

everyone (well, everyone except for the band and crew, obviously), with a new duet Kieran and I wrote titled "Never Alone". Two stagehands bring out stools for us, and a backline tech brings out Kieran's acoustic guitar.

"With this being a hometown show and the last show of the tour, I wanted to do something a little special. So here's a brand new song. It means a lot to Kieran and I, and I hope you all love it as much as we do."

I sit down next to Kieran, and though there are hundreds of people staring at us, it is as if we're the only two people in the room. Everyone is silent, and he starts to lightly strum his guitar. In this moment, I'm not really singing to everyone else here… I'm just singing to him. He starts to harmonize with me, and it's magical. While he does backup vocals every night and I hear him sing all the time, he's never sung this much during any of our shows. The slight rasp of his voice is perfect, and the song is flowing in a way that feels so right. It doesn't feel like a show—it's like when we're playing for hours in one of our apartments, without a care in the world. Like being a little girl again, not giving a shit about appearances or judgments, just enveloped in the power and catharsis of music. It's easy to lose yourself in it all—hell, I've lost myself so many times, especially recently. But right now, I'm present in this moment, singing with my best friend who I'm head over heels in love with, who somehow is also head over heels in love with me.

We sing the last note, and Kieran gives me a quick kiss. The crowd erupts in cheers and applause, and I'm more aware of the magic of this night. The magic of being able to tour around the world doing the thing I love most, with the person I love most. I wish I could bottle up this feeling and save it for those moments where I feel like I'm losing myself, but I know that's impossible. So, for now, I'm going to soak up every second of it.

kieran

"NOW, who's ready to go party?!" Delia says.

We just got off stage, and it was, without a doubt, the best show we've ever had. Some people may think that smaller venues mean being less successful, but intimate shows like this are almost always my favorite. Sure, the rush of playing huge shows where you look out and see thousands of people in the crowd is like nothing else. But with small shows, when everyone is so close to the stage, the energy is unmatched. Getting to see everyone's faces so clearly gives a level of connection that's not as possible in large venues. Plus, as someone who's not just a performer but obviously a huge music lover, I know how cool it is to see your favorite artist up close and personal. And with these small shows, you know how hard fans fought for the tickets.

I pull Emaline into my side, and she says, "I know we are."

The way she beams shows me that she feels the same way about the show as I did. She's so hard on herself, especially about performances, so seeing her revel in her magic and talent makes me incredibly happy.

"You fucking killed it tonight, baby."

"So did you, Kiki. The duet was my favorite moment. It felt like it was just us in your bedroom, not on a stage with hundreds of people around."

"Pretty cool to get to do this with my best friend in the entire world."

She nuzzles her head into me, and I ruffle her hair, even though it pisses her off sometimes when she takes so long to do it.

"So, I ordered a few Ubers to head over to the club. I packed up everyone's stuff, and I'll pile it up in my car since I don't plan on drinking too much, and you guys can grab it at the end of the night. Sound good?" Ruby says.

Emaline replies, "Sounds perfect to me."

We head to the back exit and walk outside. Our Uber is already waiting for us, and we check the license plate before getting inside. Alaina and Madison are in our Uber too, and I'm glad to have a few minutes away from the rest of the band and crew. I love them to death, but it can also be good to have a little space from your coworkers, especially when we're going to be partying together for the next few hours.

"I'm so glad you both were able to make it tonight. Getting to share these moments with you is so special." Em says.

"I wouldn't miss it for the world. My body may lowkey be dying from rehearsal, and I may have to be up early tomorrow, but none of that matters. I can never pass up an opportunity to see you living your dreams." Alaina replies.

Madison looks up from her phone and says, "I just feel so lucky to be able to support both of you and see your hard work come to fruition. It's beyond special to witness."

"I'm so grateful for both of you. Having everyone we love so much surrounding us makes the stage feel more like home," I reply.

Madison's husband Matt was at the show but wasn't able

to join us for the after party since he's working early tomorrow. I'm excited that we'll be in town for a little while because he's such a cool dude, and it's hard that he can't always be here for these fun moments.

The driver pulls up to the curb.

"Have a great night, be safe," he says.

Emaline replies, "Thank you, you do the same!"

We climb out of the car and head over to the bouncer. He checks our IDs, and we head inside.

The rest of the team is waiting for us inside, and it's time to let loose and celebrate, especially because we don't have a call time we have to wake up early for tomorrow.

Em makes a beeline towards everyone and says, "Okay, first round of shots on me, guys. I couldn't do any of this without each and every one of you, and I couldn't be more grateful for all of the hours and energy you put into everything."

I say to the bartender, "Can we get ten shots of tequila, please?"

"Sure thing, do you want to keep a tab open?"

"No, we'll close it out."

Em will not be paying for a single one of the rest of her drinks tonight.

Two minutes later, the bartender slides over a huge tray with the shots on it, and we pass them around, along with limes.

As I go to pass one to Mads, she shakes her head and says, "Actually... no shots for me tonight."

A skeptical look comes across my face for a minute, but a second later, it makes sense.

"Wait... are you pregnant?" I say.

Giddily, she says, "Yep, six weeks. I know it's early, but I couldn't keep it a secret anymore."

Em jumps up and down and says, "Holy shit! You're gonna be the best mom. I'm so fucking happy for you."

I pull Mads in for a hug and say, "I can't believe I'm going to be an uncle. I didn't think this night could get any better."

"Here's to this badass band and many more shows ahead. And to adding a sweet baby to this family," Ruby says before we all down our shots.

"Now let's go dance!" Emaline says.

Despite the exorbitant amount of energy that went into the show, she seemingly has unlimited energy. At least that makes one of us.

Madison says, "I think I'm gonna stay here by the bar and catch up with Lainie. It's been a bit, and I'm a *little* nauseous anyway."

"You sure? Do you want me to get you a ride home?"

She shakes her head. "Nah, it'll pass soon. Go have fun!"

We walk out onto the dance floor and start dancing, with sheer joy and carefree vibes emanating from Em. She works so hard, and I love getting to have these moments of letting loose with her. A few songs go by, and I decide to grab us water real quick.

"You good to stay here? I'm gonna get some water for us."

"Yeah, go for it!"

I walk over to the water station and fill up our cups. As I turn back towards the dance floor and start walking over, my heart drops. I can spot Chris from a mile away, and sure enough, he's there, steps away from Emaline. Why this fucker is here or how he knows we're here is beyond me, but if he knows what's good for him, he better not only get away from her, but leaves the premises entirely.

He says something to her, and her whole body tenses up. I start to run over, and then he puts his hand on her shoulder.

It's taking everything in me not to punch him, but I don't want to cause a bigger problem.

"Get the fuck away from her before I have someone go get a bouncer."

He laughs, and his pupils show that he's clearly high on something, and likely drunk too.

"Oh, look who's here. Guess Emmie could only get the guy who was thirsting over her the entire time we were together. I know you won't do anything to me. We're just talking."

Her breath quickens, and she's likely already having a panic attack or on the verge of one. I'm seething, and my ability to hold myself back is dwindling fast.

He leans into her. "She was saying how much she misses me."

That's a complete lie.

"Once again, get the hell away from her. Better yet, get the fuck out of this club, scumbag."

His hand inches towards her shoulder, and she tries to pull away, but he touches her. Her eyes are welling up, and I can see how everything is flashing before her eyes. Without a second thought, I shove him and say, "I said get the fuck away from her."

The rest of the band and crew have realized what's happening, and they're starting to walk over.

Chris pushes me back, and it's over for him. I never get violent, but after the horrific things he put my Emaline through, he's had it coming for a long time. And he's going to pay.

Madison grabs Em, and I punch Chris in the face, not caring that I may get kicked out or even arrested. I'll do anything to protect her. He tries to punch me back, but in his inebriated state, he stumbles and instead gets my shoulder. I knee him in his stomach and then get his face again, seeing a black eye starting to form. While I should probably stop at this point, I can't stop seeing red, and I want him to physically feel all of the pain he's put Em through. He may have thought he could get away with this, but he won't. He'll pay for what he did, regardless of whether it has repercussions for me. Two bouncers run over, and before they get to us, I push him to the ground, putting every ounce of strength I have into my punches. He's bleeding, and I don't give a fuck.

A bouncer pulls me off and says, "What the fuck is happening here?"

Ryan rushes over and says, "Sir, that man on the ground assaulted the girl over there a few months ago, and he just put his hands on her and wouldn't leave her alone. Kieran was just acting in self-defense. And I mean... this sack of shit had it coming."

They look over at Emaline, seeing her sobbing into Madison's chest.

Ruby comes over and says, "I can corroborate this. I'm her manager, and she has been through extensive therapy as a result of his actions. I know violence probably isn't the best course of action, but please let us leave without getting police involved. He was just protecting her and himself."

Clearly on another planet, probably from the combination of alcohol, whatever drugs he's on, and me bashing his face in, Chris slurs, "She's a stupid slut, she wanted me and touched me first, he's just jealous."

I have the urge to lunge in again, but Ryan holds me back.

The bouncers look down at Chris, look at me, look at Emaline, and aggressively grab Chris. One of them says, "Alright, it's time for you to get your sorry ass out of here and never come back."

He pushes them both and says, "I think they should be the

ones kicked out. I was minding my own business and she started something."

Austin, who is usually pretty quiet, scoffs and says, "Pretty sure everyone in this fucking club can say otherwise."

The bouncers are clearly taking every ounce of strength in themselves not to punch him too. He shoves them again, and they grab him more aggressively, grabbing his hands and holding them behind his back while walking him towards the door.

Ruby's eyes narrow, and she says, "And guess what? Someone was recording you, and you'll be lucky if your ass doesn't get thrown in jail."

As much as I want to see the recording and hear whatever he said to her, I know it's better not to. It's hard to see since the door is far away, but the bouncers pick Chris up and throw him outside.

I run over to Emaline and pull her into my chest. Her sobs are breaking me, and I know we need to get her out of here and get home. Countless people are staring at us, surely recognizing who we are. I'm desperately hoping that anyone who may have been recording this doesn't post it. The last thing we need is something like this getting out to the news or on social media. Especially with how the label has already been pissed at us lately.

I rub her back and whisper, "You're safe now. You're safe now. Let's get out of here, Emmie girl."

She continues sobbing, but she nods her head.

The bouncers walk back over to us, and one says, "Ma'am, we're so sorry this happened. If you would like, we can escort you through the back entrance."

"That would be great. And thank you for getting him out of here," I say.

"Absolutely, it's our job. Also, he's now on our banned list, along with a photo of him. He'll never be allowed back in this place. And we're happy to serve as witnesses if any legal proceedings arise," the other bouncer says.

Ruby looks at the rest of the team and says, "Guys, I need to get them both home. If you can Uber to my place and grab your stuff there, that would be great."

We quickly walk out the back entrance, the bouncers and Ruby shielding Emaline and I to avoid any more photos or videos.

"Get home safe, y'all. So sorry again that this happened. We hope to see you back here again sometime. We're big fans."

Emaline quietly chokes out, "Thank you."

Madison looks at us and says, "Call me if you need anything. I don't care what time it is. Love you guys."

"Thanks, Mads. I'll text you in the morning. Love you too. Get home safe."

I scoop Emaline up and walk to Ruby's car.

This turned from one of the best nights ever to one of the worst very quickly.

The sound of the waves crashing against the shore is exactly the grounding and calm I need after tonight. The beach is always our safe place, and Em asked if we could come here. I don't care that it's 1 am. I'd do anything to help her feel better. She's lying against me, and I strum my guitar. Even though it's not fully finished yet and I haven't told her about it yet, I start to play the song I've been writing about her. We usually write all of our music together, but for a change, I decided to write something on my own—and it's pretty easy when you have the perfect muse. I'm not sure if I'd ever want to have a solo career in addition to being in Emaline's band, but if there's anything this summer has taught me, it's to never say never.

Before I start to sing, she says, "What's this? I haven't heard this before."

I continue playing. "I may have written a song about you."

Even though my voice is tired and a bit raspier than usual, I don't care. I start singing, and her body relaxes deeper into my lap.

"I was searching for the light, but then realized she's always been in front of me..."

Her eyes well up, and I really hope these are happy tears, not tears from everything that happened tonight.

I pause singing for a moment. "Are you okay, baby?"

"Yes, keep playing. These are happy tears."

I know I tell her I love her a million times a day, but communicating it through music is a different level of expression.

I finish the song, and as I look down at her, I say, "What do you think, Emmie girl?"

She glances up at me. "I've never felt this loved before. Thank you, this is exactly what I needed tonight."

I place my guitar down next to me and stroke her face.

"I mean, I couldn't think of a better way to express the depth of my love for you. I've never loved someone the way I love you."

She smiles and says, "I didn't think loving someone this much was possible, but apparently it is."

I put my guitar to the side and lay down next to her, intertwining our fingers. To try to distract her from the triggering thoughts she's probably having after tonight, I start talking about my favorite moments from tour. We've definitely had some dark moments along the way, but we've also had so many beautiful ones. And that's the thing about life—painful moments can coexist with exhilarating ones. There can be phases of life where everything sucks, but even in the most challenging times, there are often bright moments mixed in.

Twenty minutes go by and Emaline says, "This is very off topic, but this morning I was thinking about how our leases are up so soon. I don't want to rush anything or make any assumptions, but I was wondering what you thought about getting an apartment and moving in together?"

I've been thinking about the exact same thing, and I couldn't be more relieved to know that she's on the same page. Some people may think it's rushing, but I don't think we are.

"I think you read my mind. It may sound a little crazy... but I've been thinking about buying a house. I know our schedules are so chaotic and sometimes we're away from LA more than we're here, but I really want to lay down some roots. I want to have a space that's completely ours, that we can make anything we want. Away from other people, having more space, and all of that. I've been saving money for years, and the money from this tour and album has definitely helped."

Please let her not be freaked out by this. The last thing I need to do is mess this up or somehow make something worse.

"That's kinda been floating through my head, too. I've been feeling over apartment life, and I think more privacy is becoming a necessity. I've been saving for a while, too, especially with holding onto my inheritance from my grandma, so I think it makes sense financially. With anyone else, I'd say that it would be moving too fast, but I've known you my entire life. I'm so sure about us, and I want nothing more than to make that even more official."

A huge smile spread across my face, and I say, "Well, I guess we've gotta start house hunting, pretty girl."

I can't believe it. I'm going to buy a home with the woman who is already my home.

emaline

A WEEK HAS PASSED since the end of tour, and today is Kieran's 26th birthday. I have a big day of celebrations planned for him, and with how rough things have been, it's going to bring some much needed joy. We're having a huge party at his parents' house tonight with tons of family and friends, including one of his best friends from college, Noah. He moved to the UK for work after we graduated, so we don't get to see him very often. Kieran spent more time with him than I did, but I've hung out with him countless times too and can't wait to see him. Kieran has no idea he's coming, and while the party itself isn't a surprise, I'm excited that this part of it will be. Before the party, we're having our Sunday tradition of grabbing bagels from our favorite spot, eating them in the park, and then the real estate agent that Ruby set us up with is taking us to look at a few houses. We've looked at a few listings online already, but haven't found one worth seeing in person yet. And, of course, tonight there will be birthday sex. And probably a lot of it.

I'm still a bit fucked up (okay, maybe a lot fucked up), over the altercation with Chris, but I'm doing better than I thought

I would be. I won't be able to have a therapy session until we get back from Paris because my therapist is booked up (the struggle of having the best therapist in the world), but I've been being really honest with everyone, especially Kieran, which has helped majorly. It's always hard for me to be honest when things are rough because I never want to bring things down, especially after the high of finishing the tour, but I know that everyone wants to help me heal. My brain often tries to tell me otherwise, but no one thinks I'm a burden. I'm surrounded by so much love and support, and I need to let myself lean into it instead of running from it. Luckily, the label agreed to push our meeting off by a few weeks after what happened, but the anxiety is still looming over me.

We haven't *officially* moved in together yet, but I've been sleeping at Kieran's every night. While many guys in their twenties have apartments that are barely a step above a dorm in terms of cleanliness and decor, Kieran's apartment is different, like most things about him. As much as I love my own room and apartment, I know with Kieran's OCD, he struggles more with being in a different space than I do, so I've been fine with sleeping at his place.

Kieran walks out of the bathroom with a towel slung across his hips. His short brunette waves are perfectly tousled, and I need to run my fingers through them.

"Alright, birthday boy, almost ready to leave? I'm starving."

He walks over to the bed and kisses the top of my head.

"Yep, just gotta get dressed. I'll change later, but a t-shirt and joggers are the move for now," he says, opening one of the drawers of his dresser.

It should be criminal how good this man looks in the simplest and easiest of outfits. I'm pretty sure that even if he was wearing a burlap sack, he'd still look like the sexiest man on the planet.

I can easily get out of this bed on my own, but he gives me his hand and pulls me up. As I stretch up to kiss him, he lightly grabs my ass. As much as I'd love to follow that lead right now, the whale sounds coming from my stomach beg to differ.

"Unless you want to deal with me being hangry, we should probably put that idea on hold until later."

"Hmm, I mean, you are pretty hot when you're angry," he says with a smirk.

I playfully flick his shoulder. "It won't be the sexy type of angry, I assure you."

He rolls his eyes and says, "Fiiiiine, I guess I can deal."

I break the hug and go slide my Birkenstocks on.

"Carbs. Now. Please."

"Whatever you want, Emmie girl."

My stomach and taste buds are thoroughly satisfied after the perfect bagel and latte, and I'm currently as giddy as a little girl at Disneyland because we are about to go into our first private house showing. Since we've struggled with finding something we like on our own, Ruby set us up with the real estate agent who helped her get her house. It's surreal that this is happening. Not only am I buying my first house, but I'm buying it with my best friend in the entire world. With all of the chaos of tour life, getting to lay down roots and have a space that is just ours, that we can make completely our own, is a dream come true. Apartment life has gotten old, and while I still feel like a kid at times, I'm excited to lean into this "big girl" era.

I don't think we are terribly picky about what we want in a house, but we do have a few non-negotiables—at least three bedrooms, an office that we can turn into a studio, an open concept living room/dining room/kitchen for entertaining, a space suitable for a workout area, a deck, a pool, and ideally an outdoor cooking space. And I certainly wouldn't complain about a huge bathroom for our primary bedroom and walk-in closet. We also want a "turn key ready" house because with our schedules, we don't have the time or energy for a fixer-upper. I'm also the least handy person in existence... and while Kieran has many talents, repairing homes isn't one of them. We're lucky if we're both able to hang art on the walls without damaging something. I think part of why we haven't found *the one* with just searching online is that we both need to feel the energy of a space in person to know if it's right. Ruby said her real estate agent found her perfect home after only visiting a few listings, so I'm hoping the same happens for us.

"Ready to go look at what could be our future home, Kiki?"

"I don't think I've ever been more ready for something. I can't believe we're doing this. In a good way."

He gets out of the car and walks around to open my door. The real estate agent is already standing by the front door of the house, and my excitement is probably palpable. Kieran grabs my hand and starts to swing my arm, and while I'm tempted to start skipping, I want the real estate agent to take us at least a *little* seriously. We walk up the steps of the house, and for some reason, the energy is similar to when I'm getting ready to take the stage.

"Hi, it's lovely to meet you both. I'm Kylie. Also, I promise to keep things strictly professional, but I wanted to let you both know that I'm a huge fan of your music. You're incredibly talented, and I'm grateful to be part of the journey of helping you find the perfect home," she says, reaching out her hand.

I shake her hand and say, "It's great to meet you, Kylie. Ruby has said such wonderful things about you, and we absolutely love the home you found for her. And thank you so much for your kind words, it means so much that you've connected to our music."

"I agree with everything Emaline said. You'll have to come to a show sometime, we'll be sure to get you on the list, of course," Kieran says, shaking her hand.

"Well, that would be absolutely amazing. Now, how about I show you this house? It hits all of your requests, and it's one of my favorites that I've seen on the market recently."

"Let's do it!" Kieran and I say in unison.

Our brains are forever almost always on the same wavelength.

We step inside, and I already love the vibe of this house. There's a bit of a foyer, which then opens up to a huge living room, complete with a fireplace. While I know that the furniture in houses for sale is often either staged or belongs to the seller, the giant couches are calling my name, and I may see if Kylie can work some magic if we decide to buy this house. There are dark wood floors, and I love that there's a combo of wallpaper and colored walls instead of all white or gray like a lot of houses these days. I get that some people like the more neutral, minimalist aesthetic, but I like a house that has a bit of character and doesn't look cookie-cutter. I don't want a house that looks like every other one in *Home & Garden Magazine*.

"Wow, this is incredible," Kieran says.

Kylie smiles. "And this is only part of it. Wait until you see the rest."

We walk through the kitchen, and all of the details are perfect. There's a double oven, and the gas stovetop is huge, including a griddle in the middle. The fridge is massive with two huge double doors and a pullout freezer drawer, with a black stainless steel finish – and it's practically twice the size of the one in my apartment. The cabinets are painted a light slate blue color, and there are stunning granite countertops, along with an island with barstools. The amount of countertop space is bigger than anywhere either of us has lived before, and I'm dreaming of all of the meals we can make in this space and all of the gatherings we can host here.

"I can imagine making us a big weekend breakfast in here."

The first thing that pops into my head when hearing Kieran mention making a big weekend breakfast is seeing two little kids at the barstools.

Kids? Do I want kids? Maybe I should think about that sometime.

"The griddle will be pretty solid," I say.

"Now, how about I show you the bedrooms and office before we check out the outside?"

We nod and follow her lead, walking down the hallway.

"There are three bedrooms, like you requested. And I think the office will really transform into a beautiful studio for you both. Oh, and there are five bathrooms. Each bedroom has an ensuite, there's a guest bathroom on this level, and there's another downstairs. Let's look at the office first."

She leads us into the office, and while it's a bit bare bones, it will be perfect for a studio. There's a desk and a couch in here currently, but I think everything could be reconfigured nicely. It's the one space where we're willing to put a little work in. And the bright floral accent wall is giving the exact creative energy this space will need.

"This is perfect. It's such a good size, but not too big," I say.

"I think it's exactly what we need for a studio," Kieran adds.

Kylie replies, "Amazing. Now, let's check out the primary bedroom. I think it will really seal the deal."

We walk down the hall, and she steps through the doorway. I'm absolutely in love with this bedroom. There are several large windows, letting in tons of natural light. The walls are a dusty rose color, and while some people may say that pink should be reserved for kids' bedrooms, I think this is a grown-up shade. Plus, screw whatever stupid opinions anyone may have about whatever we house we decide on.

The king bed is massive, and the charcoal color of the bed-frame and headboard complements the walls beautifully. There are two egg-shaped chairs in one of the corners of the room, making for the perfect little reading nook.

"A pink bedroom would be so sick," Kieran says.

There's an open door, so I peek inside. It's a massive walk-in closet, with two sides and several lighted mirrors. Kieran and I both have pretty big wardrobes, so this will be a dream. After glancing around, I walk back out.

Kylie says, "Let me show you the en suite. The shower is unreal."

As we walk in, Kieran says, "Holy shit. I've never seen a bathroom this huge. And a rainfall shower head? I'm never going to want to get out of there."

The shower could practically fit a bed inside, and a few feet away, there is a deep clawfoot tub with a distant ocean view. There's a double sink with a lighted mirror, which is going to be perfect for putting on makeup. Still in awe, we walk back out to the rest of the bedroom.

"Okay, so obviously we still need to see the rest of the house, but from everything I've seen so far, I'm absolutely in love," I say.

Kieran nods. "Same. Even though we haven't seen the full thing yet, I can already envision us living here."

Kylie quickly shows us the remaining bedrooms and the laundry room, and then we head back out to the main living space. She opens up the deck door, and there's a coffee table with a few chairs, perfect for having breakfast or reading with a cup of tea. Then, I look out and see the lawn, pool, and fire pit.

As I scan my eyes around, Kylie says, "Isn't it beautiful out here? And down the deck stairs, there's a covered outdoor kitchen area."

I can so vividly envision myself and Kieran relaxing out here on days off or after a long studio session, or having people over for a party. It's not obnoxiously big, but it's the perfect size for entertaining. Growing up, both my family and Kieran's family loved hosting gatherings, and it would be really special to have a place like this of our own where we can do the same thing.

We head down the stairs and traipse through the backyard before Kylie shows us the lower level of the house. She opens up the back door, and there's a bathroom, as well as a large workout area. While I do love a good in-studio yoga class, being able to workout at home is pretty solid.

"So, now that you've seen the rest of the place, what are your thoughts?"

Kieran says, "I mean, I think it's perfect. What about you, Em?"

"I absolutely love it. It has everything we asked for, the location is amazing... I suppose it couldn't hurt to look at other options, but honestly, if you love it too, we could put an offer in. I know the market is so fast, and I don't want to possibly miss out on this for the sake of being indecisive," I reply.

With an excited grin on his face, Kieran says, "Let's do it, baby. There's no time like the present, and considering we leave for Paris so soon, it's better to get this all situated now rather than later."

I throw my arms around him. "Oh my god, we're buying a fucking house!"

"Hell yeah, you guys are! I'll get all of the logistics situated and email over an e-sign form to get that offer sent in to the seller's agent."

Real estate gods, please let us get this house.

"Oh my god, it smells incredible in here."

We just got to Kieran's parents' house, and the aroma of home-cooked food is absolutely intoxicating. My mom is a pretty great cook, but nothing compares to his mom Maeve's cooking skills, except for my grandma's. Maeve could easily ditch her office manager job and start a catering business, but despite Jack urging her a few times over the years, she's been adamant about only wanting cooking to be a fun thing she does for family and friends—and I guess I don't blame her. It can be extremely challenging when one of the things you love most becomes your job, and I know that better than most people.

As we walk towards the kitchen, Maeve runs over to us and pulls Kieran in for a hug.

"Happy birthday, my darling boy. I can't believe my baby is twenty-six. Can you believe it, Jack?"

Jack shakes his head.

"I can't. It feels like just yesterday I was helping you learn to ride a bike. And now you're both such accomplished adults. Mind-boggling."

When we tell them about buying a house, they're *really* going to think we're adults. But that won't be happening until the offer is accepted—can't risk anything.

"This all looks and smells incredible, Maeve. Is there anything I can do to help?" I say.

"No, your mom has been helping all day, and everything is

just about done, so you both can relax before everyone else gets here. Can I get either of you anything to drink?" she replies.

Kieran walks towards the fridge. "I can take care of that, mom, you've clearly been working your ass off all day. Em, I'm gonna grab a beer, what do you want?"

"A glass of sauvignon blanc would be perfection."

He grabs our drinks, and we head over to the living room. As we're about to sit down on the couch, we hear the doorbell ring.

"I can get it!" I say.

I open the door and see that it's Noah. Kieran is going to lose his shit. In a good way.

"Well, look what the cat dragged in," I say as I welcome Noah inside.

"Holy shit, dude. What are you doing in California?" Kieran says, running over to hug him.

"I mean, couldn't miss your birthday. Especially after not being able to come to any of the shows on tour. And I've also been missing In-N-Out. But seriously, Em texted me about the party, and I had some PTO saved up, so I had to make it happen," Noah replies.

He leans in for a hug, and I say, "It means so much that you came all this way. It's been a minute since the last time you were out this way, can't wait to hear about all that you've been up to."

"What I've been up to? It pales in comparison to what you two have been doing. Pretty sick what you guys are accomplishing. I've mostly just been working. I'd been dating this girl, but it ended up not working out. Been trying to focus on myself, figure out my next career move, all that jazz."

"Sorry to hear about the dating stuff, but great that you're focusing on yourself. We've both been taking a lot of introspective time lately, too. And next career move? What's in the works? You didn't say anything about that the last time we talked," Kieran says.

The doorbell rings again, and I say, "I'll get that again. Noah, if you're still in town tomorrow, maybe we can take you to dinner? I want to make sure we have enough time to really catch up, but with everyone coming tonight, we're gonna be pulled in a million directions."

As I start to grab the door handle, he says, "Yeah, I'll be here until Monday. That would be perfect. I figured things would be a little crazy tonight."

After about twenty minutes of Kieran and I alternating getting the door, everyone has finally arrived, including Alaina. Noah, Kieran, Alaina, and I used to all hang out together pretty often in college, but I'm guessing it's been years since Noah and Alaina have seen each other. We've migrated to the dining room, where Maeve's massive spread of food has been relocated. There's a salad, grilled chicken, lasagna, roasted potatoes, bread, and I don't know how many more things. The woman knows how to throw a party... and how to make guests very happy with leftovers. Especially because everyone knows lasagna is a hundred times better the second time around. I grab a little bit of everything, trying to be mindful of how much I grab because I want to be able to eat whatever cake Maeve baked without feeling like I'm going to explode.

Being at this point in my recovery is such a mindfuck. Obviously, last month I relapsed. And before that, things had been shaky. I've definitely had a few questionable days since, but today, I haven't had a single negative thought about food or my body. I mean, I ate a huge bagel piled up with cream cheese this morning, and now I have about five different types of carbs on my plate, even though I'm wearing a crop top and we're going to eat cake in a bit.

I think that's one of the hardest things to explain about eating disorder recovery to someone who doesn't have an eating disorder. Of course, there are people with eating disorders who genuinely dislike food for a million reasons. But, there are also plenty of people like me who have eating disorders and genuinely love food and want to be able to enjoy it.

I think people assume eating disorders are a choice because of how behaviors and emotions can fluctuate so quickly. I've had spans of time where every single meal and every single day is a battle with food. But I've also had spans of time where one day is a complete disaster and the next day, I'm enjoying a burger like it's nothing. We don't get to decide where our brain is going to be on a given day. It would be wonderful if I could snap my fingers or tell myself an affirmation and make it where I magically could decide that my eating disorder wasn't going to rear its ugly head in a specific moment— but it doesn't work like that. There's certainly effort and choice that goes into recovery, and there is technically choice involved when someone engages with their eating disorder, but it's not as simple as that. They're not just choosing to struggle or choosing to thrive. And I wish more people understood that.

About halfway through finishing my plate of food, my mom walks over to me and whispers in my ear, "Take your time eating, but when you're done, come to the kitchen so you can help us carry the cake."

I'll never understand why people whisper about bringing out a birthday cake at a birthday party. I'm pretty sure it would be a bigger surprise if there wasn't a cake or some other replacement dessert. I nod and say, "Will do."

"What was that about?" Kieran says as he places his plate down.

"Oh, she spilled some red wine in the kitchen and wants me to help her so that your mom can relax."

"Do you want me to help? I can take care of it."

"It's your birthday, relax, baby."

He smirks, clearly now understanding that I'm not really about to clean up red wine, and he stops asking questions.

I finish my dinner and place my plate on top of Kieran's before I walk to the kitchen. A beautiful cake covered in dark chocolate frosting sits on a glass tray, and I can only assume there's yellow cake underneath, which is both of our favorite cake combos. My mom and I light the candles, and I pick up the cake, determined to carry it on my own without dropping it. I walk back towards the dining room, and everyone starts to sing happy birthday. As I place the cake down on the table in front of Kieran, I'm suddenly overcome with emotion. We've spent every single birthday together, but this one is different. This birthday, we're a couple. This birthday, we're stepping into this new era. We've truly been through it all, and I can't wait to see all of the other birthdays as we continue to build our life together.

"You like that, Emmie girl?"

I don't think a more unnecessary question has ever been asked.

I don't think sex has to be fully reciprocal, but having Kieran's head between my legs after giving him what he, and I quote, referred to as, "the best blowjob of my damn life," is a pretty solid reward. Before the first time we fucked, I frequently wondered what Kieran would be like in bed, especially after some of the unhinged stories he shared over the years. And let me tell you, the man never disappoints. We consistently, without a doubt, have sex that's far better than with any other person of any gender that I've ever been with.

He quickens the speed of his tongue, and while he hasn't been going down on me for long, I know I'm not going to last much more. My back arches and my feet tense up, and I try to quiet my moans.

"Why are you holding out on me, love? You know I love hearing the sounds you make."

If we're being real, despite the almost two months Kieran and I have been together, the words of past people, particularly men, I've been with continue to linger in my mind. Especially people who have said I'm too loud. But I need to stop letting that get in the way, especially because I know that letting go makes for more pleasure.

I stop holding back my moans, and it spurs Kieran on. It sends me over the edge, and I aggressively pull his head into me, not quite realizing what I'm doing.

"Goddamn, I love when you do that, Em. Now, how about you let me fuck you nice and slow while I keep my eyes on yours? Does that sound good to you, pretty girl?"

That sounds more than good. I don't think sex always has to be some deep, meaningful thing, but with us, it has made things so much better.

"Please, I need it."

He smirks. "While I would usually be tempted to tease you and make you wait a little longer, I'm pretty damn desperate. You keep lying back and letting me take care of you, angel."

It's not often that he calls me angel, and when he does, it always drives me insane, in the best way. He carefully climbs onto me, a rare moment of being delicate in bed. I love that we can switch things up like this. You never know what type of Kieran you're going to get.. His thrusts are gentle but deep, with almost every one grazing my g-spot. He reaches his hand down between us to rub my clit, once again inching me closer and closer to the edge. Our moans are almost in unison, and I can feel his body start to tense up.

"Goddamn Emmie girl, you're fucking incredible."

Despite being short of breath, I reply, "I mean, thank you, but I'm not doing anything."

He grunts quietly and then says, "Oh, but you are. Your pussy and the fire in your eyes will always do me over. I don't think I'm going to last much longer."

Smirking with a sense of accomplishment that I'm not quite sure if I deserve, I say, "Then you don't have to, babe. How about you let go for me?"

He speeds up both his thrusts and the movement of his thumb of my clit, and my orgasm hits its peak. Everything becomes blurry, but not in the dissociation or panic attack kind of way—in the kind of way that everything is cloaked in pure bliss and ecstasy.

He collapses onto me and sighs heavily before he says, "Damn, I'm going to sleep like a rock tonight."

That certainly makes two of us.

TWENTY-EIGHT

I'M SITTING in the lobby of the record label's office with Emaline and Ruby, and my anxiety has my brain running a marathon. I can only assume they want to meet because we didn't consult them before making our relationship public. Back when we first posted about it on that first week of tour, I didn't hold Emaline back despite my concerns because I never want her to feel like I'm trying to control her career. Or anything in her life, for that matter. But, part of me wishes I had slowed her down or told her to keep it secret until we could meet with the label. I hate knowing that if something bad goes down, it's all my fault. Everyone says it isn't my fault, but the moment I asked her to be my girlfriend, all of the responsibility fell into my hands.

The head of A&R (artists and repertoire) opens the lobby door. "You guys can come back now, we're ready for you."

I sigh and stand up, grabbing Emmie's hand. "You've got this baby," I whisper.

We walk into a big space that's part conference room, part regular office with a table surrounded by chairs, along with several couches a few feet away from it.

The president of the label is there, along with the VP of Marketing and their publicist.

"Great to see you all. Ruby and Emaline, you can join us at the table here. Kieran, if you wouldn't mind, please go take a seat on one of the couches, and we'll grab you in a few," the president says.

Fuck. If they want me seemingly out of earshot, this can't be good.

"Oh, okay. That's fine," I say, walking towards the couches.

Emaline's eyes narrow, and she says, "Why can't he join us?"

The VP of marketing stands up, saying, "There are just a few business things we'd prefer to keep in this inner circle. Nothing against you."

In any other situation, I'd fight it. But I've created enough problems already. I'm the reason we're here in the first place.

"Okay, let me know if you need anything," I say.

I plop down on the black leather couch, opening my phone to try to seem like I'm giving them privacy, even though I'm going to try my best to eavesdrop. Scrolling to seem incognito, I adjust the way I'm sitting to position my ear as close to them as possible.

It's hard to make out what they're saying, but I hear something to the effect of, "We know you've worked so hard to build your brand and image, and we want to ensure that you're protecting that."

I wish that I had some sort of earpiece to amplify this. The volume of Emaline's voice is nearly impossible to hear, but I think she's saying, "I know." And a moment later, it sounds like she's saying, "You're right."

Emaline wouldn't betray me. But living her dreams matters more to her than most other things, so I wouldn't blame her if she decided to either hide our relationship or end it entirely.

And maybe I should be the one to bring it up so she doesn't feel the pressure to.

Twenty painstaking minutes go by, filled with me desperately trying to make out anything they're all saying. Unfortunately, it's been all fragmented.

"Hey, Kieran, you can come on over."

I sit down next to Em, and as the label executives discuss something amongst themselves, I whisper, "I heard you saying you agreed with them about our relationship messing with your image. Maybe we should rethink things. I know how hard you've worked to build everything you have."

Her eyes look like they're going to pop out of her head.

"What the fuck? What would make you think I'd ever say that? Is this about my relapse? Are you just looking for a way out? I wasn't agreeing with them at all," she whispers.

Yet another fuck up on my part.

I put my head in my hands. "It just sounded like you were saying they were right. Of course, I'm not looking for a way out. I just want to protect you," I whisper back,

Ruby glares at us. "If you're trying to whisper, you're not doing a very good job. And what's gotten into you, Kieran? Do you really think I'd let them talk her into that?"

"No, I'm sorry. I just feel like this is all my fault, and I wanted to fix it."

Before I can add more to my sentence, the head of A&R looks towards us.

"You're on thin ice, Emaline. You're lucky that your numbers are looking the way they do. So long as things keep trending upwards, we'll keep up our end of the deal. But if anything shifts, we will reconsider," she says.

Ruby has fire in her eyes. "From my research, Emaline is currently your highest-grossing artist, and she's been putting every ounce of energy she has into her music to keep you happy. So, if you'd like her to continue to be able to perform at her best, I suggest you drop this bullshit. I'm sure you all know as well as I do that she could keep this trajectory, with or without a label."

Damn.

She's met with silence, along with all of the executives staring at each other in shock.

"We didn't mean any disrespect, we just want the best for Emaline and this wonderful career she's built. It would be a shame to put her potential at risk," the president says.

While I've tried to keep my mouth shut, I can't keep it in anymore. "I know it's not my place to say anything, but respectfully, having this meeting shows that you don't want the best for her. You haven't seen all of the blood, sweat, and tears she put into the album and into this tour. She's part of the reason you all are so rich, and might I remind you that you work for her, not the other way around. She's a grown woman who's fully capable of protecting herself. And the support of her fanbase and how positively they've responded to our relationship since day one shows that."

Ruby smirks and fist bumps me, and Em squeezes my hand, whispering, "Thank you."

The VP of marketing looks down and says, "I think we should wrap here for today. We truly value the work all of you put in, and we're grateful for the credibility Emaline's success has brought to our name. Just know that if things take any sort of downturn, we will need to have a serious conversation."

Emaline shakes her head. "I assure you, you don't need to worry about that. Now, if you'll excuse us, I have a show to go rehearse for." She looks at me and whispers, "And our part of this conversation isn't over. When we get home, we need to talk."

We step into my apartment, and Emaline is clearly pissed, but I can tell she's trying to calm herself down. She slides off her beat-up white sneakers before flopping onto the couch.

She sighs loudly. "I'm going to preface this by saying I'm not mad at you. I'm just confused and disappointed. I know you're trying to protect me and my career, but it feels really shitty to have my boyfriend seem like he's going to jump ship because some jerks at my record label aren't happy that I'm in a relationship. I need to know that you're fully in this. I know I'm not good at accepting help, but I need you to trust me that with work, I'll ask you if I need help. I'm capable of standing up for myself."

I didn't intend for it to come across as me feeling like she can't stand up for herself. With how hard things have been recently, I'm just in extra over-protective mode. But that's not fair to her.

I sit down next to her. "I'm sorry, baby. That wasn't my intention, but I can see why it would come across like that. I promise I'm fully in this. It's hard for me not to jump to protecting you, but I know you're a strong woman and can hold your own."

She scoots towards my lap, leaning into me. "It's okay, Kiki. I know you just want the best for me, but I don't want us to end up resenting each other for it. I'm grateful for the protection, but especially with shit like what's gone down with the label, I want to be the one who calls the shots. And you know that even if I don't speak up about something, Ruby always has my back."

"You're right. I've gotta work on having better boundaries

with work stuff. We're too good together both as musicians and as a couple to let shit like this get in the way."

"Exactly. And I really do appreciate you standing up for me at the end of the meeting. It was just you assuming that I wanted to end things that made me upset," she says, laying her head on my thighs.

"I promise I'll work on not jumping to assuming I know what you want, especially with stuff like this," I reply, stroking her hair.

She smiles. "That's all I can ask for, baby. Now, can we get some dinner? Fighting with the label made me work up an appetite."

"Of course we can, Emmie girl."

After almost three weeks of mostly chill bliss, including closing on our dream home, we're relaxing in our hotel room in Paris. Well, room is an understatement. It's a massive suite—a birthday gift for Emaline from our parents, me, and Ruby. We landed last night, and while we're only here for a few days, I wanted to make things really special.

Her birthday is tomorrow, but since we have the show, I figured we could have most of her celebrations today. Of course, the show will be a huge celebration, but I have some surprises up my sleeve.

"So, what's the plan for today?" Emaline says.

"Figured we could do a few touristy things. Go to the Louvre to see the art, visit the Arc de Triomphe, and I may have flown in Brie so that she can style you for dinner tonight," I say, stroking her hair as she lays her head on my chest.

She glances at me with widened eyes. "You flew in Brie? What kind of fancy dinner is this?"

"So, a friend of a friend of Noah has a condo with a rooftop with the most perfect view of the Eiffel Tower, and he's letting us use it. I hired a chef to do a dinner for us, figured we could get all dressed up and have a little Paris fairytale moment."

She sits up and her jaw drops.

"Oh my god, I have no words. I'm pretty sure I'm the luckiest woman on the planet. I mean, I definitely already was. But this? No one's ever done something this thoughtful for me. I can't wait. Thank you, baby."

"You're welcome, my love. It definitely took pulling some strings, but you deserve the best. I thought it would be smart to meet up with Brie first so you don't have to rush yourself while trying dresses on, and then we can grab some lunch and do our touristy things after."

She tackle hugs me. "You always think of everything. When are we meeting her?"

"She's ready whenever we are – she's in a smaller suite on the third floor. Want to head over? Or we can keep chilling for a bit."

"I'm not going to wait! Why wait when I can go play dress up?" she says as she jumps off the bed.

I guess that was a bit of a stupid question, considering the phase Emaline had when we were little kids, when she would refuse to wear anything other than princess dresses.

"Are you sure you don't want to kick Kieran out so that he can be surprised later, Em?" Brie says.

Emaline shakes her head.

"No, I want him here! Obviously, I'll pick what I like best, but I want to see what he thinks before I decide."

She's the most beautiful woman on the planet, regardless of what she's wearing, so she'll only be getting positive feedback from me.

Sorry, Em, guess I won't be making your decision any easier.

Emaline peeks through the rack of dresses, with a look on her face that shows she's overwhelmed by all of the options. There's a pretty wide variety of lengths, styles, and colors, and I'd expect no less from Brie.

"Hmm... I think I'll try this one first," Em says, holding a long, pink, strapless mermaid-style dress.

"Can't wait to see, pretty girl."

Brie helps her get it on and zip it, and it fits like a glove, perfectly accentuating her curves.

"Wow, you look amazing. What do you think?" I say.

She furrows her brow. "I mean, it looks nice, but I don't think it's quite *me*. I think I need a bit more princess vibes."

"Your wish is my command," Brie says, grabbing another dress from the rack.

It's a dusty blue color with little off-the-shoulder sleeves, and it's covered in butterfly appliques. I think this one may be the winner, judging by the look in Emaline's eyes.

"Oh my god, yes. I need to get this one on now," Emaline says.

Brie unzips her and then starts to open up the corset back of the dusty blue dress.

Emaline pulls off the pink dress, and I'm trying not to stare at her almost naked body.

Brie helps her step into the blue dress and magically does up the corset. This dress is absolutely perfect on her, and the shade of blue stunningly highlights her eyes. What's better than how she looks in the dress is how her entire demeanor has lit up. She starts twirling, and suddenly I'm having a vision of her wearing a dress like this but in white and a bit longer, at our wedding. I'm not sure if it's the whole buying a house together thing or what, but I've been having more and more thoughts of proposing to and then marrying Emaline—and while those thoughts used to scare me, I'm almost welcoming them now. Which feels really fucking weird to say. Not weird *bad,* but weird...*good?*

"Holy shit, Em. You look like a princess," I say.

As she beams, she replies, "I feel like one. I don't think I've ever felt this pretty. I don't need to try on any others. Brie, I know most of the time with stuff like this you have to give it back to the designer after I wear it, but is there any way I could keep it?"

"You look absolutely amazing. And I'll see what I can do."

I stand up and pull Emaline into me to dance with her for a moment. The energy radiating off of her is pure sunshine, and I wish there was a way to package up this feeling because everyone deserves to experience this kind of joy. I intertwine my fingers with hers, gently leading us, as if we're on a dance floor and not a hotel room. While she hasn't taken a dance class in years, her many years of dance training when we were younger will always shine through.

I lift my arm to spin her, and it's moments like this that I'm reminded of how worth it it all is. And I don't necessarily mean supporting Em through all of her struggles. I mean, of course, that's worth it. But, more so, my own. Being able to experience this type of joy and love makes all of the energy and pain of fighting my OCD and healing from my relationship with Jamie so worth it.

My feet are a bit tired from walking all throughout Paris this afternoon, but I don't regret it. When we're working, we don't always have time to do all of the fun, touristy, "normal people" things. Sometimes, we're only in a place for twenty-four hours. Or sometimes, even if it's not a show day, there's a day full of press stuff or recording or whatever. So, we always do our best to take advantage of these kinds of days and soak everything in. Because we are normal people—just with a really cool job.

I finish diffusing my hair and run my fingers through it. It usually looks fine when I let it air dry, especially since my hair is short, but tonight is special, and I want it to look perfect. I grab my white dress shirt off the hanger and carefully button it. I unhook my pants and start to pull them on. My suit is somewhere between a navy blue and dark teal color, and while it wasn't necessarily planned for my outfit to go with Emaline's, the colors will complement each other perfectly. After I get dressed, I walk out to the living room of our suite to wait for her.

She walks out of the bathroom, and she is breathtaking. Her hair is pulled back in a sleek bun, and her makeup perfectly highlights her natural beauty without being over-powering. She does a little twirl, the skirt of the dress floating outwards.

"Wow, Emmie. I know I said earlier that you look like a princess, but I really mean it. You're so radiant. How did I get so lucky?"

She kisses my cheek. "I think the real question is how I got so lucky to be wearing this dress and to be having this perfect night with the most perfect man who I absolutely adore.

Thank you, Kiki. And this suit is amazing. It really brings out your eyes."

"Thanks, baby. And maybe it's not that either of us is lucky. I think it's that we've both worked so hard on our friendship over the years, and somehow, it blossomed into this. Which is pretty fucking cool," I say, followed by kissing her forehead. "And as much as I'd love to stand here and admire you all night, we do have a driver waiting downstairs."

Smirking, she replies, "Pretty fucking cool is an understatement, baby. Okay, let's go. I'm starving anyway."

The driver brings us to the condo of Noah's friend's friend, and we walk inside. When we get to the rooftop, both of our jaws drop. There's a perfectly clear view of the Eiffel Tower, and a table is set up with candles, two glasses of rosé, and two place settings.

"Kieran... wow. I have no words."

I pull her into my chest. "You like it, Emmie girl?"

"Like it? I've never experienced anything like this. This is like something out of a movie. How long have you been planning this?"

"Ever since you told me about tomorrow's show. I knew I didn't have a long time to figure it out, but I was determined to do something really special. I know love isn't about grand gestures, but since we've never been to Paris, I thought it would be perfect. It's wild to me that even though I've been talking to Noah a ton with all the planning, he somehow didn't spill the surprise of him coming to LA for my birthday."

She nuzzles into me. "Seems like Noah deserves a pretty big thank you gift after making both of our birthdays so special."

Our meal was coq au vin, one of the most stereotypical French dishes—which is perfect for having a Paris fairytale evening. At the start of the meal, Emaline inhaled several pieces of baguette, which made me happier than seeing the look on her face when we first got to the rooftop.

Over the past two weeks, food has seemed a lot easier for her, which has been a big relief. I know it's not a black and white struggle and that things can change in a moment, but getting to see her enjoy my birthday cake without guilt and to see her enjoying the food here in Paris seemingly without an ounce of anxiety makes me so proud of her. I often take for granted how easy it is for me to enjoy food. I have plenty of my own struggles, but food and body image have luckily never been part of it. It may seem simple or unimportant that someone is eating a baguette at dinner in Paris, but for Emaline, it's huge.

"You're so pretty, Kiki", she says with an ever-so-slight slur in her words.

We're both four glasses of wine in, so it makes sense, especially with her being the lightest of lightweights.

"Mm, you're even prettier, Emmie girl. The Eiffel Tower pales in comparison with you sitting here."

It probably sounds cheesy or cliché, but it's true.

"You're just saying that to fit the fairytale theme of tonight. I'm not *that* pretty."

I shake my head. "I promise I'm not just saying it, baby. Sometimes, I wish you could see yourself through my eyes."

My sappiness is interrupted as a server comes out, holding a piece of birthday cake with a candle in it.

"Happy birthday to you, happy birthday to you, happy birthday dear Emmie girl, happy birthday to you," I sing quietly.

She blows out the candle and smiles.

"If you had told me a month ago that I'd be drooling over this cake and desperate to start eating it, I wouldn't have believed it. Thank you for helping me have this moment. In so many ways."

"I mean, sure, I set up this dinner, and yeah, of course I've been supporting you, but your recovery is all on you, Em. I'm glad I can help you through it, but you're the one doing all of the work. Never forget that."

She sticks her fork into the yellow cake with chocolate frosting and takes a bite.

"I know, I know. But without the support you've given me and how much I love you, I wouldn't be fighting in the way I am. Love you so much, Kiki."

I steal a bite of her cake and say, "I love you too, Emmie."

She'd kill me if she knew I was saying this right now, but Emaline is probably the cutest hungover person in existence.

Being hungover on a show day that also happens to be your birthday isn't the best, but luckily, the show isn't until 8 pm and soundcheck isn't until 5 pm, so there's plenty of time for her to hydrate, eat, and get to feeling less like death.

Since she's usually so sunshiney, it's funny seeing her all grumpy. I did warn her about all of the rosé, but she didn't want to listen. Given the current expression on her face, saying "I told you so," would be a very, very bad idea.

There's a knock at the door, which is confusing since we didn't order room service yet, and no one said they were coming to our room. I look through the peephole and see that it's Ruby.

"Hey, Rube, what's up?" I say, peeking my head out the door.

"Are you guys decent? I just got off the phone with a booking agent and have some potentially cool news. I couldn't hold it in, sorry for barging in here."

"I mean, if by decent you mean dressed, yes. Em is currently nursing a hangover," I whisper. "And be careful, she's kinda grumpy."

Emaline says, "Hey, I heard that!"

I laugh. "Guess I'm not the best at whispering. But it's not inaccurate. Come on in, Rube."

I grab another water from the mini fridge to bring to Em, along with some Tylenol.

"So, what's the news?" Em says.

Ruby sits down next to her. "You know Ember Fest? Apparently, one of the artists who was supposed to headline pulled out. I guess the album and tour caught their eye, and they want you to headline. What do you think?"

My eyes widen, and Emaline spits out her water.

"Excuse me, what? They want *me* to headline? I've never even been on one of their small stages. This must be a joke."

Ruby smiles. "I assure you, it's not a joke. They sent me a contract. I know you've been staying off your phone and social media more lately, but things are escalating like crazy. I think you headlining this festival is the start of something huge."

Ruby is right. After Em's relapse, she's been really mindful of how much she uses social media. It's understandably easy for her to get caught up in the comparison game, and I'm so proud of her boundaries, especially because being active on social media is a big thing for artists these days. She's been letting Ruby handle most of it and only checks it sporadically.

The new album has been crawling up the Billboard charts, and she's nearly number three. Tour videos have taken over TikTok. And she's on every relevant Spotify playlist that a pop artist could hope for. While Em knows some of that, I think she's also not giving herself enough credit. She constantly thinks she's lucking into her success, even though she's worked for and earned all of it.

"So, what do you say, Em? Do you want to do it?" I say.

"Of course I fucking do! But isn't that in like October? Is that enough time to prepare?"

Ruby nods. "Yeah, it's not that much time to prepare, but there probably won't be too many changes from your most recent tour set. It'll be slightly longer, and we'll spice things up a bit, but it's totally doable."

"It's plenty of time, baby. Plus, it gives you less time to get anxious about it, while still having a bit where we can chill and settle into the house."

Some of her anxiety seems to soften, and she says, "Okay, I think you're both right. I've prepared for shows in far less time than this before, and sure, this will arguably be the biggest performance I've ever had, but it's still just a show. Can I take a quick look at the contract?"

Ruby passes over her phone.

"Okay, this all seems perfect to me. So... where do I sign?"

After sharing the news about the festival with the rest of the band and crew, everyone is on a high, which has translated into our performance. We're pretty much all always high energy, but this is another level. Fans throughout the crowd are wearing birthday hats, which is the sweetest gesture. I breathe for a moment and let it all really sink in. That I'm on a stage in France with my girlfriend, for a show that sold out in under a minute.

We've only got a few songs left in our set, and it's almost time for Ruby to come out and surprise Em with a birthday cake. While we had our own celebration last night at dinner, this show is a bigger celebration.

Em looks a little confused because we're supposed to start playing "Begin Again", but none of the band is playing. Ruby walks out, and we all start to sing—including the crowd, who probably saw her before Emaline did. As I sing and glance out at the crowd, I can't help but swell in pride for the love of my life. And not just because she's my girlfriend. Because she's my best friend, and we've worked together for this since the moment her parents got her a karaoke machine for Christmas.

After she blows out her candles, Emaline says, "Oh my god, you guys. This is truly the most special birthday ever, and I'm so glad everyone is here to party with me. I have the best band and crew in the whole world, and the best fans in the whole world. Seeing you all in the crowd, even though this is our first time playing in France, means everything. It's the best gift I could ever ask for. And now, please hold while I stuff my face with some of this cake."

This kind of success and support is what I imagine every musician dreams of. And here we are, living it.

emaline

WE GOT HOME from Paris last night, and today's the day we move into our new house. It's so weird to say that. *Our house.* We're both kinda running on fumes after the show and flights and everything, but adrenaline, excitement, and a fuck ton of caffeine are what's going to get us through.

Unfortunately, we couldn't get the staged furniture we wanted, but thanks to having enough money budgeted, we decided to get all new furniture for the house—aside from the dresser that my grandpa built for my mom when she was a little girl that was passed down to me. Our interior designer managed to find furniture that matches it pretty well, and while it's not perfect, I don't care. A house doesn't have to be perfectly aesthetic, and the sentimental value matters more to me.

It was really weird getting home last night because everything in both of our apartments was packaged up in boxes, except for Kieran's bed, some clothing, toiletries, and his OCD medication. It almost feels like when I packed up my college apartment for the last time – except this time, I feel like an adult.

Well, an adult who still sleeps with her baby blanket. Don't judge me.

I walk out of the bathroom after I finish getting dressed and see Kieran pacing in the kitchen.

"Hey, Kier, you okay?"

He pauses his pacing.

"Oh, yeah, I'm fine. Sometimes I think better when I'm walking."

Having known him for twenty-six years, I know at this point that that's a lie, and his OCD must be getting loud again. But I don't want to push him too much.

"If you say so, but remember I'm always here for you."

He looks at the ground. "I promise, I'm okay. Thank you, though, baby."

I can tell he's getting in his head about moving into the house, and that all of the things Jamie said to him are probably being reactivated. But I know more than anyone that trying to force someone to talk about what's going on in their head when they aren't ready doesn't work and can make things worse.

I head back into the bathroom and pack up my few remaining toiletries and bring them out to the living room. Kieran has his remaining things set by the door.

"Ready to go start our next chapter, Kiki?"

He pulls me in for a hug. "Couldn't be more ready, Emmie girl."

I can't believe that this is our home. With all of the chaos of tour life, especially the past few months, knowing that we have this place that is completely ours to make however we want it is so grounding. Of course, there's a bit of chaos here right now with settling in, but it's a good kind of chaos.

Thanks to the interior designer we hired, a lot of things are already set up for us. We still plan on making more of our own touches over time, but for now, especially with knowing we're about to get back into rehearsals for the festival, it's perfect.

"I know we're both pretty tired, but what do you think about breaking in the kitchen and cooking some dinner together?"

We had some groceries delivered earlier so we wouldn't have to deal with going to the store.

"I think that sounds like a great idea. Watcha thinking about making?"

"How about some fettuccine alfredo with grilled chicken and broccolini? We can use your grandma's recipe. I had your mom make us a recipe box with a bunch of family recipes."

Kieran's thoughtfulness never ceases to amaze me. Aside from him, my grandma was my favorite person in the whole world, and after losing her a few years ago, I've always been looking for ways to try to reconnect with her. Even though I don't really believe in god, I do believe that our spirits live on in some way—and things like cooking her recipes make it like she's here with me.

"That was so thoughtful of you, baby. And that sounds absolutely perfect. Want me to get the grill going?"

"That'd be great. I'll start the oven for the broccolini and boil some water for the pasta. Figure we can do the sauce last since it'll be pretty quick and we'll want the chicken to rest anyway."

After I turn on the grill, I season the chicken. Watching him cook and being in this beautiful kitchen together is making me think more and more about how excited I am to hopefully marry him someday. Neither of us has directly mentioned it, but I'm fairly certain he feels the same way. In the past, I would have gotten all in my head about it, but for some reason, I'm believing it. The saying, "actions speak louder than words," really is true.

We finish cooking, and he sets the table with the set of my grandma's floral accented china that my mom gave us. Some people save china only to use for special occasions, but my grandma always said, "Life is short. Use the fancy china. Use a wine glass even if it's just for water. Why let these things collect dust when you can make every day special?" and now that we're settling into this home, I'm going to do that.

"How are you feeling about going back to therapy tomorrow?" he says.

"Honestly, pretty anxious. Shay asked me to send her an email with an update of the past few months, so that she has an idea of what's been going on before the session, so that we don't have to spend the entire time with me updating her, but I know it's going to be a lot. She's always helpful, but you know as well as I do that therapy is fucking hard. I get that in the long run it's going to help, but I know that it's going to feel worse before it feels better."

"Yeah, that's the catch-22 with therapy. It often sucks but then in the long run, it's what helps you find freedom. I made an appointment with my therapist for next week, too. It's going to be tough for both of us, but I know it's what we need. Especially with the festival coming up."

"100%. I kinda wish I hadn't taken a break from therapy, but I know I can't change that now. All I can do is commit to continuing to go back now."

"Exactly. Proud of you for choosing to do the hard things. We're in this together, Emmie girl."

It's 9 am, and I'm sitting in the waiting room of Shay's office. While this has usually always been a grounding space for me, I feel like my heart is going to leap out of my chest. I know I have nothing to be ashamed of, and she won't be mad at me for relapsing, but it still really hurts knowing that I'll have to admit it out loud. I was doing well for so long, and even though I know I've gotten back on track, it sucks to have to admit it to yet another person. I'm also not ready to have to continue talking about all of the Chris shit out loud, especially because I thought I had processed it more than I apparently did.

The door opens. "Hey Em! So good to see you, come on back," Shay says.

Well, here goes nothing.

"It's so good to see you, too. I know it's been a bit."

We walk back to her office, and I sit down on the green velvet couch. This is a familiar place, but it feels different.

"So, from reading your email, I have a bit of the lay of the land of where you've been at since our last session, but what emotions are you having right now, in this moment?"

"Honestly, a lot of different ones. Anxiety. Shame. Frustration. I know it's important that I'm back here, but I hate that it's because of a fucking relapse. I mean, I guess, regardless of the relapse, it would've been good for me to get back into therapy. But that's where I'm at right now."

"I think that makes a lot of sense. It's hard when backslides happen. But, I'm really glad you're here. I know it sounds cliché, but it takes a lot of bravery to come back to therapy. It also shows how committed you are to continuing your recovery, despite the relapse."

I catch her up a little bit more, and then she asks me to recount the night of the relapse in the club.

Deep breaths, Emaline, deep breaths.

After I finish telling her, I feel like I'm going to crawl out of my skin from the anxiety—and apparently it's visibly obvious.

"Let's pause for a moment, Emaline. I'm proud of you for sharing that. Take a deep breath, in...and...out. Now, do you remember the butterfly hug skill I taught you a while ago?"

I nod and cross my arms over my chest, placing my hands on my shoulders. I start alternating tapping back and forth on them slowly. It's a technique called bilateral stimulation. Bilateral stimulation is also part of a type of trauma therapy called EMDR that we've done before to process some of my earlier trauma, but when you're doing a butterfly hug, it's a more calming version instead of one that activates your nervous system. EMDR stands for Eye Movement Desensitization and Reprocessing, and it helps you process trauma by simulating REM sleep. Bilateral stimulation is any type of movement that goes back and forth between the sides of your body. Sometimes it's eye movements that go back and forth, but I've only ever done the tapping.

"Great. Let's keep doing that for another minute or two. I'll do it with you."

After a minute of doing it, my nervous system is a lot calmer. I uncross my arms and proceed to kick off my shoes and lie down on the couch.

"So, I know we only have about ten minutes left in our session. I figured it would probably be a good idea to talk a bit about refreshing your treatment plan. There are a handful of things that I think are important to do some more concrete processing around. If you're open to it, I think it may be a good idea to do some more EMDR, since you've found it helpful in the past. While the most recent incident with Chris is probably at the forefront of your mind, clinically, I think starting with doing more processing of the night you broke up is probably the best place to start. What do you think?"

It may seem counterintuitive to most people, but when you're doing trauma therapy, it is often most effective to start with the furthest back incidents. Shay has explained it to me like clearing out a clogged pipe. Sure, processing the recent stuff is important, but if you're not clearing out the further back things, you're not getting to the root. All of our reactions to the things we experience are a product of everything we've learned over time. Of course, trauma is trauma regardless, but the ways our brains interpret each new experience are informed by everything that happened before that, whether positive or negative.

"Yeah, I'm open to that. We've got about two months until the festival, so do you think that's enough time to do some processing while still being okay for rehearsals and all that?"

She nods and says, "Yeah, I think so. We'll make sure to have the two sessions before the festival be ones where we focus more on grounding instead of trauma processing. While things have been more difficult recently, with the amount of therapy you've done before, I have no doubts that you'll be able to regulate yourself well enough outside of sessions to still be able to do everything you need to do."

"Okay, cool, sounds like a plan."

We schedule our session for next week and then I head home.

"Oh my god, this bed is so fucking comfy. I never want to have to get out of it," I say.

"Same. I'd had my mattress since high school, and it'd definitely seen better days." Kieran replies.

Lying next to each other in this brand-new bed, in this beautiful bedroom, is everything. Change has always been hard for me, but this kind of change feels good. I'll miss some of the memories made in my apartment, but the fact that we're living together in this gorgeous home is all the grounding and confirmation I need of how committed we are. Of course, I knew that before we bought a house together, but it is an added layer.

I'm sure we'll probably go to sleep soon, but lying here together for a bit is exactly what I need.

"I can't believe we're here right now. This is actually a dream come true. As cliché and cheesy as that sounds," I say.

"Doesn't sound cheesy to me, baby. I can't believe it either. If before tour someone told me this is where we'd be today, I would've called them crazy."

He dances his fingertips along my shoulder and then places a soft kiss on my upper arm. He lets his lips linger for a moment before gently rubbing my arms up and down.

"Whatcha doing, Kiki?"

"What do you mean? Just being affectionate to my girlfriend," he says with a slight smirk that would be missed by someone who doesn't know him as well as I do.

"Is that really all you're doing, babe?"

"Well, what do you think I'm doing, Emmie girl? Since you seem to be convinced I'm doing something else."

I look him directly in the eyes and say, "I think you're trying to get me turned on because you want to fuck me, in our new bed, in our new house."

"Well, is it working?"

I smirk. "How about you reach down and find out, pretty boy?"

He reaches into my sweatpants. I shudder as he feels the wetness, the slightest touch making me sensitive. He pulls his hand out from under the blanket and slides the two fingers he used into his mouth, cleaning them off. This man will be the death of me.

"You mean to tell me that you're already fucking drenched, just from me rubbing and kissing your shoulders, Emaline?"

The slight dominant shift in his tone is going to make me putty in his hands.

"What can I say? Practically everything you do turns me on. Hard not to get turned on simply being in your vicinity. Guess I'm no better than a man," I say with a slight laugh.

He starts to roll on top of me and says, "Oh, trust me, angel. I've been with plenty of men, and you're far better than a man. Far better than anyone of any gender that I've ever been with. You make me fucking feral just by looking in my direction. You've completely ruined me, so I hope you know that we have to be endgame. Because there will never be anyone better than you. Not only in bed. In every single way."

While a younger version of myself may have fought that statement, right now, I'm choosing to believe Kieran. Because he's never given me a reason to believe otherwise.

"Endgame sounds pretty perfect to me. But, first, I want to play the game of how quickly you can get my clothes off."

"Game on, baby," he says as he starts to pull off my tank top.

In less than a minute, there isn't a single piece of clothing on either of our bodies, and with how much this man says I've ruined him, I can't wait to see how much he's about to ruin me.

He dims the lights as low as they can go without turning them off so that we can still see each other, while also having a moody vibe. He gets back on the bed, and as I sit up, he says,

"How about you lie back and let me take care of you tonight, pretty girl?"

Well, I'm not going to say no to that.

"Yes, please," I say as I lie down.

He climbs over me and starts to kiss down my body, starting from my neck, down between my breasts, down the curve of my waist, and then down to my pussy. He quickly darts his tongue over my most sensitive spot once, seemingly teasing me.

"Baby, please don't tease me. I need you."

He smirks, "Oh, but teasing you is one of the funnest parts. Love seeing you squirm. Love seeing you get as feral for me as I do for you. But, if you insist, angel."

He roughly sucks my clit, and my back arches. He lightly rubs two fingers around my entrance, and I start to buck my hips, trying to get him to slide them inside.

Between my moans, he says, "You know, baby, all you have to do if you want more is ask. I'll always do what my angel asks me to do."

Yep. Ruined.

"Please, Kieran."

"Please, what, Emaline? What do you want me to do to you?"

I, somewhat pathetically, whine, "Please fuck me with your fingers."

He gently slides them into me and says, "There you go, baby. That feel better? You like how I'm making your pussy drip down your thighs? You like making a mess for me to clean up?"

I grind on his hand, and my whimpers seem to be enough of an answer for him.

"So needy. Such a good, needy girl. Now let me clean up

this mess for you," he says, trailing his tongue between my legs again.

He first licks my thighs, not letting a drop go to waste.

"You taste so good, baby. Can never get tired of this."

He continues, the rhythm leading my breath to quicken more and more. After what was probably only thirty seconds, I say, "I need you to fuck me. Now. I'm going to come soon, and I want it to be on your dick."

"As you wish, Emmie girl." He says as he pulls his mouth off me and his fingers out of me. He cleans each one, which is possibly one of the hottest sights I've ever seen.

He climbs on top and aligns himself with my entrance. I can already sense how hard he is and how incredible this is going to feel, despite him not being in me yet.

"Goddamn, Em. Always like our first time," he groans after pushing in.

He keeps a steady pace, not going too hard or too soft. But after a few seconds, my body freezes up. Suddenly, I'm not mentally in this room anymore, and it feels like I'm on the floor in Chris's kitchen on that one night last year. My throat is tight, and tears are starting to form in the corners of my eyes.

The kitchen in Chris's house was actually the one safe room for me, which most people would think is odd for someone with anorexia. However, it had become safe for me because he was too lazy to cook, so he rarely used the kitchen. So, whenever we'd fight and he'd leave the house, I'd go sit on the floor in the kitchen until I calmed down enough to go home. But that night I broke up with him, the kitchen was the place where he assaulted me. He knew it was my safe place, so he had to take that away from me, too.

"Hey, you okay, Em?" I hear faintly.

I'm unable to say anything, frozen here, even though I'm technically safe in this moment. Kieran has never done a single thing to make me feel unsafe. But my mind doesn't care about that right now. Everything seems hazy, and I'm trapped, unsure of how to get regrounded. It's like I'm watching myself instead of being in my body, desperate to be able to move even though I have no idea how to.

I feel a cold, wet washcloth on my forehead, followed by tapping back and forth on my shoulders. I start to come back to reality, seeing Kieran there with a very concerned look on his face. I know I taught him the butterfly hug skill Shay taught me, but I didn't think he would remember.

I let out an audible sigh and sheepishly say, "I... I think I was having a panic attack."

He pauses the tapping. "I thought so. If you want to talk about it, we can. But we don't have to. Did I do something wrong? Is there anything I can do to help?"

I shake my head. "You didn't do anything wrong, I promise. I don't want to talk about it too much because I think it might give me another panic attack, but suddenly my brain felt like I was on Chris's kitchen floor again. It's like I wasn't here, even though I know I'm safe here. I'm sorry, I know you were enjoying it, and now you're left here without getting to come."

He lightly places a hand on my shoulder. "Hey, you have nothing to apologize for, Emmie. I just care about you feeling safe. Nothing else matters."

I know things like this are the bare minimum, but when so much of our world is below the bare minimum, it feels like a grand gesture. I still feel shitty about it, but I know that's because of words of past partners, particularly Chris, coming into my brain.

"Thank you. Can you help me shower? I need to wash the thoughts off of me."

"Of course I can. Do you want me to help you wash off in the shower? Or do you just want my presence there?"

"If you can help me wash off, I think that would be helpful. I know you're a safe person. My brain sometimes forgets that it's you."

He climbs off the bed and gives me his hand.

"Well, then let's get in the shower. And then I can make you a cup of tea and we can put *Gossip Girl* on until we fall asleep?"

I take his hand and stand up, pulling him into my chest.

"I think that would really help."

He helps me shower and dry my hair and makes a cup of decaf tea with the perfect amount of honey. After an episode of *Gossip Girl*, I start to drift off. And as I do, I hear him whisper, "You're safe here, Emmie girl. You're safe here."

kieran

WITH SETTLING into our new home, getting back into therapy, rehearsals, and studio time, the past two months have flown by. It's the day of the festival, and I'm a combo of extremely excited and extremely anxious. Luckily, the excitement is outweighing most of the anxiety.

About a month ago, Ruby asked me and Emaline to stay after rehearsal for a meeting. She shared that even though we just recently finished tour and have this festival, the label wants us to do an arena tour, starting in mid-January. Considering what a shock being asked to headline this festival was for Em, she was more shocked by the idea of an arena tour. I guess the label got over their patriarchal "being in a relationship means Emaline is less marketable," bullshit.

We've both had our doubts, but with the numbers for how quickly the last tour sold out, as well as album sales and streaming stats, it seems like we may sell out an arena tour. Which is absolutely wild to think about. Ruby told Em that it was totally up to her and told her that she was going to make her take a week before she gave her an answer, that way she knew it wasn't impulsive. We had several conversations about it, especially about how we both have been doing in terms of mental health, and despite knowing that it'll be a lot to handle, she said yes.

She's been going to therapy every week since that first session back, and I have been too. My OCD started to creep up again when we moved into the house. All I could think about was when Jamie broke up with me, especially because we were thinking about moving in together before that. When so many people consistently proved to me over time that they didn't think I was worthy of a long-term commitment, it was hard for me to truly, fully grasp that Emaline really wants that. That she wants me for the long haul. And, I mean, you usually don't buy a house with someone if you don't think it's going to last. So, take that, OCD.

She is announcing the tour tonight at the end of our set, and tickets will go on pre-sale in three weeks and general sale the next day. It's a really quick turnaround in my mind, but things are constantly changing in the music industry. How quickly things have been growing is a combo of being over-joyed, being worried, and it just being an overall mindfuck. As a musician, obviously, you dream of success all your life. But dreaming is a lot different than when it's happening in the moment.

Luckily, it's been mostly positive. But Emaline does still get some hate. Luckily, the altercation with Chris somehow managed to stay out of the media—because that would have been an absolute shit show. He's had a pretty bad reputation in the industry for a while, but it's still always looked on nega-tively to have any kind of drama in the press.

Em has had notifications turned off on her social media for quite some time, but I only recently turned mine off. I always had a bit of a following because of being in the band and being her best friend, but once it was public that we were dating, things skyrocketed. It's overwhelming when so many people are liking and commenting on your posts and sending you messages, even kind things. It's strange to know that so many people are so aware of nearly everything you do. It's part of how we've gotten to this point and how Emaline's career is continuing to grow, but it's still weird.

We got noticed pretty often before, but it's inescapable now. Nearly every time we go out somewhere, especially in LA proper, we get stopped by someone to ask us to take a picture or to have a conversation with us. And while we're both so grateful for the fans, it's hard when your life has been turned upside down over the course of less than a year. Sure, there was fame before this, but not the kind where you're out getting a bagel and there are people pointing their phones at you. Now that it's fall, hoodies and sunglasses have become our best friends.

We've decided to mostly lay low today since our set isn't until around 9 pm and we don't want to be too tired, especially since this set is a bit longer than the one we had with the most recent tour. We're in Chicago, so the air is crisp, and we're all sitting outside our trailer in camping chairs instead of staying inside.

We'd usually all play *Mario Party* or something like that together, but being outdoors doesn't exactly lend itself to that. So, a game of "Never Have I Ever" is our pre-show entertainment for the day. The band and crew are all always pretty unhinged with each other, and this game takes it to a different level.

Nick goes first. "Never have I ever... had a one-night stand."

For some people, that may be a risqué question. For us, it's light work. Everyone except for Delia puts a finger down.

"Wait, really?" Emaline says curiously.

Delia nods. "It's that good ol' Catholic school guilt."

"Guess that tracks," I say.

Emaline says, "Okay, my turn. Never have I ever... called someone the wrong name in bed."

The only one to put a finger down is Ryan.

"Okay, now you have to tell us the story," Ruby says.

He shakes his head. "Not much to tell. Had a drunken hookup with a chick from a bar after my girlfriend of two years dumped me. Proceeded to call the girl by my ex's name while she was blowing me, and she promptly left without a word. Only mildly mortifying."

"Well, I probably would've done the same thing if I were her, but that's actually kinda sweet. Why have you never told us about your ex?" Em says.

Ryan looks down. "Eh, I'm still pretty fucked up over her even though it's been almost a year. I don't really like to bring her up because it makes me sad."

"Fuck, I'm sorry, Ry. I shouldn't have asked. Kieran, please ask something unhinged before I make things worse," she says.

"Hey, don't worry about it. You didn't know."

I add, "Let's see if I can change things up... never have I ever fucked a coworker."

Emaline and I both put fingers down, along with Ruby and Jake. For a split second, I happen to see Isabelle and Kenzie look at each other quickly and then look away, not putting any fingers down. Something is *definitely* going on with those two. I'd bet money on it.

We've already heard Ruby and Jake's stories before, and clearly, everyone is aware of me and Emaline. Everyone continues taking their turns, and the only two people with a finger still up are Kenzie and Isabelle. Very fitting. Depending on the question Jake is about to ask, one of them may win.

"Hmm...never have I ever sent a flirty text to the wrong person," he says.

Kenzie puts her finger down, leaving Isabelle as the winner.

"This is probably a low-risk question to ask about," Emaline says.

Kenzie laughs. "Yep, I thought I was texting my now-ex-girlfriend about wanting her to come over so I could cuddle her hot body. Actually texted my dad. I was eighteen and absolutely mortified, but now we laugh about it, and now he and my mom and my sister will never let me live it down."

"Oh, I would've simply died if that happened to me," Em replies.

We all laugh for a bit, and then I say, "Well, that makes Isabelle our winner...and your prize is bragging rights, because I don't have any prizes. Thanks for playing, guys."

We're about to take the stage, and the number of people in the audience is absolutely mind-boggling. Supposedly, 100,000 people come to each day of this festival, and I'd venture a guess that there are 50,000 of them in front of this stage. Sure, I've gone to tons of festivals as an audience member, but the closest we've gotten to a festival before this was a little fair when we were in middle school. Far from the same experience.

"Holy fuck, that's a lot of people," Emaline says.

With my arms draped around her from behind, I reply, "Yeah, it is. And they're all here because they want to see how incredibly talented you are. Isn't that pretty cool?"

She nods anxiously.

"Yeah, it's really cool, but I don't want to fuck this up, you know? There's so much on the line with the new tour and working on the new album and all of it... I've never performed for this many people before, and I don't want to choke."

I gently turn her around.

"Hey, look at me, Emmie girl. Yes, it's scary playing for this many people. But it's just another show. Sure, with it being a festival, there are probably people here who aren't necessarily here to see us, but I know so many people are here because they want to see you and they love your music and want to support you. The fans love you. They want to see you succeed. Yes, there will always be shitty people who want to see us fail, but the amount of people who want to see you win is far beyond that. I know we're all going to kill it out there. Treat it like when we were kids playing karaoke in your bedroom. It's about sharing your love for music and the art you've created with the world. You are so well-rehearsed, and I know you could probably do this in your sleep. So, can you believe in yourself a little more for me, baby?"

Ruby walks towards us, which means it's just about go time.

Emaline nods. "Yeah, I can. We've got this. We've worked so hard for this, and we deserve to enjoy it."

"Damn right, we do," I say.

"Alright, ready, guys?" Ruby says, pulling us all in for a group hug.

"So ready. Let's go do this thing," Emaline replies.

Kenzie hits play on our intro music, and Emaline and I speed through our pre-show handshake. I kiss her quickly and say, "Knock 'em dead, Emmie girl," before I run out to take my place on stage.

I always thought that seeing a crowd like this would make

my OCD escalate, but it just feels right. I pick up my guitar, sling the strap over my shoulder, and take a deep breath. After I play my first notes, Emmie runs out, and I exhale. The joy on her face is everything I need to lock into this ninety-minute set. *We're really doing this.*

Between the sheer magnitude of the crowd size, the level of their energy, and the way they all went insane when Emaline announced the tour, we are all on cloud nine.

After our set ended, we changed, packed up, and headed back to the hotel for our private party on the rooftop. We all deservedly got a bit trashed. Well, more than a bit. So now Em and I are heading back to our room to chug Gatorade to hopefully stave off a hangover and then cuddle until we pass the fuck out.

"That fifth glass of wine was certainly a choice. Bed is calling my name. I don't think I'm going to bother taking my makeup off even if I'll regret it in the morning," Em says as we walk down the hall.

Before I get the chance to reply, I notice that there are two girls a few feet in front of us, all over each other, one aggressively scanning her room key.

Holy shit. Those aren't just two girls. That's Isabelle and Kenzie.

Emaline and I both stop in our tracks.

Kenzie has a lipstick mark next to her mouth, and Isabelle's lipstick is slightly smeared. I thought they were up to something, but them practically hooking up in the hallway of the hotel after we were all hanging out ten minutes ago was not on my bingo card.

Not wanting them to see or hear us, Em and I scramble to open our own room.

"Did you see what I just saw?" she says.

"If you're referring to the fact that Izzy and Kenzie are definitely about to fuck in the room two doors down, yes."

She plops down on the bed, clearly in a little more shock than I am.

"I mean, I know they've obviously gotten close on the road, but I never saw that coming."

That makes one of us.

I take my shoes off and sit down next to her.

"I didn't want to say anything because I wasn't sure if it was true, but there have definitely been signs. Towards the end of tour, it seemed like they were sitting very close one night. And then in Paris, when we got off stage, Kenzie ran from front of house to hug her, and Iz had the same look on her face that you get around me. And then this morning when we were playing never have I ever and I asked the question about fucking a coworker, they looked at each other for a second and then immediately looked away. I wasn't sure if I was reading into things too much, so I figured I'd keep it to myself," I say.

She flops onto me, clearly feeling the effects of her wine.

"Holy shit. Do you think they're a thing? Or that they're just fucking? Or what?"

She's got me on the perceptiveness. But, hey, clearly it still ended up working out.

"Honestly, no idea. I think they'd be perfect together, but I know Iz has mentioned before not really being the relationship type. So maybe they're just fucking? Or maybe they weren't fucking but are now? This must be how everyone felt about us."

"I don't want to air out their business, especially when we

have no idea what they're actually doing, but the urge to text Delia is so strong. Do you think I should say something?"

This is hard. I don't want to somehow contribute to potential band-crew drama, but considering how everyone was talking about us before we started dating, and since we saw them the way they were in the hallway, fuck it. Plus, Delia will keep quiet.

"It may be the whiskey talking, but go for it. But, I wouldn't tell anyone other than her. It'll spread like wildfire."

I pull out my phone.

EMALINE

delia. are you sitting down?

DELIA

are you pregnant??

EMALINE

absolutely not. but you have to promise not to tell anyone else what i'm about to tell you.

DELIA

oh shit...go for it

EMALINE

kier and i were walking back to our room and when we were walking down the hall, we saw iz and kenzie. not just saw them. saw them all over each other, lipstick all over their faces, practically breaking the door down

DELIA

HOLY SHIT

EMALINE

i know!!!!! i have no idea what's happening but there's no way they aren't fucking right now

DELIA

this could either be absolutely amazing or an absolute disaster...

EMALINE

for the sake of all of us with tour coming up, i
really hope it ends up amazing

Here's to hoping that keeping this secret works and that
this doesn't all blow up in our faces.

emaline

THERE ARE few things more blissful than sitting on your deck on a chilly (well, chilly by LA standards) November morning, wearing your boyfriend's sweatshirt and sweatpants, while eating the breakfast he made for you. Things have been a little hectic after getting back from the festival and now getting ready for the holidays and then tour coming up in mid-January, but now that we're settled into our house, it's truly an anchoring, grounding space.

I have therapy in a few hours, which I'm simultaneously looking forward to and also dreading—something I think only people who have gone to therapy before can understand. I know that in the long run it's helpful, and even in the short term, there are times that one particular session makes a big impact—but the whole "it feels worse before it feels better" cliché is a cliché for a reason. Having to dive into the extremely heavy work of processing trauma is so painful, but also know that it's going to be so worth it. Especially with tour coming up. I'm tired of my PTSD and my eating disorder running my life, and I know the only way out is through.

Another layer of anxiety for today's therapy is that I'm

going on *The Late Show with James Gray* tonight to play a song and talk about the tour. Not the most ideal to have therapy on a day of an appearance like that, but Shay couldn't fit me in any other day, and I'm squeezing in all the therapy I can before January.

"How are you feeling about therapy later?" I say to Kieran.

This will be his first session back after a few-month break, and I'm sure he's probably having a lot of the same feelings I did when I had my session with Shay a few weeks ago.

"Anxious. Excited. Grateful. Gonna be hard because it means having to go back to doing exposure therapy for my OCD. But even though it sucks I think I need the accountability."

"Yeah, accountability can be such a double edged sword. Obviously helps you get better, but it's hard when you have to go and be like…oh yeah I actually did do that thing I said I wasn't going to."

He nods. "Exactly. Obviously, I always want to be doing better but sometimes the OCD is too loud and I'll just say fuck it. I know that Hailie will never be mad at me if I come to our sessions and tell her that things aren't going well, but it does feel good when I get to tell her I'm doing better and she tells me she's proud."

I put my empty plate on the table in front of us.

Sometimes in dark moments, motivation comes from not wanting to have to explain why you did what you did. And obviously, it's not great if motivation is always coming from that, but you gotta take what you can get sometimes.

I'm sitting on Shay's couch, feeling a bit more comfortable than our last session.

"I know you have your performance later. I don't want to get into anything too heavy, but I was thinking about taking some time to check in on how your relationship with Kieran is going. You just had the big move, things have been going pretty quickly with you two. How are you feeling about everything?" Shay says.

"Honestly? Really good. With anyone else, I would say that the speed of where we're at is way too fast. But, with being best friends our entire lives, I feel like we skipped ten steps in our relationship. I'm not sure if it's crazy to say, but I can see us marrying each other. Every moment in the house together and honestly every moment at his side feels like we're meant to be together forever. The second night in the house, before the whole panic attack thing, he mentioned that he thinks we're going to be endgame. And while it was in the context of us messing around, I do think he was serious. Kieran doesn't say things he doesn't mean."

I haven't told very many people about that moment. I mean, there are only a few people I'll talk to about my sex life, so that's part of it, but I've also in some ways wanted to keep it between us. So much of our relationship is public, and I like when we get to have things that are just for us, not anyone else. Alaina and Ruby know, but I haven't told anyone else.

Shay nods.

"I think that makes complete sense. While you weren't technically in a relationship with him before, I know that not all that much changed for you both aside from having a label for it and having sex. I mean, obviously, the whole house thing. But I mean in terms of the speed of your relationship. In some ways, it's like you were together for years. Tell me more about hearing him say he thinks you're endgame. What did that bring up for you?"

I kick off my shoes and lie back on her couch, getting comfier.

"It completely validated all of the thoughts I've been having in my head. I've been thinking about us getting married for a bit now, and I figured we were on the same page, but hearing that solidified it more and made it real. Who knows when it will be, and while I'm not sure about many things, I'm pretty damn sure of this one."

"It makes me so happy to see you in such a healthy relationship. I know things have been rough for you mental health wise the past few months, but there's still been so much progress, especially with how you've handled this relationship. And it shows so much progress that you're really believing what he's saying and not doubting yourself. He treats you in the way you deserve, and it's so lovely to hear about."

She's right. I've been extremely hard on myself the past few months as far as my relapse and uptick in PTSD symptoms, but I've made progress in so many other ways. I've never had a relationship like this—and the fact that aside from a few moments, I haven't tried to push this love away is huge. Usually, I'd be convincing myself that the guy secretly hated me and that it wasn't real...but here I am, leaning into the love that I deserve. The kind of love that everyone deserves.

Everyone deserves a Kieran Hayes.

Well, not my Kieran Hayes, but someone like him.

I'm backstage at *The Late Show*, and while I usually love doing my own hair and makeup for shows, tonight I have a hair and makeup artist. I'm wearing a burnt orange long sleeve dress that gives the best fall vibes, my hair is up in a high ponytail, and my makeup is pretty subtle.

The production assistant opens the door. "Hey, we're on in ten. You almost ready?"

"Yep, just gotta do her setting spray," the makeup artist says.

She finishes my makeup and I head side stage. While Kieran could be back here with me, he decided he wanted to sit in the audience and get the full effect.

James Gray does his opening segment and then says, "We've got quite the show for you tonight. Let me introduce tonight's guest, rising pop superstar Emaline Rose Levine."

As I walk out, the audience goes wild, and I find Kieran's eyes in the front row. He blows a kiss, and I blow one back. Gross, I know.

"Welcome, welcome, welcome, Emaline. So glad to have you on the show tonight. You released an album that broke the Billboard Top Ten back in June, had a sold-out tour, recently headlined at Ember Fest, and tickets go on sale tomorrow for your arena tour that starts in January. Your trajectory has been pretty wild, and as someone with a daughter who has been a fan of you for years, it's so cool to see your success. How does it feel to be seeing this all come to fruition?"

"Thank you so much for having me, James, and it's so cool that your daughter is such a big fan. My fanbase is such a huge part of how I've gotten to where I am today. It's surreal to be having all of this success. I've had some experiences in the past where people tried to hold me back or told me I wouldn't make it, so getting to live these dreams is incredible."

"All of the success is so well deserved. We don't have to get into it if you're not comfortable, but you mentioned people holding you back. Do you mean people in the music industry? Friends? Family?"

While I never thought I'd be vulnerable enough to share some of my story of my experiences with Chris publicly, this opportunity is presenting itself—and I think it would be sad to miss out on potentially helping someone who is watching by letting my fear get in the way. I'm going to tread lightly and be sorta vague, but it's time to let my voice really be heard.

"Uhh, so, I haven't shared any of this publicly before. I was in a relationship with a producer, and things got really bad. He was incredibly abusive, he was sabotaging my career and friendships, and I developed PTSD after the night we broke up because of him getting physically abusive. I won't get into details because it's private and I don't want to trigger anyone, but it was one of the scariest moments of my life. Luckily, enough people on my team were on my side and saw right through his bullshit, but it fucked me up mentally. As a result, it's been really hard to trust and believe in my success. I've worked for all of this since I was five years old in my bedroom, making up songs, but the voice he put into my head still rears its ugly head at times. Therapy has been very helpful, and I'm also incredibly lucky to have an incredible support system, especially my boyfriend Kieran, who is here in the audience and is also a member of the band."

Breathe, Emaline. But don't make it too obvious.

"Wow, I'm so sorry to hear you experienced that. Unfortunately, it seems all too common that women in the music industry have experiences similar to this, and it's something that really needs and deserves more attention. I'm glad you shared this, because I'm sure it will help others who are experiencing or have experienced something similar feel less alone. Speaking of Kieran, your relationship is quite adorable. What's it like working with your partner?"

That validation is exactly what I needed. And he's right. I think this will help others, even if it's really anxiety-provoking for me to share.

"There are definitely challenges, but overall, it's so fun. We started out as childhood best friends, and getting to grow alongside each other, and now we get to live out our dreams of playing music for a living together. I wouldn't want to do life with anyone else by my side."

He nods his head. "That's so wonderful to hear, especially after what you shared earlier. You both are clearly incredibly talented, and it's special knowing the realness behind the music. I've also heard some rumors floating around about a new album possibly being in the works. Can you speak to that?"

"Well, I can't share much, but I'm the kind of person who writes music every day. Even if it's only a line or two or a poem, I'm always up to something. And Kieran brings his guitar everywhere. So, do with that information what you will," I smirk.

He laughs and says, "Well, it's time for us to take a quick commercial break, but everyone watching at home, stay right here, because after the break, Emaline will be performing her hit song, 'Wild Mind'."

kieran

CHRISTMAS IS IN TWO DAYS, and while the last thing I want to be doing right now is being in a therapy session, here I am. I've been doing weekly sessions ever since we got back from the festival. I'm definitely doing a lot better than I had been, but OCD isn't something that magically disappears, even if you've been working on your healing for years. We leave for tour in two weeks, and Em and I have been working on our mental health as much as we can so that we're able to be fully present.

When we first settled into the house, I had an uptick in my obsessions and compulsions, mostly connected to fearing that Emaline would somehow decide she didn't love me anymore and would want to move out. There have been a bunch of different compulsions connected to it that fluctuate, but the one my therapist and I have been working on challenging most is me having to tap my fingers together six times before I get in bed. My intrusive thoughts tell me that if I don't, Emaline will die in her sleep. Which I know is pretty impossible, but OCD isn't logical. It's the exact opposite.

"So, I know last week we got down to you only tapping

your fingers together one time before getting in bed. How was that experience?" Hailie says.

"Well, not as bad as I thought it would be. It still brought up a lot of anxiety. But I was able to do some paced breathing, and it helped enough for me to be able to go to sleep."

"I'm really proud of you. I know doing exposures like this is hard, and it's great that you're continuing to commit to them despite that. How would you feel about trying not to tap your fingers together at all before bed at least one time before our next session?"

That sounds like a panic attack waiting to happen, but I know that the only way to truly beat my OCD is to continue doing these exposures, including the ones that are most terrifying. Plus, I know that I have Emaline to help me cope if the anxiety is that intense.

"I don't feel great about it, but I'm willing to try it at least. Can't promise I won't end up doing it, but I'll try," I say.

She nods. "That's all I can ask for. Trying is what matters most. Of course, it's great when you're able to complete the exposure, but trying is progress, too."

Sometimes it feels like I'm failing if I try to resist a compulsion but I'm not able to—but she's right. I could easily not try at all.

"Thanks, I needed to hear that."

"Well, before we start to wrap up, are you excited for your first Christmas in your new house with Emaline? I know you've spent plenty of Christmases together before, but I'm guessing this feels a little different."

We decorated the house the day after Thanksgiving, and it was one of the best feelings ever. Christmas has always been our favorite holiday, and getting to make these new memories together has felt so special. Our moms each gave us some of our family ornaments, including ones that we made in school

as little kids. We also got plenty of our own, and as we decorated the tree, I kept thinking about how one day, we may get
to pass those ornaments down to our own kids... if we decide
to have kids. Considering we're not even engaged yet, that's a
conversation for another day. But it's a really nice thought to
have.

"I'm so excited. We both have had our gifts for each other
wrapped up under the tree for over a week, and we're hosting
both of our families, as well as some of the band and crew who
don't have somewhere to go for the holidays. We're gonna
make a bunch of cookies using Emaline's grandma's recipes,
and I think it's going to be exactly the magic we need after the
challenges we've had this year."

She smiles. "That makes me so happy to hear. You'll have
to show me pictures during next week's session. I'm sure the
house looks beautiful. It's been so lovely to see your relationship continue to flourish. We have to wrap up here in a sec, but
anything else important that you wanted to get to today before
we look at the calendar?"

"Nope, I think that's all for today."

We schedule our next session, and I drive home.

The living room floor is littered with crumpled-up wrapping
paper – the sign of a perfect Christmas morning. While
Christmas definitely isn't just about gifts, gift giving is definitely one of my love languages, and getting to see Em's reactions to what I got her was a present in itself. My big gift for
her was a dusty rose colored acoustic guitar she's been eyeing
for months. It was in desperate need of tuning, but she immediately played it.

One of my favorites from her was box seats for the Yankees' season opener. You may not peg us as baseball fans, and if you did, you'd probably think we were Dodgers fans because of growing up near LA. But when we were at NYU, we started getting nosebleed seats for the Yankees every few weeks. There's an app where you can get super cheap tickets the day before or day of, and while they were almost always in the highest row of the stadium, we still loved it. The game happens to be the same weekend as our show at Madison Square Garden, which I suppose is probably part of why she got them.

"Hey, babe, I've got one more gift for you," Emaline says, scooting closer to me.

Considering there's nothing left under the tree, I'm not sure what it could be. With a puzzled look on my face, I say, "Do you have to go grab it or something?"

She climbs into my lap and says, "Oh, it's a different kind of gift. Maybe your favorite one of all."

She grinds her hips into mine and kisses my neck.

"Fuck, Em."

"Can I take this off?" she says, grabbing the edge of my t-shirt."

"Please do," I reply.

She pulls it off quickly and then kisses down my chest, getting to my abs, and then untying the drawstring of my sweatpants with her teeth. I think I see where this is going, and I'm definitely not mad about it. She pulls at the waistband, and I lift my hips to help her pull them off, along with my boxers. She gets on her knees next to me on the couch and leans over my lap. Her tongue swirls around the tip of my cock, and I breathe in sharply. She looks up at me as she sinks her mouth down, and the fire in her eyes alone could nearly put me over the edge.

"Goddamn, angel."

The wholesome vibe in front of our fireplace is the exact opposite of the vibe we had in the living room this morning, but in the best way. We did a potluck dinner, and now we're all eating our body weight in cookies. Em insisted on making five different kinds, and despite it being an extremely lengthy process, I couldn't say no to her.

I can never say no to her.

Madison is five months pregnant, and it was really fun getting to spoil her, Matt, and their soon-to-be baby girl, even though we're having a baby shower for her right before we leave for tour. She's sitting in Matt's lap on the couch, his hands on her belly. I can't wait to be an uncle soon, and I know her and Matt are going to be the best parents. And our mom and dad have both been in full grandma and grandpa mode, which has been so sweet to see. It's wild to think that next year, there will be a little baby here, too.

Isabelle has a complicated relationship with her family and basically never goes home, so she's here, too. Ryan also stopped by, saying he was desperate to be free from his family after being "bombarded by a million and one questions about tour and why I still don't have a girlfriend." I know that a lot of people don't have supportive families, and I'm so glad that Em and I both do—our biological families and our chosen family as well.

Em and I are both sitting on the floor, my back against the couch, and her sitting in my lap. We're wrapped in a fuzzy blanket, and if you had told me six months ago that this would be happening right now, I would've called you insane. I rub her shoulders, taking in all of the carefully placed decorations,

noticing the perfect combination between our childhood ornaments and our new ornaments.

My mom walks over and gives us mugs of homemade hot
cocoa. "There aren't words for how happy it makes me every
moment I see you two together. I know you both have gone
through some difficult things, and getting to see your joy is
everything a mother could ever hope for."

We both say, "Love you, Mom," in unison.

While Em is in shock after realizing what she said, my
mom and I are beaming. Sure, my mom has been like a second
mom to Em for her entire life, but she has never called her
mom. Our lives have been intertwined from birth, but every
time there's another new moment to share, or a moment that
we had together as best friends but haven't had yet as
boyfriend and girlfriend, my love for her grows deeper than I
ever thought possible.

I can't imagine a life without Emaline—and with how our
love has continued to blossom every day, I know that someday
she will be my wife. Which will be the luckiest day of my life.

emaline

AFTER TWELVE SHOWS, we're inching closer and closer to being halfway through tour.

We're currently in Nashville, one of my favorite cities in the country—which, with the nickname Music City, I guess that makes sense. We have a few days here, with a show at Bridgestone Arena tonight, a day off to record tomorrow, and a small show at the famous Bluebird Cafe on Saturday.

With this tour, a lot of mental health stipulations were put in the contract, including no back-to-back shows, more days off than most tours, and scheduled time for a weekly therapy session. The label wasn't pleased with that, but we gave them an ultimatum that they luckily agreed to. Kieran and I have both done a lot of work on our healing over the past few months, and we want to make sure we're able to maintain that progress. Sure, some artists can do back-to-back shows, even several nights in a row, and stay mentally healthy, but for me, that's not possible. Aside from the label, I'm so grateful that the rest of my team, especially Ruby, has been totally on board with it all. It's made the tour a bit longer than it would be with more back-to-backs, but it's honestly better for everyone involved. Tour life is grueling on your body, and everyone still gets paid on days off and travel days, so it's a win all around. Plus, the extra days off mean that everyone gets to actually explore most of the cities we're in, versus just seeing the hotel or having a meal.

While tonight's show is definitely the bigger show in terms of audience numbers and ticket sales, the Bluebird Cafe show means more to me. All of the supporting acts are local female artists and bands, and fifty percent of the proceeds are going to a nonprofit that helps people struggling with eating disorders get treatment. From ticket sales alone, even with Bluebird only holding about ninety audience members, we've raised $5000, and I have a feeling that we'll raise more on show night.

Eating disorder treatment is exorbitantly expensive, and as a result, the vast majority of people with eating disorders never get the care they need and deserve. In the United States, eating disorders are the second-deadliest mental illness, second only to Opioid Use Disorder, and yet so few people are able to recover because of a wide variety of barriers. I'm very privileged that my family was able to pay for me to get the care I needed and that I now have the kind of income where I can pay for my own therapy, but for so many people, that's not the case.

I remember being in residential treatment in high school, and one of my roommates had to suddenly leave because her insurance cut her off because she was at a "healthy weight," even though she was still really struggling with behaviors and wasn't doing well.

This organization helps people in a lot of ways, whether it's connecting them with a treatment center, therapist, or dietitian who donates care, helping them pay their deductible so that they can use their insurance for treatment, organizing travel, or helping them figure out what their insurance covers.

So, getting to do these kinds of benefit shows is a big priority for me, even if it means not making much money on the show. I always make sure the rest of the band and crew are paid the same, regardless. I know that's not something that every artist can do, but I'm grateful to be in a place I can, and I will always make sure to use my platform for good, especially as it continues to grow.

We're in the green room and just finished playing a game of Twister, very reminiscent of the early shows of last year's tour. Except this time, instead of me winning, it came down to Ruby and Austin. With it being an arena, the green room, dressing rooms, and catering area are all separate, which is nice for being able to spread out.

"Hey guys, dinner is ready in the other room. We've got about two hours until go time," Ryan says.

Kieran stands up from the couch we've been sitting on and gives me his hand.

"Hot chicken and mac and cheese are both calling my name," he says.

"Me too, and the collard greens. I wouldn't want to only ever eat comfort food, but it is one of my favorite parts of Nashville."

I take his hand and stand up. We head over to the catering room and load up our plates, trying to be mindful not because my eating disorder is saying no to eat too much, but because I'm about to be jumping around on stage for ninety minutes, and vomiting during the set wouldn't exactly fit the vibe.

He pulls a chair out for me, and we both sit down and start eating.

Between bites, he says, "It makes me so happy to see you enjoying food, Emmie girl. I know things aren't perfect, but you've worked so hard over the past few months in therapy, and it shows. I'm so fucking proud of you."

I'm proud of me, too. Recovery is fucking hard, especially after a relapse, but it's so worth it. I still have moments where negative body image creeps in, but I haven't had urges to restrict in months, which is major progress.

"Thanks, Kiki. It feels really good to be able to nourish myself without a second thought. I mean, obviously, I think about it somewhat so that I make sure I'm fueling my body in the way it needs, but you know what I mean. I'm so proud of you, too. I know you still have intrusive thoughts pop in, but the fact that you've been able to stop doing so many compulsions that you had been doing for years is so major."

"I think something about us becoming a couple flipped a switch, for me at least. There are times when my OCD has fixated on our relationship, but with how secure I feel with you, it makes it feel safer to challenge those difficult things. I know that you're not running anywhere."

He's right. Sure, we've always been each other's biggest supporters, but this is different. Knowing that you have a romantic partner who loves you in the way that Kieran and I both love each other and that that love is unconditional, regardless of how dark things get, makes it easier to work on yourself. Not that it's easy by any means, but it's easier.

"It's hard to believe how much has changed all because of one night in New York," I say.

Last night's show was pretty wild. It was completely sold out, and while I've now played a ton of arenas, it's never not shocking to see that many people in the crowd. It's tradition to be given a custom jersey from the Nashville Predators, the hockey team that plays at Bridgestone. They gave it to me halfway through my set, and I wore it for the rest of the night, even though it made me pretty sweaty.

Despite the late night, Kieran and I are both up pretty early, walking around Centennial Park before a recording session. I've needed to be more mindful about the places I go and when I go to them, if I don't want to get swarmed by fans. I know I'm not an "overnight success" and that I've been working at this for years, but the speed of my growth over the past year makes it feel like it's been overnight.

"How are you feeling about getting the last track done today?" he says.

"Really good. This album, being all duets with you, has made it extra special, and I think it's made it easier to be okay with imperfection. I always love recording in Nashville, too. Just a different vibe than studios in LA."

He nods, keeping my hand intertwined with his. "I agree. I don't think I'd ever want to live here, but it does have the best energy for writing and recording. Obviously, there are a lot of creatives in LA and other cities, but Nashville is such a hub for music, and it's so inspiring."

"Exactly. I don't think I could deal with living in bachelorette central 24/7, but it is a fun place to visit, especially for work. Want to take one more lap and then head over to the studio? I know our session is in like an hour."

"Sounds good, figured we wouldn't want to walk too much and get our legs too tired anyway."

We continue our walk, taking a bit longer than intended because I had to stop and pet almost every dog along the way, including a little yorkie named Tidbit. Her owner told us that every pup in her litter had size names like Chunk, Tub, Morsel, and Niblet—which is one of the cutest things I've ever heard. Maybe someday we'll get a dog, but definitely not until this tour is over.

As we get closer to the car, I say, "Speaking of those tired legs you mentioned earlier... Can I get a piggyback ride? My legs technically aren't *that* tired, but it's been a bit since you've given me one."

He crouches down and says, "Hop on, Emmie girl."

"Okay, I didn't completely love how that sounded, but I think I'm getting closer. Maybe the third time will be the charm?" I say.

We're at Blackbird Studio, one of the most iconic recording studios in Nashville. Artists like Taylor Swift and Brandi Carlile have recorded here, which is pretty sick to think about.

While some artists like to record an album all in one studio, I've been enjoying that for this album, we've recorded in a bunch of different cities. I think it adds more to the story of the album, even if the listeners don't necessarily know that. We're almost done with recording the last track of the album, and we're finishing the outro. With twelve tracks on the album, it's been a journey.

"Sure, one sec," Quinn says.

While she's usually based in LA, we've been flying her to the cities where we've been recording since she's our most trusted recording engineer.

"Okay, ready whenever you are."

I lay down the vocals, and then she presses play.

"Em, to me, that sounds absolutely perfect. What do you think?" Kieran says.

"It'll probably shock you guys that I'm happy with it after just three takes, but yes, I think it sounds great... Does this mean we're done with album four?"

My progress in therapy is definitely showing because with album three, there were some parts that took fifteen plus takes. Which, I guess, isn't completely unheard of, but was definitely inefficient and unnecessary. It wasn't that none of the takes were good – it was that I couldn't stop overanalyzing every single nuance.

"Fuck yeah, it does!" Ruby says as she runs over to hug me.

Quinn laughs, "Well, all of you are done. My work continues, especially since there's still mixing and mastering. But, congratulations, you two. It's always an honor, and this project felt extra special to record. You better buckle up, because after how well album three did, there's no telling where this one will take you."

When we proposed the idea of an album of duets to my label, there was some pushback. But we came to a compromise that if they let us do this one, we'd give them another more "regular" album, which I was planning on anyway.

Kieran, Ruby, Quinn, and Ryan all crowd around me in a group hug, and in the most literal sense, I can feel the support and love surrounding me. I can feel how these people truly want us to win, and that they truly believe in me.

And it's moments like these that prove how wrong Chris was. That prove I am talented, and that he was an abusive shitbag who was threatened by me. I've heard through the grapevine that he's been completely blacklisted as a producer, and few things have been more gratifying than knowing he's crumbling. While I don't usually wish ill will on others, he fucking deserves every bad thing that comes his way.

Ruby says, "She's right, you guys. It may feel like this is the top, but I promise you this is just the beginning."

A year ago, I would've responded to that with self-deprecation, but today, I think I actually believe it.

This really is just the beginning.

kieran

WE'RE BACK in New York, and after lots of thinking and planning, I'm proposing to Emaline tomorrow. I'm scared shitless. Not because I think she's going to say no. I know she's going to say yes. But I want the plan I've created to go perfectly, because she deserves the perfect proposal.

A perfect proposal for a perfect girl.

I had her ring custom-made, and I really hope she loves it. Over the years, she's mentioned different gemstones that she likes, and I know she loves Madison's ring, her grandma's ring, and her mom's ring, so I tried to take inspiration from that. And with knowing her for this long, I know her style pretty well.

She has always liked vintage jewelry, and frequently wears pieces that were passed down to her from her grandma, so I figured something vintage-esque would be perfect for her. The center stone is morganite, so it has a peachy, pink-ish tone. The setting is rose gold and oval-shaped with a scalloped edge, and small diamonds surround the morganite. The band is also encrusted in diamonds, and it sparkles almost as much as her eyes do. While I very much don't view her as "property" and don't subscribe to those traditional ideas of marriage, I do love envisioning the ring on her finger, signifying our commitment to each other.

But despite all of the plans for tomorrow, today, I have to stay present so that I don't give anything away. I've managed to keep it a secret from her for this long, and I'm determined to keep it like that.

Today's the Yankees' season opener, so we finally get to use the tickets Em got me for Christmas. It's still a little chilly in New York with it being the end of March, so she's wearing a baggy crew neck with "Yankees" embroidered on it, along with a pair of jeans and a Yankee hat. My outfit is similar, except I'm in a hoodie, and my hat is backwards because apparently women think that's more attractive for some reason... at least according to Emaline.

"Ready to go see whatever fancy food they have in the box suite, pretty girl?" I say.

She pulls me in for a hug and places her chin on my chest, looking up at me.

"I mean, yeah, but I also can't wait to eat a pretzel and a hot dog. I'll definitely eat the fancy stuff, too, but it wouldn't be a baseball game without the classics."

I drape my arms around her. "Definitely. And the beauty of not having a show tonight is that we don't have to worry about feeling too full. Bring on allllll the snacks. And hopefully the Yankees kicking some ass. But also snacks."

Despite the possibility of being noticed, we decide to take the subway to the stadium for old times' sake. We got a few questionable looks and phones pointed at us that probably were people knowing who we are, but no one came up to us.

With the variety and quality of this food, you'd think we were at a party at a fancy restaurant, not a Yankee game. Although with the face value of the tickets, I suppose that checks out.

Of course, they did the typical pan across the stadium with the camera and point out celebrities at the game thing and showed us. At least with being in a suite like this, we've been able to enjoy the game instead of being overwhelmed by people wanting to talk to us or take pictures with us. I like when we get to have "normal" moments like this together because at the end of the day, we're still just normal people who happen to be famous. Which is still a weird word for me to attribute to myself, even though it's true.

They're in the bottom of the ninth inning, and we've each eaten a hot dog and our body weight in popcorn, as well as sharing a pretzel with cheese sauce, a french dip sandwich, and vanilla ice cream with rainbow sprinkles. We've both had a few beers, and we're definitely feeling it, but also still at a publicly appropriate level of drunk, where we'll be able to make it back to our hotel safely.

"Let's fucking gooooo!" I cheer.

The game is tied 5-5, but after a line drive by the Yankees, the bases are now loaded, making the recipe for a potential walk-off grand slam, or at the least, a pretty good chance of getting one run and winning it. But a grand slam would be the perfect end to the night and an already great game.

One of their top hitters steps up to the plate, and Em and I are at the edge of our seats. The pitcher throws what I think should have been a ball, but the ump called a strike. The next pitch leaves his hand, and the hitter swings and hits the ball, in what is almost certainly a home run. We leap out of our seats, and the ball goes over the fence, leading the entire stadium, including us, to erupt in cheers and applause as all of the runners go around the bases and cross home plate. They win 9-5, and Emaline jumps up and down. I scoop her up and swing her around, and then she plants her lips on mine. It warms my whole body and amplifies the joy and excitement of the win that much more. While I'm tempted to deepen the kiss, I know that we're in public, and that can wait until later.

I plop her on the ground and say, "Well, that was quite the Christmas gift. Thank you, baby."

"It ended up being a gift for me, too. I forgot how much I love watching baseball. It's bringing all of the college nostalgia back," she says.

"Same. While I'm glad we're not broke college students anymore, I do miss little traditions like that."

She nods, "Yeah, but now we get to make new traditions. Which is pretty cool, too."

Today's the day I'm going to make Emaline my fiancée, and I'm both a ball of nerves and overwhelmed with excitement. The challenging part is trying to make it seem like a normal day, even though it's definitely not.

Tomorrow we're playing a sold-out show at Madison Square Garden, so Em thinks that us going out to dinner is a celebration of that.

The plan for the first part of the day is to eat bagels I had delivered, walk through the Strand Bookstore, and then come back to the hotel to get changed. Then, we'll take a taxi to Brooklyn and get an early dinner at Cecconi's, an Italian restaurant with one of the best views of the Manhattan skyline. After that, if everything goes according to plan, we'll walk around a bit, and then I'll propose in Brooklyn Bridge Park at sunset. Faye will stealthily get photos of the moment, along with Ruby videoing it, so that we have the memory captured forever. With working in live music, they have both gotten pretty good at going unseen, so I'm hoping that is the case today as well. That and that our dinner reservations go according to plan and there aren't any delays, since sunset is a rather short and specific span of time. My phone vibrates.

NOAH

How ya feeling about today, man?

KIERAN

Anxious as hell. But also so fucking excited. Can't believe it's happening. I know she's gonna say yes so IDK why I'm so worried but I am

NOAH

Hey, it's a big day and you've spent a lot of time planning it out, so it makes sense that you're anxious. But try to be as present as you can and enjoy every moment. So fucking happy for you

I know I'm likely going to get a million and one texts today, but I'm trying not to pay attention to them too much since I don't want Em to get suspicious.

"I'm so excited to walk through Strand. Come to think of it, I don't think I've been there since we graduated. I'm so glad we went to the game last night and that we're having a day just for us today," Em says after placing her empty plate down on the table.

"Me too. I'm happy for so many reasons that we built in more days off on this tour. It's nice to be able to enjoy things and not feel so rushed or like the only part of a city I'm seeing is a stage in an arena."

I throw away our plates, and we both get our shoes on and head out. Our hotel isn't terribly far from the bookstore, so we decide to walk and take in the combo of crisp spring air and warm sunshine.

Bookstores are always grounding for me, so the decision to start the day with this was both because I know Em also loves bookstores, but also because I knew it would be a good way to calm my anxiety.

We walk in, and as we usually do in bookstores, we go our separate ways to wander. I feel my phone again—one of those million texts that I know will pour in over the next few hours.

MADISON

sending all the good vibes for today!!! it's going to go amazing. matt and i are both so sad that we can't make it tomorrow, but we'll be there in spirit <3

KIERAN

Thank you!! Feeling anxious but ready. I know you'd both be here if you could. I'll be sure to send plenty of pictures and videos. Can't talk much rn but I'll text you later on. Love ya

MADISON

love you too, kiki!!

Madison is now eight months pregnant, so while the rest of the family is coming to the show tomorrow, she has to hang back in LA with Matt. I couldn't be more excited to know that my niece will be here in a few weeks. Assuming she doesn't deliver too early, we'll be back home just in time.

I make my way over to the rare and out-of-print section and slowly look through the shelves. It's really cool thinking about all of the character and history these books have, and not only because of their content. And there's nothing like the smell of old books.

After about ninety minutes, Emaline finds her way over to me, her hands full of books.

"Find anything good, my love?" I say.

She nods. "I may have gone a little overboard. But with all of the travel, I've been reading books so quickly, so I think it's justified."

"Have you ever needed justification for getting a pile of books? I'm not sure I've ever left a bookstore with you without you having at least three books," I smirk.

She shrugs. "Guilty as charged. Did you find anything, babe?"

I show her the journal I'm holding and say, "It was more of a look at books vs. buy a book kind of day. But I did find this journal. I needed a new one, and I really like the cover."

After how much Em loved the song I wrote back in July, I started writing more of my own music, which has been really therapeutic.

"Can't wait to hear the songs you write in there. Now, can we go check out before my arms fall off?"

Our taxi is currently stuck in traffic on the way to the restaurant, and I'm about to lose my mind. This plan has been timed practically down to the minute so that we can be sure to catch sunset, and if this doesn't let up soon, I'm fucked.

"Hey, it's fine. I'm sure they'll hold the reservation," Emaline says.

Apparently, my anxiety is palpable. And I need to make it seem like it's only about a reservation... not about the fact that

I'm about to propose to the love of my life, and I need it to be absolutely perfect.

I place my hand on her thigh and say, "Yeah, I just hate being late, especially at a fancy place. But you're right, it'll be fine."

The traffic finally opens up, and I quietly breathe a sigh of relief. We pull up to the restaurant, and I get out of the taxi first. After I get out, I give Emaline my hand to help her stand up. She is wearing a short pink dress with slightly poofy sleeves and a slightly poofy skirt. It's covered in 3D floral appliques, which, unbeknownst to her, will complement her ring beautifully.

Emaline is always gorgeous, but tonight she is pure radiance. Her long blonde hair is in a half-up high ponytail with waves all throughout. Her makeup is mostly muted, with the exception of bright pink lipstick, and just enough eyeliner to make her blue-green eyes pop.

"Good god, I'm a lucky man, Emaline," I say.

She scans her eyes over my olive colored suit and says, "And I'm a luckier woman. You clean up nice, baby."

We walk to the entrance of the restaurant, and I open the door for her. We're a few minutes late, but so long as they're able to get us to our table more or less immediately, timing should be fine for catching sunset.

"Good evening, do you have a reservation?" the hostess asks.

"Yes, we have a table for two for Kieran Hayes," I reply.

"Perfect, we have your table ready. You can follow me."

She takes us to our table, and we have an impeccable view of the Manhattan skyline. Sunset is around 7:15 pm and it's currently 5:30, so we should be in the clear, so long as no other delays happen.

"I can't believe we've never come here before. This view is

stunning, and everything on the menu sounds so good," Emaline says.

I resist the urge to say the cheesy cliché that she's more stunning than the view.

"Yeah, I don't know how I'm going to decide what to have. Almost too many options. Would you maybe want to get a few things to share?"

She nods. "That sounds like a smart idea. It's not exactly like we live around the corner anymore, and food FOMO is arguably some of the worst kind of FOMO. Especially because I've had far too many years of missing out. Gotta start making up for it."

We order a bottle of chardonnay along with the truffle honey whipped ricotta crostini, bucatini cacio e pepe, branzino, and roasted broccolini.

After the server fills up our wine glasses, I say, "Cheers to selling out Madison Square Garden, words I've always dreamed would come out of my mouth."

She clinks our glasses together. "Cheers, baby. We fucking did it."

I've always been hesitant about claiming some of this success, but she's right. *We* did it. And not just me and her. The entire band and crew. None of this would be possible without every single person behind the scenes. Which will also be true of this proposal.

"We really fucking did."

We eat our dinner, and while I have a plan for dessert later tonight, we each get an espresso and share an order of cannoli.

The server gives us the bill, and I leave a large tip before we head out.

With each passing moment, my anxiety and excitement continue to increase—with the excitement mostly edging out the anxiety. Unless there's somehow a rainstorm or Ruby and

Faye got lost somewhere, there are pretty much no more logistics to worry about. Now it's all in my hands.

"So, what's the plan for the rest of the night, Kiki?" Emaline says as we walk out of the restaurant.

"I was figuring we could walk around a bit and catch the sunset, and then maybe grab a drink at the hotel rooftop bar? How does that sound?"

Not a lie, just omitting some steps in between.

She intertwines her fingers with mine. "That sounds perfect. The sunset is going to be so pretty tonight."

And the sunset is going to be made prettier with a ring on her finger.

We walk through Brooklyn Bridge Park, and we make our way over to a waterfront spot that has a clear view of the bridge. In my head, I'm cheering because there aren't a bunch of bystanders around who will get in the way. I've been sharing my location with Ruby and Faye all day, so that I didn't have to risk texting them and ruining the surprise if Emaline saw.

We talk for a few minutes, and out of Em's line of sight, I notice Ruby and Faye in the distance... which is my cue to do the thing that has been on my mind every single day since that night we hooked up last year.

I try to keep my cool, but my heart is racing and tears start to well up in my eyes. And it's not from fear. It's from sheer, overwhelming love.

The kind of love I didn't know existed in real life.

The kind of love I never anticipated to find in my best friend but am so glad I did.

The kind of love that makes every single challenge I've ever faced worth it.

The kind of love that words can't possibly fully capture... but I'm going to do my best to find some that at least show a fraction of it.

I take Emaline's hands in mine, and try to gather my composure and words, since I kinda have to be able to speak to propose to her.

"Em, I never imagined I'd experience the kind of love I have for you and that you have for me. And I certainly never thought I'd fall in love with my best friend. But, somehow, even though I didn't fully realize it until last summer, here we are. Completely head over heels, and getting to live our fucking dreams together. And ever since that first night in New York, I've had another dream, a dream that I'm hoping we can make happen together."

I reach into my pocket to grab the ring and get down on one knee.

The biggest smile spreads across her face, and happy tears form in the corners of her eyes. And that look is all I've ever wanted and needed.

"Emaline Rose Levine, will you marry me?"

"Yes. Yes. Yes. Of course, I'll marry you, Kiki!"

I slide the ring onto her finger, and it fits perfectly. I pull her into my chest and we kiss. It's a relatively chaste kiss, given the fact that we're in public, but it's one that's dripping in joy. We break the kiss, and she looks at her hand, closely observing all of the details of her ring.

"Kieran, this ring is so beyond beautiful. I've never seen anything like it. When did you get it? How long have you been planning this?"

Faye and Ruby come out of hiding and sprint over to us, both crying.

"Oh my god, you guys. What are you doing here?" Em says.

"Kieran had us come and get some photos and videos. I'm so fucking happy for you both. So fucking happy. Show me your ring!" Faye says.

Ruby throws her arms around us both and says, "I've been

secretly hoping for years that this would happen. Before either of you mentioned a single word about being into each other. I've somehow always known. And I couldn't be happier for you two. I've never met a more perfectly aligned couple."

They both take a few more photos and videos, and then Emaline takes a selfie of us showing off her ring. I've never seen her as joyful as she is right now, and I'm so glad we'll have this memory captured forever—we can't bottle up this feeling, but we can relive it in our minds every time we look at a picture or video.

"Okay, I don't want to rush us, but we may have a bit of a party of sorts waiting for us back at the hotel. We'll do an official engagement party back in LA after Madison has the baby, but our parents are here, Noah and Alaina are here. I wanted to make it special," I say.

"Oh my god, you put so much thought and effort into every single moment of this. And it's beyond special. It's more than I could have ever dreamed of. You're more than I ever could have dreamed of."

Last night felt like a movie. The energy of everyone's excitement for us was intoxicating, and I'm absolutely on cloud nine now that I get to call Emaline my fiancée. And now, we're about to play a sold-out show at Madison Square Garden.

We haven't posted anything about the engagement online yet, and I'm leaving the ball in Em's court on that one.

She decided to wear an all white outfit tonight, one that Brie brought over to the hotel this morning. I didn't want to assume that she'd want to wear white tonight, but I asked Brie to get some options to surprise her with in case she did want to. Emaline chose a strapless crop top covered in white feathers, along with a pair of sequined white trousers. It's very reminiscent of the outfit she wore on the first night of last year's tour – the night that changed everything for us.

Her hair is up in a sleek high ponytail that I'm hoping I can pull later. But I won't dare mess it up right now.

We have about thirty minutes until show time, and she's sitting in my lap, holding my hand. Every time I look down and see her ring on her finger, my heart swells. Not because I own her, but because now I know for certain that she's going to be with me for the rest of my life. I mean, I guess part of me has always known that. But now I *really* know. And it won't just be as best friends. It'll be as husband and wife.

After all of the attention last night, everyone has been giving us some space to be on our own today, which has been nice. It was amazing being surrounded by all of the love everyone has for both of us, but it's also great to have some moments where we're alone and can soak up what that means—since at the end of the day, this commitment is about just the two of us, not anyone else.

Twenty minutes go by, and our new production manager, Ava, peeks her head into our dressing room. Kenzie is still our front-of-house engineer, but since we're playing such big venues, we've expanded the crew to better support that.

"Hey, guys, we need you backstage in five," she says.

Emaline pops up and says, "Cool, we can head back now."

"Ready to do this thing, Emmie girl?" I say.

"Beyond ready."

I can see why so many artists say there's nothing like playing MSG. The energy is different. And seeing all of the banners for the massive acts that have played here before us hanging up makes it clear that I'm not dreaming, and this is really happening.

We play the final note of our first song, and I take a moment to take in the massiveness of the crowd. Nearly 20,000 people are here to see us tonight, and one of the things that I love almost as much as seeing them scream our lyrics is seeing the community they've built with each other that goes far beyond our music and our concerts. They truly take care of each other, and seeing the love and support they have not just for our music but also for their fellow fans is so rewarding and inspiring to see. And sure, I think Emaline has really fostered that community over the years, but it's something that the fans themselves have built.

I see comments and posts on social media every day about the friendships they've found as a result of the fandom, which in some ways is more rewarding than the music accolades. Yeah, selling out iconic venues and having massive album sales numbers feels great, but knowing that you've been a small part of people finding community and connection matters more. I know how lonely and scary this world can feel at times, and it's so powerful that their connections transcend our art— which is kinda the whole point of why we do what we do.

Emaline grabs the mic and says, "Good eveninggg, Madison Square Garden! I'm Emaline, and I'm so glad you're here tonight. We have a great show lined up for you, and I hope you all have the time of your lives. But before we play more music for you, I have a huge announcement to make, and you all are the first to hear. If you've been to my shows before, you all know that after I introduce myself, I always introduce Kieran as my boyfriend. But tonight, for the first time, I get to introduce him as my fiancé. We got engaged last night after the most beautiful proposal, and we're so excited to party and celebrate with you all tonight. New York is a very special city for us both, and the energy you all are bringing tonight makes it more special."

The already loud cheers of the audience get even louder, and I couldn't be happier.

When she pauses for a moment, I pull her into my chest and kiss her. We're not usually big on onstage PDA, but I think this moment warrants it. And, in this moment, as I stand on stage at MSG, kissing my fiancé, surrounded by bright lights and a sea of people who are here to see us live out our dreams, I truly feel at home.

Because I don't think home is a structure or building or a house—it's a feeling. A feeling that I'll never take for granted.

THIRTY-FIVE

emaline

A YEAR AND A HALF LATER

AS I STAND in front of a full-length mirror and touch up my lipstick, it's really hitting me. I'm about to walk down the aisle and marry my best friend in the entire world.

After we finished tour last year, we started wedding planning pretty quickly. While for us, marriage doesn't technically change *that* much and we know that regardless of a legal document, we'd be committed to each other for life, I've dreamed of a fairytale wedding ever since I was a little girl. And after months of planning and lots of stress, our fairytale is moments away from coming true.

I'm wearing an ivory a-line style dress with a sweetheart neckline, dropped off-the-shoulder cap sleeves, and a cathedral length train. It's covered in lace, along with 3D butterflies like the dress I wore in Paris, along with beading and a corset back. My hair is in loose curls, and the front is pulled back and loosely braided. For accessories, I have a tiara with pearls and beading, a long, simple veil, and my grandma's pearl earrings that she wore on the day of her wedding. My makeup is simple, with a hint of sparkle in my eyeshadow and a subtle pink-nude lip.

With a day full of all eyes on us, getting to have these few minutes where it's just me is a much-needed bit of solace. I used to hate being alone, but over the past year and a half, as I've continued to do more work on my mental health, I've come to enjoy it at times. I still prefer being around others, especially Kieran, but being alone is no longer something that brings me anxiety. It's a time where I find connection with myself, instead of feeling like I have to be defined by things I'm doing or people I'm with.

Our wedding planner knocks on the door.

"Hey, Em. Ready to go become Mrs. Hayes?"

"Fuck yeah, I am."

Our venue is a dream. We decided that the hotel in San Diego that we stayed at last year, the same one we went to on vacation as kids, would be the perfect place to get married. The ocean has always been the most grounding place for us, so having an oceanfront view was an absolute must.

We walk to the door that will open up to the ceremony space in just moments. My dad is waiting for me, tears of pride and joy already about to run down his face.

"I know you're not a little girl anymore, but I hope you know that you will always be my little girl," he says.

"Dad, you can't make me cry before I get down the aisle."

He hugs me, and then I hear the music transition to an acoustic instrumental version of *18* by One Direction. Some may think it's cheesy, but the song really captures me and Kieran's love story.

Our wedding planner grabs the handle of the door, and my dad and I interlock our arms. As the door opens, all of the guests stand up and look towards me. My eyes immediately lock with Kieran's, and he's already crying. He's wearing a pink suit, and he easily looks more handsome than I've ever seen him. I finish walking down the aisle, and my dad hugs me before shaking Kieran's hand.

Alaina is my maid of honor, and Madison and Ruby are my bridesmaids. Noah is Kieran's best man, and Matt and Ryan are his groomsmen. We wanted to keep the bridal party small so that things weren't too overwhelming. Stevie, Madison and Matt's daughter, who is now a bit over a year old, is our flower girl. I'm sad I didn't get to see her walking down the aisle, on account of me being the last one to walk down, but watching her walk down yesterday at the rehearsal was one of the most precious things ever. Seeing how Kieran has been with her ever since she was born has made me so excited for when we eventually, hopefully, have our own kids someday.

As Kieran takes my hands in his, it takes everything in me not to start bawling happy tears. I haven't seen him since this morning because his one wedding request was us not doing a first look, which I was glad to oblige. It would have made some things easier for photos, but I care far more about the sentimental parts of our wedding than I care about the ease of capturing it all.

"Hi," he says quietly with a smile.

"Hi," I reply, squeezing his hands.

The officiant leads us through the ceremony, and now it's time for our vows. This may be the moment when I can't hold back my tears anymore.

"Kieran, I'll try to keep this short because you know I tend to ramble sometimes. And because I've told you a million times in a million different ways how much I love you with all of my heart and soul. You know me better than anyone. Sometimes, I think you know me better than I know myself. You've been with me through every single one of the darkest moments I've experienced in my life, and your support for me has never once wavered. Though it took me so long to admit it to myself and to you, I know that I've loved you since the moment I learned what love was. Honestly, before I knew what love was. You bring out the best in me, and it's been the greatest privilege of my life to get to grow up alongside you. The love and life we've built, and the way we get to live out our wildest dreams together, is something I thought only existed in books and movies. But now I know it's real. Here's to the first day of the rest of our lives. I couldn't be more honored to become your wife, and I promise that I'll love you with every fiber of my being for the rest of our lives."

He gets choked up after hearing my vows, and my own tears start to flow. Like she's read my mind, Alaina passes me a fluffed-out Q-tip that she must have stuck in the pockets of her dress. It's a hack she learned on social media, and it's the perfect way to wipe away these tears without ruining my makeup.

After Kieran and I both collect ourselves for a moment, it's his turn.

"Emaline, I'm not sure how I'm possibly going to top that. But, in fairness, I think that's a theme for almost everything you do in life. You're the most talented, accomplished, wise, caring, witty, intelligent person I've ever met. It's hard to believe there was ever a time when I was afraid of loving you or afraid that you wouldn't feel the same way. Because here we are, in front of all of our family and friends, celebrating the limitless love we have for each other. You've been through things that no one should ever have to, but you've committed to your healing in a way that has helped you not only reclaim your life but also help others. I can't imagine anyone better to do life with, and I can't wait to continue to grow with you by my side. While I know that this marriage isn't the beginning of us and our love, I know that it is the start of our next chapter, and I know that every single new chapter with you has been more fulfilling than the one before it. The love I have for you grows stronger each and every day, and I can't wait to continue an eternity of loving you and having you as my wife."

After we exchange our rings, I'm reminded of little me and little Kieran, playing in my childhood bedroom.

And I think that's the most beautiful part of our love. That even though we denied it for so long, or chalked it up to loving each other as friends, it's always been there. We've always been it for each other. We've always been each other's biggest fans. We've always been each other's constant.

I don't think you need to know someone all your life or have them start out as your best friend to have a beautiful, loving relationship, but I do think that it's what makes our love the force that it is. The kind of love that so many search for, but often never find.

epilogue

one year later

EMALINE

SO MUCH HAS HAPPENED since we got married last year. We've released our fifth album, and today, we're going to be playing our fifteenth sold-out show at Madison Square Garden.

For this tour, we decided to do residencies in several cities, instead of doing the typical city-to-city thing. It's mind-boggling to me that less than three years ago, selling out one show at MSG was a huge moment.

And now, here we are.

I won a Grammy for best pop vocal album, and the same album is on the verge of going multi-platinum—words I never thought I'd be able to say.

The past few days, I've been feeling a little off, and my period is also late. And while I doubt I'm pregnant, I've decided to take a pregnancy test just to be sure. It's probably that I'm tired from all of the shows, and I know that periods can be late for so many reasons. But I'd rather be certain.

Kieran and I haven't exactly been trying to conceive, but we also haven't exactly not been. I got my IUD out a few months ago, and we've decided to see what the universe wants to do. We know a lot of people put pressure on themselves, especially early in marriage, to get pregnant, but for us, it's kinda an "if it happens, it happens," thing.

I didn't want anyone to suspect anything, so I told Kieran I wanted to take a solo walk to have some recharge time, which is pretty usual for me. And when I did that, I wore a hoodie so that no one would notice me, and I swung by CVS and bought two pregnancy tests.

Since Kieran and I have still upheld our tradition of him not seeing me in my show outfit until I'm fully ready, I'm able to take the pregnancy test without him being suspicious. I go into the bathroom and take out one of the tests. While I'm still pretty sure I'm not pregnant, I'm a bit anxious regardless.

After I bring the test back to the vanity in my dressing room, I decide to hit record on my phone, so that I can get my reaction if it is somehow positive. I wait the two minutes the instructions say and then hold my breath as I pick it up.

There are two blue lines.

Holy shit. I'm pregnant.

I take the other test to be certain, and sure enough, that one is positive as well.

I'm so glad I don't have any makeup on yet because I can tell I'm about to cry. And these are happy tears. I couldn't be happier. With the tour almost done, it's perfect timing, and we are also in the most financially stable position we've ever been in. I know that many people don't have the privilege to have the financial resources that make pregnancy and being a parent easier. Not that it's going to be easy by any means, but I know we'll be more supported than many folks are.

I know Kieran is going to be the best dad ever, and I can't wait to see his reaction. I don't think he'll be expecting it at all...especially because I know I wasn't.

But in this moment, it's so special to know that only our future child and I know about their existence. So, I'm going to soak this up, at least for a few minutes.

A few minutes with just me and my baby.

KIERAN

EMALINE

hey baby, can you come bring me some water?

I grab a water bottle from the green room and walk over to Emaline's dressing room. I knock on the door to make sure she's not in her show outfit yet, not wanting to ruin our tradition.

"You can come in!" she says.

Her face looks a bit tear-stained, and I'm worried about what could be wrong. I know things have been a bit chaotic with all of these shows, but it seems like she's been handling it all well. So I hope it's just allergies or something.

"Are you okay, baby? It looks like you've been crying?"

She pops up with a smile.

"So...uhhh...I probably should have come up with a more creative or special way to tell you this." She picks something up from the vanity. "But, baby, you're going to be a dad."

Holy. Fucking. Shit.

It's a positive pregnancy test.

I throw my arms around her, scoop her up, and swing her around.

"Oh my god, you're going to be the most incredible mom, Emmie girl. I know we haven't fully been trying, but I've really been hoping it would happen soon. I can't believe we're going to have a tiny human who is half me and half you."

She squeezes me tightly, and though I'm sure it's not pregnancy causing it yet, she's glowing.

"I didn't think it was possible to love you more than I already did, but the thought of you holding our baby or running after them is somehow making my love bigger," she says.

I place her down on the ground. "I feel the same way, angel. I think we're going to be pretty cool parents. And this little baby is going to be surrounded by so much love. Well, they already are. But considering how loved we are, this little peanut will be loved even more."

I place my hands on her stomach, and her eyes are welling up again.

I lean down to her belly and say, "Hi baby, your mommy and daddy already love you so much."

She places her hands over mine, and nothing has ever felt so right.

We don't want to tell anyone that Em is pregnant yet, so we're doing our best to hide the excitement. Luckily, we're able to pass it off mostly as being excited about having this fifteenth sold-out show at MSG. Which, don't get me wrong, we're over the moon about that, too. But when you just found out you're going to be parents, suddenly the biggest achievements seem to pale in comparison.

After our pre-show handshake, we head out and play an incredible set. We know this stage and set like the back of our hand, so we're able to soak it in and have fun, which is what being a performer is all about.

About three-quarters of the way through the set, we have a pause between songs, which is when Emaline usually reads some signs and talks to the crowd. But while earlier she knew something I didn't know, now I know something she doesn't know. They are about to raise a banner with her name and "15 Consecutive Shows at The Garden." She's one of only a few artists to have this honor, and it happening on the night we found out we're having a baby couldn't be more perfect.

She starts to read a sign but then stops in her tracks. She sees the banner starting to be raised, and her jaw drops.

"Oh my god. This is so unreal. I can't believe this is happening. This wouldn't be happening without each and every one of you, and I don't think I'll ever be able to fully express how incredibly grateful I am for my fans. Some of you have been here from the beginning of my journey, and some of you are brand new, but you all matter the same. Thank you for your support and for letting me have the coolest job in the world."

Breaking our "keep the PDA off the stage" rule, I run over to Em and swing her around.

Here we are, once again having one night in New York change our lives.

Because ever since New York, we've never been the same.

acknowledgments

Writing and publishing Ever Since New York has been a journey unlike anything else I've ever experienced. This process has been so fulfilling, and I wouldn't have accomplished this without the many incredible people who are in my corner.

To both of my parents, for instilling a love of reading and writing in me from when I was a baby. Every night, my mom or dad would read a story to me – often more than one. I also was always creating stories, and they listened to them intently, even when they were silly or nonsensical. Weekends were filled with library trips, and at home, I also had several full bookshelves. They also invested in me attending a creative writing camp for two summers in middle school, a gift I will never forget.

To my mom, thank you for the hard work you have personally put into healing our relationship over the years. It's been a gift to share the process of getting this book out into the world with you, and your reassurance when I've experienced writer's block is invaluable. You've never seen my writing as a silly little side project, but instead as a passion. Thank you also for instilling such strong feminist values in me and fighting for what is right even when it's unpopular, which was an undercurrent of this book.

To my dad, thank you for always encouraging me to be a leader. Spending so many hours on the sidelines watching you coach baseball games showed me the power and fulfillment of giving time to your passions, even when it's not your full-time job. Also, thank you for always fixing the computer when I'd inevitably give it viruses from Limewire as a kid, allowing me to get back to working on whatever story I was writing that day.

To my brothers, Mark and Sean. Seeing you both pursue creative projects throughout my childhood and now adulthood has been so inspiring. Making music without a label is hard work, which has also given me confidence in this self-publishing journey.

To my Grandma Rita, who is sadly no longer with us. Thank you for our weekly Barnes & Noble trips – always fueling my love for reading and, as a result, fueling my love for writing. I didn't know it at the time, but those trips led to my goal of seeing my book on a bookstore shelf someday.

To my Aunt Ilene – while you haven't directly been a part of my journey of writing this book, your love for writing and our times of being email penpals when I was a kid, always reading the stories I would send you, gave me the foundation for getting where I am today.

To my best friend Francesca, whom I met at writing camp, for always being my biggest fan, even when adulthood and living in different states have made it so that we can't see each other as much as we would like. I'm so blessed to have experienced girlhood with you, and I'm so glad that we both have rediscovered our love for writing as adults.

To every mental health professional I've encountered in my healing journey, especially my current therapist, for helping me find healing that has allowed me to channel my own lived experiences into this story. While this story isn't a self-insert or about my life, I pulled bits from my journey that I wouldn't have been able to without the power of therapy.

To the founders of NovelBound, Sophie and Madi. I credit the wonderful community you've built for being able to complete this book. Additionally, thank you, Sophie, for creating the most beautiful cover art. You took my loose idea and ran with it, making something better than I could have imagined.

To my writing besties, most of whom I found through NovelBound, especially Taylor, Landry, Tori, Dessie, Samantha, and Kym, for giving me so much motivation and confidence, and always willing to lend a listening ear or give me a much-needed laugh.

To all of the other members of NovelBound, thank you for your constant support, inspiration, and affirmation of my identity as a writer.

To my beta readers, thank you for giving such useful feedback and for helping me make this story better than it was when I sent it your way. Your willingness to volunteer and take a risk on reading and critiquing a work is greatly appreciated.

To Land of a Thousand Hills Coffee & Social Edgehill location, for being the place where I wrote and edited most of this book, providing the best vibes and perfect English Breakfast Tea. In addition, the genuine interest each employee has shown in this book, before I even completed the first draft, has made this book feel real and like something I can be proud of, instead of just some words on a computer screen.

To my amazing social media community, thank you for cheering me on through so many phases of life. The excitement each of you has shared about my writing journey gave me the confidence to pursue self-publishing.

Thank you so much to my phenomenal editor, Sabrina Grimaldi, for your wisdom and guidance throughout this process. I was terrified of starting the editing process, and you have given me an experience that is truly collaborative and respectful. You helped me make this story far better than when I first sent you an early draft, never making me feel like my book was bad, always framing it as an opportunity to improve an already strong story. Also, thank you for saving me from many a late-night feedback spiral, reminding me of my talent.

Lastly, to anyone holding this book, thank you for taking a chance on me. I hope that some part of this story has helped you feel seen or has helped you see something in a different light. In addition, I hope that if you have ever felt like "too much" or "too broken" to be loved, this story has shown you that healing can coexist with the pursuit of love. Thank you for reading.

Colleen McNamara is a writer and therapist who believes that the best love stories are messy, imperfect, and unfiltered. Originally from New York, she now lives in Nashville. She is a proud Directioner and Harry Styles fangirl at heart, and when she isn't writing, Colleen can be found curled up with her kitten Harry and a cup of tea, immersed in a good book.

Connect with her on social media: @colleenmwerner